The Ripples and the Tapestries

To Paul —
with thanks
Lyz

Lyz Harvey

authorHOUSE®

AuthorHouse™ UK Ltd.
500 Avebury Boulevard
Central Milton Keynes, MK9 2BE
www.authorhouse.co.uk
Phone: 08001974150

© *2009 Lyz Harvey. All rights reserved.*

No part of this book may be reproduced, stored in a retrieval system, or transmitted by any means without the written permission of the author.

First published by AuthorHouse 6/1/2009

ISBN: 978-1-4389-7901-4 (sc)

This book is printed on acid-free paper.

This was written in appreciation of all those whose ripples have intersected with mine, and whose tapestries have combined to illuminate the bigger picture - I can never thank you enough.
Go with my love on your own journeyings ...

Introduction

Searching ...

It's so much her usual swooping style, I hear her voice reading it to me, rather than my eyes scanning the page. Just as well. They were already brimming with tears even as I slit open the large envelope addressed to me.

F.A.O. Troy Treadwell -
<u>To be opened when I am dead</u>

Inside, her exuberant handwriting covers the white expanse of the copier paper in orderly rows, liberally scattered with exclamation marks, dashes and parentheses.

> *Hey there, Troy! Hope you're not weeping buckets already – weep not for me, old thing – I've just gone ahead and solved the eternal mystery, while you've (hopefully) got <u>years</u> ahead of puzzling it out for yourself.*
>
> *No use beating about the bush with the "to be opened" bit. You agreed to be my literary executor ages ago when I had no idea that I was ever going to publish any of my scribbles. Nor have I, so here we are now with the actual situation that we discussed hypothetically over a bottle (or even two?) of Medoc one evening.*
>
> *It's up to you what happens to the pile of papers you'll find in the back of the wardrobe – they're in a couple of purple box files & hopefully still in order, as I left them.*
>
> *Well, no-one else knows of their existence – not even (or <u>especially</u>!) the other executor. Smuggle them out and take your time deciding what to do. There are many hours of sweat and tears written into them, and I trust you won't just bin them.*

I pause, remembering that evening, soon after Paul had left her – the mingled relief and terror, the elation and pain. By then, I was living near enough to go to Cress's flat to give her the support she'd needed in the few years since we'd met up again at that fateful school reunion, and now could provide more and possibly - eventually - an alternative.

With her given name Cressida, and when we were heavily into Shakespeare at school, I became Troy - and the names had stuck, although I could never quite work out whether I was really the similarity or the antithesis. Other reunionites remembered us as the pair we'd always been until life intervened, and it was strangely comforting to find so many of them did. Our closeness revived, we'd negotiated our way around the distances and met when we could, phoning in between times.

> Make sure the diary's in there too. I don't want Greg getting any notions that his mother's wierder than he already thinks.

Ah ... Greg. Yes, well, that would be understandable, whatever the circumstances.

Our lives could not have turned out more differently. I'd embarked on the expected marriage route, but fortunately extricated myself before too much damage had been done i.e. no offspring to clutter the career I'd begun to carve for myself as a very minor contributor to gardening magazines just at the time when gardening began to build up as a pastime for everyone. I happily fell into that comfortable (and rewarding) niche and began to travel the Continent and then the world, describing other people's gardens.

Cressy had, I discovered when we met again, managed to survive almost two decades of marriage to Paul, taking comfort and refuge from his and Greg's attitudes by consuming immoderate amounts of that refuge of the middle classes contained in French bottles, brought back through customs by Paul on his business trips, augmented by her weekly supermarket order which he never bothered to check.

He was successful. So successful that she had no need to work in any accepted sense of career fulfillment, although she found plenty of voluntary occupations to make her feel useful. Once Greg had left for University she began to write. At first it was solely an outlet for her pent up emotions - a catharsis she acknowledged as being very necessary to focus her bitterness and sharpen her skills with words; then the writing brought her comfort as she began to exercise her latent but very vivid imagination. She wouldn't show me any of her work, though.

"One day ..." she would tease "... but not just yet."

> *If it ever sees the light of day you must - absolutely <u>must</u> - preserve my anonimity. Publish it as your own, invent a nom de plume, <u>anything</u>. I know I can trust your discretion. Just imagine - if it's a success, I want to sit up on my cloud looking down, having a good old chuckle watching <u>you</u> spend the royalties, not the nightmare of seeing Greg wasting the sweat of my brow on his tarty girls. He'll go the way of his father, just mark my words!*

Oh Cress, my darling love. No more of the gentle banter that would have us both collapsed uproariously laughing into the small hours on nights when your depressions could no longer be ignored. No more texts at all hours, staving off your loneliness. I don't, can't, *won't* believe that you have really gone. I look around this room where we've shared so many moods in the last (is it really only three?) years; surely I hear you singing under your breath in the kitchen as I sit here re-reading your letter.

I played so much of the long game that it became second nature, and passion lay no longer smouldering, but buried under a close blanket of familiarity. We could, and often were, mistaken for siblings, for surely no mere partners would find such delight in one anothers' company? Not even a kiss had been exchanged - ever - but I can remember each and every hug as we greeted one other, and recall in detail every time we wandered down a street arm in arm as we talked. And talking was the balm that soothed. You quoted George Eliot and even had those favourite words written, framed upon a background of seeding dandelion heads -

> *"The comfort, the inexpressible comfort of feeling safe with a person: having neither to weigh thoughts nor measure words, but to pour them out just as they are - chaff and grain together - and a*

> *faithful hand will take and sift them: keep what is worth keeping, and, with a breath of kindness, blow the rest away."*

If only you had known, Cressy, if only I had been able to tell you - but you were too bruised by life's vagaries for me to go down that route. Betrayal leaves such deep scars that I was unable to eradicate them swiftly – hence the 'long game' that never quite allowed me to lose hope, but kept my sincerest feelings from risking hurting you again.

> *I hope you find someone who will take care of you as you did me. I wish I had been able to be the person I felt you hoped I could become in your life, but tempting though you were for a time, it would have only been as an escape - and I couldn't run the risk of that well-rutted track from the frying pan into the fire, could I?*

There's such an agony in this; did it mean that all the time she actually *knew*? ... and ... and ... I can read no more, lost in a tumultuous daze of thought, tears streaming, until - I *definitely*, unmistakeably, feel a hand on my shoulder in that gesture I know so well. It lasts only a moment – in its brevity even, so typical of her ways – yet as comforting as the actual gesture had been in reality. But, I pull myself together – she's *not* here; *this* is the reality, this room I shall never see again, this void in my life. I quickly stuff the letter back in its envelope and into my jacket pocket. There will be time – too much time – to read and re-read it later.

I have no idea how long I've been sitting with her letter in my hand but, collecting my scattered wits, find that the purple box files do indeed reside at the back of the wardrobe. The arrangement with Greg has been that, under his supervision, I could collect any personal effects. Whatever sixth sense dictated that I would need to arrive two hours early has stood me in good stead, but the time for Greg's arrival is drawing perilously close.

Cautiously I leave the flat. Good – no sign of him arriving early. I put the files on the floor behind the passenger seat, covering them with an apparently carelessly thrown travel rug and drive into the next street, positioning myself where I will see Greg's sports car arriving. I keep him waiting several minutes before I ring the bell, having driven at speed round the corner to the vacant space a few car lengths away from the door, in order to arrive convincingly breathless after running up the stairs.

Generosity is not in his nature. He queries every book, every CD I gather up to put in the sports bag I've brought. Not that there were many. I take the framed George Eliot from its place on top of the bookcase.

"May I have this as a memento?"

He shrugged.

"It's hardly an old masterpiece, is it? No accounting for taste."

I wanted to spend as little time in his company as possible and am soon ready to leave. He is still sifting through dressing table drawers - for any hidden treasure, no doubt, but I know that Cress has deposited her best jewellery at the bank, in an uncharacteristic mood of caution before she left. Not that I am going to tell him that - let him find out for himself and earn his right to be executor. He accompanies me to the door, making sure nothing else disappears en route, I think sourly, as I leave for the last time.

My own place has always been a haven – of sorts; that is, when I can be bothered to tidy away the piles of papers and matters requiring my attention. I give the purple box files a prominent place on the table at the side of my 'work station', as I so grandiosely call the fourth-hand desk bought from the charity shop across the road. Cressy had moved into what I called a gracious flat in a Georgian house near the park, after leaving the marital house full of memories for Paul to rattle around in, and populate intermittently with Greg and his friends.

"No use demeaning myself in any way – this is the standard he needs to maintain for me after all those years" she'd said firmly "and if it costs him more than he wants to pay – so much the better!" Attagirl! I was so proud of her resilience at that time, although at the same time suspecting it was an armour of bravado; but we could build upon it, I'd hoped.

My own flat, by contrast, is tiny - above a small gift shop in a busy side street just off Chiswick High Road. I'd never entertained her there – not through any feelings of inadequacy on my part or fear of snobbery on hers, but simply that hers was so much more comfortable and spacious.

I enter the side door, arms full with the box files and the sports bag of books and CDs, ignoring the day's post on the floor, and shuffle up the stairs into the main room. My filing system is overflowing from the seat of the Victorian nursing chair, so, as I manufacture space on the desk, I sigh at the thought of an enforced attack on the chaos. But not today – no, definitely not today, although I make room for George Eliot on the mantelpiece.

Filling the kettle in the tiny kitchen I gaze out over the back yard scattered with piles of packaging from the gift shop below me. It could be worse, I've always thought – worse being, in my scale of snobbery, a fast food takeaway of some description. I need the solace of strong coffee as I read the last part of her letter.

... Now, before I descend into maudlin, and just in case anyone queries my state of mind at the time of writing, I need to tell you that I've noticed one or two strange episodes of late. To say I'm worried is somewhat of an understatement.

As you may perhaps eventually guess, the 'other' side of my life (which you don't know, are unlikely to understand, and of which you certainly wouldn't approve, I suspect!), has brought me great comfort of late. But, as I put into the mouth of one of my characters - from yourself, an "air of amused tolerance will suffice".

Please read it. Carefully and considerately, winnowing chaff and grain ...

And now I really must go to pack my clothes for the trip. Whatever made me agree? I have no wish to be seen as one of the international faces of charity, but maybe they'll allow me some shopping time as part of the deal.

So, no long farewells. If events prove that I was right to spend so much precious time producing all this, then I can't resist saying that maybe you will

The Ripples and the Tapestries

> *also come to know that there really was more to it all than meets the eye ... !!!*
> *Much love as always, my dear guide, philosopher and friend -*
> *Cress xxx*

I had returned home to an emptier life - or so I thought. But what if Cress was right and what if there *is* more to it ... to what ...?

Some weeks later, with emotions slightly less raw, I find myself with time to spare and, setting the diary on one side, with a glass and a bottle of Chilean red from the off-licence to hand, opened the purple file marked

PART ONE - THE RIPPLES

Another handwritten note was inserted after the title page.

> *The characters are of my own choosing, as is the 'what if?' attitude towards the plot. But as I researched the background for the first part of my 'fantasy' novel I uncovered genuineness and remarkable skills among people who were as devoted to their 'calling', as they saw it, as any orthodox priest.*
> *I found the project developed an energy of its own ... this is well-documented by other authors who say "the characters took over" and indeed I found this - but I also found that whole passages were taking place as I wrote about them e.g. Sonia's act of generosity was being carried out by a friend <u>at the precise time of writing</u>. What would logically explain that? Once could be called coincidence, but there were others.*
> *I found myself having conversations with people, which provided material I needed for the part I was currently working on - again too many for coincidence. Books began to arrive in my life unbidden - literally falling off library or bookshop shelves, but with information which saved me hours of research. Having always been (as you*

well know) a spiritual sceptic, I was introduced to people (mostly via fundraising events for the charity), whose whole way of life encompassed these things, and they seemed so normal and genuine that I found myself <u>in spite of myself</u> becoming a tentative believer.

<u>Now</u> the scariest thing is the predictive element occuring so often in the second part.
So, if you're reading this before you expected to, then just let's say I had a premonition ... and all I ask is that you read with as open a mind as possible ...
C.

the ripples

1

The Secretary breathed a sigh of relief.

"I'll swing for that woman one of these days" she muttered under her breath, watching from behind the curtains as the Chairwoman and the other two cronies departed, making their way to where George awaited his employer, holding the car door open.

Turning to Elsie, an amiable sort who let nothing upset her on principle, and Janet, who would not say 'boo' to the proverbial goose, she looked from one to the other.

"What do you propose doing about *that*, then?"

"There's nothing we *can* do, Margaret," replied Janet "we'll have to amend the constitution, as she said."

"But we're the ones who have to bear the brunt of the complaints, and it's so *unfair*."

"She's within her rights, I suppose" ventured Elsie "Being Chairwoman and having the casting vote and all that, but it's always the same – she invariably manages to get her own way."

"… and all I can do is put it in the minutes as proposed and carried – just because she had her friends here. We never see them when we want some practical help with the fundraising."

"Well, if it's any comfort, it's not just *our* Committee."

Disconsolately they started to gather the coffee cups and biscuits.

Lady Sonia had deigned to nod haughty acknowledgement to her two acquaintances, their roles having been played so that she had again won the day, and sat back in her car with an irritated air as the chauffeur arranged the rug over her lap. Village life is becoming so tiresome, she thought. However, she saw it s her duty to direct those who would otherwise get bogged down by their own incompetence – and duty was something she had certainly never shirked.

Perhaps in the New Year she would revise her schedule and stand down from the most boring committees. She had set a standard, after all, and surely they could continue without her, providing they followed her precedents. As one's years advanced, being a pillar of the community was somewhat of a mixed blessing. Tapping George on the shoulder, she directed him to drive to Guildford – she would spend half an hour at the small gallery she had recently decided to patronise. There was always room at the Hall for another local watercolour of quality.

George, knowing which side his bread was buttered, had long ago cultivated an expressionless response, and respectfully murmured "Yes, m'lady" as all good chauffeurs are trained to do, resigning himself to missing coffee and chat in the kitchen with Annie and Doris.

※

It was, to outward appearances at least, just like any other day at Woolston Hall, and, apart from the extra preparations for Lady Sonia's birthday in the following month, he planned changes that would be taking place gave no hint of the cataclysmic upheavals to come from the unplanned ones.

She, Lady Sonia that is, had decided it was to be a celebration reminiscent of years long past, when the Hall was the focal point of so many business calendars, and invitations were much-coveted accolades of success. Preparations for *this* event, Lady Sonia's seventieth birthday (to be celebrated by all and sundry, like it or not, on Christmas Day – no matter how inconvenient) had begun in October, with lists of guests and food, programmes of shopping and ordering. Every taste catered for, every eventuality covered even before it might be thought of as a problem – aspects of hospitality for which the Hall had become renowned in Sir Geoffrey's time.

Annie emerged from the pantry with yet another armful of ingredients.

"What is it this time?"

"Florentines. I've been drying the tins ready to store them."

Doris paused, hands on hips, arching her aching back, then wiping a wisp of hair from her brow with the back of her hand. She was the epitome of the old-fashioned middle-aged cook-housekeeper, surveying the scene in the kitchen with a practised eye. The kitchen was undoubtedly the hub of the household, jealously guarded by Doris as her domain, and she deferred only to Lady Sonia who, as her employer, was the only one allowed to voice opinions. It was an empire to be proud of and with standards to be zealously maintained.

"I shall be glad when that girl from the village starts. Work Experience

I think they're calling it. Well, she'll get plenty of experience here for a couple of weeks. Enough to put her off work for life, maybe."

"Think of all the experiences we've had over the years, and we're still part and parcel of the Hall ..." mused Annie, pouring mugs of tea for the two of them. "Come on, it's ten-thirty, and we can have this before you start mixing. Let's have a look at the paper for a few minutes, then I can start the coffee for upstairs when her ladyship returns."

They settled into companionable silence for what had become their morning ritual in the past few years since the regime at the Hall had changed. Doris's mind was full of today's list of tasks – after the Florentines, she would start mince pies. Dundee cakes were already wrapped in greaseproof paper and stored, and the heavy fruit birthday cake was upside down in its container, halfway through the daily spoonful of brandy that prepared it for the later layers of almond paste and icing.

The notice board in the kitchen was full of different handwritten lists, carefully arranged in sequence equally carefully adhered to, ticked and filed away – a system that had worked well when the Hall was in its heyday. Doris was glad she had retained them – it made life easier now she was a little, well, more mature. Methodical, reliable, unflappable, she had needed all those qualities to survive Lady Sonia for so long. The mainstay of the domestic scene, her lack of further ambition had been exploited for ore years than she cared to remember, but she cherished and totally believed a conversation once held many years ago when Lady Sonia had been recovering from an illness that had meant a short stay in hospital.

"The food was certainly not suited to my taste, and I just couldn't wait to return to my own diet, Doris. Stay in my service and you'll never want for anything for the rest of your life."

Well, there were definitions that changed over the years, of what Doris might want, but she saw no reason to doubt those words and the intention behind them. On the whole she had been happy enough – at least until recently. Now, however, the order of things had definitely changed and showed worrying signs of becoming unbearable, no matter what incentive there might be to stay on.

The problems centred around Benjamin's wife, of course – Lady Sonia's daughter-in-law and were especially worrying when Victoria (whenever her indomitable mother-in-law was out of the way) tried to insist on reorganising minor domestic matters that had been running perfectly smoothly for years- under the pretext of 'updating'. Doris had already come very close to telling her employer that she could not be expected to work for two mistresses.

Doris rose, with effort, and resumed her place at the other end of the table, checking the assorted ingredients. Annie looked up at the clock, folded the paper, hastily drank the last of her tea and started to assemble the coffee tray. Small and neat, she darted around the kitchen. Hanging her apron behind the door, she glanced in the mirror, patting a strand of her fading auburn hair now streaked with grey. Whatever had happened to the real Annabel Waite, she wondered, as a reflection of a stranger looked back at her from the glass – where was the girl who had once been so happy? Sometimes her life had seemed to consist solely of different performances; the current one of 'devoted Lady's companion' having definitely been the most demanding, and so lengthy tat she had almost forgotten who her real self might be. A small shiver made her turn away from the reflection and back to the task in hand.

The Hall occupied a significant part of the Surrey countryside – near enough to Guildford to be convenient, yet distant enough from the M25 to feel completely rural. The last two miles from the nearest motorway junction wound through smaller lanes to bring the traveller to the village then beyond, to large wrought iron gates set in a semicircular sweep of rich red brickwork, bound and capped by Portland stone to match the architectural style of the Hall. The Gatehouse, set back slightly from the driveway just inside the gates, no longer needed to perform its original function; modern communications linked the intercom by the gate with the big house.

The landscaping of the nineteenth century had favoured an avenue of limes leading to the well-kept grounds surrounding the house. A slight curve in the drive led to an air of mystery about what lay ahead. In late spring, with high banks of rhododendrons providing a backdrop behind the newly-leaved trees, it was an approach possibly at its best – but even in winter when the bare trunks and branches were starkly outlined against the dark shrubbery, it had a grace and beauty.

The Ripples and the Tapestries

The Hall was a very distinct example of its time. The gateway had echoed this, but older and more mellowed red bricks formed the main square building with single storey wings at each side; gables rose a the front outlined with stonework in an enthusiastic tribute to the architect's whim; imposing bay windows jutted their solid shapes, and crenellations against the contrasting brick and drainpipes formed exclamation marks, emphasising corners protected by more stonework..

The garden boundaries were marked by a profusion of stone urns. Long-established walkways with herbaceous borders meandered through the grounds, punctuated by statuary. The gardens had always been a significant part of the charm of the Hall, particularly in the days when Sir Geoffrey was in his heyday. To be invited to the house parties was an honour, and greatly appreciated by other businessmen. Grottoes and nooks were the scene of many a deal being conducted in the utmost privacy. More 'personal' usage was also a feature, but discreetly so, of course, with never a hint of scandal reaching the ears of Lady Sonia – it was essential to protect good standing with the couple, to say nothing of running the risk of blighting potential business opportunities.

≈≈

Wheeling the coffee trolley into the drawing room, Annie paused just before her usual discreet tap at the half open door. She could hear Lady Sonia's authoritative tones fro he far end of the room, as she explained yet another nuance of etiquette to the hapless Victoria.

Sharply featured, elegantly dressed and immaculately groomed, her Ladyship sat straight backed and formal at her writing desk with a pile of lists, giving total concentration to the task in hand. Her hands were slim claws, bearing the weight of several heavy diamond rings of flawless quality, matched by discreet diamond studs in her ears. Se ad taken care to ensure that hallmarks of quality and value had emphasised her improvements in life at every turn, and years of observation and practice had honed her air of good breeding, so that she truly appeared to be 'to the manner born', with not a trace of the flatter vowels of her provincial upbringing ever betraying her origins – of which, of course, she never spoke. With the wealth and standing she had acquired ensuring that she carried weight in the levels of the community she chose to honour with her presence, she had chosen committee work wisely. Significant enough to be household names, yet offering duties not too onerous to be fitted into the demands of providing the correct setting at the Hall to give the perfect backdrop for the business deals, charity work fitted well into forming a list of significant contacts. Sonia understood well what made the wheels of her current world go round, but was not too bound up in the work to weigh up its usefulness, and decided that the village could well do without so much of her time from now on. Bu confirmation of these thoughts could be left until after New Year – it was time now to concentrate on the matter in hand.

Vicky, sitting at her side, looked totally bored – alert enough only to become artificially animated when her mother-in-law turned to her for confirmation that she understood a particular point. Her seventh month of pregnancy did not suit her at all. She had none of the bloom that sometimes happens even after a difficult first trimester, and her sallow skin appeared out of condition, as did her short dark hair, listlessly flopping forward into her eyes, needing constant flicks into place behind her ears.

A young woman given to sulkiness, a pout almost her constant expression these days, she shared none of the joyful anticipation that her pregnancy seemed to bring to her husband and his mother. Their expectations of a son, the continuity of a dynasty that had long been planned by Sonia and her late husband, meant that they were completely blinkered. Only once, soon after she suspected she might be pregnant, had Vicky wondered whether to point out it might not be a son, then she had adamantly refused the information when it was later offered by the doctors, just in case Ben chose to use it as an excuse not to marry her. Vicky's ambition was almost as ruthless as her future mother-in-law's had been at her age, and it would be soon enough to face that hurdle when the child was born.

But Vicky felt cheated. She had intended to have at least a few years of getting accustomed to the new life she had married into, and seeing what she could get from it, before deciding whether motherhood was to be her choice or not. There was no doubt that she would have eventually persuaded Ben that they should marry – he was besotted by her, and she knew just how to keep him interested, but the unexpected

The Ripples and the Tapestries

pregnancy had hastened the wedding, as even in the first years of the new millennium some old-fashioned values still lingered on in families where outward appearances mattered. The wedding had not been quite the lavish society affair she had craved, but grand enough to make most of her erstwhile friends envious, and she had decided that life in Ben's private rooms at the Hall would be worth any inconvenience of living under the same roof as his mother.

Unfortunately, she had found that once she was married her role had subtly but swiftly changed from that of the cherished love of Ben's life to becoming an understudy for Ben's adored mother. Why had she not seen the warning signs sooner, she was to ask herself increasingly frequently as time passed.

Sonia was a force with a momentum so powerful that no scope for anything other than acquiescence was possible, and Vicky, young enough to wish to assert her independence yet unskilled in knowing the ways and means that might achieve it, had to bow to her mother-in-law's wishes at all times. It had hurt that Ben had taken his mother's side in all differences of opinion, ad it was only the thought of their eventual inheritance of the Hall that prevented more stubbornness on Vicky's part. She learned her role, but grudgingly, and eventually the mantle of resentment began to fall on her in a grey cloud of depression. All she could do was keep her hope projected forward to a time when her manipulative mother-in-law's powers would inevitably fade.

Annie was about to withdraw discreetly from the drawing room when Sonia's imperious tones made her obediently turn back.

"Tell George I shall need the car after all, Annie – sharp at two o'clock. He will be taking us to Guildford."

Annie, with years of practice, betrayed no reaction to the command other than a dutiful nod. No use explaining that it was George's afternoon off duty, no use trying to tell Sonia that George had made plans to take his mother for a birthday treat. Sonia had spoken; Sonia must be obeyed. Not surprisingly, chauffeurs came and went fairly rapidly after Sir Geoffrey's death, unable to cope with the unfeeling demands of his widow. Sonia decided not to notice the faint stiffening of Annie's posture. She knew full well it was George's free afternoon, but sometimes chose to remind her employees that their employer was in control. It felt good to be in charge of people's lives.

"You may pour the coffee, Victoria." Sonia never used the diminutive. The girl was looking pasty again. Such a pity that today's young women went to pieces. Pregnancy was a natural process, for Heaven's sake, but at this rate when the waiting ended it would not be a moment too soon.

Sonia turned to the guest list again, checking the three sections – house guest, visiting family and close friends, expected villagers and local contacts.

"The success of any function on this scale depends on meticulous planning, and imparting to the guests a thorough understanding of their participation. In that way, everyone is clear about what we expect from them – departure times are just as important as punctuality in arrival."

Vicky handed Sonia her coffee. She knew that she was being groomed for a time when she would be expected to take over these duties – under Sonia's watchful eye at first of course, then eventually she would be trusted on her own. It could take years, but while Sonia was still around Vicky could not expect to be allowed a free rein. It was proving to be a more difficult role than she had envisaged, but the rewards were so great that she had rationalised it to herself as a learning and qualifying process – her Master's degree in Mistress-ship, as she had once described it to a friend in an unusual moment of levity; Vicky was not renowned for her wit or her sense of humour.

Downstairs again, Annie sighed as she picked up the house phone to speak to George. Doris stopped chopping the nuts for the Florentines. Hearing Annie's part of the conversation, she gestured in sympathy. Poor George. How long would *he* continue to bite his lip and endure the treatment? True, Sonia had an amazing ability to keep some employees longer than would have been thought possible, but it seemed to have more to do with the employees' needs for a job than their conditions of work.

2

Barbara looked again at the invitation as dusk fell. How many more gatherings would she attend, she mused, pouring another large gin, and splashing a token amount of tonic into the antique cut glass tumbler.

As Sonia's oldest friend she had been honoured by a handwritten letter, outlining her expected part in the preparations – three days prior to the birthday her usual room would be available. Inwardly she sometimes felt manipulated, but outwardly she always took care to co-operate with whatever arrangements Sonia chose to make, however inconvenient it might be to her own private schedule. It had paid dividends in the past and, after all, she did have a genuine fondness for her friend after the long years of seeing Sonia make the most of her own opportunities in life. In fact, Barbara had learned a great deal over the years, and her own achievements made life more comfortable in ways she could never have foreseen when they first met, had there not been the background of the Hall from which to make the contacts on which her comfortable position in life rested.

It was certainly a long way from the drab house she had called home, in the drab post-war town where they had both attended the same school - although four years difference in age had meant that they did not actually form any friendship until later, meeting at a time when they briefly worked in the same office. Sonia had left to further her prospects, Barbara had stayed for a while, but they did not lose touch, as, apart from the common bonds of school and training, they had discovered a similarity of background. Barbara's openness had enabled Sonia to confide in someone for the first time in her life, and although Barbara had not had to suffer the stigma of a father who left her mother for another woman, she herself had lived without a father from the age of twelve, trying to absorb her own widowed mother's grief. Having exchanged their experiences at that early age, it was a measure of Sonia's trust that she knew she could rely on Barbara's discretion, and nothing ever went further than their own private conversations.

It's strange how life turned out, Barbara thought, glancing around the opulence of her flat, relishing the contrast between the 'then and now' of her life. Who would have thought that a girl from her ordinary background would have reached such a pinnacle of comfort? Once having decided that her destined path in life had little to do with the shorthand skills in which she had trained, but everything to do with her own brand of public relations, she accepted her clients good advice and generosity, and had earned the essential London base many years ago. Had she been given to introspection she might have linked the missing father figure in her life with her own readiness to accept favours. However, it was one part of herself that she successfully kept hidden from Sonia, knowing that Sonia was capable of a cold ruthlessness that would end even the oldest friendship if it were deemed necessary. Sonia, for her part, never gave it a thought. As she never went to Barbara's flat, and their only contact was when Barbara's assistance was needed for conferences, she was best left in ignorance.

※※

Other parts of Chiswick had changed, but this had been a good investment and would most probably always be regarded as the better area, close to the park yet within easy reach of the High Road. Barbara looked round the room and smiled fondly; she was pleased with her taste in this high ceilinged room with its elaborate cornices and period marble fireplace. On the wall opposite the tall sash windows the Georgian glass fronted cabinets reflected the lessening glow of the setting sun, their displays of delicate porcelain figurines shown to best advantage within the frame of burnished mahogany. On the mantelpiece an exquisitely gilded French clock took pride of place; a jeweller's display case contained so many small delights of gems and miniature gold charms nestling cheek by jowl with a few Faberge pieces. Whichever direction one looked there were delights, and everything contained so many memories of so many rewarding times.

Barbara drew the heavy velvet floor length drapes. These days she loved the onset of winter and the excuse to retreat into 'hibernation mode' – her only concession to her sixty-six years. Another party at the Hall – well, it would be a date not to miss, and would give her a chance to meet Benjamin's wife again.

What *was* her name ... oh, Victoria, that's right. Such a scheming little minx she'd appeared to be at first, but Sonia would carry on training her well, and would, no doubt, get her to a stage of being a worthy successor. Sonia had seen potential in her and had encouraged her beloved Benjamin to settle down. When he showed reluctance she had even thought of suggesting to her prospective daughter-in-law that the age-old ploy of feigned pregnancy might be used, she had once confided in Barbara. Fortunately nature took matters into its own hands, and although the result was a hastier entry into married life than any of the concerned parties had hoped, nonetheless it all showed signs of great promise under the ever watchful eye of the mistress of the Hall. Barbara settled into her chair with the footstool, a table just large enough to hold the latest novel she was reading, ash-tray, bottle and the tall crystal glass. Time to relish the thought of the forthcoming Christmas Day that promised to be like no other ...

Jacqueline's preparations for Christmas ground relentlessly on, but she enjoyed it more this year than for as long as she could remember. She had relaxed into her marriage now and had confidence in the feelings that had proved themselves well-founded. At first it had seemed incredible that any man had even shown the slightest genuine interest in her.

"A twice-married thirty-something with two children by different fathers" was her flippant self-deprecating comment when Richard once asked her how she would describe herself, but was taken aback by his vehement response.

"Don't *ever* put yourself down like that – *I* see a woman of courage and great depths, and I know you'll be capable of achieving anything you set your mind to."

Oh, he was the most perfect man for her, and she had daily reminders that this was so. It was not because he had so rapidly started to tell her of his conviction that he wanted her in his life forever, but he was prepared to wait until she was ready for him, no matter how long it took. With this emotional security obvious and available, Jacqui was ready far sooner than she had anticipated after the events of the previous years. The longer she knew him, the more Richard proved rock solid and supportive without being over-protective. Soon she could no longer imagine life without him, and they slipped away one weekend to a quiet wedding that had none of the publicity her first had attracted, nor any of the mixed feelings of her second. Any doubts, she realised, had largely been due to anticipating her mother's disapproval of what she would, no doubt, see as only a slightly more acceptable husband than the first had been.

Sonia, of course, had very fixed ideas of who was suitable for either of her twins, and Richard would have been better advised to have turned up first in Jacqueline's life – it would have saved much heartache and bitter feelings. But timing is everything and at least he had come on the scene at a time when Jacqui could appreciate his qualities, and she was able to announce their wedding to Sonia - although only after it had taken place.

While Richard was busy establishing his past as junior partner in the country medical practice, Jacqui was able to care full-time for Tim and Ella. They planned to have their own child at a later date, but there was no need to hurry – let the two older ones settle into the reassuring normality of their newly formed family life, and forget the traumas of the past; she was thankful that even having Sonia as mother-in-law had not daunted Richard from marrying.

"You must take no notice of how she treats me," she had said as they travelled to the Hall for the first time as a family "it's something I can cope with, so please let me deal with it in my own way."

Richard said little, but inevitably noticed Sonia's obvious preference for her son, and what could only be described as a barely tolerant indifference to her daughter. However, Jacqui's relationship with Ben was loving and warm, as was to be expected from a twin sister, and she offset his tendency to be a 'Mother's boy' very well. A succession of girlfriends through the years had been expected by Sir Geoffrey, his late father, and the subject of many references to Benjamin being a 'chip off the old block' and other innuendos – well out of earshot of his wife, of course.

Sonia's attitude had been that she tolerated rather than welcomed the prospect of another woman in her son's life, and vetted them all for suitability of class, financial background (gold-diggers abounded in some circles) and potential succession to herself. Her reactions were invariably heeded – which did not mean to say that her precious Benjamin encountered only the pure and suitable girls his mother wanted, but he soon learned that there was a vast difference between the sort of girlfriends he could bring home to meet the family, and the ones with whom he could have active and non-meaningful relationships. In other words, the normal way of life for those young men with whom he had rubbed shoulders at school and through his undistinguished time at University.

Jacqueline met a few of them, and warmed to some more than others, naturally, but became less involved as her own life produced its significant demands of marriage at a young age. Ben had clumsily offered support, but had been unable to offer any practical help with either her divorce from Zak, or during her bereavement after Anthony's death - his loyalty to their mother getting in the way of his natural feelings.

Time passed, and as Jacqui became less in touch with her brother due to the twists and turns of her own life, she had not been party to the early stages of Ben's relationship with Victoria. In fact, due to the circumstances, she was only introduced just before the imminent wedding was announced at the informal betrothal dinner at the Hall, where she sat quietly wishing above all that their father could be at her side. Shortly after the wedding, when she discovered that the haste was due to Victoria's pregnancy, she offered friendship, as was natural between sisters-in-law and as a mother to a mother-to-be, but received little by way of warmth and responsiveness from the bride.

At the time of Sonia's seventieth birthday Ben had been married for less than six months, and it was not turning out at all as he had expected. He had always found Vicky to be moody, even more so now she was pregnant, but he expected her new way of life to provide a welcome distraction from her physical condition. Sometimes he wished that he had not been so stupid as to rush into the marriage - but having confided his predicament to his mother when Victoria had announced her pregnancy, Sonia had seized the opportunity to gain a daughter-in-law who at least appeared to have the potential to be trained for her position at the Hall. The pregnancy was a bonus, and the expectation that Sonia would soon have a grandson was uppermost in her mind when she firmly told her son that it most definitely was the right time for him to settle down and produce the next generation of Woolstons.

Ben had acquiesced readily enough. He was tired of playing the field, felt sufficient emotional attachment to Vicky to sustain a permanent relationship, and vaguely thought that everything would settle down without too much effort from himself. When the marriage developed early teething troubles as all marriages can, it was unfortunate that it was Lady Sonia in whom he confided. Sonia, also unfortunately, appeared to relish this, welcoming the knowledge that her son had not left her, and that she was still the prime love in his life.

Jacqui observed all this intermittently from the sidelines, but realising she was unable to do anything to improve the situation, wisely kept her thoughts to herself. Yet she felt sad that her brother could not have the easy and rewarding fulfilment that she and Richard had. It was Jacqueline's nature to want everyone to have good things in their lives, and to help people discover what they might be. She had touched on that happiness and fulfilment with Anthony, her second husband, then had it snatched away by the accident. Now she had a second chance with Richard – life was good, and she knew how to value and cherish the quality of their love for each other.

But now it was Christmas Day – and not only that, but also Sonia's birthday celebrations. The car sped along the roads towards the Hall. It would only be a thirty-minute journey with no commuters on the motorway at this time of day. The children sat in the back seat, half-dozing after the excitement of the previous evening's anticipation, then the ritual of sleepily rousing, feeling the weight of a full Christmas stocking on their beds, and contentedly murmuring "he's been!" before shuffling back into cosy happiness for the second part of the night's sleep.

This year, of course, it was to be a different Christmas Day. The normal routine was to travel to Woolston Hall in time for lunch with their grandmother. Sonia's personal habit was always to rise early to attend morning service in the village church with Benjamin, then return to the Hall, where Jacqueline's arrival with the children would coincide with drinks before lunch, and gifts would be exchanged in the drawing room. With the Christmas tree set up away from the fire, and painstakingly trimmed by Doris and Annie with festoons of tinsel, strings of lights, and fascinating miniature toys hanging from every available branch, it was instant Christmas wonderment.

Last year Jacqui had cherished the moment when Tim and Ella, eyes shining, stepped into the drawing room and saw the 'magic tree' as Tim had always called it, with neat piles of parcels around the foot. They were carrying Granny's birthday presents and rushed in, insisting on giving them to her even before they had taken off coats and mittens.

Whatever Sonia thought of her daughter in private, she'd had the grace to put on sufficient pretence in front of the children. Welcoming them with a somewhat formal peck on each cheek, after accepting their gifts she asked what Father Christmas had brought. Tim had proudly showed her his new watch and had been asked to "Tell Granny what time it is".

Saving him from the embarrassment of having to admit that he had not yet learned how to do that, his sister Ella came toddling up to Nonny, as she always insisted on calling her grandmother;

"Nonny, look, look!" waving a doll destined to be her favourite toy of all time, a creature of lurid coloured clothes, brown limbs and face. Sonia flinched, but forced a brave smile as the flailing arms threatened to dislodge her spectacles. Sonia had, from her birth, felt strangely drawn to the child – an unexpectedly emotional bond that she had never felt after her own pregnancy. Not that it resulted in anything other than a slightly warmer response than she afforded their mother. Anything more would have been seen as a sign of weakness, and she was the last person to encourage closeness that could lead the way to over-familiarity in any form.

"Oh … lovely, dear, now do be careful …."

Jacqui retrieved her daughter and led her to look again at the Christmas tree.

"When Mummy was a little girl like you, Uncle Ben and I always helped put the decorations on the tree. See that little glass trumpet? It's ever so old. And the glass balls with the crinkly edges? – they belonged to *my* granny."

The small girl had stood, finger in mouth, trying to think of her Mummy as very little – gave up the task and squatted to look at the packages in their Christmas paper with bows. Soon both children were engrossed in the presents.

That was last year. This year, of course, Sonia's birthday party was to eclipse any routine Christmas celebrations - the family would be part of a very much larger gathering. Richard knew how much effort his wife put into maintaining the link between the children and her mother, and how she hoped that one day the children would be able to achieve what she herself had not, and a better relationship would result.

Sonia was not a naturally affectionate woman, but Jacqui ensured that Granny was part of daily conversations at home, even though the children saw her only a few times each year, mostly to commemorate birthdays. She herself made a weekly telephone call to her mother, always including the children, with a piece of news they could 'tell Granny'. Sometimes Sonia appeared to be responsive and Jacqui would raise her hopes that one day their relationship would become easier. As ever, her mother's usual vacillation between what appeared to be indifference and animosity was puzzling.

Jacqui had sat back in the car seat as they drove to the Hall, musing about her life. She had grown up in the knowledge that her twin brother Ben was Sonia's favoured one, and indeed had never questioned it. Her father's his love for both his children included a special element for his daughter, which provided compensation for what his wife could not. It seemed, if not entirely natural, an arrangement that at least appeared to preserve a balance in the family.

Jacqui's second husband Anthony, the hypnotherapist and father of Timmy, had had his own theories, but could do nothing except sustain

The Ripples and the Tapestries

Jacqui's faith in her own beliefs that one day Sonia would somehow warm to her daughter. Experienced and skilful in picking up clues, Anthony suspected that there was an area of Sonia's life that no-one knew about. He'd already seen how secretive she could be about events that did not add to the image of perfection she decided her life had to be – even to the point of denying illness. A chauffeur had once made the mistake of referring to a visit to a private clinic that had been made. Sonia overheard the remark as she entered the kitchen to give orders to Doreen, and saw this as a gross betrayal of trust. Her tirade led to his dismissal, which was to be expected - and when she had to have regular treatment for a few months, she told no-one anything other than that she was "going into town for a shopping spree", which would necessitate staying overnight then having a few day's rest when she returned home.

Anthony had never had the chance to get further than the suspicions about Sonia's past – perhaps as well, Jacqui sometimes thought – she had noticed that those who tried to come too close to her mother would not last long as friends. Barbara was the only one who had survived as Sonia's confidante, and being the soul of tact that she was, had managed to steer a tricky route of maintaining that friendship, but also being a favourite person in Jacqui's life, too. Anthony's car accident after only months of marriage was a tragic blow, and Jacqui had to concentrate all her energies on the pregnancy Anthony never had a chance to know.

Then came Ella's birth and yet again trying to cope with her own life as a single mother. It was Barbara, her mother's friend, who stepped in and gave most comfort to Jacqui in those terribly bewildering months.

Jaqui shivered slightly at the memory and firmly told herself to concentrate on the day of celebrations ahead.

3

Sonia had spent an hour after attending the morning service at the church, dictating and dominating (her two favourite pastimes), and receiving several satisfactory telephone congratulations on achieving her three score years and ten. A late breakfast had been served for all those in the house, as the buffet would be available for the afternoon party, then the family evening meal would take place once all the visitors had left.

After breakfast, dignified enthusiasm had greeted Benjamin's disclosure that he had ordered 70 rose bushes, to be planted at the appropriate time. As an immediate gift, he had bought his mother an exquisite gold bracelet set with rubies, that Victoria had chosen. They both basked in her favour. Barbara had triumphed with her traditional gift of handmade Swiss chocolates plus, this year, to commemorate her friend's special birthday, a dainty pair of antique silver sweet tongs to complement them.

Annie and Doris went to the large dining room with Lisa, putting the final touches to the buffet, checking the various flower arrangements, making sure the glasses were sparkling – part of what was once their usual house party routine from years ago, when a buffet would be provided for the guests on the day of departure. Lisa, just fifteen, and experiencing her first time at the Hall, was terrified of Sonia, and very nervous, but proud to have been chosen - Sonia chaired the School Governor Committee, so the Head Teacher had known how imperative it would be for him to select the right girl for the occasion. Lisa's neat hair and carefully discreet makeup perfectly set off the formal uniform of black skirt and white blouse, and she looked far more mature than her years. Benjamin had already noticed her, thought Annie, more attuned to those things than Doris, and she determined to keep a discreet eye on the girl – the last thing they needed would be any scandal, and Annie's deep mistrust of men guided her protective instincts.

Vicky had been ordered to attend Sonia's preparations before the gathering, scheduled for 3 o'clock, began. They made their way slowly up the wide staircase an hour before the first guests could be expected, even Sonia's dignified pace slowing to match Victoria's eighth month pregnancy need. It was her only concession these days to the expected arrival of her grandchild. She had been more irritated than she cared to disclose by Victoria's 'below par' pregnancy, and hoped that it would soon pass when the child was born. The nursery had been prepared well in advance, in a room that was part of Benjamin's suite, and fortunately well out of earshot of Sonia's rooms. The child would be part of the family when she, Sonia permitted – with none of that over-familiarity that seemed to be encouraged these days.

It would be too tiresome if Victoria became a doting mother, but Sonia somehow thought that was unlikely – she enjoyed the trappings of affluence too much to allow motherhood to intrude, and would soon be putting her energies into the plans Benjamin had for the Hall.

"Not the lilac, after all, Victoria" she commanded "it makes my skin look sallow. I will wear the dark blue dress - and find that pink pashmina dear Benjamin bought me last year."

She lay on the bed for precisely seven minutes, eyes closed, while the garments were found, then opening them, found she was slightly dizzy. Shaking her head slightly, she sat up carefully and decided to ask for assistance from Victoria, rather than dismissing her to prepare herself. Swiftly recovering, and having changed her dress, Sonia tried several pairs of heavy diamond earrings for effect before she decided on wearing the daintiest, to complement the silver thread embroidery on the fine cashmere.

"We used to call them stoles fifty years ago" she mused, sitting at the dressing table, while Victoria was busy with tail comb and spray. "Dances were known as 'hops', there were no such things as teenagers, and gentlemen accepted 'no' for an answer."

"It sounds dull to me" Victoria commented.

"You knew where you stood;" snapped Sonia acidly. "We had backbone, and standards. Something I want *you* to develop with regard to Benjamin's projects. The Hall has always been associated with quality. We may be new money compared with some of the families around here, but we certainly know how to conduct ourselves."

Even on this day, Sonia could not resist seizing an opportunity for training, Victoria thought, sullenly. It made her shudder and wonder if she was, after all, in the right place. Coming from an unremarkable local professional family, but determined to improve herself, her social ambition had apparently resurrected memories of the young Sonia, and this mirror image had formed an instant recognition when they first met. Sonia had seen in Benjamin's choice a worthy successor to her role as Lady of the Hall, and had set out to train Victoria to be her equal as a hostess, in preparation for Benjamin's business plans.

But could anyone be as ruthless at the core of her being, yet with that deceptively charming exterior, as Sonia had been, her daughter-in-law wondered. According to Ben, even Sir Geoffrey's final illness had never prompted a softer part of his wife, although she managed to retain a façade of caring in the presence of his private nurse. Victoria wielded the comb with a momentary lack of concentration.

"Don't pull, girl" Sonia snapped "now hold the mirror so that I may see the back properly. I thought so – do that part again, you've made it unbalanced."

Victoria sighed, straightened her back momentarily then bent to her task again, but at last completed Sonia's coiffure to her liking.

"There you are. Do you wish me to come downstairs with you?"

"Of course not. You may inform Benjamin that I am ready and we will make our appearance at three precisely. As it is two forty-five now, that leaves you time enough to get yourself prepared."

The young woman took heed of the note of dismissal in her mother-in-law's voice. She walked heavily along the corridors to the rooms she shared with Benjamin, and the adjoining dressing room that had been converted to make a nursery. Using the house phone, answered by a busy Annie, she announced that Lady Sonia was expecting her son in her room, then sank on the bed for one glorious moment of relaxation. Thank goodness there was only a month or so to endure this awful undignified physical state, where she felt like nothing on earth, where her moods were uncontrollable, and where the last person she wanted to see was her husband.

"Please God, let it be a boy, then I won't have to go through all this again" she prayed for the thousandth time. No time for dwelling on that now, though – no time for anything but a quick change of dress and refreshing her makeup. Reluctantly, with ill-grace and a supreme effort she rose and went to the bathroom.

※

Barbara was greeting and surreptitiously supervising the guests as they started to arrive at the Hall for about two forty-five, as instructed. Over thirty had received their invitations some weeks past, with very mixed reactions, as they realised that their own family traditions would have to be totally disrupted to accommodate Sonia's schedule. Husbands had grumbled, grandchildren had been puzzled and resentful, but it made no difference - husbands and wives concocted various excuses to justify the expected response and rearranged their own plans to suit the obligatory attendance; to step out of line would have social consequences that would affect lives for their foreseeable future.

"Like a command performance" was the least offensive comment expressed by many of those 'privileged' to be on the list. Selected W.I. members, fellow members of the charity committees chaired by Sonia for many years, the Vicar and his wife, head teachers of schools, representatives of the village clubs and societies which, if Sonia never actually graced them with her attendance, welcomed (at least in theory) the approval her invitation bestowed.

Neighbours were represented by a retired Colonel, and business connections by erstwhile 'captains of industry' with their wives. The guests stood around or sat in the drawing room, talking in low tones, clustered in small groups by the fireplace, by the grand piano, by the tall spruce tree firmly braced in a large tub and festooned with all its decorations. An air of tension mingled with the boredom, but most managed to conceal their resentment.

Barbara had let it be known that Sonia would appear at three o'clock precisely, and as the clock ticked on the last arrivals came breathlessly into the hallway.

"Barbara! How well you look!" Richard had a soft spot for his mother-in-law's best friend, and gave her an affectionate hug. "Say hello to Auntie Barbara, children."

They happily obliged, showing the small toys they had smuggled in

their coat pockets, knowing she would join in their conspiracy. Jacqui gave her an affectionate hug and a whispered
"We'll have a chat later if we can manage it."

But with time ticking away there needed to be a hasty disposal of coats and gloves, then the family joined the other guests in the drawing room, shaking hands with a few, before Barbara stepped in, with a finger to her lips.

∽4∾

The subdued chatter died as all the guests turned to look through the doorway. Sonia, with studied effect, came slowly and elegantly, down the curved staircase, one hand resting lightly on the balustrade, the other tucked warmly into the crook of Benjamin's arm. Following at a discreet distance was Victoria Jane. For a fleeting moment at the bottom of the stairway, as her mother paused, Jacqueline thought she looked quite fragile – but it *was* only an impression, and it *could* be a trick of the light ...

As Sonia entered the drawing room a spontaneous chorus of "Happy birthday to you" started from the corner where the choirmaster (representing the choir) sat at the piano and his wife (representing the Mothers' Union) stood by his side. Tension eased as the tune was taken up, fell apart raggedly at the line "happy birthday dear ..." with a mix of "Sonia, Lady Woolston, Granny, Mummy or Mother" depending on the connection of the singers, then a rousing last line of relief when all joined in with

"... Happy Birthday to *you* ..."

Sonia acknowledged the ripple of applause, sank into a large chair with a table at the side, and was soon busy with the procession of gift-bearers led by her grandchildren. The brave few who had brought nothing but themselves were glad to see the distraction of the trays of sherry brought round by Annie and Lisa, then replaced by further trays of champagne. Doris appeared, wheeling a dumb waiter with the magnificently iced and decorated cake, encrusted with yellow sugar roses and ribbons. This was the signal for Benjamin to clear his throat and tap a pen on his glass for attention, as he prepared to make a speech.

"Welcome to each and every one of you" he began in a pompous tone. "As you know, my mother has today reached her three score years and ten, and it is fitting that so many of her friends have been drawn together to celebrate the event. It was, I am sure, no accident that her birth coincided with another great birthday ..."

The Vicar drew in a sharp breath, but Benjamin continued, oblivious to any potential offence.

"... and to commemorate her own significant day, a donation will be made to the village church in order to provide a new set of vestments, which will match the altar cloth she donated at the time of my father's death."

The Vicar looked startled, then pleased.

"... this gesture is so typical of my mother. Her generosity over the years has become well-known throughout the county and beyond. Every time anyone enters our church or attends a service they will be reminded of this."

Sonia allowed herself to pat her son's hand, and smiled up at him – an indulgent, self-satisfied smile that no-one could fail to notice.

"The connections with the world of business forged by my parents, have been passed on to me and will be maintained at every opportunity. I am glad to see them well represented here today."

This drew a nod of acknowledgement from the three prevailed upon to attend by their socially climbing wives, who simpered and preened in their finery.

"Finally, I had rather hoped that my wife would have already chosen to present us with an impeccably timed contribution to the next generation ..."

Vicky refused to meet her husband's eyes and looked away from the glances of a less than tactful few, all strangers to her. None of her own friends had been invited, nor had that even been suggested, yet she would have given anything to have had someone present who was not family, someone who remembered her as she used to be, just for reassurance and an understanding glance.

"... but it was only a fleeting thought. How could this day be shared with any other – it belongs solely and indisputably to my mother and no one else, so I ask you to rise and toast the grandest woman in the county – Sonia, Lady Woolston."

Glasses were raised, and Sonia rose to formally make the first cut into the cake before it was taken away to the dining room. Chatter resumed, Sonia held court, and soon people were drifting into the dining room to make inroads on the food. The delicious savouries, prepared so lovingly by Doris and Lisa proved too tempting to ignore and disappeared surprisingly rapidly, given that many local guests had already consumed their Christmas lunches. Small bite-sized sandwiches, tiny quiche tartlets and cream cheese roulades could not be resisted, and settled surprisingly well on to full stomachs, when accompanied by sherry, champagne and wine.

༺༻

Vicky was glad of a chance to sit down after the toast. Jacqueline noticed this and went to her side.

"Anything you'd like to drink? A glass of water?"

Her offer was accepted gratefully. These days neither sherry nor champagne was palatable, and her obligatory glass sat untouched on a nearby table.

"I'm not prying, but if you're finding anything too difficult these days and I can help, do let me know. The last few weeks always seems to be such an endless stage."

Vicky managed a wan smile at her sister-in-law, then pulled herself together with an effort.

"Oh, but I *am* coping. Your mother is such a wonderful inspiration with her 'show must go on' approach, so I'm doing the same. I'm sure I will soon recover, and of course there will be the Nanny to help."

Jacqui remembered her own optimism as she had awaited the birth of Tim, trying to retain a 'normal' life for the benefit of her first husband, the wayward rock star who demanded his wife's total attention - when he remembered to come home. Ben was as likely as Zak had been to be intolerant of disruption, but now was certainly not the time to enlighten his wife. She returned with the water.

"Don't forget, I'm only a phone call away."

Her sister-in-law nodded.

Ella trotted over, her hands extended to show her mother how much chocolate had melted before it reached her mouth.

"Nonny gave it to me" she announced proudly "and Timmy's is even worser."

"Worse" her mother automatically corrected. " Come along – we need to wash this off. Timmy? Timmy – come with us … Do excuse us, Vicky."

Watching the little group steering through the guests, Victoria wondered again if she herself was really in the right place, with the right people, in the right life. She felt a shiver of something that felt like foreboding, and wished that she could disappear for a rest. The baby felt so heavy in her womb and everything took so much effort – another month of this was a huge mountain to climb.

She noticed that some early leavers were making their way to Sonia's chair to say farewell and congratulate her, having done their duty. Hopefully the rest would not take too long. One blessing of insisting on this day was that most people wanted to return to their own homes as soon as they decently could, and an hour was sufficient for most to feel they had done their duty, delivered their good wishes and have seen and been seen by the ones who noticed these finer points of etiquette. No sooner had the first bold few said their farewells than the majority took the opportunity to ask for their outer garments, and soon Annie and Lisa were dispensing coats and wraps, and ensuring no-one left anything behind.

✥

"Victoria!"

Ben's voice came nearer. Aware he was under Sonia's watchful gaze, he bent to murmur discreetly in his wife's ear.

"Yes … yes. No, I'll be fine" she assured him. Moving as swiftly as she could she went across to Sonia and helped her mother-in-law to her feet. Sonia looked pale under her make-up and her eyes were dull, but she shrugged off any assistance once she was standing.

"I will rest for a while. Benjamin – attend to the remainder of our guests, Barbara will help you. Victoria - come upstairs with me and I will be down for dinner as usual."

The journey upstairs was slow, with many pauses for breath, but Sonia refused to allow Victoria to call Annie for help, or even Barbara. On reaching her room, she swayed and nearly lost her balance, but her daughter-in-law managed to steady her and help her to the bed, where she sank back on the pillows. Removing her shoes, Victoria made Sonia comfortable under the coverlet and noticed that a little colour was coming back into her cheeks.

Victoria was never very comfortable with other people's illnesses, and the thought of the indestructible Sonia succumbing to anything serious was unthinkable, so her bedside manner consisted of vaguely patting the bony hand lying on top of the counterpane and awaiting further instructions. None was forthcoming, so when Sonia's eyes closed and her breathing settled, she moved away from the bed and slipped out of the room. Her own chilliness had returned after the exertion of climbing the stairs with Sonia, and she walked through the corridors to her own room to collect a wrap for herself.

The guests had almost dispersed. Annie and Lisa had closed the dining room door and were starting to clear the debris of the elegant buffet. Jacqui was getting the children into their coats and Richard was shaking Ben's hand, formally thanking him for his hospitality.

Barbara longed for a cigarette. Once the little family was out of the way, she thought … these days one had to be so careful not to offend, particularly with Richard being a doctor. In any case, she was very fond of Jacqui and the way she had survived the unfair bias of her upbringing. It was a puzzle to her, close friend though she was, that no real reason had ever come to light for Sonia's blatant favouritism of Ben and overt resentment of his twin sister.

"I'll run upstairs and say goodbye on behalf of all of us" Jacqui said to her family, "get in the car and I'll be with you in just a minute."

A soft tap at her mother's half open door brought no response, so she pushed it open and walked in to leave a gentle kiss. Leaning over the still figure she immediately sensed that something was not right – not right at all. No faint breath against her cheek. Jacqui reached for her mother's hand, tried to locate the pulse spot on her wrist, then felt the side of Sonia's neck.

Victoria - where was Victoria?

Grabbing the house phone she waited an age, it seemed. Benjamin answered, irritated, then was stunned into silence.

"Ben, get Richard – I think mother's … quickly … *quickly … please* come up here."

5

"You totally stupid girl! I *knew* I should never have let an idiot like you get your hands on him ..... what sort of daughter-in-law are you ...... can't you see I'm not well ...... what *am* I doing up *here*? ...... you had no right to leave me ......"

Sonia's thoughts had screamed inside her head as she found herself gently floating up to the ceiling, moving in a soundless vacuum she couldn't explain. Her limbs were without sensation – or appeared to be, as the ceiling was there but she had no feeling of bumping against it. Now, looking down, she saw herself lying peacefully on the bed, apparently asleep. Why was she *here* when she should be *there*?

"Get me out of here! Benjamin, Barbara – help me to come back!"

The phone – that would solve it. One ring and her beloved Benjamin would come running and take care of everything. She looked down again and tried to reach out ... but nothing in her arm responded. It must be part of whatever she was dreaming ... if she shut her eyes then it would all be back to normal. But even her eyelids would not obey. She felt trapped. There was no pain, not even an ache, just this ridiculous situation where she was pinned up against the ceiling, unable to speak or move, and with nobody there to see her predicament.

There was a tap at the bedroom door. It opened - how *dare* anyone enter without receiving her permission ... Jacqueline moved quickly to the bed and bent down.

Sonia, at first puzzled, then horrified, watched her daughter's reaction – the way she held her mother's wrist, the way she felt for a pulse in her neck, the swiftness with which she seized the bedside telephone - and the urgency with which she then ran to the door and shouted for Richard to come quickly. Benjamin came rushing into the room first, then Richard, followed by Annie at a discreet distance, and Barbara, of course – all showing great concern.

Benjamin falling to his knees at the side of the bed, trying to get warmth into his mother's hand. Richard did what Jacqueline had done – felt her pulse, raised her eyelids, then shook his head gravely at the waiting family.

Having at first thought she looked asleep, now her body actually began to look lifeless, thought Sonia, yet it could not really be so – all that was needed was for it to be joined up again with the real Sonia who was *here*, waiting, floating above. She kept trying to pull against the force that held her apart from the empty shape on the bed, but nothing in this new situation would respond. Helpless, she continued to watch the scene below.

Her own doctor appeared, recalled from his early escape from the party. He used his stethoscope, checked pulses and, looking very serious, spoke to all of the assembled family in the room. Sonia couldn't hear what he said, but Jacqueline turned to her husband and wept. Richard put his arm around her, comfortingly. Ben, looking stony faced, gazed long and hard at his mother's body, then suddenly clenched his fists and turned swiftly away and out of the room, shrugging aside Victoria's attempt to hold his hand, snapping something under his breath at her, so that she visibly cringed. Barbara moved over to Sonia and patted her hand helplessly, tears streaming down her face.

The looks on their faces were the looks that people wore in old movies, Sonia thought. It was all too bizarre, when here she was, desperately wanting them to look up so they would see her and bring her back down.

Why were there no attempts at resuscitation? What was the doctor thinking of?

There should be ambulances and people rushing around with equipment and shocking her body back into life, instead of this attitude of acceptance. Again and again she tried to make herself heard, but it was no use, obviously they could not hear anything. Eventually she was forced to accept that she was wasting her time and became resigned to a situation that she only half understood – not wanting to acknowledge the full implication of something she had never encountered in her beliefs about the process of death.

Was she destined to spend eternity in this ridiculous space? Hovering around in her room for evermore? Eventually the fuss beneath her calmed down. One by one the family left the room until only Jacqueline remained.

Her daughter's face was full of love as she tenderly stroked Sonia's cheek and tucked a stray wisp of hair into place.

The Ripples and the Tapestries

"Oh Mummy, I *do* wish you peace at last. Please forgive me if I haven't been the daughter you hoped for. I hope you will be together with Daddy, and happy again."

A discreet tap at the door, and Annie entered with two men in suits whom Sonia had never seen before.

⁂

Sonia became aware that she, of all people, was powerless to do anything. It was an alarming thought that she had no control over anything for the first time for many decades. Then just as the implication dawned of the undertaker's men coming into her room, the ceiling apparently dissolved so that she could move through and she passed into a void.

A small part of her still wanted to return to her bedroom, which was now growing smaller and more distant. Sonia tried to reach back, to clutch the edges of the dissolving ceiling, but there was nothing to feel, nothing to hold, no sensation in her fingers.

All the walls had evaporated and she could see Ben pacing along the corridors outside his room. Jacqueline and Richard were moving down the stairs, then to the kitchen where Doris was fussing around, trying to distract the children from asking too many questions. Now even the Hall, with everything and everyone in it seemed to be getting even smaller, as if she were looking at the scenes through the wrong end of a telescope.

Everything became a velvety blackness that should have been threatening, yet somehow was not. It was warm and soft, and immensely soothing – a feeling as if she was being drawn into the softest feather down – no pain, no anxiety, nothing but peace. A pinpoint of light in the distance was drawing her towards it, as if it was a powerful magnet - yet lights did not magnetise, so why did it feel that way? The light continued to exert its influence. Powerless to resist, she felt an increase of speed as the light grew larger and brighter, then she was being rushed along through an upward vortex of brilliance towards … towards … where?

There was an impression of moving through warmth and exquisite perfumes, sounds like no others she had ever heard, colours like no others she had ever seen – all fleetingly, tantalisingly passing before she had time to dwell on them. Vast oceans passed beneath her and mountain ranges appeared in grey mistiness, too far below to endanger her progress. It seemed endless and very strange. She was aware of robed figures appearing and melting away as soon as she had focussed on them. Strange buildings appeared in the landscape and were soon lost to sight. She had no indication of how her flight was taking place – it just seemed to happen. It *must* be a dream.

Then at last all movement stopped.

Sonia found that she was standing in a meadow of luxuriant grass, with drifts of many exquisite flowers appearing at her feet in the most incredibly beautiful colours that she could never recall having seen anywhere before. A fringe of trees lined the edge of the meadow, which extended as far as she could see, gently undulating and with a warm perfumed waft of a breeze that hardly stirred the grass, yet which set the intense colours of the flowers shimmering and dancing before her eyes. But it was the lake that captured her attention. It was like no other lake she had seen – fathomless, dark and mysterious, reaching from a distant point somewhere unknown past the horizon. A boat appeared from a misty distance, moving silently without any apparent method of propulsion and slowly, with dignity, coming to rest at the bank a short distance away.

A figure appeared at the helm of the boat and motioned to her to step in. Sonia hesitated and looked around, wondering if she had a choice. She wanted to stay with the flowers in the meadow and reflect on what had happened. But even as the thought passed through her mind it detached itself and floated away like a wisp of gossamer. She had no choice.

Her arm was steadied as she stepped into the boat and she lay down on soft seating, closed her eyes and let matters take their own course. She had no resistance left, and felt as if she could sleep forever. Time seemed to have ceased, and in any case there was no way of measuring it. It could have been hours or minutes - or even days, she thought, as the gentle movement lulled her into another sleep. Rousing later, she thought she saw another bank where there were some indistinct figures

The Ripples and the Tapestries

who melted away when they saw her - all except one, who helped fasten the craft to a tree at the bank, and offered a hand to assist her out of the boat, before escorting her along a path.

This countryside was different – another meadow, certainly, but the grass was as closely cut as the finest English lawn. No wild flowers here, but at intervals there were drifts of plants and flowers she recognised – large hostas, sweet-smelling freesias and lilies, all somehow emerging from the edge of the trees in a way they would never have been landscaped on Earth, and again with the intense colours that almost dazzled her. The pathway took a turn at the end of a copse, and looking ahead, it led to a marble house built in the classical style. They walked up a flight of shallow steps onto a balustraded area that extended around the building, then through a space between two pillars that led inside.

The interior was light and cool, and the whole atmosphere was very similar to ancient Grecian paintings. A gathering was in progress in a vast hall that lay behind the façade, and gentle conversation could be heard, as well as music. Sonia momentarily expected it to be a welcoming party, but she was not allowed to stop. Her escort whisked her through corridors, then in through a doorway to an anteroom where there was a couch, and motioned her to sit.

She tried to see who her guide had been, but he was wearing a hooded garment that shaded his face, and melted away before she could focus properly. Sitting on the couch, she tried to recall all the events of the day, tried to connect things one to another and make sense of it all, but it became too much, so she gave up, wondering what would happen next.

❦

Waking later, Sonia found she was lying in her own bed. She tentatively stretched her arms then her legs, and found to her amazement that she could move more freely than she ever remembered doing since she was a young woman. Sitting up, she looked around cautiously. The room was the same, with the curtains half-drawn together. All her usual possessions were lying on the dressing table – the jewel case, the silver-backed comb and brushes, the photographs. Relieved that it had all been a dream - or a nightmare - Sonia reached for the telephone to summon Annie to attend to her. But there was no phone. She looked around with more attention to detail.

All looked very normal … and yet … and yet … there was definitely something different. Glancing upwards, she noticed with surprise that the walls appeared to have no limits - they just disappeared into a vague golden mistiness of gossamer threads. A trick of the light, she assumed, suddenly feeling very tired again, so she sank back into her pillows and allowed drowsiness to overtake her once more. But when she woke later and optimistically looked around what seemed so familiar, it was the same appearance turning out to be the same delusion.

Where *was* everyone?

A thought struck her that was so odd she dismissed it instantly, but then it came back again – was it possible that this was *death*? But no, it couldn't be – where were the trumpet fanfares? Where was the welcoming party of all those who had been waiting to see her? Where were all the Heavenly hosts, the choirs of Angels, the Cherubim and Seraphim?

It was a pleasant enough setting, of course it was – but could this be what was meant by the house of many mansions? Surely not. Yet here she was, in some sort of a replica of her room at the Hall and with no-one to greet her – not at all what she had been led to expect by the Church's teachings.

Cautiously she tested the floor with one foot then both, then found she was able to rise swiftly and naturally - no need for the light cane she had been using lately – and moved across the room to the door, intending to summon Annie or Benjamin – anyone. But it had no handle or any visible means of opening it from inside and showed no sign of yielding to the firmest push. Moving across to the window she could see that the view outside was certainly not the view she was used to seeing from the Hall.

This was pleasant enough – gardens, countryside and even a glimpse of some far-off expanse of water, although whether it was lake or sea was impossible to tell, and in the far distance beyond a hint of mountain ranges. But - no gentle English hills rising into the distance, no village roofs visible a mile away, no lodge by the gateway …

… it most definitely was not Surrey … not England … not home.

6

Frantic haste gave way to a whole range of mixed reactions at the Hall. Richard had waited in the room until Sonia's own Doctor returned, hastily summoned back from his fireside where he was just starting to relax from attending the birthday party. He examined Sonia's body, confirmed Richard's report, made notes, then went to discuss matters with Ben.

Jacqui had retrieved the children from the car and was waiting with them in the drawing room that had so recently been full of people paying tribute to their hostess. It was unbelievable. The children, sensing that they ought to be solemn, actually were, but were very pleased when Doris came to ask if they would like to have biscuits and a drink with her and Lisa in the kitchen. Jacqui gave her a grateful smile.

"A massive stroke" Dr Hartley pronounced, when he came down the stairs. "She wouldn't have known much about it, really – who was the last one to see her?"

"Vicky took Mummy up to her room" Benjamin said as he followed behind. "Where is she? I haven't seen her – do *you* need to see her, doctor?"

"I should, for the paperwork. And in any case I should check up on *her* – don't want her going into shock at this stage, do we?"

"I'll go and find her first – I just want a word ..."

Ben went back upstairs, his tumbling thoughts in free-fall. She couldn't. Not Mummy. She wasn't ready to die – *he* wasn't ready to let her go. There was so much she had to do before she handed everything over to him. She couldn't leave like this, not with the baby about to arrive, and how would he cope with Vicky? Vicky – why oh why did it have to be *her*? What an *idiot* she was. She'd be nothing without Sonia to steer her, advise her and make sure she maintained the standards ... by the time he reached their room he was even more full of frustration and anger.

Vicky waited, sitting hunched wretchedly on the bed, recognising the footsteps along the corridor to be Ben's impatient rush. She was not, however, expecting the door to be slammed and to be the subject of his towering rage.

"*My* mother – the one woman who understood me" he fumed, "and you couldn't even be trusted to take care of her for five minutes. You must have *known* she was ill. You couldn't even be bothered to lift the phone. You think you're going to run this place? – you're not fit to take over a market stall."

Even with the door shut, he could be heard from the head of the stairs. The tirade went on and on, with his wife flinching at every phrase, unable to speak, and certainly unable to defend herself. She cringed at every word, hoping he would stop if he saw how much he was hurting her, but her reactions only served to increase his fury.

"Don't sit there snivelling, you wretched girl. If it wasn't for the child you'd have been booted out long ago, as well you know. You've made things ten times worse for everyone …"

A knock at the door while he paused for breath made him come to his senses.

"Ben!" it was his sister, who was truly appalled by what she heard as she came up the stairs followed by the somewhat embarrassed family doctor.

"Ben – you need to come and deal with things downstairs. I'll join you when Dr Hartley's seen Vicky."

୶୨ଓ

The doctor tactfully avoided any reference to what he had overheard and dealt with the necessary questions as briefly and sympathetically as possible, asking Victoria if she had noticed any unusual signs that Sonia was not feeling well, but she was too upset to say much. He offered to send her to hospital, but she adamantly refused, insisting she was just tired, even though it would have been tempting to take that line of escape – but no, it wouldn't be worth the risk of adding further fuel to Ben's rage. The Doctor reluctantly gave her a sedative and persuaded her to lie down.

"I would have preferred her to go to the hospital to keep an eye on the situation, but I'll call back in the morning" Dr Hartley said to Jacqueline who had waited outside the room. He watched Victoria sink into an exhausted sleep.

"If you're going now, could you tell Richard I'll be down in a moment and could you find out if Barbara can take over?" Jacqueline asked him. "We must take the children home, I want to reassure them and help them get used to things."

She went back to Sonia's room and knelt at the side of the bed, stroking her mother's hair, holding her hand, tears falling as she whispered a few words to the still figure. Getting to her feet when Barbara joined her, they both stood quietly holding hands for a few moments.

"Can you stay with Mummy until they come to … to …?" she choked back more tears. "I really must get the children back home."

"Of course I will. They need you. I'll look after things here, and keep an eye on everyone."

They embraced, and Jacqueline took one last look.

The journey back home was such a contrast from the excited anticipation a few hours earlier. Their mother sat in the back of the car with the children, reassuring them with warm cuddles, but there was no hiding the fact that Richard and Jacqui were subdued.

"Will it mean we won't ever see Nonny again?" Ella asked.

"She'll come and see you when you're asleep. You'll dream about her, then you'll know she's been."

Tim felt suddenly grown up.

"Will she be with Gramps?" He could just about remember his grandfather's kindly ways and the smell of his tweed gardening jacket. Geoffrey had died just before Tim was two, but there had been a strong bond between them and a special photograph was always in his room at home – Gramps bending down to hold his hand as they walked in the garden at the Hall, not many weeks before the heart attack claimed him.

"They'll be together now, and probably walking in a garden, smelling the flowers" Jacqui responded, picking up his thoughts. She gave him a gentle hug. The death of his grandfather, then later his stepfather, who was also abruptly taken from his life just as he was really getting to know him - too many changes and losses for a child his age, Jacqueline feared, but she had done everything she could to help him accept and understand. It was a difficult period for them both, but her pregnancy had helped to heal the sadness that Anthony would never even see his child.

The arrival of his little half sister had been a blessing in many ways, and although Jacqueline had little support from her mother she attributed that to her mother's continuing grief, hidden behind a mask of seeming indifference. Staying with her policy of remaining in touch, her patience eventually produced results, and Ella, once introduced to her Grandmother, proved to be a child that Sonia unexpectedly warmed to (providing of course that she did not have to encounter her too frequently), and the old rift at last had showed signs of beginning to heal.

≈≫

Jacqui hoped that none of Ben's rage had been audible downstairs. She was a great believer in adult conversations, particularly emotional ones, remaining just that – for adult ears only. The children dozed, snuggled up against her, one each side, in the warm car, and the quiet minutes gave her time to ponder that scene. Her brother could be volatile, she knew, but even making allowances for the shock he too must have been feeling, there was no need to round on his wife in that way. It did not bode well for that relationship, she mused – but perhaps things would improve once the baby arrived and they could settle down as a family.

Arriving home, the holly wreath on the front door of the neat house in the suburbs looked welcoming. Richard helped Jacqui carry the children out of the car and into the warmth of their sitting room. Putting them at each end of the long sofa, she covered them with the bright crocheted blankets she kept downstairs for times when security and comfort were what an upset child needed. She and Richard sat drinking hot chocolate, talking in low tones and making sure the children were undisturbed, not wanting them to wake on their own. Richard held her hand.

"You were a brick" he said tenderly "thank you for looking after Vicky like that."

"I hope she'll be alright. The doctor seemed to think that a few hour's sleep would help, but Ben's attitude worried me more than I can say. I'm just glad I was there."

The Ripples and the Tapestries

"Shock can have some really strange effects, Jacqui – fortunately he'll be kept busy with the funeral arrangements, and it will all blow over, I'm sure. All we can do is wait to hear from him about what he needs us to do. Phone by all means – but not tonight. Let's concentrate on the children and you."

The rest of that evening was occupied in looking after the children's needs and making things as normal as possible. Later that night, emotionally drained, Jacqui dreamed as she eventually slept fitfully. Her father was there, and walking with Anthony her second husband. They held out their hands to her, then moved away. After that, the second part of her night's sleep was easier.

❧

Barbara had taken over from Jacqueline's vigil, but once she was satisfied that Victoria was truly asleep, had crept downstairs again. Vicky had slept for a couple of hours, then woke alone, with a stabbing pain in her head, and a dull ache in her back shooting down her legs. The awful scene with Ben came flooding back into her consciousness as she tried to ease herself into a better position, then the ache became more insistent.

"No, please no …" she muttered through another wave of pain "I'm not ready, I can't …"

She waited a while longer, terrified of what she instinctively knew was about to happen, and her own unpreparedness. Carefully walking slowly down the stairs she could hear Ben and Barbara in the Library - thankfully realising he was not on his own gave her the courage to face him. Pushing the door open she saw them sitting either side of the fireplace, brandy glasses in hand, Barbara with the inevitable full ashtray on the table at her side. But thank goodness Barbara was there – it was another woman she needed at this moment.

"Oh God, it's that bloody wife of mine, the one who killed my mother."

Vicky's face crumpled with humiliation as she clutched the door handle, pain surging through her body.

"Barbara, I think I … I need … " she caught her breath and sank to the floor.

However much Barbara had to drink, she always seemed to be able to function when there was an emergency. The ambulance eventually arrived, but Ben refused to go to hospital with his wife who wept and screamed when he came near, so it was Barbara who accompanied her.

Three hours of confusion later, Victoria gave birth to a healthy girl. Barbara telephoned the Hall just before midnight to tell Ben the news. There was no answer, except from Annie who was sitting by the extension in the Lodge and who reassured her that he had safely gone to bed, not adding that he had staggered off with another bottle, even though she was sure Barbara would not have turned a hair at the news.

Barbara saw that Vicky was settled down for the night, made excuses to her and the hospital staff for Ben's non-appearance, ordered a taxi and returned to the Lodge, where Annie was waiting for more news.

It took another hour and several brandies to relay all the details. Barbara and Annie had become well acquainted over the years of Barbara visiting the Hall to assist Sonia; there was nothing to draw them into a close friendship – that would have been inappropriate in Sonia's eyes, who always had firm lines of demarcation drawn for her staff. Because Annie's position was more that of maid than companion, whenever Barbara visited she was expected to wait on her too, although Barbara was careful not to make her tasks too onerous.

Once the facts of the birth had been dealt with, the two women sat in the cosy front room of the gatehouse, reminiscing over good times and difficult ones. Annie confided that she felt it might be time to move on now that Sonia had died.

"I'm under no illusion about how things would be – even if Mr Benjamin said he wanted me to stay on, the new Mrs Woolston would feel that I was forever comparing her with her mother-in-law. I'm not intending to do it straight away, in the circumstances, but I won't hang on indefinitely. The next few days are going to seem very strange, though."

"It's not every day you have a death and a birth in one family. Come to think of it, it's not every day that someone becomes an orphan and a father within hours. I'd like to help, so I shall offer to stay on and assist Benjamin with practical things, give moral support, even though he may think he doesn't want that. We don't want him to go to pieces, but I do urge you to reconsider, Annie – things will be difficult enough for them."

"There's nothing now to keep me here. I only stayed because I promised Geoffrey …" Annie checked herself, but unspoken words hung thick in the air.

Barbara looked at her curiously. The familiarity was out of character and she sensed that Annie might have been about to add something that she could have regretted the next day, but they were both exhausted by the tensions of the day, to say nothing of the turn events had taken, and she let it pass.

"Come along then, time for bed or we'll be fit for nothing in the morning. We're going to need all our wits about us, dealing with birth, death and everything in between." Her brisker tone prevented the possible descent into shared confidences. Annie responded, albeit reluctantly – wishing, not for the first time, that she herself had someone close and trustworthy to talk with.

Barbara eventually dozed off to sleep in the spare bedroom at the Lodge that Annie had prepared for her while waiting for news from the hospital, rather than risk disturbing anyone at the Hall. She slept fitfully after hazily sifting through a jumble of thoughts. Benjamin could be dealt with in the morning, and by the sound of it, would not be in a fit state to do a great deal until the day was well under way. Thanks to the promptness of the funeral directors, Sonia was safely in their Chapel of Rest in Guildford. Official paperwork could not be dealt with until after the holiday period was over, which meant that the funeral arrangements would probably not be made for another week or so …

She slept soundly enough until Annie came through with coffee, then walked over to the Hall to have a shower and exchange the long maroon bead-encrusted dinner dress which had seen so many fraught situations in the last twenty four hours, for something more practical.

Benjamin had appeared, somewhat shamefaced, for a very late breakfast, and seeing Barbara's expression swiftly contacted George to take him to the hospital. Victoria sat in bed in the private ward feeling as miserable as she could ever remember. Her daughter lay in a crib, having been in the baby ward for the most part of the night. There had not been much chance of Victoria getting any sleep, though, the events of the past day kept running through her mind, and on top of that, the natural hormonal changes and emotions of giving birth were making her head spin.

She heard Benjamin's footsteps outside the door. It opened slowly and a huge bouquet of flowers appeared, waving slowly - it was Ben - hoping that Vicky would not remember they had been on display at the birthday party. Sheepishly emerging from behind the flowers was Ben's face, looking blotched and apprehensive. He moved over to the bed and bent to kiss his wife, with a waft of peppermint breath to disguise any trace of last night's brandy and the morning's 'hair of the dog'.

"Darling, I owe you the most abject apology – will you ever be able to forgive me? Where's our daughter? I need to see if she's as beautiful as you."

Vicky was disarmed, as indeed she wanted to be. At this stage of their marriage Ben's apologetic moods were to be responded to and treasured, with the upset never referred to again, giving time for both of them to forget the cause. They both spent a long time discussing their daughter, neither really wanting to broach the subject of Sonia's death.

But eventually, Vicky held Ben's hand and asked what had happened after she left. Ben stood up abruptly and walked to the window, not answering immediately, until, taking a deep breath, he tersely informed her that she would not have to answer any more questions from the doctor, the certificate had been signed, and he expected her to be well enough to be at his side for the funeral, which would take place after New Year.

Then, subject closed, he returned to the seat by the bed and dutifully gazed at his daughter again, only leaving when she woke and Victoria said she was going to feed her.

7

Sonia woke, still somewhat dazed. Looking around with a feeling of unease, she realised that what she vaguely remembered was indeed no dream after all. As before, it certainly appeared to be her room, but with no ceiling – just the walls rising into a mist. No familiar sounds of domesticity, no discreet tap at the door with Annie bringing her breakfast tray. She went over to the window and looked out, hoping against hope for the usual view across the Hall's familiar parkland, but again it was the different scene of an unknown landscape. What was she supposed to do? It was impossible to think that if indeed she *were* dead – she shuddered at the thought - that this could be her situation for evermore.

Then she recovered her old equilibrium and felt her normal reactions rise to the surface - in fact, it was *unpardonable* if that were so – at the very least she should have been given some sort of explanation – was there really nothing to do but wait? No, it was definitely *not* possible – it had been a nightmare and she was still in it – she had not woken at all. A feeling of irritation started to dominate, and the longer she waited, the stronger it grew. No telephone by her bed, the door still would not open, and there appeared to be no-one about within call.

It most definitely was not what she expected, and most certainly was not good enough. By the time there was a discreet cough behind her, she was more than ready to demand explanations in her usual authoritarian style.

A diminutive figure stood respectfully at a distance. He was no more than five feet tall, although as he had a slight stoop he could possibly have originally been taller, and he was definitely on the portly side. Thin wisps of pepper-and-salt hair were revealed as he took off a cloth hat of indeterminate design and stood holding it in gnarled hands. He was dressed in a charcoal grey robe that was circled by a knotted cord and finished in an uneven hemline just above bare ankles, his feet in worn old leather sandals. Presumably some menial sort of monk, Sonia thought. He looked almost hesitant. She interpreted this as not being used to speaking to a lady.

This gave Sonia the upper hand - servant class without a doubt - but at least he was someone she could make use of …

"And who might you be?" she snapped.

"I'm your Guide" he said, with a slight bow "and although we've hardly ever been in touch through your life, you'll soon come to realise that I've been with you at all times, just waiting for you to want me."

His voice had a lower class accent that Sonia realised, with a start, was reminiscent of the area where she had been born and raised; those cadences she had eliminated from her own speech, the vowels so different from the cultured ones she had worked so hard to acquire.

I *must* still be dreaming, Sonia thought – I'm probably running a fever, which would account for the muddled thinking and the visual distortions. She turned back to the bed, only to find that it had gone, replaced by her study at the Hall – again with the walls disappearing into the mist. Her desk was there, with notepaper and pens – looking as if she were about to start her usual morning's correspondence.

"You won't need your bed again because you won't need to rest," the strange man said. "You're here to learn and understand."

"I most certainly am not! Please put everything back in place, summon someone senior to help me, then be on your way. Whoever you are, you are not one of *my* employees, so kindly leave and you will hear no more of the matter."

"Ah – I thought so! You don't realise what has happened" he said, taking no notice of her instructions. "Now sit down and listen carefully - this sometimes comes as a shock when people are not prepared for the journey. I'm afraid there's no easy way of putting it, and I don't want to upset you – it's just that you had to come here so suddenly. This is the Afterlife and, like I said, I'm your Guide."

Sonia looked as she had never looked at any stage in her life - totally non-plussed. To have vague suspicions was one thing, but to have the confirmation of death thrust at her in this way destroyed all the hopes that the whole thing would turn out to be the nightmare she felt it to be.

"You are trying to tell me that I have *died*? But I am here in the Hall. I have only to call Annie and she will be here with the coffee and everything will be back to normal. It's Boxing Day, Barbara and I are expected at the Nelson's for lunch, then on to Jacqueline's for tea with the children. No, what you say is totally impossible. Now *go* - before I get *really* upset."

The Ripples and the Tapestries

"But Sonia …"

"How *dare* you be so familiar! On whose authority do you speak? Get out, get *out*! You do not look like any Guide and you certainly do not speak like one! Who are you supposed to be guiding and where? You come here to my room dressed in the oddest clothes that would disgrace even the gardener at the Hall, and you try to dictate what I shall do? Get *out* I say!"

He withdrew to a respectful distance, as the fury Sonia usually reserved for incompetent tradespeople was unleashed. It was just as he'd feared when he read the advance notice from Above that it was her time to be called – this one was going to take longer, and he would need all his powers of persuasion to get her even to the point of starting the work she had to do. There had been no opportunity to work with her during her Earth life, as she had made no contact with him. She had no real spiritual side – oh yes, he had seen her attending church regularly, but knew that it was for her own ambitions and not for her genuine spiritual development.

Sighing, and clasping his hands under his robe, he prayed as he faded away from the room.

"Oh dear Lord, please help me. These sudden ones are always the worst (give me a nice contemplated suicide any day). Lord, I tried to be gentle but she's so arrogant. I'm going to leave her with the angels for a while until she's calmed down, then I'll return to try again. Amen."

❧

Immediately, Sonia had the oddest feeling – as if her thoughts were being enfolded in soft downy wings. This soothed Sonia for a while, as did the realisation that she was once more on her own, but in spite of the comforting sensations, she still rationalised that she was dreaming and would wake up. But now there was undoubtedly a niggling doubt. What nonsense, she told herself, and having decided that indeed it *was* a dream, determined that she would take advantage of the opportunity and see if she could go outside for a breath of fresh air. Her thoughts had not stopped veering from one thing to another. Perhaps this would help.

Stepping through the French windows she found herself in the most delightful garden. Wandering among the herbaceous borders with all the flowers at their peak, it seemed to her gardener's eye too good to be true. Flowers changed as she approached, which was odd in itself – but flowers? On Boxing Day? These borders were June borders. Maybe they were in a large dome of some sort of perpetual climate, like the Eden project in Cornwall she had visited with Barbara last year. Yes, that was the only possible explanation, and condensation would explain this wretched mist everywhere, indoors and out, yet the light had an intense quality that she had never seen anywhere else on earth.

Sitting on a smooth wooden bench, trying to piece together her vague impressions of all that had happened, she could remember no pain – no, she mused, it had started with a bright light and warmth. Then there had been a feeling of travelling over mountains and rivers, coastlines laid out as if on a globe. All as if she were taking off in a plane in some way, but with no feeling of having to look through an aircraft's window. The light had become brighter and brighter until she felt that it and she were one, and she must have fallen asleep, only to wake and find that although there were certain similarities to her rooms at the Hall, there were also major differences that made it feel not quite genuine.

But the Afterlife? No, it *couldn't* be. That awful little man would have to find a way to prove it to her before she believed him. All her life she had understood and followed the Church's teaching, so of course she *knew* what lay ahead. It was precisely that understanding that had led her to be so significant a part of worship in the village, setting an example to all. It was one of the things that was so comfortable about village life – the division between churchgoers and those who did not get involved – one could conveniently forget the ones not seen on Sundays and simplify the village contacts, leaving room for other, more important things. In that traditional setting it was important to have a vicar who was also a traditionalist, and of course she used every influence she or her fellow churchgoers had to maintain that – the village would most certainly not respond to any of the more radical ideas that were around, and the merest whisper of the possibility of a woman being considered, for instance, had ensured that any number of significant strings had had to be pulled. Consequently, the current vicar was under no misapprehensions about his position and what he was expected to do. Moreover, any slight step out of line would earn him an imperious note from the Hall – Lady Sonia had many ways of organising even her spiritual life to her own taste. The thought that she might have to reconsider aspects of her belief was not something she was really prepared to contemplate.

The angels' wings persisted and eventually performed their task of soothing her, so that a slight curiosity ousted some of her resentment, and turned into resolve - if there were to be a challenge, then she would rise to it – she had never been afraid of meeting challenges head-on, from whatever quarter they came.

❧

He was waiting when she returned, and motioned her to sit at her desk. Surprising herself, Sonia did so without protest.

"Have you had a nice walk?" he enquired solicitously. "You need to know that although we'll be working closely together it won't be without its rewards, and knowing you've been such a keen gardener I arranged for you to have the best place for your stay."

"For my stay? Does that imply that this is only a temporary arrangement? For heaven's sake, please tell me what exactly I am to expect."

"Dear *Lady* Sonia, if that's how you like to be addressed, I'm only too happy to explain, but please try to listen without interrupting me.

"As you now know, you're in the Afterlife – in other words, your soul has left its last body behind on Earth and you had a long journey to this place, which is called the Review Centre. It's where souls come to review their life, and their guide (that's me, of course) helps them to assess how many of their life's lessons they have learned. Later, …"

But he was not allowed to pause for breath before Sonia rose to her feet, her old attitude to the fore, her voice icy.

"I have never in my life heard such arrant nonsense. How dare you talk to me in this way when I know full well what the system is! None of this sentimental New Age rubbish, if you please – I had enough of that from my daughter. I have attended church for many, *many* years and I know that without doubt what is waiting for me is a place in one of the Lord's many mansions and, as is befitting one who has done so many good deeds, I shall be sat on the right hand of God Almighty Himself. If you continue to harass me in this way I shall not be answerable for the consequences."

She stalked out of the doorway and returned to the garden. This time her guide briefly cast his eyes upwards, muttered, and after apparently receiving approval, plucked up courage and followed her, his sandals flapping slightly in his haste.

"Dear Lady Sonia, please hear me out. This is all very new to you, but it's what you *have* to do and I can't change things. Look, let me show you something - it will help you understand." So saying, he stepped nearer and took her hand.

Before Sonia could open her mouth to protest she felt enveloped in the soft downy feeling once more and an impression of immense speed, but then it was all over very quickly and she suddenly found herself breathless and dizzy, in the corner of the kitchen at the Hall.

⁂

Annie and Doris sat at the large table in the kitchen. It was piled high, as every available space was - occupied with glasses and china, overflowing ashtrays and remnants of the feast that Doris had prepared for her deceased employer's birthday party. Lighting another cigarette – absolutely forbidden behaviour in any part of the Hall at all times among servants - she kicked off her shoes and drew up a chair to put her feet on.

Sonia stepped forward to remonstrate, and to find out why clearing away after the party had not been finished, but they totally ignored her, except for Annie giving a little shiver. Horrified, Sonia realised they could not see her. However awful the thought that she was indeed dead, it must be so. The conversation confirmed it without doubt.

"Have they all gone, then, Annie?"

"Just old Mrs Nelson waiting for George and the car because she's had several sherries too many. I found her quietly snoring her head off in the corner of the drawing room, so I organised Lisa into looking after her. He should be here in a minute and they can all go home."

"With Mr Benjamin sulking through several bottles in the Library and now Miss Victoria in hospital with Miss Barbara, we'll be safe for a good few hours yet. What a way to end a party – a death *and* a birth!"

Doris felt her mood suddenly lift, and continued.

"Look, I've been thinking, Annie – this *could* be the perfect timing. We've agreed that neither of us could ever face working for Miss Victoria and that's going to happen sooner than we thought, in the circumstances. Get Madam's funeral over and done with, the Nanny installed and I'll hand in my notice. You might be needed for a while longer, I suppose …?"

"I may be *expected* to stay on, but there's no reason why I *should*. Sonia's death has released me from all obligations, I'm ready to start living my own life and I certainly intend doing just that, and as far away as possible. The only one I shall miss is Jacqueline – and the children, of course - but I want to have a retirement I can enjoy, and the sooner the better."

The two women carried on chatting about possible dates for the funeral, and what might be needed for the arrangements for guests, but it was all too much for Sonia. She had heard more than enough, and aghast, turned to find the little man at her side.

"Have you seen enough for now?" he enquired. She nodded, bewildered.

The speed, the sensations happened again, and they were returned to their previous setting in the garden.

8

"Let me explain more ..."

Sonia reluctantly decided to hear what he had to say. There *had* to be some explanation for the scene she had just witnessed. It had been torture to hear and see two people she had trusted for so many years, behaving as they did – only hours after the party had finished.

"First tell me who you are" she said firmly. "You do not seem to be a person of any significance, but you appear to have certain skills and I may as well use your name."

"My titles wouldn't mean anything to you, and my actual name is of no importance, but you may call me Master, and I'm your teacher in the Afterlife."

Sonia thought she had no reserves of energy left, but at this she raged yet again.

"*Master*? No-one is *my* 'master'. What a preposterous idea! You look like that down and out person Geoffrey once brought back with him from some Eastern trip - *he* turned out to be a real help in the garden, which was his saving grace – but I have yet to discover yours! Now get your explanation over and done with so that I may have some peace. And I shall name you Fu – *Mister* Fu – after the gardener!"

There was a small sigh – perhaps of resignation.

"Whatever you say, Lady Sonia - *whatever* you say on the matter, if it helps you do what you're here for. Now I think you've just had proof that you're indeed finished with that Earthly life you occupied for exactly seventy years. I'm sorry it had to be such a shock, but sometimes swift pain is better than prolonged discomfort. While you're going through these first stages of adjusting to your situation, you might find it helpful to know you're allowed to have as many visits to your old life as you wish. You only have to say and I'll come with you - the sooner we can get to the point of you *really* starting work, the better. It quite often helps people get another perspective on what we're doing. But be warned – you may not experience what you hope to find."

"I have nothing to fear from returning. I have led a blameless life, as you will hear. What we saw and heard Annie and Doris talking about was a natural shock reaction to the loss of their dear employer. They will soon come to their senses." Sonia snapped.

The little man looked at her quizzically, decided not to pursue the matter and resumed.

"Now - the work I mentioned. We need to look at the effect you had on other people's lives – good and bad. Then there are the lessons ..."

Sonia's mouth opened, but he hastily continued.

"... you see, during your life on earth, you had certain tasks to accomplish and we need to examine these life lessons to see if you did indeed learn them. If there is evidence you didn't, then we examine your life in more detail, and see how and why you missed out on the opportunities. When all this is done you're allowed to move onwards, and then the next part of your work will be to decide the lessons you are to learn in your next life."

"You are talking the same nonsense I had to hear from Jacqueline and her friends. You cannot *possibly* mean that my beliefs are wrong after all these years. You're turning the Day of Judgement into something resembling a therapy, and I *won't* have it!"

The little man's face fell. As Sonia turned her back, another prayer silently formed itself on his lips.

> *Dear God,*
> *<u>please</u> give me the wisdom to choose the right words -*
> *and the strength to continue.*
> *Amen.*

Aloud, he said,

"What you can't remember is that this is a process that you've done before - when you've left one Earthly life you've returned here, then moved on to a new one in order to improve your soul's understanding. As you probably know, the word for this is Reincarnation.

"I know in your last earthly life you enjoyed keeping a journal, so I've provided you with one here. As well as that, I'd like you to make a start on the lessons. Usually people are asked to list the Ten Commandments and explain how they have observed them. But with you we will try something more refined and intellectually befitting."

Sonia was about to try another bout of huffiness, but somewhat mollified by the implied compliment of recognising that her knowledge was above the ordinary, decided to keep quiet.

"There's no hurry" he continued "just let your thoughts flow into your journal, and in the meantime you'll have the best of everything brought to you – ask and it will be provided, as we always say. For now, I suggest you take another walk in the garden and enjoy the chance to rest while you can."

⁂

It was some time before Sonia came back to her room, and looking around saw no sign of the little man. Breathing a sigh of relief, she crossed to her desk. A journal lay in front of her – the new leather bound one, bought for the inaugural year of her seventies – and surely there could never be a better time to start it. She sat down, reached for her pen and started to write, hoping to feel the peace and pleasure she had always felt as she consigned her thoughts, hopes and wishes to paper, as if to her dearest friend.

The journal of Sonia, Lady Woolston, of Woolston Hall, near Guildford, Surrey.

Apparently I have died. This seems an utterly ridiculous statement to make, but I have now been shown incontrovertible proof that it is indeed so, and I must accept it.

I will admit I was a little taken aback when I learned I had to have a companion with whom to share my thoughts, but he has provided this, my journal, and I will insist that my privacy be respected. If this ever gets discovered it should make fascinating reading ….

I am in a large house of some sort, which has been made to feel like my drawing room as far as possible, although the architecture here is very strange. There are no ceilings, so when I refer to a doorway I mean an opening between two pillars whose tops are shrouded in far distant gossamer cloud. Quite beautiful. There is no need for practicality here, of course, as there is apparently an even climate.

The garden is a delight, although I have only explored a small part of it so far. The little stream is perfect. It emerges from under the steps that lead down from the doorway, sparkling and glinting in this special light that is so bright, yet does not make one's eyes ache. It tumbles down among grassy banks and over pebbles that look as polished as any semi-precious stone.

If Jacqueline were here with me, no doubt she could identify each and every one, and bore me to tears with the so-called healing properties they are supposed to have. Such nonsense, I once told her – the only properties they have are to provide comfort to those who believe the mumbo jumbo. Only precious stones are worth polishing and should be set in precious metals, to be admired, and worn with discretion.

But I digress …

Looking around me I can see many flowers that I do not recognise. How interesting, and how my friends in the Ladies Gardening Club would beg me for cuttings if only I could take some back. The gardens seem to be haphazard in their design, which surprises me – I would have thought that things would be more ordered, somehow. There are some areas which are most definitely overgrown, too, but perhaps they give scope for those who wish to perpetuate their earthly pursuits.

Apparently this place is called the Review Centre. They have recreated my drawing room so that I feel completely at ease. I have been told by the little man (who, incidentally, suggested I call him "Master" – such nonsense – I informed him I would name him Mister Fu, as he looks vaguely Oriental) that when I feel ready, we can start on a task of great significance.

From what I can gather at this stage, we are all born into a life where we have the opportunity to improve ourselves. The task is to look at one's achievements and discuss them. When this Mister Fu is satisfied (which I cannot imagine will be too difficult, as my achievements speak for themselves), I will pass to another stage for what I can only regard as some sort of recycling process of my soul. Another life ahead? Will I remember all this? I will keep this journal to record whatever happens and try to take it with me, if indeed I do return to another life on earth.

All this nonsense about how I lived my life and how I affected others will quickly be sorted out when he learns how I fought for my position in society and retained it, in spite of many handicaps. I was always engaged in good works of one sort or another, and the donations I made, or ordered Geoffrey to make on my behalf, will keep any recording angel very happy for a very long time, if one is judged by the gratitude one receives in life.

As for personal achievements, I hardly know where to begin, there are so many throughout my life. In fact it seems to have been one long spell of success after another – overcoming my childhood illnesses, marrying the man who gave me the potential to enter the lifestyle I could foresee as my destiny – and yes, I know I made the most of that potential – socially and financially.

Geoffrey had his share of the bargain too, of course, and I was wholeheartedly devoted to him for all those years, even when I discovered what he was pleased to call his "little indiscretion". (Hopefully we will not need to discuss that).

But I run ahead of myself and there is no place for that in my new journal, so it is certainly time to change the current of my thoughts, and after another rest I will begin to write what the wretched man wants. Then perhaps I can move on before I get too bored with the whole thing.

❧❦

Mr Fu was also writing. He sent a memo to God:

> *Dear God –*
> *To be quite honest, when I received the summons I thought 'You've managed to do it again!' –*
> *I know I did a good job with all those other formidable ladies, but I really don't wish to make a career of it!*
>
> *When it was nearly time for Lady Sonia to enter the Afterlife, I thought I'd prepared myself thoroughly, but I will admit to some qualms as she came over. As part of fitting in with whatever my recently-passed-over human related to in their Earthly life, I've chosen to get her started on a journal. The first exercise will be a good way to find out the scope of her self-delusions.*
> *I've already realised there will be no point in being too gentle with Lady Sonia or she would treat me as*

arrogantly as she has treated most living people. No doubt there will be tantrums, and she may try to bother You with small matters. I can only apologise in advance.
All will be well eventually – as You know.

Your most devoted Worshipper -
Angel Prince of the East, Master of the Higher Realms.

(Now also known as 'Mr Fu'!)

9

Not surprisingly, the atmosphere at Woolston Hall was tense in every respect, whichever permutation of family or staff encountered each other.

"Thank goodness we have our work to get on with" Doris said to Annie several times in the next day or two "even though I seem to be catering for people with no appetite, or who are liable to leave the table at a moment's notice."

"They're having to handle all sorts" Annie agreed. "Routine's impossible."

It would be even more unlikely when Victoria and the baby returned from the hospital. The Nanny would be arriving soon and would need to be settled I,n and catered for. Doris's work was now punctured by many sighs. The hours seemed endless and the funeral date had yet to be set, although it seemed that it was unlikely to be this side of the New Year.

Annie busied herself keeping out of Benjamin's way as much as possible, except at mealtimes – she did not want to be at his beck and call. The task of sorting Sonia's clothes and carefully packing them away between layers of tissue paper, in boxes that George then took up to one of the attic rooms, could take some time to complete. The jewellery had gone straight into the safe, of course, a few pieces awaiting dispersal to various homes as part of the distribution that would take place when Sonia's Last Will and Testament was made public knowledge.

Ben realised that he would have to spend many days, if not weeks, getting back into Vicky's good books. Although there had been his apology, and her apparent acceptance, in the hospital, he knew he would have to tread warily for a time. What a fool he had been - but totally justified at the time, he thought, on his second night in the Library in front of the fire with the brandy at his elbow. He slumped morosely into the leather chair unable to do anything other than focus on his loss, unable to summon the mental resources to shoulder any more responsibilities for that day.

The door opening made him start, but when he saw it was Barbara he relaxed and vaguely waved a hand towards the drinks cabinet in the corner of the room.

"Help yourself, Auntie Babs" he slurred "it's all yours at the moment. Things will change, of course, when my wonderful doting wife returns complete with nappies, bottles, potties, prams, buggies and sacks full of clothes. No more drinkies then for the Daddy, so make the most of it." He slumped further into his chair, and Barbara wondered how many drinks he had consumed since dinner.

"How is the baby?" she enquired. "Are you and Victoria any nearer choosing a name yet? Or several?"

"D'you know, Babs, it never occurred to me to think of girls' names. All I could think of was that it would be a boy. Vicky didn't want to know beforehand, said it was unlucky, so we didn't take up the offer when they did the umpteenth scan. Wish I'd known so I could have got used to the idea – keep wanting to call it Charlie!"

"Don't do anything so foolish, for heaven's sake. You're in your wife's bad books as it is. These days, not being there for the birth is a black mark against *any* father, let alone not turning up until the following morning, *and* with a monumental hangover. You're going to have to buy something very special for your wife to get rid of those memories."

She poured herself a drink, waved the heavy decanter enquiringly in Ben's direction, and receiving a response, walked across to top up his glass. She was now wondering if it had really been a good idea to volunteer to stay through the intervening days between now and the funeral, but felt that she might somehow be a stabilising influence. It could be a last tribute to her lifelong friend. But for all her composure, Barbara too was in shock. Fifty years of friendship was not to be dismissed lightly.

"You know" she mused to a half-aware Benjamin, attempting to change to a different subject, but one that might arouse his interest. "I never thought when your mother invited me for the first business weekend all those years ago that it would lead to such success. Sonia certainly had a flair for entertaining and making sure that everything went smoothly. She'd done smaller things before they moved here, of course, but this house was the perfect setting for exclusive negotiations. Even when you children had arrived, it all carried on like clockwork. Victoria will be doing the same, no doubt, with the conferences you're planning?"

The Ripples and the Tapestries

Ben grunted.

"She'd better not try to wriggle out of it. Mother groomed her and spent hours going over every little detail of every event – she kept detailed diaries, you know. Pretty remarkable woman, my mother ... oh God, I *miss* her ... I don't know how we ... "

Barbara knew that Ben was close to his mother, but the anguish and panic in his voice alarmed her with its intensity.

"*You* have to be the head of the household, so you must *not* go to pieces. Drinking won't help, either, you know, although you'll be excused for a day or two longer before people begin to fear the worst. Now tell me what you propose doing about the Nanny."

Ben twisted in his chair, but Barbara's brisk tone made him drag his scattered thoughts together. No use antagonising her as well, he realised, so he resentfully outlined the plan.

"She's been contacted and can come earlier than planned, after all. When she arrives the day after tomorrow, I take her to the hospital to meet Vic, then everything will be set up here for them both to return when the brat's got the all clear from the medics – turns out she wasn't as premature as we'd all thought, but not enough to start tongues wagging in the village."

So that was it, Barbara thought, remembering the haste with which the wedding plans had been put into action. Those months of Sonia intensively coaching Victoria in how to run the Hall made sense now - done in case she might not be interested, or even have time to learn, after the birth. No wonder poor Sonia had looked pale by the time it was her birthday.

Barbara lit another cigarette and let her thoughts silently wander, making no pretence of prolonging conversation with Ben. So that was the way the wind blew – he had no confidence in Victoria's commitment to the business plans, and no wonder. Certainly she was a girl Barbara found it difficult to warm to – no generosity in her manner, and a sulky sullenness when she was thwarted that did her no favours at all. Maybe she would rally round when it eventually dawned on her that she was mistress of the Hall, and it was her responsibility to ensure that things carried on.

Barbara felt a foreboding about the future that she could not shake off – of family harmony, and of the Hall and all it stood for. Would she herself continue to be seen as helpful or would Ben's wife see her as interfering? What a sad end to a family of whom she had grown so fond … but then she mentally shook herself – what nonsense to look on the negative side when there was also so much potential. Of course things would not be the same – but it did not have to be the worst scenario: it had the potential to change for the better, particularly if she could make herself indispensable. She too could adapt to whatever lay ahead if she just took her own advice and tackled one day at a time, concentrating on whatever task she undertook.

≪≫

Jacqueline's kitchen was warm and bright. Outside, Boxing Day's hard frost had covered everywhere in a sparkle of candy coating, the winter sun was casting its light across the lawn and the birds were already busy at the bird table. It lifted her spirits immeasurably. Richard was eating his usual toast and honey, while the children still slept on. They had hardly stirred when they were eventually carried up to bed, and although Jacqui had spent the night sleeping fitfully in order to hear the slightest murmur, it was not Tim or Ella who caused her restlessness. She worried about her brother and how he would be able to adjust – not only to the massive changes that fatherhood would bring, but also to the fact that Sonia would no longer be there to maintain a steering role at the Hall.

Richard needed to go to the hospital minor injuries unit for a short time, on duty to see any emergency patients, although there were rarely too many of those just after Christmas, and it meant that he would probably be back by lunchtime. They could all go for a walk after lunch, she thought, smiling across at him over the rim of her cup. In response to his enquiring look she responded.

"I continue to think that I must be the luckiest woman in the country to have met you."

"What's wrong with the whole world?" he teased. "You've demoted me in a sentence!"

"You understand so much, yet you hardly had a chance to get to know my mother properly."

"Put it down to my renowned bedside manner, darling, and please can we have some of your famous soup when I return – all that heavy Christmas food is lying like a lead weight!"

He blew her a kiss as he swung cheerily out of the door, then returned to tilt her head towards him.

"And don't take any nonsense from that brother of yours - refer him to me if he wants you to do too much. By all means go there for a day or two before the funeral if it would help, providing I'm there with you – I'll phone my parents straight away to see if they can look after the children here. No more than that, though" he added firmly " *you* have to have time to adjust, too."

Jacqui smiled up at him appreciatively and started the chores, thinking about what was to come. They knew about the technicalities that might mean the funeral could not be sanctioned until the authorities were satisfied that nothing improper had taken place. Fortunately her mother had seen Dr Hartley not too long ago, over a minor matter, so once offices were open after the holiday arrangements could be made and people notified.

She wondered how things were at the Hall. Ben was not the best person to rise to a crisis – his mother was the one who had always steered him through anything unpleasant, but at least Barbara was there to help. Jacqui loved her brother in spite of the way his attitudes sometimes betrayed the effects of Sonia's unfair bias and favouritism. Underneath his 'must be top dog and centre of attention at all times' attitude she knew he was and always had been very fond of her. Once, when even his beloved mother had overstepped the boundaries and yet again punished Jacqueline unfairly, he had interceded on his sister's behalf.

"*Don't* interfere with what you don't understand" Sonia had snapped - with such fury that he had hidden in the attic for the rest of the day. When Jacqui found him she made him promise not to do it again – she was used to the regime and felt she was tougher than Ben. It still mystified her. There was not, and never had been, any obvious explanation for Sonia's attitude. Fortunately, Jacqui had been protected by her father's love, and remembered him with the huge sense of loss that six years had done nothing to lessen.

She felt deeply saddened that her relationship with her mother had never been better than a thinly disguised veil of tolerance on Sonia's part. When Jacqui had been betrayed yet again by her first husband Zak and decided to divorce him, it was to friends she was forced to turn for help and support as a single mother. Sonia ignored her for many months. Having disapproved of the marriage in the first place, she was not going to play any supportive role in its painful end, and certainly had no wish to provide accommodation at the Hall for either her daughter or her infant grandson. When the publicity died down and the public's interest in picking over the excesses of yet another pop musician, Jacqueline was eventually allowed to resume contact and Sonia never again mentioned the marriage.

When Jacqui remarried, Sonia tolerated Anthony because any branch of medicine was a respectable profession, even though she herself was wary of psychologists. The thought of his additional skills in hypnotherapy made her wince – not for *her* this dabbling about in people's minds; but it paid well enough and Anthony himself was charming. His death had been so totally unexpected, yet the news that Jacqueline was expecting his child helped them as they grieved.

Those had been very dark days, when she had more than once wondered how anything could ever be worthwhile again. But incredibly it proved to be the start of a sequence of events that had led to the eventual meeting with Richard, briefly standing in as practice locum doctor. The healing began and they both carefully built a relationship that they knew would stand the test of time. Sonia's death was the first major crisis life had given them since their marriage, although already Jacqui knew her confidence in Richard was well founded. She poured another cup of coffee and waited for sounds that the children were waking, wanting a diversion from her thoughts.

Sure enough, before long the children crept downstairs, rubbing their eyes and yawning. With the resilience of the very young, they were soon engrossed in their presents, then Ella organised Tim into a game of Nonny playing with the angels which meant a lot of racing around up and down stairs with arms outstretched.

≈≈

When Jacqueline phoned to speak to her brother, Barbara took the call and became quite emotional. Jacqui had been the first to ask how *she* was feeling, and show genuine concern.

"I shall feel much better when all this is over" admitted Barbara when her voice became steady once again "but at least there's plenty of practical work to do. Are you able to come here before the day of the funeral? I know it's a cheek to even ask, but I also know it will help so much, as Victoria will be busy with the baby."

"Richard's parents will be having the children for as long as necessary, bless them, so we can both be at the Hall for a couple of days to do anything that's needed. Poor Ben, he's got so much on his plate."

"Poor Ben needs steering away from the brandy decanter at the moment" Barbara replied tartly "and to be perfectly frank, I'm not the one to help him with that – I've had more years of practice than he has!"

"I'm sure it will all settle down. Don't be too hard on him – or *you*, for that matter. It's time for lunch, so I'll have to leave you for now. I'll be in touch every evening if you need some moral support or anything else, but do feel you can phone at *any* other time – whether you want help, or just a chat."

The family afternoon passed with much healthy exercise and laughter. The children adored Richard, and he them, and their time together was always full of fun. It just proved how life can and must go on, Jacqui thought, no matter how devastating the circumstances; and in the scale of things, she felt so much more able to cope with her mother's death. Sonia had at least reached her biblical 'three score years and ten', whereas Anthony had been cheated of that fullness of time.

❧❧

Some semblance of routine resumed at the Hall. Ben visited Victoria in the late afternoons, having spent office hours dealing with the myriad aspects of officialdom and paperwork necessary to steer events to their conclusion. Weekends and official holidays made this the worst time of year for a death in one way, but it gave the family some much needed breathing space. The date for the funeral was set for the fourth day of January, announcements were made in the newspapers, letters were written to all Sonia's contacts who would need to know. There was the dreadful poignancy that the contact list was the one Sonia herself had so recently used for the scores of Christmas cards.

Ben had decided to make amends to his wife, at Barbara's prompting, and had rushed to a jeweller's in Guildford as soon as it reopened. An exquisite gold necklace set with pearls and small amethysts seemed to be the ideal gift for Victoria – both to mark their daughter's birth, and also to get back in her good books.

Victoria had confided in a senior member of the nursing staff at the hospital, explaining her misery at Ben's immediate reaction to the arrival of a daughter instead of the planned-for son. Ben had been called into a private meeting to be firmly made aware that he had to be careful to guard his comments, and he genuinely determined to turn over a new leaf and become the exemplary new father. Nanny had been contacted and was due to arrive almost immediately. It was as well that arrangements for the nursery suite at the Hall had been completed well before the end of October - so that it would not interfere with the birthday preparations, of course, and as another example of the planning and organisation in which Sonia had revelled. She had also interviewed the Nanny, and Clair Frost had come with the highest recommendations. She was a mature and experienced Nanny who would be able to handle the most delicate situations, and although secretly a little frightened of her, Vicky knew she and the baby would be in safe hands.

֍

Working together in the kitchen gave Annie and Doris plenty of time to speculate on how Victoria would fare in her late mother-in-law's shoes. Doris had found her willing enough to learn the routines, but out of her depth when it came to understanding the finer nuances of household management. On the occasions when Sonia had left her to take responsibility, Victoria tried to cover her own inadequacies with an autocratic manner that was often infuriating and always unnecessary. Doris was the one mostly on the receiving end, which she correctly attributed to nervousness on Victoria's part, but nonetheless it caused many silent smarts. The worst occasion had been when she attempted to cover an oversight on her own part by blaming Doris for lack of co-operation, but fortunately Sonia had, at least publicly, ignored that. Whether or not she had privately taken Victoria to task over the issue had of course never been revealed, but Doris had been very indignant.

The Ripples and the Tapestries

Annie and Doris took to spending time in the evenings at the gatehouse, after dinner. Their friendship developed a new closeness that had not been possible before, when their duties tended to give them time off separately. In any case, Sonia would have firmly taken steps to discourage too much familiarity between the housekeeper and her personal companion.

"When the funeral's over I'm going to insist on being called by my full name at long last" Annie said during a conversation on the first evening they were on their own. "I've always hated Annie more than I can say!"

Doris was startled.

"D'you know, I'd forgotten about that. When you were in the village I always thought Annabel was the prettiest name, but why did you change it if you didn't like it?

"Sonia did that. Told me it was too pretentious for someone who had no cause to have airs and graces, and that Annie was a traditional servant's name."

"I know it was many years ago and attitudes have changed, but how could you agree?"

"I suppose I was having some sort of breakdown - the Vicar's wife and Lady Sonia got me sorted out between them. Looking back, I must have been too weak to argue, but anyway, nobody argues with her Ladyship, do they? Sorry - argued – so I agreed to anything. It was a better post than I had at the school, after all, and it eventually led to more than I could have ever dreamed would be possible."

She lapsed into silence, and Doris assumed she was referring to the benefits of being a Lady's companion, compared with the mundane routine of supervising the infants' class. Annabelle, however, was silently, wistfully, remembering passion and excitement, secrecy and intrigue.

"One day I'll tell you the whole story, Doris, but not now – not yet."

And with that her friend had to be content.

10

"Mister Fu! – I *cannot* get accustomed to your gliding up behind me, nor do I intend to. Please do *not* make a habit of it in future!"

Lady Sonia had decided that if there was no way of avoiding the obnoxious little man, as she thought of him, and that she did indeed have to do the work he had set, the best way of handling him was to keep him in his place – which of course would be as she had always treated the least significant people in her life.

"Dear Lady Sonia - I just wanted to say that I'm so pleased you've started recording things in your little journal, but we'll soon need to begin the serious work – the first Task. It's only when these Tasks have been done, that we can look at your life and see if we can uncover the details of how you have learned your lessons."

Sonia bridled. He sounded positively patronising about her journal – and no-one, but *no-one*, had ever dared to patronise her and lived to tell the tale. He really was quite awful, yet he was apparently her only contact in this place, so rather than be left in solitude she decided to try to be reasonably pleasant.

"Lessons? You sound like my wretched daughter and the sort of thinking she dabbled with. The church taught me that I was put on earth to achieve, and to make use of my talents, and surely I have done that over and over again, benefiting countless other people. I have always believed in leading from the front and setting an example to which others may aspire. I also learned that when I died, providing I had led a virtuous life, I could expect a long blissful rest waiting for the Resurrection Day, when all the great and the good will find themselves together for evermore. Naturally, I expect to be one of that assembly. It will take me a long time, if ever, to get used to this situation, and I still cannot understand why everything is so different."

Oh dear Lord, he thought, that self-righteousness will have to go before anything else, and it's going to be so painful for her. But she will have to do it, or she will never believe what she sees and the result will be that the next stage will have less effect. There was no use trying to hurry the process. He'd had many stubborn people through his hands since time began, and although he pretended to grumble when another came his way, he really found a great deal of satisfaction in accompanying them through a difficult time, then seizing the moment when arrogance turned to humility and rewarding it with kindness and peace. In the meantime he would have to be firm – even stern, or she would inevitably try to overrule him.

"Dear lady, you'll find there have been many simplistic notions over the centuries, fed by leaders to the masses, in order to keep them happy and in their place. Heads of organisations always do this, and heads of various religions no less so. Now – I'd like you to do the first written exercise for me. It will have to be done before you can move on."

"Oh no, I have met you so-called Socialist thinkers before - all you can think about are the downtrodden masses and it is utter nonsense! The masses have to have leaders; people of my status are natural leaders; it is the natural order of civilisation. Now, if there truly *is* no alternative, I am prepared to do something that helps to make sense of why I am here, which will allow me to move on to where I *should* be, but before we start I must point out that I will retain my faith and trust in the teachings of the Church I know, come what may."

He ignored her protestations and folded his hands under his robe.

"I'm here to help you understand how it all fits in with the greater scheme of things and it will become clearer as we do the work. The first task will simple – I'll give you one of the Great Laws which tell how people are expected to interact with one another in their Earthly life; then I'd like you to pen your thoughts on how it has been part of your own life, and how it has affected those around you."

"I have no fears about any of your laws" retorted Sonia "I am sure I will have heard of them, and if, as you say, they are foundations of life, then I can expect them to fit in with any teachings of the Church to which I have adhered."

Mr Fu produced a small scroll from the sleeve of his robe and unfurling it, read aloud a short statement.

"Do as you would have others do unto you."

"Well?" Sonia asked, expecting more.

"That is the first one - nothing more, nothing less."

"But this is infantile!"

"Well, yes – you see we need to go back to the beginning. All the examples you can think of, and also how they affected those involved. Please do as I ask, dear lady. Contemplate the statement deeply and you will find the true implications. Don't be taken in by the simplicity, because in this, and the other tasks that I shall give you later, lies the whole purpose of life."

~~

Sonia sat at her desk with the scroll in her hands long after Mr Fu had departed. It was typical! She was willing to expound her theories and argue her points, exercising her intellect as indeed she had done on many committees and in many meetings throughout her life. Now here was this dreadful little man taking away all that fun, bringing her to the very basics and depriving her of the opportunity to impress him with her erudition.

Well, as a first exercise it was going to be easy enough, thought Sonia, and there was nothing else to do with her time. She copied the sentence into her journal.

"Do as you would have others do unto you."

She wrote pages. She wrote of hospitality, of generous gifts. She described acts of unparalleled magnanimity until Mr Fu returned, just in time to witness the last graceful flourish of her pen, then laying it down, she turned to him triumphantly.

"There you are – now may we please move on?"

He read her work thoughtfully, pacing the room as he read, sometimes shaking his head with a rueful expression, sometimes frowning, then sent up a silent prayer that he might be guided to choose the most tactful words for what he had to say next.

"I do appreciate the insights you've given me, dear Lady Sonia, but I'm afraid it's unfinished. These are just examples of things you were able to do because of your wealth. Were people's lives made better by exchanging expensive gifts on an escalating scale? Also, I did ask you to describe what the consequences of these acts were - in the lives of all those they affected."

"I should have thought it was obvious!" she retorted. "They were all without fail exceedingly grateful, and yes, they did find ways of repaying me, for which I also expressed gratitude in due course. It is the current commerce of friends and acquaintances at any level."

"I don't doubt that, but please remember we're looking at what ties in with a true principle of life, not these current so-called civilised ideas.

"Perhaps we should make it even simpler - tell me about something you once did for no other purpose than that of being kind; then maybe we can discuss the results together."

Sonia wondered whether to argue the point, but reluctantly picked up her pen again. After a great deal of cudgelling, her brain eventually remembered a very minor event from the past that she had forgotten years ago and would nowadays dismiss as nonsense – a moment of what she shamefacedly thought of as weakness, and had forever kept secret, when she impulsively thrust a ten pound note into a street musician's box, just because a tune reminded her of a happy moment in childhood.

Mr Fu was much more delighted with this than with the pages of notes she had written out before.

"But I cannot say *how* it affected that man's life, because I never saw him again!" she said, puzzled.

"That's just the point, you *don't* know for certain, so it was an act of true generosity. Whenever we work in that way it becomes a demonstration of faith in the Higher Powers. Would you like to know what happened?"

Curiosity aroused, she nodded before she could stop herself.

"The musician treated his friends to a drink …"

Sonia snorted contemptuously.

"No, no – let me finish: he had reached a really low point that day when you walked past, and his self-esteem was practically non-existent. What you did gave him renewed faith in himself and he was able to hold his head up high and treat his friends, rather than being dependent on handouts. That proved to be a turning point in his life – he saw that he wanted to be able to do that every day. He realised that if he could play that well when he was at his lowest point, he might be even better if he worked hard at his music. He made up his mind not to waste his life, went on to join a group and eventually began to earn a real living wage. Nowadays he's training other drop-outs to use their musical skills."

"Is this really true?"

Mr Fu nodded vigorously.

The Ripples and the Tapestries

"This is why it's such an important idea – it's never simply the deed itself, but its repercussions that spread like ripples in a pond, after a pebble has been dropped in. Now please record that in your book so that they may be referred to again."

※

Sonia, surprising herself, did as she was told. However, the success of approval prompted her to ask about the next Law. Knowing this would be much more difficult, and too much haste would lead to a need for painful proof, Mr Fu attempted to abide by his decision that it was not quite time for the project. Of course, this led to trouble - she tried to insist, he resisted, she fumed and would not be swayed.

Eventually, after getting close to offering up a heartfelt prayer to be delivered from the task, he decided it might be used to prove a point, and somewhat reluctantly produced the next scroll from his sleeve.

"I warn you, dear lady, that unless you approach this task with the greatest humility, you could be very disturbed by the consequences."

"Why - is there trickery in this one?" Sonia asked suspiciously.

"No trickery at all - this is just the other side of the coin, so to speak."

He handed her the small scroll, with the words
'As you sow, so shall you reap.'

"This time I want to apply the subject to attitudes – both your own and other people's. Think hard about other people you have known and worked with, and be honest – have you *really* been aware of their true attitudes towards you, or have you made assumptions?

"It's an idea that should start you thinking of *how* people treated you in your Earthly life in the way that they did, and more importantly, *why*.

"Your last visit produced some surprises and has maybe started you wondering if you know everyone as well as you think you do? Have you always listened to what people want, or have you imposed your own will? Have you encouraged people to use their initiative, or have you kept them in their place?"

Sonia frowned. This was taking her into deeper waters than she cared to admit. But then she straightened herself in the chair, remembering how she had, in the past, made even bishops and cabinet ministers quail with her sharp thinking (and even sharper tongue when necessary) – so she, of all people, would not be intimidated by a shabby little man, whatever fancy titles he gave himself.

He left her to mull over her thoughts while he wrote out his next report, prefaced by a memo:
> *Dear God –*
> *Sonia has a phenomenal tendency to argue things out to suit herself! Hearing people's <u>true</u> opinions may be the only way to prove that she is mistaken, however upset she becomes. As ever, I shall continue to seek signs of humility, before moving to the next stage.*
> *Thank you for answering my prayers –*
> *as always, your Angel, Fu*

⫷⫸

Time was non-existent of course, so it could have been hours, or even days later, measured by Earth time - Sonia was still sitting there, deep in thought - when Mr Fu returned. Nothing had been added to the second statement she had copied from the scroll.

"*As you sow, so shall you reap!*" she quoted, sneeringly. "You wretched man! This means nothing to me! I have spent a lifetime of giving and yes, I have received service in return – that is what wages are for, although it would appear that some have forgotten that simple fact, judging by the behaviour of Annie and Doris."

"Are you really having such great difficulty seeing yourself as others saw you? Have you received willing service? If not – why? Could it be that you have taken advantage of your position as employer and exploited those who have no choice?"

Sonia started to look mutinous, so he changed tack.

"Let us think of something else – forgiveness. Has there been a time when you felt you'd been let down or something really bad happened, and you wanted revenge in some way."

Sonia immediately shuddered.

"My father - he betrayed my mother and abandoned me."

"Ah, precisely so - and did you ever forgive him?"

"Forgiveness? My mother never let me speak his name again. She was bitter and hated him, so I naturally followed suit."

"But did you actually *want* to do that? Forget what your mother wanted you to do - did *you* ever try to get in touch with him later on, to hear his side of things?"

"Well, I did wonder once or twice, I suppose, then I was too busy getting my own life sorted out. I eventually heard he had died years ago, so of course it was too late by then. I think he used to send me birthday cards, but my mother hid them and I only found one by accident when I was clearing out some old papers."

She looked almost wistful for a moment, then became her normal brisk self again.

"What good would forgiveness have done? We wanted him to suffer as we had done, reaping what *he* had sowed" she added triumphantly, expecting to have scored a point and prepared to encounter an argument she felt she would eventually win. But her strategy was transparent.

"Exactly – that's just what can happen! But I want you to think about the possible positive aspects if you had met? You *could* have attempted to understand, and in doing that, everyone concerned would have had the chance to forgive and heal old wounds. Life is all about opportunities to perpetuate good, and undo bad. Your suffering was just as prolonged as your father's, just as wasteful, and achieved nothing but bitterness that damaged all concerned."

Sonia flung down her pen in a fit of bad temper and stalked out into the garden. Some of this was going to get very uncomfortable, she realised. If only there was a way out of this wretched 'work' as he called it. If only she could see her own darling Benjamin again and remind herself of how a parent and child relationship could and should be.

The more she thought, the more she longed to do that. Could she, dare she, ask for another trip to the Hall? The last visit had been awful, seeing and hearing Annie and Doris betraying her and plotting now she was gone, after she had shown them nothing but kindness over the years. How did Mr Fu's theory fit in with their behaviour? But seeing Benjamin would provide her with the reassurance she needed. He would be grieving, but would also be strong and dependable – a son to be proud of, demonstrating what her training could achieve.

Mr Fu appeared, as if he read her very thoughts. Although he knew what she was about to ask, he also knew what would be the consequence. So be it – he would be there, as he always was and had been.

"We will put aside the work until later, dear lady – I think you've done enough for now, and I didn't intend to upset you. Are you certain it's to be Benjamin this time?"

Sonia nodded. The thought of seeing her beloved son, yet not being able to speak any words of comfort to him was almost too much to bear, but she steeled herself to be content with whatever peace of mind it brought to her, and prepared herself for what was now becoming a familiar transition from the Afterlife to an Earthly location – the speed and the soft wings.

❦

This time it proved to be her son's bedroom and Victoria was sitting on the bed, sobbing.

"I do hope that girl is not going to be a dreadful disappointment" thought Sonia from her vantage point at the far side of the room. She had hoped that Victoria would by now be showing signs of her mother-in-law's own dignity and ability to hide undue signs of emotional upset. "After all those talks I gave her on how to put on a brave face and disguise her feelings, now here she is, snivelling at some imaginary little problem. Ah, that's better," she thought, seeing Victoria start at hearing Ben come into the bedroom, and moving swiftly to the stool at the dressing table, pretend to be engrossed in brushing her hair.

Ben sat down on the bed and asked how the baby had been. How thoughtful, Sonia thought – her son was such a tender loving husband.

"I'm not seeing very much of her. Clair keeps telling me I need to rest, so I only see her at feeding times."

"Nanny knows best, they always say, so for heaven's sake stop moaning."

"It's all very well for you – you were brought up by one, so it's normal, I suppose. We didn't have that, and I can't get used to the idea. It feels as if she's not my baby at all."

"Look, we're paying a great deal of money for her. Clair came highly recommended and we agreed that we would do it this way. Anyway, you're obviously getting back to normal, so the sooner you help with all the work, the better. Now, we must choose the names, because I may as well register her birth when I collect Mummy's certificate."

Victoria shuddered.

"I know she was born the same day as your mother died, but do you *really* have to be so tactless?" Her voice rose, hysterical tears not far away. "Is that old witch's death going to haunt her for the rest of her life, so that she can never have a birthday without us all being reminded of it?"

Ben strode across the room and taking her by the shoulders, turned her round on the stool to face him. Bending low and menacingly, he looked fiercely into her eyes.

"Don't ever – ever – speak like that of the woman who gave me everything. You are fortunate that you received her approval and that somehow she saw in you an eventual worthy successor. Because you are my wife, you will act like the wife I need and be a testimony to my mother's judgement and training. If you feel you can't live up to those standards you may as well pack your bags and leave at once - and don't imagine I'd lose much sleep over that! I'm rapidly getting tired of your miserable whining about how difficult everything is – get up and actually do something useful, for once in your life!"

Victoria cringed under his grip and looked aside, but he roughly cupped her chin, forcing her to look directly at him as he spoke.

"Now – we will have Sonia as one name, of course, Margaret for my father's mother's memory, and that leaves you with the main choice. See how generous I am when you start to behave?"

Victoria managed to draw breath and tremulously said "Lucinda."

Ben squeezed her jaw viciously, then contemptuously withdrew his hand, strode out of the room and returned to the Library, his inevitable refuge away from baby noises and his wife's tantrums.

Sonia was appalled, yet there must be something that justified it – undoubtedly something his wife had done that had driven him beyond human endurance. She looked down at the dejected new mother and muttered darkly to herself.

"You cannot even begin to know unhappiness, compared with mine. Pull yourself together and make an effort – if I could climb my mountain, then you can surely cope with this molehill! Mr Fu – we shall return, I have seen enough!"

But Mr Fu had other ideas and, determined to let the point be made in as explicit a way as possible, he took the unwilling Lady Sonia downstairs to the Library.

11

Barbara had found plenty to do, supervising the arrangements for the funeral gathering in just over a week's time. Replies and condolences had been pouring in since the public announcements, and she fielded the media questions with skill – not in order to protect Ben, but simply to do the job effectively. She could not trust him to handle the press in the right way, even though all they wanted was a summary of Sonia's local achievements. The danger of an over-zealous reporter just happening to ask one too many questions might prove to be too much, particularly if he had been hiding in the Library, where she knew he kept the reserve supplies of brandy, and it was preferable to be cautious.

Her own needs continued to be propped up by regular but discreet consumption of alcohol, and supplies of her favourite slender cigarillos – although as a concession to the presence of the baby in the house, her smoking was confined to the Library, where often her need for escape coincided with Ben's.

"Have you noticed anything wrong with the heating?" Victoria asked that evening, joining them after dinner. She had eventually overcome her weeping sufficiently to feel she needed company – any company, even in that atmosphere. "It doesn't always work effectively. Sometimes I feel really cold in some rooms, but it appears to be fine in the nursery."

"Oh, as long as *that's* all right" Ben looked viciously at his wife, still in the aftermath of his earlier bad mood. "We could have howling gales blowing through every nook and cranny and no-one would turn a hair, just as long as the *nursery's* not affected. Of course, it could just be my mother coming back to haunt you – has *that* occurred to you?"

Sonia wondered fleetingly whether she could indeed be seen in the corner behind the desk, but a small chuckle from Mr Fu made her realise it was impossible.

Barbara decided to ignore Ben's sarcasm and eventually his moody silence started to ease as the brandy took effect. With the decanter passing between Barbara and Ben – Victoria forced to abstain because of feeding the baby – they became reflective, and talk turned to speculating about Sonia and her childhood. Victoria asked Barbara how she and Sonia had become friends, although she had heard Sonia's version; but it was a safe topic of conversation, and she was beginning to realise how friendless she was in this household – better to get into Barbara's good books rather than antagonise her. Ben slumped lower in his chair and soon the drone of voices lulled him into sleep.

❦

"It spans several decades, but it's not a long story. You probably know that we both came from the same town – and in fact had attended the same school, although four years difference in our ages meant that we did not meet there. No, that was not to happen until my first secretarial post at Woolston Manufacturing - Geoffrey's father's firm. Although Sonia was by then already rather grand, we got on well and she enjoyed training me as much as I enjoyed learning. Well, when she and Geoffrey got married it broke many hearts, but it was a wise choice for him. Her father knew her capabilities so the marriage received his blessing, and he hoped it would settle his son down. Too many sailors found life very tame after the War ended, you see, but with a wife and a good business, Geoffrey could turn his energies to helping his father."

"Did it work out like that?"

"Oh yes. Well, at least on the surface. The truth was, Sonia was very, *very* ambitious. Now that's a great asset when your husband is due to inherit the fruits of his father's labours. Geoffrey was used to travel, so it was natural that he should take over the sales side and Sonia decided she could develop the contacts he made, so that their business clients became social and loyal friends. She did it very cleverly, of course, so that their large family home retained an air of a privileged club, and when they moved down here to the Hall, the most favoured were invited to the weekends."

These occasional weekend gatherings – no more than six each year, Sonia had informed Victoria as part of her grooming to become the hostess of similar events - had been extremely successful, as much because of their exclusivity as the actual events themselves. It was the normal hospitality of an English country house weekend, with (weather permitting) recreational walks, tennis, croquet - golf at the nearby club, that sort of thing. But the secret was in the careful selection of the guests and the opportunity for developing contacts of the right sort.

The sum total of the financial deals that took place on the lawns, or as men walked along the shrubbery paths, was immeasurable. Because of the loyalty their hospitality engendered, Geoffrey and Sonia survived the slump of world markets in the eighties – assisted, of course, by investments in other deals that had come to Geoffrey's ears, as a trusted and generous friend would expect.

Barbara continued, telling Victoria about the distinguished guests and the gifts they brought, especially the Eastern contacts. Geoffrey made a point of reserving one place at each weekend for a foreign customer – not as an incentive, but a reward, and only after contracts had been agreed and signed. The Arab or Asian or Japanese Director would arrive for a weekend of impeccable hospitality and return home with his tales of traditional English country life – feeling that this could be bettered only by contact with Royalty.

Sonia was in her natural social element, and revelled in running the events smoothly and efficiently. Barbara had been drafted in to help one weekend, having in the past assisted with local meetings and proving that her discretion could be relied upon. Barbara found that Sonia's ambition was infectious and, as her eyes opened to a world beyond her limited experience, she determined to make herself readily available and totally indispensable.

"I don't quite understand the timing of all this" Victoria ventured during a pause when Barbara's glass needed a refill.

"It started to develop when they lived at the Manor – Geoffrey's father's house, then he died. It was when they had been married for over twelve years and thinking of moving to Surrey after Geoffrey's father's death that Sonia realised she was pregnant. That caused a gap in the hospitality side of things, so I lost contact, except by letter, for a while. Then after things settled down, Sonia asked me to help with a particularly significant event that involved Governmental dealings, and we have never lost touch since."

"I know she always spoke so highly of you, and said you were her most loyal friend."

❧❧

To her astonishment, Barbara suddenly lost her poise. Tears welled up and spilled unchecked down her cheeks. Then, even more appallingly, she began to sob – huge heart-wrenching sobs that woke Ben.

"What on earth …" he mumbled, but a warning glance from Victoria for once stopped him saying anything further. He sank back, listening reluctantly - totally unprepared for the result of days of tension and grief that had eventually unleashed this deluge of tears and guilt.

"I'm not the person you think I am" Barbara said when her anguish abated slightly. "Oh please let me tell you and get it off my chest, then you can throw me out and I need never come here again."

"But Mummy always said it was your second home." Ben ventured, earning another frown from his wife.

"She wouldn't have said that if she'd known how I have abused her hospitality all these years. I must tell you, so you can decide if I'm fit to attend her funeral."

"Well, *what* happened … ?"

Barbara took a deep breath and began in a low tremulous voice.

"Sonia is – *was* – the dearest friend I ever had. More than she ever knew. We had so much in common – both our fathers leaving home because they had found other women – yes, we shared that disgrace, we found out later. In those days it was a stigma that was impossible to cope with, and Sonia's mother insisted that she had to leave school, in case her friends found out and told *their* mothers – and that was why we never met. I believe she was ill for several months, and avoided being forced to return to school because her age meant she could leave. She went to secretarial college, trained, and became ambitious.

"I'm telling you this because it happened to me too, and it made me hard – very hard. I became single-minded about being independent, and as soon as I could, I left home, determined that no man would ever treat me as my mother had been treated. I was so bitter. No boyfriends – who needed them? Everything I would ever need I would provide for myself, with no obligations. I suppose I was one of the early women's libbers.

"I worked. Every penny I earned I spent on improving my lifestyle, my skills and my knowledge. *I* was not going to stay in a small town, waiting for a 'Mr Right' as the saying went, bringing up babies and waiting for the tell-tale signs that he'd had the best of my life and was now ready to move on to someone younger.

"Sonia's meetings gave me the opportunity to learn about the things that really make the world go round, and how to act the part of sophisticated assistant to the 'nth degree – and I *was* only acting, as I was terrified of men. I became known as the 'English ice-maiden' because I would not yield to the blandishments of the guests, but I eventually learned to enjoy the power that came with that – oh, *how* I enjoyed it! Then one evening I was trapped in a situation I couldn't avoid, with one of their best-known clients – and I was no longer a virgin."

Victoria shuddered, but fascinated, continued to listen, as did Ben – trying to focus through his alcoholic haze.

"He had been very forceful and I had marks to prove it – I realised very quickly that it put me in a winning position. I could have ruined him - I knew Sonia trusted my integrity, and I also knew that he had a reputation to maintain in his own country. So, when he pleaded with me, I threatened to tell Sir Geoffrey, then eventually promised that I would not tell a soul, provided I had significant recompense. Within two days of him returning home I received a handsome gift – a portfolio of shares. No note, no admission – a gentleman's agreement that he trusted me to honour.

"It gave me a great deal to think about. For the first time, I realised I had real power, and that maybe, now that I had nothing to lose and everything to gain, I could turn this episode to my advantage. By the time Sonia moved down to Surrey I had built up a small but very exclusive clientele – only four or five - none of whom knew about each other, and who were all captains of industry willing to pay handsomely for 'quality' time with me.

"Eventually their generous gifts kept me in very pleasant circumstances, but it was all very low profile and intermittent – nevertheless, I made new and even more influential contacts here at the Hall and we would arrange to meet in a discreet hotel some distance away. I was happy with the way I could control these men and their basest feelings, in a way my mother had never been able to do with my father. I had found a *very* satisfactory way of having revenge on the whole of the male population – and although I gave good value for money, I betrayed the true meaning of love. Fortunately, Sonia never found out – never even suspected.

"When I stayed at the Hall, the code of honour (if that's what it should be called when it's betrayal of a friend and trusting employer) meant that I never gave a hint of anything devious, by word or by look, when one of my 'gentlemen' was one of the guests.

"My flat in Chiswick, my porcelain collection, my watercolours, my clothes, to say nothing of my bank account – all have been provided by my disgraceful behaviour to someone who trusted me. Oh Sonia – can you ever forgive me?"

Silence fell, broken only by Barbara's muffled sighs. Such was the effect of her words that the chill the others felt on their souls numbed their thoughts.

※

It was a miserable journey back to the Afterlife, made with increased foreboding about Sonia's reaction. Her guide began to wonder if he had overdone the shock tactics and muttered a quick prayer under his breath, asking for help in finding the right words when the inevitable attack came. Sonia waited until she was sat once more at her desk.

"Did you take me there deliberately? Knowing that woman would reveal her sordid past?" she eventually said in a strange, taut voice, "What do you make of someone who lives that sort of life? To think that I have left her so much in my Will … all my Dresden collection to add to her own …"

"It is not my place to judge your friend, or anyone else for that matter. I am here to help you see things in their true light and I tried to warn you that it would sometimes involve surprises that you would rather not know."

"But now I *do* know, and you have destroyed a precious memory of someone I believed to be a dear friend."

"She herself has provided the disillusionment, and I would like you to consider the reason why she had to seek revenge all her life. Could it be that like you and your mother she couldn't forgive? Now would you like to be left to your thoughts, or would you prefer to discuss this further?"

"Go away, you cretin! Get back to your garden and do what you're supposed to be doing! I don't need to dwell on this betrayal – how

The Ripples and the Tapestries

dare you subject me to this kind of humiliation!" Eyes blazing with a white-hot fury, she suddenly thought of a further tactic. "Who is your superior? I shall put in a complaint so that I need never see you again!"

Sonia could not escape the turmoil of her thoughts. She turned to her journal and gazed bleakly at the next page, wondering if her practice of writing would help to ease this particular problem.

Why could I not see what was taking place? Was I too naïve, or too busy? I wonder if Geoffrey knew? All these men and their wives, and from the best families, too – if word had leaked out, we would have been the laughing stock of the county, the business could have been ruined, and it would all have been such a disgrace. I spent my youth trying to escape humiliation and to have it so nearly catch up with me is too awful to contemplate.

I blame Geoffrey for encouraging me to bring Barbara back into our lives. I could so easily have engaged a local girl with a few brains, and trained her exactly as I wished. If I have any control over who I meet in this Afterlife, Barbara is now most definitely not on the list.

To think that poor Benjamin had to hear all that when he is least able to cope with any more shocks just proves that she has no concern for anyone else's finer feelings. As for her plea for forgiveness – that is totally out of the question, from whichever side of the grave you view the situation. Never could I forgive such betrayal, and that is the end of the matter.

Well, Mr Omnipotent Fu, I will persist in my trips back to the Hall in order to show you how my son rallies round, as I am sure he will once this unpleasantness has worn off. The letter I left for him to hand to Jacqueline will give him strength to rise above any petty opinions, safe in the knowledge that the empire founded by his grandfather and developed by the partnership his father and I shared, will help him prosper for the rest of his days.

He will father sons in the future, no doubt, and they in turn will maintain the family name and position.

❧

Mr Fu stood looking over Sonia's shoulder as she was engrossed in her writing, and left, shaking his head sadly. He knew the contents of the letter, as he knew everything that had happened in her life, having spent her lifetime waiting for a call that never came. There *was* no plea for a guardian angel when a soul was housed in a stubborn, arrogant, invincible body such as Lady Sonia.

Inevitably, more storms lay ahead. He penned another memo.

> *Dear God –*
> *Thank You for Your help with the visit.*
> *I will work on the forgiveness factor, then take her back just once more before the funeral – she needs to see her daughter's reactions to the letter. The effects of that particular time bomb should make her realise what nothing else has done so far.*
>
> *If she puts in the complaint against me she has threatened, then please take it with a pinch of salt – hopefully by the time it reaches You, we will have resolved the matter.*
>
> *Yours as ever, devotedly -*
> *Angel Prince/Mr Fu*

12

It had been a low-key New Year as far as the adults were concerned. Tim and Ella had greeted Richard's parents with glee, looking forward to having their undivided attention for a few days.

Jacqui and Richard viewed their journey with mixed feelings as they travelled to the Hall two days before the funeral – Jacqui was hoping her brother would soften towards her when she was on the spot, getting involved with the preparations. He'd had such responsibilities thrust upon him, and although she was sure he would be fine in time, the tension fairly crackled when she telephoned Ben, and meant she had kept the calls brief and practical.

"I'm so glad you've been able to come and give me moral support – I've a feeling I'm going to need it" she said as she realised just how much she had come to rely on Richard. He was always there, with his incredible gift of saying or doing the right thing at just the right moment. He also had the gift of not being too protective, and that was infinitely more precious in a way. Her life had taken some hard twists and turns, and she needed to remind herself that she had fought against many odds in order to retain her independence. A husband, however well-meaning, who took even a fraction of that hard-won strength away would have been doing her no favours.

Richard patted her hand lightly.

"Whatever happens, we're us, and what we have is pretty good. It's the end of an era, and everyone will be getting used to the idea."

"Mmm, just hold my hand when we go through the door, will you? Then I'll be fine."

Annie looked harassed when she welcomed them in, taking their coats.

"You're to sleep in your old room Miss Jacqueline, and coffee's just been put in the drawing room. I'll get George to take your things upstairs. Were the roads busy? Now, please excuse me – I'm needed in the kitchen."

In the drawing room, pouring the coffee, they were joined by Vicky, who looked pale and tired.

"I thought I'd better do the honours when I heard your car – no-one else is up this morning. We had a dreadful night last night."

"Isn't she settling well?"

"Oh no – not Lucy! She's as good as gold, Nanny says … No, it was something else, but I can't tell you now … Oh, here's Ben after all – I didn't realise you were awake. Coffee?"

Polite conversation, the traditional refuge of the English in tensely emotional situations, came to their rescue. Richard expressed formal condolences to his brother-in-law, Jacqueline showed sisterly concern at the strain Ben was showing, reminding him they were willing to undertake any tasks that needed doing in the remaining two days before the funeral. Ben explained Barbara's absence by saying she had been overdoing things, but hoped she would be well enough to join them all at dinner that evening.

When Jacqui showed keen interest in the baby, Victoria took the opportunity to take her up to the nursery where Nanny ushered them in.

"Lucinda Sonia Margaret Woolston, this is your Auntie Jacqueline."

Jacqui peeped into the crib and exclaimed with delight, commenting on her looks, her hair and all the tiny details new mothers long to hear. Vicky at last felt she could relax, and happily received the compliments on her baby's behalf. Soon they were exchanging experiences, Jacqui's natural warmth and interest eventually beginning to soften the reserve and defensiveness that Sonia's constant denigrating had built up.

Jacqueline had realised this might be the root of the problem – it was an obvious thing for Sonia to set out to do, to perpetuate her own feelings and create a divide between brother and sister. She was therefore so glad of the opportunity to show she felt only genuine regard for the little family, and hoped this baby would do much to fill the gaps left by her grandmother's death, as time went on.

They eventually retraced their steps downstairs and Ben readily agreed to spend time updating Jacqui after lunch, then she would be able to contact people later. He had found it hard work with only intermittent help from his wife, which was due, of course, to strict orders from Clair the Nanny who was adamant that new mothers had to obey her regime. Although Barbara had been willing to step in -

after the previous night's embarrassing episode Ben hoped she would need to spend most of the day resting in her room, until he could face her without disgust. Soon Jacqui was ticking off more items on the main list of things to be done, and prioritising those that remained.

Vicky had wondered whether to say anything about Barbara's disclosure, but eventually decided against the idea, hoping that Jacqui would forget the earlier reference to the disturbed night. She continued to be plagued by thoughts of it – not least because it put her late mother-in-law in a different light entirely. How could that go on for so long, right under that would-be aristocratic nose? Was Barbara being fiercely protective of her friend, or was it to protect her own interests? Whichever had been the case, the result was conspiracy on a remarkable scale.

She glanced at her watch and lay down on top of the bed. Time for the rest that Nanny was insisting she should have each afternoon in order to be able to feed the baby adequately. Ben resented this, as he seemed to resent most things connected with the new regime. Maybe if Lucy *had* been a boy it would be different and Ben would be more pleasant. Well, it was too late for thoughts of 'what if' and she had enough adjustments of her own to make - to motherhood. Her parents would be able to visit when their cruise holiday ended. That would be something to look forward to. Marriage was not turning out to be anything like she had imagined it would be. What would Lucy be like in ten years from now? Would she have to take second place with a younger brother around? These and other random troubled thoughts eventually subsided and Victoria dozed fitfully for an hour.

⁂

Barbara heard Annie's discreet tap at the door, murmured "Come in", and looked up ruefully as the tray was set on the table by the window and the curtains partially drawn back.

"Sorry I'm such a pain – these migraines are hell."

So that was to be the official line, thought Annie, knowing Barbara and her habits better than Barbara gave her credit for. In fact Annie suspected many things about Barbara that were unknown to anyone else now that Sir Geoffrey was dead.

"Do you have your tablets handy?"

"Yes, it's easing now. Annie, do you have a moment?"

"Well, yes – what is it?"

"I'd like to think that there will be a chance for me to slip into Guildford tomorrow, to buy a gift for little Lucy, and doing that will lift the gloom a little. Would you be able to come with me?"

Annie felt it would suit her own purposes very well, so she agreed to the trip, if it could take place immediately after breakfast, leaving the rest of the day free to prepare for the following day's event – the funeral.

※

Barbara felt much better later that afternoon and was so pleased to hear another gentle knock at the door just as she was wondering whether to put in an early appearance downstairs.

"Auntie Babs! Are you feeling better now? I thought you might be ready for another cup of tea."

"Oh, Jacqueline! I am so glad to see you."

They had always had a closeness dating from the intermittent occasions of Jacqui's childhood when Barbara relaxed for a day after the business weekends at the Hall had finished. She had enjoyed the company of the little girl who was so solemn for most of the time, but had the capacity for so much love. This satisfied any latent maternal tendencies that Barbara might have had, for motherhood had never figured in her life plan.

Of course she had been apprehensive about Jacqui's first marriage, but was wise enough to keep her thoughts to herself, so that later, when Jacqui had been having problems with Zak and was being hounded by the press, eager for more of the sordid details she needed, she had been able to give her a place to retreat to, in her flat. Privately, Barbara had thought this was what she should be having from Sonia, but she willingly gave Jacqui whatever she could. Jacqueline had always been less favoured in Sonia's eyes than Ben. No wonder Geoffrey had always tried to make amends – sometimes, Barbara thought, to the point of over-compensating.

They hugged now, relieved to have each other to turn to.

"You are so fortunate to have Richard" Barbara said "I really think he might have been the person to bring you and your mother closer in time. She would listen to him, whereas she was always wary of Anthony. Didn't approve of the hypnosis, she said, but I think she was probably scared."

Jacqui smiled at the thought of her mother being scared of anything or anyone.

"Most of mother's generation don't approve of it. He did sense, though, that she'd hidden so much from her past it had formed a thick layer of control. She felt safe if everything in her life was predictable, and gave short shrift to anyone who stepped out of line."

"Particularly since your father died."

"True. Oh Barbara – I do miss him so much." Jacqui buried her head in her hands.

They both wept - for their memories of a man who, although far from perfect, had meant something special to each of them and both thought of him with fondness and gratitude.

"I wonder if they're together now …" mused Jacqui. "I suppose I shall never find the cause of my mother's dislike, but I do wish them both peace and happiness. Perhaps Mummy will find it in her heart to forgive me for whatever I kept doing wrong. When I was little I always wondered why she treated me so harshly. It wasn't too bad when there were people around – visitors, you know. But when we were alone she ignored me as much as possible, otherwise, something I said or did would work her up into one of those terrible tempers.

"It was awful, and when Daddy was there, somehow it was even worse, although she never let him see her hitting me. She would say the most hurtful things to me and threaten to kill my pets. I could never understand why, and I really did try to be a good girl. Daddy would comfort me afterwards, and spend time with me until he was sure I wasn't upset, but somehow he never seemed able to prevent her punishing me, no matter how unfair it was."

"Barbara held her hand and squeezed it lightly, not interrupting the flow of something that Jacqui obviously needed to talk about.

"When I met Anthony I'd managed to forget a great deal of this. You know how my marriage to Zak, and all that publicity had left me - I was just about holding things together for Timmy's sake. Anthony helped me to start piecing things together, and I learned the reasons for many of my reactions. It explained a great many things that had puzzled me for years – why I felt so much shame when things were so obviously not my fault, for instance. But I never really got to the bottom of why my punishments were always so much more severe than Ben's – much more than you would expect from an ordinary favouritism situation."

Jacqui hung on to Barbara's hand as if she were drowning. Barbara waited patiently.

"The only real clue was found when I went for hypnotherapy with a friend of Anthony's. I was taken back - regressed - to a time when I felt happy. It was a summer holiday when I was about eight or nine. Ben and I were staying with my Aunt and Uncle. It must have been the time when Mummy was ill and we were suddenly sent away. They were so kind to me. I was outside a door, going to the kitchen for a drink, then I heard them talking. They must have thought I was playing outside.

'What can you expect from someone like Sonia, coming from that disgraceful family background? Her father didn't leave home on a whim, you know. He must have had that other woman for years, and his wife never knew.'

"At this point of the session I screamed and became very agitated. The hypnotherapist helped me come round safely, but I couldn't discuss it with him. I just needed to get home, and it was two days before I stopped shaking. I never went again – what other disturbing secrets might come out?

"We eventually pieced it together. They were talking about my mother, and the Grandfather I never knew. I had always been told he was killed in the War, and had built up this idea of a courageous soldier - a strong, upright man who would fight for his country and family. Suddenly I was totally disillusioned, when the memory of what I'd overheard was unearthed.

"Anthony helped me to sort it out as the shock wore off. It *was* a shock, too - instead of a war hero, my Grandfather had suddenly become a disgrace. What must it have done to my mother? Anthony said that a normal reaction would be a desire for my mother to protect herself from any more pain. Her father had betrayed both mother and daughter, so the young Sonia might well think that the best way to deal with life and relationships would be to control everything she could.

She even controlled your father by making herself indispensable in his business.

"It seemed to make sense, put like that. My poor mother couldn't handle the pain she had been feeling inside for so many years. The illness she had when I was away for that holiday was never referred to – by anyone – and it was not the sort of thing I could ask her about directly, was it?

"After that, when we returned home, I would hear her sobbing in the night. Night after night it went on. My father's voice would soothe her, and it eventually stopped. She stayed in her room for days on end. I remember she only ever wore long sleeved dresses after that, but I couldn't connect these things at the time. Children were only allowed to see what adults thought they ought to see in those days. We were sent away to school soon afterwards, and that helped me, as it was a means of escaping. It set a pattern, though, and Anthony explained how my first marriage had also been an escape – anything rather than return to that unhappy house.

"Ben coped much better, of course. Mummy was more tranquil when he was with her. It must have been a strain for her, all those years of keeping up pretences, being hostess for all Daddy's business guests. If it hadn't been for you, Barbara, she might never have got through it.

"When Anthony helped me to realise what had been happening, I decided to see if there might be a way I could help her. I kept it low key, of course, but I made sure I was in regularly in touch. It wasn't easy. I know that with my first marriage I'd given her plenty of things in my life to be scathing about, but I couldn't bear malice towards someone who was as sick as she had been. I clung on to the hope that if I loved her enough it would eventually smooth things out. But then when Daddy died, it made her very bitter."

Barbara had been listening intently as she drank her tea and gradually returned to her normal self. She held Jacqui's hand silently for several more minutes, then gave a reassuring pat.

"Time helps us to see things in better perspective, Jaqui, but try not to let the old hurts get stirred up. Only one more day to go, my dear, then it's the funeral and we can *all* start getting on with the rest of our lives. I'm so glad you're here and I'll be able to help you out tomorrow,

I promise, after I've been to buy a gift for Lucy – isn't she sweet? And *that's* a telling remark from a crabby old woman who never had any time for children!"

"Nonsense Auntie Babs – I know you've always had a gift for it and my two adore you - you know that, as will Lucy. They are three very lucky children with a fabulous Auntie. Now I'll wait for you to get ready and we'll go downstairs together."

Jacqueline knew that practicality would be the best antidote to her emotional conversation and busied herself with the remaining phone calls that afternoon, while Richard persuaded Ben to go for a walk around the estate, to 'blow the cobwebs away'. Ben found it was good to have another man to talk with, and the fresh air helped him to think more clearly than he had been doing for some days. They discussed many topics, and even found common interests – anything other than the recent events. The early setting sun lowered itself through the distant trees, and long shadows were cast over the winter fields.

Richard breathed deeply as they walked back up the driveway.

"Running an estate like this must take an enormous amount of time" he commented.

"That's why it's essential that my wife plays her part. If she doesn't recover soon she'll have to start taking the happy pills, or everything will fall apart."

"I'm sure she'll start to feel better after the funeral – it's always like this while you're waiting for that to take place. A sort of limbo, with everything put on hold until the final farewell. Didn't you feel that when your father died?"

"Not at all. Mother held everyone together and ran the whole thing like one of their business weekends, as indeed it almost was – more business contacts here than family. There will be some of those this time, too – the church mob in full force and the Mothers' Union no doubt, then there's the village side - the Women's Institute, the Gardening Society, the Parish Council – there'll be many more people than you saw on her birthday; another excuse for the social climbers to take advantage of who they rub shoulders with. I just want Victoria to do her bit, and do it properly. It's not too much to ask, surely?"

Richard took the question as rhetorical, as they entered the side door and made their way to the drawing room to see how the others were faring.

The evening passed pleasantly enough with the aid of a good meal, and light relief in the form of old family photo albums, and an early night seemed to be the best plan for them all, they agreed.

Apart from Ben, who needed to spend time in the Library.

13

The next day, the day before the funeral, again dawned bright and cold. After a more sociable evening, the emotional pace had changed and tensions returned. Ben and Jacqui were scheduled to spend an hour at the vicarage, going over last minute details of the service. Richard had previously asked Ben if there was a possibility of including the carefully selected quotation Jacqui had made. However, Ben emerged looking very satisfied and relieved, Jacqui tearstained and sad, saying she'd like to walk back to the Hall on her own. When she caught up with Richard she explained.

"He has written the eulogy for mother - no need for anyone else to add anything, so it will all be done with dignity as befits her memory. Mother wouldn't have wanted any of that emotional stuff, he said."

Defeated, Richard busied himself, helping Jacqui with some last minute preparations for the funeral, followed by a stroll together in the grounds before lunch.

"Ben's attitude has begun to puzzle me" she mused. "He seems to have taken everything on board and won't take any advice or even suggestions. He's so … so … well, bossy, and that isn't how he's been before."

"Don't forget, he has huge responsibilities now, and your mother was very much a guiding light with all her experience over the years. The way she ran the day-to-day life at the Hall was something he knew he could rely on, so that he could concentrate on the family business – now he knows that Vicky will have to take over that role, and he must be wondering if she will be able to cope with that and the baby as well."

"Doris and Annie don't need much supervision, though. They've been running the show admirably for years, and I'm sure they will give Vicky every assistance they can."

"Well, I'm sure they will offer it. I just hope she has the good sense to accept. She's young, and not used to dealing with staff, so it might appear as if she's treading on their toes. But I'm sure it will all settle down in time."

Walking back to the Hall, Jacqui telephoned the children again. Their chatter about games and feeding ducks in the park near home gave her a warm, comforting sense of the loving family she and Richard had created out of the chaos and grief of her past. Jacqui hoped that Victoria would soon start to experience that glow of achievement once the next few days were over.

⁂

Annie had returned after the Guildford trip more than ready for the cup of tea that Doris was always ready to make in the kitchen.

"Did you see what Barbara has bought Lucy?"

"No – we went our separate ways, then met again later, and it was gift-wrapped. I had to spend ages at the bank, and … oh, I'll have to tell you later." Annie restrained herself as Victoria appeared at the kitchen door.

"Is there anything I can get for you, Mrs Woolston?"

"Doris - Nanny says that she needs to know if tomorrow will affect her routine."

"All I can say is that I will *try* to make sure that everything goes like clockwork - but as long as she understands that it's buffet for lunch, and dinner will be served half an hour later than usual, then perhaps she can be a little flexible in the circumstances."

Victoria lingered in the doorway.

"It all seems so strange without my mother-in-law. Such a short while ago we were all here seeing how the preparations for her birthday were going … "

But Doris was not to be drawn into sentimentality, or even any level of conversation, and her tone of voice did not encourage either.

"There's a large portion of that cake left, and I don't know what I should do about it. Wouldn't be seemly to serve it at the wake, I suppose, but it will keep until you can decide. Now will you excuse me – there is a great deal to do to get everything just right."

When Victoria had returned upstairs, Annie looked quizzically at Doris, eyebrows raised.

"I know, I know. But I can't pretend to like the girl, and I don't want her thinking she can make a friend of me, if that's what she was trying to do."

"Maybe it was just loneliness. She doesn't seem to have made any friends at all since coming here, and life can be pretty boring when you have nothing to do."

"She'll soon have more than enough to do when we hand in our notice. I'm just glad I won't be around to see what she makes of it – she'll have Lady Sonia turning in her grave, no doubt. Now help me get lunch ready and we'll have a talk later."

෴

"Oh, Richard, thank goodness we've got a little breathing space" Jacqueline fell back on the bed and held her arms out to her husband, hoping he'd join her.

Later, leaning on one elbow, he turned to study the framed photograph on the mantelpiece, then looked quizzically at his wife.

"That was taken one summer when everything was good, for a change, except for Mummy, who was ill. Ben and I were packed off to various relatives in turn, and we had a lovely week by the sea when all the Aunts, Uncles and cousins met up in a big house they'd rented. We'd have been about 8 years old then, and what I remembered most was the laughter. Everyone seemed to have so much *fun*."

"Poor little girl" he said tenderly.

"I've got over the worst now. It doesn't feel like a knife twisting every time I think of what I put up with, and I've also forgiven myself for not having the guts to stand up and tell her about the hurt. So, there you are – living proof that the therapy worked."

She finished lightly, on a purposefully higher tone of voice than she actually felt, for it did still hurt if the memories caught her unawares.

"Come on, Richard - let's put on a suitable expression and make our way down for a drink before dinner."

෴

It was a tense evening, although the flow of some very good wines helped to ease matters. Until the last few days Benjamin and Richard had been on fairly formal terms, having met only briefly at the register office wedding the year before. Ben had disapproved of his sister's choice of husbands even more than his mother, and it was with reluctance he had attended her third wedding, representing the family. However, the previous day's walk had helped break the ice and he was beginning to accept his third brother-in-law, and realise that this time Jacqui had indeed found the right man.

After the meal drew to a close, Victoria peremptorily told Doris she would not be needed further, then gave Jacqueline a slight frown of impatience as she murmured words of appreciation to offset the somewhat sharp dismissal. Jacqueline had always been quite fond of Doris, and over the years had seen just how devoted to Sonia she had always been, always patient, never objecting to her time being used to the utmost. But at least Sonia always made a point of saying thank you when she dismissed staff for the night. Victoria would have done better to learn the same standard of courtesy, Jacqui thought – no point in setting up unnecessary animosity with either Doris or Annie, or life might rapidly become less pleasant.

They all settled down to coffee and brandies by the log fire, then at a moment when all were apparently individually lost in thought about what the following day would bring, Ben made a sudden announcement;

"Well, I thought we might as well get the sordid details out of the way. I've got a copy of the Will in my desk and I suggest we read it."

"But don't we have to have the Uncles here?" Turning to Richard, Barbara explained that the Uncles were Sonia's cousins, solicitors working in partnership.

"Oh that will take place later for the official reading, and we can keep that very brief. Don't want people hanging about unnecessarily. No, it will be better to get it over and done with now."

He left the room, returning moments later from his office, carrying an envelope.

"Didn't really want the Hollywood suspense treatment with everyone sitting round, and I'm sure there will be no surprises. Let's be dignified about it, I thought, and the Uncles agreed when I phoned them – they're also the other executors, after all - so we get first reading now, and the formal reading will be done in the usual way. Then it's just the straightforward work after that, making sure everything's implemented."

The Ripples and the Tapestries

Jacqueline felt slightly uncomfortable, as did Barbara, she was sure. Uneasiness spread through the group, but Ben's determination to do it this way was obvious. He opened the envelope, and began to read.

❦

The Will was the usual format ... their mother was of sound mind etc., then after stating there would be amounts set aside for the executors (Benjamin and the Uncles) to cover expenses, the bequest to Doris was the first item to cause a raised eyebrow from Ben.

"Fifty thousand pounds to Doris Forrester for her loyal service."

He paused. "I personally think that's a bit much. But Mummy always was so generous."

"At the express wish of my late husband, the vintage Bentley is to be given to Robert Higgs, in memory of his role as chauffeur for so many years. If he chooses to sell it back to any member of the family, he must receive a fair price.

"Well, of course we'll offer – I'm sure he'll need the cash at his age – just leave that to me."

"My complete collection of forty-eight Dresden figurines kept in the glass case in the drawing room, is to be passed on to my dear friend Barbara, who has always admired them so much.

Barbara looked unsurprised, as Sonia had made no secret that they were to be hers eventually.

"For my grandchild, the descendant of Benjamin my son, and as yet unborn at the time of making this Will, and to any future grandchildren bearing the name of Woolston, I have set up a sum of £3,000,000 in trust, which will be managed by my son Benjamin, the details of which rest with my lawyers.

Benjamin cleared his throat slightly, and glanced towards his wife at this disclosure assuring the safe future of their child, then resumed ...

"Although neither Timothy nor Ella bear the family name, nevertheless they have been allocated a sum equivalent to ten percent of the Trust i.e. £300,000, which will be theirs when they each reach eighteen years of age. There will be no additional amount for any further children born to Jacqueline."

At the mention of her children's names, Jacqui had stiffened, and as the sentence was completed she stifled a sharp intake of breath. Richard, who had been standing, put down his drink and moved to her side, a reassuring hand on her shoulder. Ben appeared to need to concentrate on the paper in front of him to the exclusion of all else, shifting it slightly, and avoiding lifting his gaze to any of the faces around him. He cleared his throat again and once more resumed.

"The remainder of my estate - all businesses, Woolston Hall and all possessions - is bequeathed to my son Benjamin, for his unfailing support throughout my latter years, and in the knowledge that he has found a worthy successor to me in his wife Victoria, to perpetuate the name and continue the Woolston line in the family home."

The air had become electric. A long pause followed as they each digested the import of the last ten seconds of the reading. Ben eventually went over to the sideboard and poured himself another brandy, returning to the group by the fire. Barbara sat motionless.

Richard tightened his grip until his knuckles whitened, but Jacqueline hardly noticed the force he used. The colour drained from her face, then returned with a quick flush as she turned to look at her brother and saw a fleeting expression of triumph in his eyes.

She looked at his wife - and Victoria, for her part, momentarily bore a look that would have been worthy of her late mother-in-law. Superior smugness and awareness of power had dropped over her face like a mask – a mask that only the _very_ wealthy can afford to wear, unafraid of retribution.

Turning back to Jacqui, Ben added "There's another document here, in a sealed envelope addressed directly to you, Jacqueline, and marked 'Private', so you may prefer to read it in your room."

It was a suggestion of dismissal Jacqueline decided to take. She walked out of the library without a word, head held high, and it was left to Richard to take the proffered envelope and follow her upstairs, wondering what more awaited them, but knowing that even if it were the worst disaster in the world he would be at her side to help her in any way possible.

Hands trembling, Jacqueline sat on the bed, looking at the envelope, tears in her eyes. It was indeed marked *'Private'*. Underneath, a phrase was added - *"to be opened only after my death and after my Will has been read."*

"Do you think I will learn now?"

"About your mother's reasons?"

Richard asked in their shorthand of shared understanding and closeness. He, most of all, knew how she had constantly wrestled with the demon of her mother's dislike and victimisation, puzzled and hurt. Drawing her close to him, he added

"Whatever we find out, whatever the results are – just remember that we face this together, you and I. You are never going to feel isolated and unloved ever again as long as I draw breath."

The letter was cold and formal.

> *To Jacqueline Gray, nee Woolston:*
> *When you read this letter I will be beyond your reach. Had I been alive and this secret had come to light, no doubt you would have thought of making some sort of pathetic attempt to "understand" me.*
>
> *You will have heard the terms of my Will. That should give you understanding enough, and the knowledge that I can affect you even after I have gone gives me some satisfaction.*
>
> *The facts are as follows:-*
> *By the time I was unexpectedly found to be pregnant at the age of 38, it was too late to take medical steps to deal with it. However, I determined to make the best of the situation, and insisted your father and I moved to a home more befitting our ambitions – the Hall. I had*

been booked into a private nursing home for the birth. Inevitably, Geoffrey was away on one of his business trips, so I dealt with all the arrangements on my own.

Then, only hours after going through the rigours of giving birth to Benjamin, I had a visit from my husband, who at least had the grace to be very agitated. No wonder. He confessed he had been keeping a mistress, who had died in childbirth only two days before, leaving a surviving daughter he had promised to care for.

Money always helps to find a solution, and he had already made arrangements for me to leave the nursing home with one child, and arrive at Woolston Hall with two.

As he had already spread the news to family and friends that I had given birth to twins, I was presented with no choice in the matter. In the meantime, I was to be denied any visitors on the grounds of exhaustion. If I refused to go along with the deception, he would make up some story about postnatal depression, ongoing mental health problems, and he would eventually divorce me. Social ruin loomed, and he knew me so well – losing face was the one thing I dreaded.

Lying there in the nursing home, I had time to think overnight. Something good had to come out of this appalling mess. Eventually I realised that if I agreed, I could be in control forever and I could make Geoffrey pay for his actions for the rest of his life. More than that, I could and would make sure that he was tortured daily. He would have to see his daughter bear the hatred that I could never publicly inflict upon him.

Life at Woolston Hall was a new beginning. Outwardly I became the mother of twins, in a large house with servants, including a Nanny for the children, so that I soon returned to my usual role. The business weekends continued, with Nanny and her charges accommodated in the Lodge. I could live a life of my own choosing - I only had to mention something I wanted, and Geoffrey would *provide it, not daring to oppose me in case I revealed his deception.*

But I hated his favouritism of you. Benjamin was an amenable child, but you were different. Not so surprising when one considers the mother you had. You are, however, reasonably intelligent, so I need not go into further detail – you can piece things together for yourself.

Therefore it will not surprise you that I have made my Will as I have – you are no flesh and blood of mine, but have been a daily reminder of a deceptive husband and the result of that immorality. I recommend that you be careful of who else knows the truth – your father took it to his grave. I was tempted to do the same, but in the end decided it should be the only legacy you will receive from me.

Sonia

The letter dropped from Jacqueline's fingers, and momentarily Richard felt her weight against his shoulder increase. They had been sitting side by side on the bed, and now she turned suddenly to look at him. He felt for her hand, but she pulled away, then gave a short, bitter laugh.

"You haven't married a Woolston, – you've been saddled with a b……."

He covered her lips with his fingers, then recoiled as she bit him and flung herself on the bed hitting at the pillows, her voice rising hysterically with sobs and incoherent words. He held onto her, until her world ceased falling apart.

It could have been an hour, or several, but he continued to hold her, stroke her hair, and tend to the woman he loved going through an agony at which he could only guess. When she had experienced the worst, he raised her tear-drenched face in both of his hands and told her, earnestly,

"Never forget – *you* were conceived in love. You were no resented accident, and your father *proved* that, through all your time together. You've lived through the worst punishment and absolutely nothing now can hurt you as much."

He hushed her until she slept exhaustedly, wrapped in his arms.

14

Sonia's time in the Afterlife had paused. Time, in fact, had no meaning there, and in any case, there was no means of measuring its passing. She explored the ceaselessly changing setting in the grounds and enjoyed the scenery, but missed contact with people. Was this all there was to it? This everlasting solitary existence?

Her task of writing continued. Mr Fu also asked her to write about her understanding of the five virtues – goodness, judgement, love, wisdom and truth - and explain how she had attempted to apply these to her life. They would discuss it at length - but he would leave before she could make up her mind whether or not he approved of what she had said – it was very frustrating for someone who had lived in a culture of effort and reward to find that the end never appeared in sight.

She tackled Mr Fu about this, summoning him to appear and explain.

"Dear lady, you *will* be able to move on when you've finished this part of your task. As I explained earlier - *you* have to assess your life and the effects you had on others, in order to see if you have learned the lessons you were set to learn. It's no use expecting me to do the hard work for you!"

"But as I was not aware of the existence of any of these so-called lessons at the time, how could I set out to learn something if I didn't even know what it was?"

"May I remind you again of the simplest message of all?" Mr Fu said, summoning his utmost patience. "The message that love is the key to everything, no matter where you were born, or in what circumstances. You must have heard that as the basis of many sermons over the years.

"I think it's summed up by this quote – *'So many gods, so many creeds, so many paths that wind, while just the art of being kind is all this sad world needs.'*

"Love is kindliness, and Earthly lives can demonstrate that, by treating others as we wish to be treated. Every opportunity that comes along is an opportunity to do that."

"But I still say that too many people would take advantage of the situation. The world would never survive!"

"Not if they were all treating everyone as they wish to be treated themselves."

"No, it would never work. You don't understand civilisation. You are most certainly basing your ideas on some outdated concept of ancient times, when people were simple-minded compared with today's sophisticated outlook."

"That *was* when the world began – but simple-minded? Think of the great civilisations of the past – think of where so-called 'modern' learning has its roots. Egypt, Asia, China, Greece, Peru – think of the scientists, the astronomers, and the medical knowledge that has been learned, lost, and had to be rediscovered later. Thousands of years cannot be dismissed lightly, dear lady."

"Well, if it was so perfect, what happened to end it?"

"People began to forget the true purpose of their existence – that they needed to work together for the benefit of all. Their baser instincts came to the fore and they became greedy and ambitious. For a while it didn't seem to make any difference, so they didn't stop to examine their motives, and the greed continued and increased. Think of the way that all kinds of discoveries eventually began to be used wrongly – to benefit individuals first and foremost, and to gain self-glory – inevitably, corruption was the result. Then mankind lost sight of the lesson of love and kindness."

"So why were there no reminders?"

"Oh but there were. They were brought by the Messengers who were sent to all quarters of the Earth - at various times and as part of all the major faiths. At first there was no need of them, with the whole population working together with mutual respect for each other and their needs, sharing everything. However, whenever corruption has started to get to a dangerous level, many Messengers have been sent. But they have always been seen as threatening the new system, so many of them were banished - or worse - so that the greediness could continue.

"Then the greedy people began to acquire more and more earthly power. Fear replaced love. People did things because they feared the consequences, not because they loved the ones they were doing them for, or superstitiously felt their actions would in some way protect them. As the centuries brought us towards the so-called sophistication of today, the blanket of corruption solidified into ignorance."

Sonia could keep quiet no longer.

"But the *churches* survived in order to teach people how to behave! That is why religion is so important, and why people like me are needed in order to set others an example of righteous living."

Mr Fu paused for a while before he answered.

"You shared a birthday with one of the greatest Messengers. What happened to Him? He was sacrificed in order to demonstrate who actually held the power. His resurrection was another message - that even death cannot kill the messenger and the truth. The desperate sadness of the human race is that some of them subsequently corrupted that message for their own ends, set up an alternative civilisation and called it religion.

"It became divided and subdivided over the centuries, as people who had glimpses of the real truth struggled to put that message in a more convincing way and relate it to their lives at the time. Ways were devised of proving that love existed. Someone decided that money could be used as proof, so people could give money and not have to actually love their fellow man. They did not even have to see where the money went – not even if it went into the wrong hands, as it often did."

A picture came into Sonia's mind of a cathedral she had once seen on a television programme. Not an inch of its interior was undecorated – gold everywhere, jewels set in crosses, in the crowns on the figures of saints, and on the sumptuously embroidered robes of the priests who conducted the service. The camera panned to the exterior of the building and showed how it was set in the worst of the city's slums, with people in ragged clothes begging for money from the visitors to the church who were coming to donate more money.

She firmly pushed the image away.

"What nonsense! The world is full of feckless individuals who have to be directed by people of my class, in order to make them productive members of society. That is our duty – to save them from themselves. Read my notes again and you will see how the system works."

"I have indeed read your notes again, and I was going to ask you to reconsider them in the light of some of the things we have seen on the visits back to your home. You may have been able to justify everything to your own satisfaction, but I notice that asking for forgiveness has not been part of your understanding."

"*Forgiveness*? Why should I ask to be forgiven? For what? Every good thing that happened to me in life has been as a result of my own determination and single-mindedness. It was *I* who made the good things happen, after that awful start. I am proud of my achievements, and the way I have made the most of my God-given talents."

"But at whose expense? Has your single-mindedness meant that you had the best interest of others at heart at all times? Have you ever overlooked others in the preservation of your own progress?"

He momentarily sent a wordless thought up to God and, receiving a surge of strength back in return, had the courage to continue.

"For example, what happened to your mother, Lady Sonia?"

"How *dare* you attempt to distort things – my mother had everything I could possibly give her, and ended her days in the best nursing home in the county."

Standing and drawing himself to his full height, Mr Fu appeared to increase in stature and suddenly became an impressive figure. Not one to be trifled with, Sonia realised uneasily. His response was stern.

"Your mother died alone and loveless, knowing only that she had a daughter who was almost always too busy to come to see her. She protected you, though, to the very end - *her* end – telling the staff how proud she was that you had made your way in the world, never revealing how many tears she shed in the prison of her room, nor how every day she hoped you would walk through the door."

Turning on his heel he swiftly left.

The Ripples and the Tapestries

Although Sonia was startled, nonetheless she was very, very angry. It could simply not be true. The staff at the nursing home had fussed around her when Sonia returned to thank them personally for the care they had given. One after the other they had all said the same thing – "she was so proud of you."

Was it possible that she had secretly been unhappy? That last visit, on her birthday ... Sonia remembered how she had had to prise her mother's twisted hands from her own as she said goodbye.

"I'm late as it is, Mother. I have to get back to prepare for Geoffrey's business lunch. The staff will take care of your flowers and I've paid for a special cake. I'll be in touch – just let me know if there's anything you need."

"*You* ... Sonia ... *you* ..." the voice quavered and weakened.

"Now don't get sentimental, I can't stand it. Just enjoy your day and look at all your cards. I *must* go."

But that was just the way things had worked out, Sonia told herself. No use wasting time over guilt – she had done more for her mother than many others would have done – no expense spared, and she had always made sure that Jacqueline and Benjamin had written their thankyou letters for those appallingly cheap little gifts their grandmother had insisted on sending them each Christmas and birthday without fail.

No, forgiveness was something that had to be sought only when actions were *unjustifiably* unkind. True, she had resented her mother for a long time – for her weak will and illnesses – but she had amply recompensed her later on. What else was this wretched man going to find in her past?

Sonia looked slightly apprehensive as Mr Fu returned suddenly, muttering under his breath as he bustled in "*...really have to find some way of doing it, Lord – does she actually know what it is?*" and sitting down at her side he leaned forward earnestly.

"Lady Sonia, can you tell me what forgiveness means to you?"

"Weakness! It's the one thing I disagreed with within the church's teachings. I regularly had to take the Vicar to task and remind him that if you lived a blameless life, or set things to rights as soon as you could, you need have no guilt, and therefore no need to ask for forgiveness. Strength of character and beliefs mean that God is always with you, helping you to act correctly at all times."

"It is, if I may say so, a very simplistic way of looking at things. But we won't continue to argue. I think that painful though it's going to be for you, the time is ripe for me to take you back again. You don't seem to have understood the message at all, as yet. You saw what your staff thought of you, you heard how your daughter-in-law referred to you, and as for your son being devoted and loving – well all I can say is that he appears to be almost as selfish and arrogant as his mother!"

Sonia wanted to get away, and half rose from her chair. To her horror, she found her wrist held in a strong grip, while Mr Fu continued.

"There is someone you have intentionally hurt very deeply, very recently. In fact you have hurt and puzzled her all through her life, and what has made it worse is that it was nothing *she* herself had done, but an act of revenge on someone else. In spite of your treatment, she loves you. But your recent action has endangered that – and if she loses her love for you because of what you have told her, she will have a far more difficult life ahead than she deserves. If, however, she can still find it in her heart to forgive you, I ask you to learn from her example. It will make your work here much easier. So much depends on her."

≈≫

They made the journey - Sonia with a heavy lump in her heart, uncertain of what the outcome would be. She did not want to see Jacqueline, knowing that the letter would have had its full impact. She had known, even as she wrote the letter, the intention was to crush her for ever with a burden of knowledge that could never be told, and destroy the innocent victim of her husband's actions as a last act of revenge. Surely no love could surmount that.

With a start, she realised that it had been personal weakness that led her into the trap of wreaking revenge on an innocent person. Revenge - the very thing that she had been able to discuss dispassionately with Mr Fu, without realising that for a great part of her own life she had been so glaringly guilty. There was no pleasure in this journey to Earth, and Sonia felt an unaccustomed knot of dread tighten in her chest.

They arrived in the bedroom at the Hall, with Mr Fu still holding her wrist. There was no escape. Sonia could never tolerate weeping and

The Ripples and the Tapestries

emotional outbursts – such weakness – but they saw that Jacqueline had woken from her disturbed sleep to find Richard was still awake, waiting in case she needed him. They were lying in bed, talking through some of the implications of the letter that lay crumpled on the bedside table.

Suddenly Jacqui sat bolt upright, shaking, and drawing up her knees clasped her arms around them, as she used to when she was a child. Sonia steeled herself for the outburst of rage she had intended to provoke, but was totally unprepared for the expression on her daughter's face – she was smiling!

"Richard – I've just realised – she's set me free! All these years I've spent so much time trying to remember something I'd done that was so dreadful it would be the reason for the way she treated me. Now I realise there *was* no reason.

"I was the scapegoat, not the one responsible – all I did was to be there, a daily reminder of my father's unfaithfulness and great love for another woman.

"Oh, *poor* Mummy. I knew she was tormented – her suicide attempt was proof enough of that. If *only* I could tell her that it's all right. I may not be her daughter, but she's the only mother I ever had."

"But it verged on criminal …" said Richard.

"Yes, it may have done, but Daddy was able to see me, and he loved me so much. I could never have known *that* love if he'd sent me away somewhere else. He must have gone through agonies over the decision, and for the rest of his life."

Now that Jacqueline had found her answer, she gently lay down and snuggled back in Richard's arms, a smile on her lips. To her astonishment, Sonia saw a warm rose pink mist spread across the room from Jacqueline's side of the bed. It enveloped her unseen mother in its depths and she looked at Mr Fu.

"*That*, dear lady, is love and forgiveness."

And they returned.

༺༻

Sonia was very thoughtful for a long time, and Mr Fu knew that it was wise to let her sort out her own conclusions, waiting to join in conversation, but not until she was ready to communicate. Even her journal lay untouched. Eventually she looked up to find him sitting not far away, studying her intently.

"… after all I did to her …?"

"Love knows no limitations. Jacqueline has found her answer, her true answer, and it has brought her happiness. Limitations are brought about by narrow mindedness and negative thoughts.

"*You've* been the one who has been limited – by the heavy burden of hatred you carried around, and you've never been able to let go any part of it because you were unable to meet your own father again, forgive him, and set your mind at rest. You and your mother perpetuated the hatred, and neither had the means to see how he could be forgiven."

Sonia thought about this for a while.

"Would it be possible to meet him now that I'm here? He must surely be around somewhere?"

"We have your work to complete before we can even think about things like that, and you must not look on the possibility of that sort of reunion being an incentive – true forgiveness must come from the heart, not the head."

"Do I even know how to forgive?" Sonia looked bleakly at her guide.

"Let the love come through from wherever you have buried it. Don't even worry about what to call it – when you feel the warmth and the one-ness, you will know."

15

Jacqueline and Richard did not go downstairs for breakfast. It had been a long night, but he knew that later on, when Jacqui had half woken again and wept, it was not for herself, but for the waste of all those years when Sonia had tormented her husband by ill-treating his love-child.

Jacqui did not doubt that her father's love for his mistress was great – great enough to make him want to blackmail his wife, but he had done something impulsive that, once set in motion, could not be undone without the destruction of the lives of all concerned. All of them – Sir Geoffrey, Sonia, Jacqueline and Ben were trapped into a lie that could never be told while the originators were alive.

Sonia's bitterness had lasted all her life and she had deliberately, vindictively, planned to play her trump card at the time of her death – not content with writing Jacqueline out of her Will, she had finally revealed the cruel secret of her illegitimate birth and the deception of her parenthood – but only at a time when she knew she herself was unassailable, and in a manner that precluded making amends.

"Will you be able to cope with today, Jacqui? We could go home and everyone would understand if we said you were ill."

"No, I'll be fine. Would you do one thing for me, though? I need you to have a word with Ben. He may feel uncomfortable about the Will, but can you reassure him that it's perfectly all right with me, without telling him anything about Mother's secret, of course – at this stage, anyway. Now is most definitely *not* the time."

Ben and Victoria had not slept well either. The triumph that Vicky felt when she heard that Ben was to inherit everything was the reaction she had told herself she was waiting for. Yet it was a hollow victory. She was beginning to realise that what Sonia had made look simple – the daily running of the Hall, the organisational skills, the expectations of the various strands of village life – were not duties that could simply be taken over and run as smoothly by anyone else, especially by herself. In short, she was beginning to develop a fear of what life might hold from now on.

Ben had stayed downstairs with the decanter until well into the night, and had woken with the consequences of yet another hangover.

Victoria was glad of Lucy's needs, so that she could escape into the nursery, where even Ben could not come and throw his weight around – Clair the nanny ruled in there.

She woke him as she was about to leave the bedroom, left him to shower, get dressed and go downstairs alone. At least in this household it was easy to avoid each other, she thought, as she made her way along to the nursery, then later to pick at breakfast.

※

"I shall be very glad indeed when today is over." Doris stacked the breakfast things in the dishwasher and turned to check that the coffee trolley was prepared.

"What time will Lisa arrive?" asked Annie.

"She's due in half an hour, so I suggest that we have our break before then, because it will be all systems go after that."

They had reason to be satisfied with the smoothness and efficiency of the preparations, and allowed a few minutes to sit down with their usual cups of tea and plate of biscuits.

"We'll have to be careful about when we hand in our notice, Doris, but we mustn't leave it too long. I suggest this evening, after dinner."

"And before he sees off too much of that brandy. He's getting too fond of that, and his mother would most certainly not have approved."

As ever, there was not too much that escaped Doris's notice.

"Miss Jacqueline looks washed out this morning, but calmer, in a way" she continued. "She's such a sweet natured girl, in spite of all the past tragedies she's had – makes you wonder why some people seem to get all the troubles in the world. It always seems to be the good ones, too."

"Perhaps they're the ones best able to deal with them. I do like her husband. He was a tower of strength on Christmas Day – so calm. I'm sure he'll be the same, whatever happens in their lives. They were just made for each other."

Lisa arrived early and Doris ran through the programme with her.

"Everyone attending the funeral who is not family will go straight to the church. There will be some family members arriving here ready for the cortege – they're Lady Sonia's two cousins and their wives. They'll have had a long journey down the motorway, so, as Annie is going to the service to represent the staff, you will greet them and make sure they're made comfortable when they arrive. Drinks to be served for them, or coffee if they prefer, then they'll return for the buffet. That will be served in the dining room, the same as we did on Christmas Day."

Lisa pulled a face.

"I feel that she's around, watching."

"Nonsense! You've been seeing too many late night films, my girl. The only spirits here are in the drinks cabinet, now give me a hand with emptying the dishwasher."

Her matter-of-fact approach gave the girl confidence, as did a motherly hug, and they were soon too engrossed in their work for Lisa to have any further fears.

※

The small church was filling rapidly, even half an hour before the service was due to begin. People from the village, from the various organisations with which Lady Sonia had been connected nationally and locally, people from the business world – all about to pay their last respects. Conversations in subdued whispers, discreet nods of heads, then a stir of expectancy as the vicar moved down the main aisle with his servers, to meet, turn, and lead the procession to the front of the church.

The coffin was covered with the most magnificent flowers – huge white lilies in profusion with cascades of delicate yellow and cream freesias set against rich dark green foliage. Benjamin and Jacqueline headed the mourners, with Victoria and Richard following, then the Uncles and their wives. Once they had settled in their pews the service began.

※

Sonia had begged to be allowed to attend her own funeral, and watched entranced and triumphant, Mr Fu at her side, floating near the organ loft. She was gratified by the elaborate display of flowers on her coffin, by the well-rehearsed choir, and by the sight of so many people attending to pay her their last respects. It was a fitting service indeed. The hymns had been chosen well, all of them sung to well-known tunes so that there would be none of the embarrassment of non-regular churchgoers struggling to join in. The lesson, read by Benjamin, included his mother's favourite reference to 'Heaven's many mansions.'

The Vicar began his address.

"It is with gratitude that I receive the honour bestowed upon me by Lady Sonia of conducting this service. She had determined that it should be in this, her local church - yet another demonstration of how she had always remembered her own humble origins. Never too proud to overlook local matters, there are examples of people sitting here who would not be where they are today, were it not for the intervention of her Ladyship …" his gaze swept seemingly innocuously across the congregation, pausing for a split second as he reached Annie's gaze, Sonia noticed, feeling satisfaction and hoping that Annie would feel ashamed at her loose talk with Doris.

"… and I know it is an old-fashioned expression, but she was a true pillar of the church and all that it stands for."

He had obviously spent a great deal of time ensuring he neglected no-one's connections. He recounted acts of generosity that encompassed everything from the stained glass window installed in memory of her late husband, Sir Geoffrey, and omitted nothing that their benefactor had done for the church and the village. It was a list that sounded worthy of the greatest in the land, and as the Vicar drew it to a close, he exhorted each and every one there present to emulate the woman they had all been privileged to meet or to know.

❦

Jacqueline and Benjamin sat in the family pew with Victoria and Richard. Jacqui held Richard's hand tightly, looking pale and drawn but determined to retain her composure, trying to forget the hollow

The Ripples and the Tapestries

sound of the Vicar's words now that she knew so much more about her mother. She wanted desperately to hang on to good things to remember, and consoled herself that the public things were true and good, no matter what had happened in Sonia's personal life.

Ben sat with an air of what could only be described as smugness. His position was becoming clearer with every day that passed. Now he was destined to take his place as titular head of the community, Victoria would have to take her share of the burden. She would have to take over the committee work that his mother had done for so many years, and would soon find herself so occupied that she would have no time for moods and sulks. By the time summer came she would no doubt be thriving on it, and why not? She was being provided with a lifestyle that many women would envy, so she had no option but to co-operate. He wondered what exactly had been the contents of his sister's letter – not good, judging by the state she had been in, when she and Richard had appeared, just before the cortege approached the Hall for Sonia's last short journey.

Victoria herself wished she were anywhere but here, sitting on this hard pew, just days after her child had been born. Ben had insisted she attend. She felt nothing but anger towards her late mother-in-law – anger that Sonia had stolen the show in the most appalling way possible at the birthday party; anger that Lucy had been cheated of the attention that should rightfully have been hers at her birth; anger that Sonia had not hung on long enough to allow Victoria to ease herself gently into the new life; anger that Ben held her responsible for his mother's death.

Richard sat beside Jacqui, her cold hand in his, willing her not to give way. She had surely had enough to deal with in the last twenty-four hours, and it was not over yet, but at least she would be spared the formal reading of the Will, having had the preview the night before. However, even that had paled into insignificance alongside the contents of Sonia's letter. He was not surprised by his wife's reaction after the initial shock. Jacqui was always the one who saw under the surface of anyone's actions and her compassion for her mother, after all the years of Sonia's ill-treatment of her, was so typical of the woman he loved. He would do his utmost to make sure that his wife and her children wanted for nothing, and above all, he hoped that one day they would be able to have children of their own. But not yet. Not until this pain had eased out of her life a little.

Also sat in the family pew was Barbara, in deep mourning. Black always became her; she had the complexion for it. Her looks were still striking and reminiscent of her heyday, and there were a few surreptitious glances in her direction, resulting in fingers eased round shirt collars by elderly gentlemen, no doubt with memories of their own to entertain them through the service.

It eventually drew to a close. The family party followed the coffin and bearers out of the church as the organist broke into his rendering of the triumphant 'Zadok the Priest', Sonia's favourite piece of music, and the strains followed them along the pathway to the graveside for the private interment alongside her husband, while the rest of the congregation filed outside and stood talking. The much briefer graveside ceremony was soon over and the mourners returned to make their way to the Hall.

⁓⁓

Many of the assembly were there for reasons other than lamenting the late Lady Woolston. Some were blatantly curious to see inside the home of the woman who had run their organisations. They had heard descriptions from a few privileged committee members, but now here was a chance to see for themselves. There was the county set, of course – not friends, naturally, but it had been felt that a token few making an acknowledgement would be appreciated. Businessmen and their dutiful wives attended, either to say farewell to an era or hoping to receive a welcome from the new regime.

Eventually the main party was seen arriving outside the Hall with the Vicar, and a respectful hush greeted them as they entered their large country home. Benjamin and Jacqueline moved among the gathering, shaking hands and murmuring thanks for their condolences.

"I don't know half of these people" Ben had commented to his wife "but it just shows how widely Mummy was respected."

The trays of sherry circulated and when everyone was holding a glass, Ben asked for silence and proposed a toast.

"To Sonia, Lady Woolston, now resting in the peace that is her due."

The Ripples and the Tapestries

"Lady Sonia ... to Sonia" echoed around the room.

Sonia, from a high vantage point, could not resist a self-satisfied smirk. It had been a very gratifying funeral, and one that people would talk about for years to come, no doubt. So many of the great and the good in attendance, so many wonderful tales of her life recounted so that all would know what a benefactor had lived in their midst.

But there was more to come – snatches of conversation drifted upwards.

" ... the end of an era, thank goodness ..."
" ... absolutely ruthless in business dealings ..."
" ... *now* we can get on, without her interference ..."
" ... certainly didn't understand democracy ..."
"... those awful meetings when she over-ruled us ..."
" ... she only did it if *she* could benefit ..."
" ... personally, I could never stand her ..."
" ... no *real* breeding, of course ..."

Unable to believe her ears, Sonia dared to look at Mr Fu, who thankfully showed no sign of hearing the appalling comments, and they retreated to the conservatory, where Barbara and Jacqueline were sitting in the heavily scented atmosphere among the lush foliage.

Benjamin had done his duty, and emotion threatened to take over, so he had excused himself for a moment and hastened through the library door. The strain and the alcohol consumption of the last ten days had taken their toll. Victoria saw him disappearing and followed him into the library.

"For heaven's sake, Ben, you have guests to see to. You go on about my responsibilities – what about yours? I'm not going to cover up for your lack of manners – I'm going up to Lucy."

"Oh, no you don't - we pay a huge amount of money to that wretched Nanny so that you *don't* have to see Lucy all the time. Stay here and deal with the guests – *I'll* let you know when it's appropriate to leave."

"I would only be a minute ..."

"No doubt that's what you were saying when you left my mother ill and alone, with no-one to comfort her in her last moments. Don't ever forget that you did that – *I* won't."

So this was the way it was to be - Victoria thought wretchedly - always the danger of being reminded that in Ben's eyes she was responsible for his mother's death. Then, with an effort worthy of her late mother-in-law, she straightened her spine and walked swiftly through to the conservatory, smiling that smile she had learned early on from Sonia – the smile only on the lips, not reaching the eyes and making no direct contact with other people. It bespoke of other things to be done, more pressing needs than those of ordinary mortals, aimed at giving the impression that if one then became the object of her attention, it was an honour bestowed.

Jacqui was there, with an arm around Barbara, who had eventually found the situation very difficult to cope with now that her own secret had been divulged to Ben and Victoria in those unguarded, brandy-fuelled moments. She wished that she'd not said a word and was glad that Jacqui didn't know.

But Victoria, fuelled with malicious spite, came across them, and in her raw state of nerves she had to lash out at someone.

"I'm surprised you don't feel contaminated, Miss Goody-goody Jacqueline - being in the same room as that whore."

Jacqui looked startled, as much by the unprovoked attack as by the actual words.

"Don't tell me you're another one who didn't know – she must have really enjoyed laughing up her sleeve at the lot of you. Providing her services for all those businessmen and making a nice profit, too."

Barbara looked horrified.

"I didn't mean to …"

"Of *course* you didn't. It just goes to show how stupid Sonia must have been, not noticing what went on under her nose. Maybe she had some appalling secrets herself."

Jacqui thought of the letter and shivered, but leapt to her mother's defence.

"Vicky, *please* … I don't know what you're talking about, but my mother was a very special person, as you must know from Ben. Any troubles she had were not paraded in public, as above all she had dignity. I intend to do the same and keep her private life private. I'm proud to have been born a Woolston, and all who bear that name, whether by birth or by marriage, should respect her memory. We know you're upset as well, but for goodness sake, please try to be kind."

The Ripples and the Tapestries

❧

Sonia looked down on the scene. All the scathing comments, the betrayals from people she had known for years, had been sending shock waves through her soul. But the biggest shock was the way Jacqui had, after all the years of being the scapegoat for Sonia's wrath, and within hours of knowing the reason for Sonia's hatred – *Jacqueline*, of all people, had been the one to defend her. It would have been easy for her to divulge her mother's secret, easy to use Victoria to upset Benjamin - but she had kept quiet – even though it meant that she would give up her legal rights as first-born.

Sonia experienced something that felt like a physical thunderbolt. She turned to Mr Fu, her face betraying that the moment of realisation had come.

"Oh, what *have* I done?"

"You were human, dear lady. Come – it is time to return to the Afterlife. Now we can start your work properly."

❧

The last glimpse of her old home was the red winter sun setting over the copse to the West, casting a glow on the frost covered earth. The shadows of bare trees lay long and low across the fields and people were starting to walk to cars parked in the sweep of the drive.

Fortunately, she was spared knowledge of a final secret that would have broken her completely - Mr Fu's intervention had been timely.

16

Annie and Doris cleared the debris in the kitchen. There was no-one else left in the Hall now apart from Benjamin and Victoria, Nanny and Lucy. Jacqueline and Richard had decided to return home after the scene in the conservatory – she felt she had heard enough for one day, and the Uncles, having decided there was no need for a formal reading, were heading back home, after arranging an appointment at the London office with Ben and his accountant for the following week. Barbara had also decided to depart – to the security of her home in Chiswick where she could phone friends and safely sink into despondency and memories of times past.

&

"Shall we have ten minutes with a cup of tea?"

Annie settled into her chair by the table as Doris poured their drinks.

"When shall we tell them, then?"

"As soon as possible, I'd say – when we've served dinner and cleared away - then we'll hand in our notice. Did you see how upset Miss Jacqueline was? Couldn't stay for even a minute more and you can't blame her, after the way she's been treated. Very upset, little Lisa was when she overheard what was said in the conservatory by Mrs Woolston. Didn't expect it from posh people, she told me – she could get that sort of thing on the telly."

"Just as well Miss Jacqueline's got that lovely husband to take care of her. You can see he wouldn't let anyone harm her."

"Wish I'd had a man in my life who was like that – I wouldn't be sitting here now if I had."

"I did – for a while. In fact that's what I want to tell you – the full story of how I came here and how I found love. I think you should know now, so that we have no secrets - yet it *is* a risk."

"What on earth do you mean, Annie?"

"Well I *want* to tell you, but I'm also afraid it will upset our friendship if you see me in a different light."

"Oh, for goodness' sake – I'm not going to fall out with you, whatever it is. You know me – if I don't like something, I'll say so, then it's gone. I don't hold things against people for evermore."

Annie paused, took a deep breath, and gazing into her half empty cup, eventually started.

"I can still never think of Surbiton without a shudder. The assault had been awful, and the Police in those days, unkind and uncaring – no cosy suites for interviewing victims, no sympathy – more of an attitude of 'she must have brought it on herself'. No offer of support - even when it was found that I was one of several women attacked, but the only one prepared to be a witness. Yet it proved to be the making of me in a strange way.

"As you know, I lived at the edge of the village. Just after it happened, even going to the village shop became an ordeal. People would move aside, seemingly not wanting to be contaminated. One or two brave souls would say "good morning" as I passed, but it was hardly meant as a conversation opener. I soon gave up the attempt, lapsed into depression and relied on a weekly trip into Guildford to obtain essentials. For the remainder of the week I hardly ever ventured out, except to the doctor's once a month for my next prescription. I lived day by day and some days the numbing feeling wouldn't arrive until the dose had been doubled.

"My one constant caller was the Vicar's sister. D'you remember her? She was his housekeeper at the Vicarage. Every Tuesday afternoon there would be a knock at the door, and I would hide. A note would be pushed through the letterbox, saying she hoped I was managing and if there was anything she could do in the meantime, I should let her know ... then she would call again next week.

"One Tuesday I opened the door, intending to tell her to stop pestering, but somehow I found myself inviting her in and was able to begin to talk about things. A few months later, not long before the court case, I'd managed to become less dependent on the tablets, and to show signs of wanting to return to a more normal life.

"Much later, I learned from Lady Sonia that the vicar had preached to the text of '... *inasmuch as ye do it to the least of my brethren ...*' and he delivered a sermon rich in examples of how even the humblest citizen could do things that would surely be recorded ready for the next life, and rewarded in this. Coincidentally, it was only a day or two

The Ripples and the Tapestries

before he went for his monthly afternoon tea to Woolston Hall. Also coincidentally, only the previous week he and Lady Sonia had attended a meeting of the School Governors, where they had been forced to discuss what to do about this Miss Annabel Hartley who might feel she was entitled to resume her previous duties in the infants' dinner hall each day.

"Well, we know how her mind would have worked - her interest in me was more for herself, but it would look so generous to any outsider if she took me under her wing. She would certainly have acquired a willing assistant. She knew my background, of course – no family, no ties, rented house, and low paid work at the school, where they didn't want me to remain in contact with little children. Meek, biddable, and above all *grateful* – I would be an ideal person to help in the house. Whether or not this act was recorded in Heaven, it would surely be noted in the village and brought to the attention of the Bishop, no doubt - which would also impress. I'm sorry if I sound cynical, but as the years went on, I could see how she always took advantage of the situation and I had no choice."

She cleared her throat and dabbed her eyes while Doris poured more tea for them both

"I came here as soon as the court case was finished, although my evidence was insufficient and the man walked free with a smirk on his face. I was an object of charity, but to tell you the truth, I didn't much care one way or the other – not even when she said she would change my name from Annabel to Annie – and at least being busy stopped me brooding. I lived in the Lodge and kept it prepared and ready for visitors, as well as doing work over here. As Lady Sonia had intended, I really was eternally grateful and prepared to do anything to demonstrate that gratitude.

"Sir Geoffrey knew who I was, of course, but took little notice. Our paths seldom crossed, with him being away so much. Then about a year after I had moved in, he called at the Lodge one evening to deliver a message from Lady Sonia, intending to carry on for a walk. It was the second anniversary of the actual event, and I was feeling low. I was in tears when I opened the door, so it seemed natural that he offered to comfort me - a friendly arm round my shoulders - that was all."

Annie paused, stirring her tea slowly and wiped a tear with the back of her hand. Doris froze, her own cup halfway to her lips, and looked across enquiringly.

"I know, I know … Oh Doris, he was a real gentleman, and it was just a warm hug that I found comforting. It didn't feel as if he was about to take advantage of me, or anything like that, and I never expected it to be repeated. But of course, it was, and finding he was welcome, he returned again … and again."

"I *never* guessed, dear. You always were one to keep yourself to yourself, and you both must have been so careful. I can't say I blame Sir Geoffrey, because you were an attractive woman – you still are."

Annie carried on, lost in her own thoughts.

"It went on for years, and it meant so much to me - I really loved him and he knew that. One evening, while Sonia was staying overnight in London on one of her prolonged shopping trips, Geoffrey surprised me by outlining a financial arrangement he'd made for my benefit. 'A secret trust fund' he'd said. 'But if I go first, you won't be able to collect until after Sonia's death, and provided you've not left her. That way *nobody* need ever know - except you, me and the lawyers who've set it up.'

"It kept me tied to Sonia, of course, but that had advantages too. Knowing that my nest egg was safely tucked away and gaining interest has given me a sense of security. I just continued to work and was the soul of discretion at all times. The arrangement continued until Geoffrey became too ill to continue his secret visits. Oh Doris, that was the worst - it was agony to see him when I took up the meal trays and not be able to do anything. He knew how much I loved him, though. It was terrible when he died, but I couldn't show what I felt in case Lady Sonia suspected."

❧❦❧

Doris was stunned. She had never suspected anything like that. Indeed, why should she? Annie worked in the Hall, mainly upstairs doing Lady Sonia's bidding, then returning to the Lodge when her duties were finished, keeping herself to herself. The ultimate in discretion indeed, but in a way she was quite glad that there had been something

The Ripples and the Tapestries

more worthwhile in Annie's life than just the daily round of work. She had known about the attack all those years ago, of course, but that was something that could happen to any woman in an unguarded moment. It had been village gossip, and filtered through to the Hall, then died down. Annie had come to work there later, but Doris had just thought she was very reserved, not realising she had been ill and depressed.

Her friend broke into her thoughts.

"I've been in touch with the lawyers this week now that Lady Sonia's died, and the trust fund has been looked after very well. There's more than I thought possible, so I've decided to take a holiday in Spain and look for a place to buy – would you come with me? Two heads are better than one!"

Doris was startled.

"*Could* we? Go on holiday, I mean? I know there's supposed to be something in the Will for me – Madam referred to it often enough when she wanted me to do extra, but I'm not one to count my chickens …"

"Don't worry so much – my treat, if you've been left nothing, and we'll go Dutch if you have!"

For the first time in her life Annie understood, and was beginning to enjoy, what was contained in the feeling of power, of being in control, and the freedom it brought. This was what Sonia had known all her life, she mused. Now it was her turn.

"Here's to freedom" she called across the table, raising her cup "and God bless dear Geoffrey for making it possible."

17

Sonia's work continued when Mr Fu felt she was ready. He allowed her to overcome the initial shock of what she had seen and overheard at the Hall, although he was careful not to fall into the trap of allowing her to rationalise things to a point of absolving herself from all blame.

But if he had stage-managed the whole event he could not have done better. He sent heartfelt thanks to God. She *had* to see and hear the incontrovertible truth and realise that the image she had of herself had been almost solely in her own mind. Self-delusion is the hardest thing to unravel, he thought, remembering some of his past cases.

His next intervention had to be judged carefully. Too soon, and she would resurrect her anger: not soon enough, and she would have retreated into her armour of denial. He prayed for guidance and was advised to catch her unawares.

The flowers did the trick. Entering her room he stepped forward with the armful of freesias and lilies.

"Oh, my favourites!" she exclaimed, startled, and before she could bite her tongue. She buried her face in their fragrances, yearning to be back in her own home, back in control – anywhere but here.

"Dear Lady Sonia - I know I made it hard for you. It had to happen that way, believe me. We can talk later. But first take your flowers, have some refreshment and let us enjoy each other's company. Then you can spend some time in the Healing Temple and experience what that can do."

It was bewildering. But suddenly it was easier to obey than to argue. Feeling child-like, she saw that delicate china had appeared on the table, accompanied by plates of dainty food, exquisitely presented to entice her appetite.

"I know we don't actually *need* to eat, but sometimes you have to remind yourself that good things are not lost forever. Now, how do you like your tea - Indian or China?"

Sonia could not help it. She laughed. Perhaps more of a damp smile at first, but the sight of the little man seriously waiting, teapot poised in one hand, cup and saucer in the other, was more than she could resist. At first she tried to suppress it, but then yes, she laughed!

They talked of other things. She began to feel more human now than at any other time since she had come into this strange Afterlife. Mr Fu seemed to be a different person. She *could* afford to relax a little now he was less authoritarian. For his part, he began see the social Sonia emerge from under the crusty defence she had worn for so long – the Sonia who had once charmed dinner parties for decades. Aware and adept at selecting just the right anecdotes for the occasion on Earth, she had lost none of her old skills.

She felt safe in pitching the conversation at ecclesiastical events, having noticed that he was not in favour of the stuffier aspects of the church - tales of the village school Nativity plays, the visiting party of evangelical Vicars who danced in the aisles to a Reggae beat, the carol singers who had received too much hospitality too early, falling over each other as they rang the doorbell at the Hall, then couldn't sing a note. Innocuous in their actual content, Sonia added details and subtle hints to the stories with perfect timing. Soon Mr Fu was holding *his* sides and roaring with laughter.

"You look more like Friar Tuck!" Sonia chuckled, delighted by the effect she was having, as she embarked on yet another tale of parochial scandal.

Eventually, when they had exhausted the dainty sandwiches, featherlight cakes and both pots of tea, they sat looking at each other across the table.

"*Please* tell me what I am doing here." Sonia's voice was lower, more earnest. "Do I really have to go through this? I don't know if I can deal with any more of it. *Is* there more, and can … can you … *please* … help me?"

Mr Fu recognised the moment he had been waiting for.

"There may be a little *more*, but there will be nothing *worse*. Everyone has to be dealt with differently, and I decided that it would be best for you to get the worst over to start with. Now you are more receptive our next task is to look at *why* people around you should have acted in that way, and how it could have been prevented. But be assured, you will be helped at every stage, and the first thing to do is to go to the Healing Temple, where your emotions will be soothed."

The Ripples and the Tapestries

Taking Sonia's arm, he led her to a doorway she had never noticed before. It opened into a beautiful wild flower meadow where a gentle rise led to a building of classical proportions and appearance. Mounting the steps that led to the entrance, they walked through from the heat of the day into a cool marble interior. It was vast. Marble pillars reached up to the misty ceiling, and elaborately designed stairways led to upper galleries of book-lined walls, reaching as far as the eye could see. The floor was also cool marble, a checkerboard pattern in darkest and lightest grey. As they entered they could see many figures on couches, surrounded by various other figures in robes.

Mr Fu handed her over to a figure robed in blue, waiting inside. As this being took her hand Sonia felt a warm tingle run through her arm, she was led to a vacant couch and a gesture indicated that she should lie down. The couch proved to be soft and yielding. A pillow was placed under her head, and settling herself comfortably, she attempted to use the 'switch-off' technique that had stood her in good stead whenever she had to face unpleasant medical procedures in her life. This time, however, it didn't succeed - her senses seemed to be heightened, if anything. Yet her body was relaxed and her mind seemed increasingly at ease. Hazily wondering why she felt no actual fear at handing herself over to strangers, she waited, eyes half closed.

Then she found she was rising above the couch, and could look down at her body. Fascinated, she saw several figures move across calmly and efficiently, to position themselves at her head. It was unlike any earthly operating theatre – here, there was just a feeling of calm peacefulness and purpose in which everyone involved was sharing. No spoken instructions were necessary. One figure stepped forward and ran a glowing finger around her skull above her eyebrows. The bone and hair dissolved, revealing a tangled mass of what looked like wires.

From her position above she could feel absolutely no sensation. The team dealt with the mass as she herself had once sorted the tangled threads in her Grandmother's sewing box in her childhood. They were teased out and carefully untangled until they lay on the pillow, softly glowing, pliable and glistening.

When they were all in neat strands, another team moved in. One carried what looked like a blueprint. This had been bought over from the Library shelves, and the new workers referred to it frequently.

Gradually the strands were woven together into the most beautiful three-dimensional construction, with subtle changes of colour blending smoothly one into another. It was as exquisite a work of craftsmanship as she had ever beheld. She watched in awe, entranced.

Eventually, all was done. The chart was checked for a final time, the first figure was recalled to restore the skull and hair, and when all was complete Sonia felt herself gently pulled back from her height above the couch, realigned with her body, then lowered carefully until the two merged perfectly.

Lying there, she found that the only sensation she could experience was one of utter calmness and peace. It was bliss! Thoughts came into her mind and out, like small fluffy clouds across a blue summer's sky, none of them staying long enough to engage her interest completely. A smile played about her lips. She wanted it to last for ever.

As if in a dream, she felt herself raised from the couch and discovered that any movement she made was now somehow smoother and lighter. It felt as if she glided across the marble floor. Approaching the doorway, she saw Mr Fu waiting with a warm smile, hands outstretched. Turning to thank her helpers, she found they had already returned to their next task.

∽∾

Sitting back at the table, Mr Fu volunteered an explanation.

"What you've just experienced, dear lady, is something that will also help you in the future. The Healing Temple is actually available to all - one of the links between Heaven and Earth, so that even people in their Earthly life can access it, although they have to have help from people who are aware of these things through developing their long memories of times past. When you return to your next Earthly life you'll discover more of these links if you take the opportunity to develop your own awareness. The workers in the Healing Temple are those who have the finest minds and the greatest skills, whether they work on mind or body. The shelves full of books are resources – not only for the types of treatment, but they contain the files, or pattern books, of every soul who has ever lived. The blueprint you saw is part of your individual pattern book. It contains your physical, mental and spiritual health patterns, and it also holds the details of why you made your choice of family and lifestyle."

Sonia looked at him, wonderingly.

"Do you mean that I do actually have choices?"

"There is always a choice, as you will see later on when you decide on the lessons you choose to learn in your next life. You will be given many, many opportunities to learn these lessons – they only stop when you have proved your learning and can move on to the next one. By doing that you will be working your way to eventually becoming a higher soul. As you progress through a lifetime you will have the opportunity to link directly with some of the Upper Realms, such as the Healing Temple.

"We (and by 'we' I mean peoples' guides) can help people come to the Temple, even in their Earthly lives – they just have to be led to the doorway and have their helper wait until the task is done. The only problem for those on Earth seems to be that they find it difficult to understand that they're entitled to ask for help. That was why even here, I had to bring you to a point where *you* voluntarily asked for help - and you did, as you sat there in distress."

Sonia listened intently. She felt that all the years of emotional tensions had been erased. No longer was she looking for the hidden meaning behind every word he uttered, suspiciously wondering what demands would be made on her that would be irksome and unfair. The years of warped and distorted thinking had been cleansed from her mind, and she wanted to learn more.

She had been given the ability to think clearly, and understand how her friend had helped. Her friend? Good gracious! Had she consciously thought of him in that way? But she was now seeing Mr Fu in a new light, and he was indeed friendly and gentle, genuinely caring what happened to her.

"As for your treatment in the Healing Temple, some people describe it as having had a mental spring-clean. I suggest you go out into the gardens and spend a while enjoying your new outlook on life before we resume our work. You may meet some people who will interest you."

Sonia needed no urging. Feeling light as a feather, she trod down a path that felt cushioned with moss. The colours were even brighter than she had seen them before, and all her senses were fresh and alive.

The scents from the flowers mingled as she walked down the pathway towards the edge of the garden. A group of people stood and sat at the bottom of a grassy slope, and as she came nearer she thought she recognised one.

This figure turned … then … arms outstretched, came to meet her.

"Gran!" she breathed delightedly.

"Sonia! "

Their embrace brought a feeling she had long forgotten, but now recognised … it was love. Pure and simple. A love that asked nothing, and needed nothing. It was without past and without future, a coming together in one present moment.

Love.

~18~

Life at the Hall eventually settled down, although Vicky had felt at the time that she would never be able to handle the multiple tasks that each day brought. She had panicked when Doris and Annie's bombshell dropped on the day of the funeral, after dinner. Every time she thought of that dreadful scene she inwardly cringed, knowing that she was at least partially responsible, and that there was truth in most of the things the two had said.

Ben had been apoplectic.
"Of all the … Annie – you ungrateful woman! After all the things my mother did for you over the years – she must be turning in her grave at this very moment. As for you, Doris, I cannot *begin* to imagine what you're thinking of. What about my wife's needs – who is going to take care of things here?"

"I will, of course, leave you and your solicitors my forwarding address" Doris said with dignity "but I can't stay here any longer. Working for your late mother was often difficult, but nothing compared with what's happening now. I've tried making allowances, but you're both so rude and indifferent I can't take any more and my mind's made up."

"And *I'd* like you to remember that my name is *not* Annie" Annabel interjected "so please make sure you use Annabel from now on. It was your mother who changed it – to keep me in my place, would you believe. There are many things you have no idea about, but Doris and I have reached our limits, and that's why we have both decided to go."

Ben rounded on his wife.
"It's *your* fault – I *knew* it would happen! You've got no idea how to treat servants, or anyone else for that matter. You're just a selfish spoiled little bitch who's good for nothing to me or anyone." He charged out of the room, banging the door, disappearing into the library once more.

"But Doris – couldn't you possibly stay on for a few months?" Vicky pleaded, the humiliation of her husband's critical words far less distressing than her panic at the thought of having to engage someone else at such short notice. "It's much too much for me."

"I'm sure you'll find a solution" Doris replied tartly "as a matter of fact, a few *days* would be too long, Miss, as I would never be able to work for you – at least your mother-in-law tried to be a lady in every sense of the word. You have no idea how to treat people fairly and I'm very sorry that it had to come to this. We'll be leaving in the morning after breakfast."

"But you will forfeit your right to any more pay, and you won't get any references."

"It will be worth every penny, believe me" retorted Annabel "and as for references, I don't think that will be a problem – I've had enough of being a doormat, so I'm never going to work for anyone else again. Fortunately I'm not in a position to need to …"

Doris swiftly interrupted before her friend was goaded into revealing things she would later regret.

"We've got all that packing to do. Let's go or we'll be here all night."

Later, sitting among Annabel's cases in the Lodge, they paused and looked at each other. After all these years of biting their lips to prevent their thoughts escaping, their new powers suddenly struck them.

"We've actually done it! Now, no-one need ever talk to us like that again."

"I shall be glad to leave this place behind" said Annabel "too many memories – time to let it all go and move on. I kept my word to Geoffrey and stayed with Sonia – now it's a new life ahead. Spain beckons, and I think I ought to be able to find something to keep me gainfully occupied. Let's have the holiday first, though, to get over all of this."

⁓⁓

Their taxi left the following morning, leaving behind an air of great consternation. But of course, Doris was right – Vicky *was* able to find an agency replacement at short notice, the new housekeeper proved to be adequate for the task of running the domestic side of the Hall, with help from a local girl, and Nanny kept the nursery running smoothly and with a rod of iron, as before.

Ben chose not to take too much notice of the changes. He eventually made his peace with his wife, and a handsome pair of earrings to match

The Ripples and the Tapestries

her bracelet were received with a semblance of gracious forgiveness, thus establishing a style of exchange that would, over the years ahead, build up into an expensive array in Victoria's jewellery box.

※

Preparing for bed one evening, Vicky sighed - she sighed a great deal nowadays, and pouted and sulked. How tiresome of Ben to have to deal with the execution of his mother's Will – at just the time when they should be planning their holiday programme for the next twelve months. Having been cheated of their annual skiing break because of her pregnancy, Vicky felt she was entitled to look forward to a compensatory early Spring visit to golden beaches. Nanny would care for Lucy so they could have a fortnight of peace after all the upheaval over Christmas and the New Year. Looking in the mirror above her dressing table, she saw she was frowning, and applied another streak of night cream on the offending area, massaging it in with fingertip movements, erasing the faint line. She could see the reflection of Ben's back as he undressed in the adjacent dressing room.

"Don't you think you *could* manage to spare a couple of weeks in March? Surely there can't be too much to do if your Uncles help out as they're supposed to?"

"That's the whole point. The last thing I want to do is to leave them with any actual effectiveness. They're better off with no discussion - just sign what I prepare and send it off in all our names to keep the accountants happy that it's all above board. As long as they get their recompense and don't have too much to do, they'll pat me on the back and tell me what a chip off the business-like old block I am."

"But we *always* said we'd go away" Victoria pouted. "I shall be bored to death with just Nanny and the baby rattling around in this house, with you up to your eyes in probate and legalities. Then I suppose you'll need to have another business trip."

"Go to your sister's in Portugal, then, and take Nanny." Ben's exasperation showed in his voice. "How about after your medical check? Get the all clear, and it will be perfect weather for young Lucy in that part of the country. We haven't got any seminars booked. Then you can return here, pick up the threads and it will be 'all systems go' again."

"I'll let you know when I've thought it through" she responded sulkily. Switching off her bedside lamp, she turned her back as Ben came into the room. He tentatively put a hand on her shoulder as he slid into bed, but she produced no response apart from a muttered "Good night", and sighing, he turned away from the communal centre of the bed into what was becoming firmly his solo territory, night after night.

Having made the token gesture, Ben was in fact content to drift off to sleep, letting his mind wander through his list of possible outcomes to his mother's bequests. Her friend Barbara's revelations had been unexpected, but were of no importance now – as she'd said at the time, those involved were now mostly beyond any possible embarrassment. So the porcelain would be a fitting bequest, would retain the connection between her and the family, and no doubt would return to Woolston when she died – if they offered to forget the whole embarrassing episode and give her the opportunity to be a Godmother for Lucy at her Christening.

The other actual bequest was the car. That had been a surprise, but no doubt had been discussed by his mother and father, before his father's death. He'd had many years of Wilkins' service before he pensioned him off. Well, it would depend on how the offer was put, but really made no difference to the outcome. Wilkins would want the cash, no doubt, to fritter away at the Cross Keys, so all Ben had to do was find out the value of the old car, halve it, then make up some story about how he had already found a buyer who was only prepared to pay this amount. Being a simple soul, Wilkins would accept this, he was sure and Ben would keep the books straight. Old habits die hard and there was no room in Benjamin's business heart for sentimental generosity.

Doris's bequest would be posted on to her, and with no hurry, in the circumstances. She had known about it for a long time – not the actual amount, but at various times in her working life, Sonia had made reference to it, in order to keep her loyalty, no doubt. Strange that his mother hadn't left anything to Annie, but perhaps she felt no obligation towards her after what she saw as her years of charity towards the woman, and in any case Annie had proved that she deserved nothing.

It *was* strange, though - Ben was not usually receptive to other people's moods, but he had noticed a gleam in Annie's eye, and a certain sort of – well, he would call it 'cockiness' in anyone else – in the days after Sonia's death. He had been looking forward to the moment in the library when he had privately told her of her legacy – thinking it would wipe any smirk off her face, to find she had been left nothing - but there was no such effect.

As for his sister ... but Ben did not want to dwell on any serious problem areas at this point, so decided he would defer that topic until the morning. He firmly turned on to his sleeping side and let the effects of the brandy waft him into unconsciousness.

Victoria, on the other hand, was now wide awake, having summoned up the necessary tension to repel any possible advances from her husband, and now finding it difficult to unwind. To make matters worse, for some inexplicable reason she could not rid herself of the recurring nightmares that had started just before the funeral, on the night that Ben had handed over the letter to Jacqueline. They were dreams of drowning and suffocation that would wake her in the night. The apprehension was now as bad as the actual dreaming. Ben's breathing regulated then became deeper, and when she felt it was safe, she succumbed to the temptation of slowly and noiselessly opening the drawer of the bedside table, feeling for the glass of water on the top surface, and swallowing the tablets that she hoped would give her some sleep.

❧

The Uncles, James and John, sat patiently waiting on the large leather sofa in the outer office. Ben's receptionist had supplied very good coffee, and the brothers were content to sit and reminisce discreetly about family events. A phone call had warned of Ben's delay, but eventually he arrived, full of bonhomie and affability, shaking the hand of each in turn.

"Come in, come in. Make yourselves comfortable."

The file was waiting on his desk, copies of the Will inside, which he passed to the Uncles. They took the papers and settled in their chairs, adjusting spectacles and taking pens from pockets – keen to impress, to appear as efficient and prepared as any of the Company legal team that Ben employed.

"As you will see, there has been no alteration since the original date of the document, which is quite recent. My mother was a great believer in regularly revising and updating her Will, and this was done with the Company solicitors as she approached her seventieth birthday."

They read carefully, nonetheless. The sheets of paper represented control of a vast financial empire, in addition to a personal fortune, and the property. They nodded together at the bequest to Doris "such generosity" they muttered, and again at the outlined disposal of the car "a very nice way of doing things".

"You'll buy it back, of course?"

"Oh, of course – apart from anything else it has such sentimental attachments."

"Yes, yes, very right and proper."

Eventually they reached the end of the document. Uncle James cleared his throat.

"Benjamin, old boy, I don't want to pry, but being executors we're in a position, I suppose, to ask questions … John – you've noticed the same thing …"

"Jacqueline."

"Exactly. Now I know she wasn't your mother's favourite, but she's left out completely on a personal level. Surely that's a grave oversight. No pun intended, of course" he added hastily, as he felt a nudge from John.

"There's the trust fund, Uncle James."

"Ah, the trust fund for the children – and with such very clear instructions on how it is to be managed. Well, perhaps it was something to do with the husbands Jacqueline managed to acquire – although I must say this new one struck me as being very pleasant. Still, blood's thicker than water, and who better than her brother to look after her interests. I'm sure you'll see that she's not without some personal mementoes of Sonia. Jewellery or something, no doubt …"

"But even if the new husband doesn't leave her in the lurch, Ben, you will make sure she's not overlooked – now or in the future, won't you? Trusts have to be handled carefully. I do wonder what was in Sonia's mind when she set up something that in effect would reduce the value per capita if Jacqueline increased her family - almost as if she didn't want any heirs unless they carry the name. Silly, really. You can always change a person's name. *That's* been done before, in many industrial families."

"I always said our brother had married a woman of unfathomable depths...."

They lapsed into silence.

Ben, arms resting on the arms of his chair, carefully placed his fingertips together.

"Now can I ask *you* something, Uncles?"

Without waiting for their answer, he carried on.

"I know how much of an onerous task this Executor role can prove to be – particularly with an estate of this size, so I've decided to offer you the services of Gerald French our Company solicitor. He has his own secretary who is the soul of discretion, to take care of all the boring administrative details - writing letters, making phone calls – you know the sort of thing.

"You can be kept up to date by post, instead of having to come here, and you would have nothing more to do than sign the forms. Your rights as Executors wouldn't be affected, of course. So what I wanted to suggest is that you leave it all to me. If that's acceptable, then I'll get you to sign this, as a formality – just to keep French happy."

James and John scarcely hesitated. Relief that they need not take an active part was uppermost in their minds, any reservations about the ethics being overruled by an overwhelming desire to leave their brother's family alone. They had endured Sonia's patronising attitude for years, and felt no real warmth towards her son. As for his wife, they had only been aware of Sonia's favouritism extending to any decision Ben made. Their own wives had only met Victoria twice before, at the wedding, then at the funeral, yet often made comments about her manner – none of them terribly favourable.

Jacqueline was the only ray of hope in the family, they had decided, on the journey to the City office. Now *she* had a spark of Geoffrey in her, they agreed – a little rebellious, to be sure, but that stemmed from an enquiring mind and a reluctance to accept the status quo – that was what had made Geoffrey such a good businessman at the time when taking a fresh look at business techniques was a novelty.

He had taken the family business into places in the world that his father could never have foreseen venturing, and moreover, he had built up respect, even among rivals, for the audacity with which he handled deals. Straightforward transactions were boring, but an element of the unorthodox brought a glint to his eye and a willingness to strike a deal that always seemed to benefit him even more than in the obvious way. Thus it was that when the company prospered in those post-War years, so too did Geoffrey's private fortune, with shares and business opportunities that he encouraged to be part of his way of life. True, not all of the shares proved to be golden eggs, but he had a knack of intuitive response, so that he usually offloaded any doubtful ones before they became an embarrassment, and retained some that proved to be golden indeed.

The Uncles made the journey north together, reassuring themselves and each other that they had done the right thing.

"Far better to do it at this stage. I wouldn't want to cross swords with Benjamin over even the slightest thing."

"No, certainly – he's got a streak of his mother that hates any other point of view. D'you remember when we were on holiday that year …
"

The rest of the journey passed in reminiscences of times past, but not missed.

19

A much calmer Sonia looked up as Mr Fu came into the room where she waited at her desk, not knowing what to expect. Mr Fu knew he could be gentle, with no need for the stern attitude he had used before, now she had seen for herself the repercussions of her life on Earth.

"I'd like you to write a summary of what you have learned from your last visit to Earth. Don't forget – having been to the Healing Temple, there will be no pain associated with this, and in fact you will find your thoughts are crystal clear. Once you've done that, you will find that the next task falls into place."

Immeasurably heartened to hear there would be no painful memories, Sonia started to write, and found that it was indeed so. It was as if she were writing about a character remembered from a film. More than that, she could see what choices had lain open to her in every situation and how, by making the choices she had, she had gone further and further along a track that led to – well, where *did* it lead?

***

She paused, and a clear picture came into her mind … it was of a great mountain, the peak of which was hidden in mist and clouds. On the flanks of the mountain were many well-worn tracks, along which people were moving at varying pace. Sometimes the pathways were smooth and wide, sometimes narrow and rocky, and had to be negotiated with care. Partway up the mountain she could see a small but busy town with a vast area of commerce – a marketplace that stretched as far as the eye could see. Some of the paths led straight to it, others went past, then back. As Sonia watched, fascinated, she could see that the marketplace was very appealing to the travellers – some went straight there and were swallowed up immediately, losing sight of their path; others hesitated, then yielded to the temptation of the bright stalls and retraced their steps, until they too were absorbed in their delights.

Suddenly she found herself standing in the heart of the market. Everyone seemed to be shouting. It all merged into a general cacophony

– she could hear as many languages used as there were people there. Hundreds were bustling about, and it seemed to have developed into a kind of frenzy – there were even people grabbing what they wanted, snatching it away from those more hesitant. She noticed that the stallholders appeared to be very harsh, ungenerous people who had no time to do anything other than grasp money from the outstretched hands, thrust the goods at them, then turn to the next buyer.

A number of steeples and towers rose through the clusters of the stalls, some of which even encroached onto their steps. For a few moments it was fascinating – Sonia could see so many things which would have attracted her in her Earthly life – exquisite paintings and jewellery, rich silks and embroidered satins, but she longed for a peaceful place to sit down and collect her thoughts, and turned her back on it, fighting her way out from the noise, the crowds and the smells.

The vision faded.

⚘

For a long time Sonia pondered on what she had seen, then resumed her task with a new energy.

I am ashamed of the things I wrote in this book when I first came here. I don't even want to open those pages. But now I can see how necessary it was for Mr Fu to help me go through all the upsetting visits, even before going to the Healing Temple. I would never have believed that my family and friends would behave like that behind my back, unless I had actually seen for myself.

I have tried to stand back and see why they have behaved in such appalling ways, and the only common thread running through their lives, much as I detest having to admit it, appears to be me …

It's as if they had to develop secret lives in order to escape from me. Was I so very cruel? I had high standards, and I was very critical of anyone whose behaviour did not match those standards, and certainly did not suffer fools gladly. The Church's teachings, as I interpreted them, just confirmed what I thought – and when someone is convinced that they have God on their side it is so easy to become intolerant of others.

The Ripples and the Tapestries

I wonder what would have become of Barbara if I actually <u>had</u> found out about her other interests? I would most certainly have ruined her socially, and she would probably have had to return to some obscure little house somewhere. But by doing that, I would have lost a friend whose generosity and loyalty has never been in question in many respects —such as the help she gave to Jacqueline when I wanted nothing to do with her; and the way she has been a tower of strength for Benjamin. Without her, life would have been far more difficult for everyone.

Victoria is completely out of her depth. I'd rashly assumed that I would be around for a long time in order to 'train' her, but really that whole project was a pretence – I didn't intend to let go of the reins at all. I'd manipulated the whole situation so they would marry and I would have a runaround daughter-in-law to carry out my bidding - and of course I justified all this as being something that would benefit Benjamin. I have indeed done her a disservice and there is no way of putting things to rights now – I will just have to trust that she will be able to rise to the occasion.

I can see clearly where I went wrong with Benjamin. I used those children so unfairly. As for what I put Jacqueline through, I shall never be able to think of her childhood years without regret, however distant it seems. My only excuse is that I was so damaged by events in my own life. Worst of all, though, I can see no opportunity for making amends and asking them to understand and forgive me. I am now out of reach. Will there be a way of having a second chance, or does this have to repeat itself generation to generation, for evermore?

Jacqueline showed me what pure forgiveness and love is – it's not just saying you are sorry – it's generosity of a kind that doesn't even recognise revenge.

I can see that Geoffrey was a loyal man, in his own way. He remained steadfast as far as I know – or if he didn't, was at least discreet enough not to let me discover anything else after his affair with Jacqueline's mother ended. I'm now beginning to wonder if I actually drove him to seek it – I was so ambitious that I had little time for him, except as the power behind the throne. Can I now forgive him for the wrong he did? Although really it hardly seems to matter, now that I know what great wrongs we are all capable of in our lives.

But through meeting my Gran in the garden I have now been reminded what it feels like to be loved unconditionally and to love in return. Is it possible to have that feeling with the others I should have loved in that way? Can it be, in spite of what may have happened? Can I hope there may be more meetings? I would really like to meet my parents if I can – will it be allowed, and will they be able to forgive me? I'd risk that, if I could just see them once more.

I'm not sure about Geoffrey at this stage. How could he forgive what I did to his love, and to his daughter? It would be a superhuman task …

Mr Fu intervened at this point, having been keeping a watchful eye from a distance.

"They have been learning about their own lives, don't forget, and there can be no meetings until you have both reached the same point of understanding. This makes sure that even though you've had the most negative relationships with people in your earthly life, they too have been given assistance with understanding theirs. All you have to do is let the love come through from wherever you have buried it. Don't even worry about whether to call it forgiveness or understanding, just let it flow."

⁂

Sonia's work continued. Mr Fu frequently accompanied her for walks in the garden, talking as they went, discussing a wide range of matters and always giving Sonia more food for thought. She had at last realised that although other people's points of view did not necessarily match her own, it did not mean that she had to try to win arguments, and that she could in fact reach an amicable conclusion by agreeing to differ. With so many of the topics they aired there was no right or wrong – just differences. When weighing up the alternative plans of action she could have taken in the past, she found that there was no implication of guaranteed results – any course could have led to success or gratification of some sort, or equally, whatever she chose to do would have led to failure. After all, whenever someone else was involved, they too had a choice of reaction.

Sometimes as they walked Sonia thought she caught sight of other people in the distance. Some of them even looked vaguely familiar but faded out of sight as soon as she looked more intently, so she supposed it must have been a trick of the light.

Mr Fu was pleased with the progress she made and felt that soon she would be ready for the next stage, although there were many instances that Sonia remembered each time she started writing, and they had to be recorded and examined.

"Will Daddy have been able to forgive himself?" she asked her guide. "I'm sure that he must have been desperately ashamed, or he would have tried to get in touch after leaving. Maybe he died before he had the chance to track *me* down. What will have happened to him? Will he have been able to reach this stage? How does the system work? Will I *ever* be able to set things right with everyone I have wronged?"

He could see how much these and other questions puzzled her, and sent another memo:

> *"Dear God –*
> *as You will have noticed, she is progressing very well with the work. I feel it is time for a large reward, if it can be arranged. There are so many loose ends to tie up that otherwise we could be here for Eternity.*
> *Your humble servant and walker of interminable pathways -*
> *Fu, Angel Prince of the East*

One day they walked through a different way without noticing the surroundings, until they came to a grassy slope leading down to a small stream among banks of azaleas and rhododendrons where a figure emerged on a path ahead, and sensing a presence ahead, Sonia broke off her conversation and looked up. Hardly able to believe what she saw, a lifetime of waiting dissolved into nothingness as she paused, then ran – yes, ran – to her father; to be swept into his arms and the safety and warmth of the love that she had been without for so long.

Then, miracle upon miracle, there was her mother – fit and well, and happy to embrace both of them, the past just a vague painless memory. And in due course they were joined by so many others – people Sonia had known in her life and left behind; people she had neglected and forgotten; people who had met her only briefly, but who wanted to share their love. It was a joyous happening. Surrounded by friends and acquaintances, old and new, she revelled in the unaccustomed warmth of openness and genuine regard of one person for another.

Then the throng parted slightly as a new figure appeared on the fringe of the group and made his way to the woman who stood happily smiling. He was tall and handsome, the Geoffrey she remembered in her distant dreams, and he was holding out his hand, clasping her to him in an embrace that was at once familiar, yet strange. No hidden agendas this time, no bargaining involved – for either of them. They looked deep into each other's eyes and knew that they would meet again, next time in a situation where they could heal their differences with love and understanding.

Mr Fu discreetly left the scene.

༺༻

Sonia's next entry in her journal was deeply reflective:

I don't know if I will be able to take the memory of this pure love with me when I return for my next life. Maybe it's what causes the void that we all seek to fill in our hearts. I have learned so much about life through the process of what people experience as death.

I had begun to look back on my life as a waste, yet there must have been a purpose behind it, in the same way that there will be a purpose to my next Earthly life. Mr Fu says there is always an element in anyone's life of developing characteristics that others need to encounter, in order to promote their own spiritual growth. I realise now that Jacqueline is a prime example of that, and that much as I wish I had not treated her as I did, yet she had chosen that path – as I will have to choose my next path and the lessons I have to achieve in a lifetime.

That will be the next part of my work here. I am, naturally, very apprehensive, but I am sure that I will receive the right guidance from Mr Fu. If only I could take this journal with me when I return to Earth! If only everyone could – it would save so much time! We have to flounder our way through life on Earth, not knowing the purpose of why we are there until it is too late, for some. But again, it must be a matter of choice – we all have opportunities presenting themselves.

If I had one thing I could wish to take with me it would be a memory of the vision of the pathways up the mountain – it seemed to give the key to all understanding of what life is about. What a reminder that would be of how easy it is to become distracted from one's true path.

As I did.

20

The first dilemma after the funeral had been for Jacqueline to decide whether or not to tell Ben about the contents of Sonia's letter. She and Richard returned home and discussed the implications at length, from every possible angle, including the legal one that she would be entitled to challenge the Will, as the elder of Geoffrey's two children.

"I could never do that – it would mean that I would never see Ben again. He would be so hurt, and I certainly don't want to take away their life and everything they live for. It would be a betrayal beyond all reason and I couldn't live with the consequences."

"What about telling him, though? Don't you have to let him know?"

"It would be awful to have any secrets. I think it would be better to have it out in the open, than have him imagining all the wrong things. It's not the sort of thing one does on the phone, so I'll go to see him as soon as I can. Maybe I'll be able to see how things are for them generally, as well - I've been worried about the way he speaks to Vicky, and that's not good. A bit of moral support from her sister-in-law might not go amiss."

"What if he decides to tell her about the letter? Would that be a problem?"

"Oh my love, I want to get rid of any suspicions and secrets. There have been too many of those in the family for years. I've nothing to fear from anyone. It will make me very happy to tell him, that's all – what he chooses to do with the information will be up to him."

Richard breathed a sigh of relief – he wanted Jacqueline to have peace of mind above all.

"You'll never want for a thing if I have my way."

"I'll never want anything other than knowing you are my life" she whispered, as he held her closely to his heart.

When she travelled back from the Hall on her own a few days later, having seen Ben, she felt lighter and less burdened than at any time she could remember. It had been the right thing to do, although she'd sensed he felt uneasy about the purpose of her visit when he showed her into the Library. She had wanted to prepare him for yet another shock, but there was no preparation possible that she could think of, so once they had sat down and exchanged polite enquiries about health and the baby, she fell silent at his question about the purpose of her visit and handed over Sonia's letter without a word.

He recognised the envelope from the night before the funeral, when he gave it to his sister after reading the Will, and extracted the letter cautiously. He'd wondered at the time whether Jacqui would tell him what it contained, but other events had proved too demanding and he had forgotten to ask about it. If it had crossed his mind later, he supposed it might be some information about a private bequest to his sister that had no place in the Will. As he read the letter, however, Ben felt the blood drain from his face, his mind in turmoil.

His immediate reaction was that the emotional content passed him by – the fact that their father had betrayed their mother in that way did not really register in his consciousness. All he could think of was the possibility that Jacqui, now disclosed as the firstborn, might have an idea of the legal implications that could ruin him, if she chose. He wondered if she realised what power she had – it could mean an end of everything for him and his family, if she decided to contest the Will on those grounds.

He looked up at his sister, to find her watching him apprehensively. She held out her hand without saying anything and they sat for some time, each deep in their thoughts.

"I had a copy made for you to keep" she eventually said, retrieving the letter from his other hand. "And here is a letter I had drawn up by my solicitors stating that I shall never, at *any* time, lay claim to any part of the estate left to you by your mother. They don't know the reason, but hopefully it will reassure you. My children have their trust fund, and Richard will take care of anything else we need. Now, may I see little Lucy before I return home?"

Ben nodded, dumbfounded. His first thoughts were for himself, then for his child and the son he hoped to have at some stage in the future. He had always known Jaqui had a generous nature (and in fact had traded on this more than once as they grew up together) but he was unprepared for this degree of generosity, and knew that were he himself in the same position, he could not have been so altruistic.

The Ripples and the Tapestries

The shock of being handed back all he lived for, within minutes of feeling it could be under threat, meant it would be a long time before he managed to think about his father's actions and the effects on his mother. Then, when he did, he sat morosely for some time before carefully filing the letter from Jacqui's solicitors, to be dealt with at the earliest opportunity. A visit to the nursery to see Lucy, and a brief chat with Victoria helped Jacqui feel grounded again.

❦

She had left the Hall with promises to keep in touch, and, true to her word, made a point of phoning Victoria regularly to hear about Lucy's progress. Occasionally she would be able to speak to her brother, and although she sensed it was more difficult for him she knew it was only a matter of time before he could trust that she had meant what she said, and once again relax into the relationship they had before.

Six months later Lucy's Christening was the next occasion when the Hall saw a celebration party, but then it was with Richard and the children, and by then Ben's unease had eventually given way to a realisation that his sister had genuinely turned her back on the family wealth, and was content with her life as a doctor's wife and being as good a mother as she could be for her own children. He telephoned her one night to let her know that he had chosen not to breathe a word of the letter's contents to a soul, and had destroyed his copy. Jacqui breathed a sigh of relief.

The Company solicitor had received Jacqueline's official letter with a mixture of feelings – relief that the Company was safe in one pair of hands, as splitting it would have been a difficult and prolonged business, and regret that her decision would prevent sharing out a significant profit in courtroom fees, spread among his professional contacts.

❦

As Vicky was never told the contents of the letter, she found Jacqui's acceptance of Sonia's bequests an example of extraordinary but very welcome family loyalty that allowed her, as Ben's wife, to occupy and run the Hall as the 'lady' following in her mother-in-law's footsteps.

It proved not to be the ecstatically happy experience she had set out to achieve when she determined to marry Ben, but she had plenty of time to herself once she had organised several new staff to take the brunt of the work - although the turnover was frequent, due to her high-handed treatment and inability to respect other people's feelings. She had none of Sonia's knack of enticing staff to stay on, with implied promises of rewards to come, mixed with exquisitely judged comments that brought about a sense of insecurity so that they did not become complacent.

The Christening went well. Just a small family gathering, to which Barbara was invited. This was Jacqueline's suggestion, and it suited Ben's plans of eventually seeing the return of the Dresden collection to its original home. Barbara made a suitably lavish gift of one of the antique porcelain figurines, the sight of which made Victoria shudder when she opened the exquisitely wrapped package, remembering the way in which it had been earned.

Jacqui's life continued to unfold into episodes of peace and fulfilment after she had mourned Sonia's passing, and the waste of so much that could have been better. But she continued to think of her as 'mother' - for that was who she had been for thirty-two years, and she found that the letter had given answers to so much that had puzzled her for a lifetime.

In practical ways too, a door had been opened and eventually she might decide to trace her birth mother if she chose – as Richard said, for medical reasons, if nothing more.

Time also passed at the Hall, and as she grew older Lucy started showing unmistakable signs of inheriting something of her father's stubbornness and her mother's tendency to sulk if she did not get her own way. Nanny left, exasperated by the way Ben reinforced his daughter's behaviour by denying her nothing and contradicting anyone who tried to discipline her. A succession of au pairs took her place, none of them lasting long enough to form any bond with their wayward charge, and Lucy rapidly learned that when she grew bored, she could mischievously tell her father tales of their wrongdoing – real or imaginary, and they would disappear in favour of another one who would try to ingratiate themselves with her.

By the time Lucy was three years old she had learned to be a manipulative, spiteful little bully, with a range of tactics employed to get her own way if she was thwarted by anyone, including a smile that switched on briefly when she was successful – although it never reached her eyes.

21

Sonia had felt nothing but peace as she walked into her husband's arms in the garden. It had been the only meeting, but the only one necessary for peace of mind. Whatever difficulties and estrangements they'd had over the years completely evaporated, and they were simply two souls joined together in the unblemished love that each soul has for another in the Afterlife and the realms beyond.

"Why is this so different from Earthly love?" she asked Mr Fu as they sat discussing these matters, and others that would help to prepare her for the choices she would make.

"When souls return for another life on Earth, they carry with them memories of the life here, which is the purest feeling that it is possible to have. But these memories rapidly fade from consciousness the moment they are born, and so-called civilisation teaches people to accept less than the purest form of love. People are deceived into confusing gratification with love. But if they *do* meet another soul with whom they have shared time in these realms, then they feel a special bond, and try to recreate that feeling."

"I never felt that with Geoffrey in my Earthly life."

"No – you were a new soul in each other's lives. Next time you will recognise each other at the deep level you have experienced here, and events will probably prove happier than in the life you have recently left."

"I always dismissed the thought of 'soulmates' as Jacqueline used to refer to it, along with all her other nonsense."

"The term has been subjected to over-use and has therefore become another cliché – but one of our discussions was about the way that clichés contain the greatest truths. That may be one of the facts you rediscover when you return for your next life."

"Do I have to go back? Why can't I stay? It was all so difficult and unrewarding, even though I had great riches – it felt bleak and empty for so much of the time, although I kept busy with charity work. Surely I have done enough?"

"You have to have many lifetimes, in order to learn the lessons your soul needs. The quicker you learn, the easier it will be to choose the lessons for your next life. We are approaching the time when you can select those. Once you have done that, you will be able to choose what setting you need."

"What do you mean by 'setting'? Do *you* help me?"

"The family you choose to be born into. You make that choice, with the help of the patternmakers – I can only advise, not predict. Now I suggest that you spend time with all the people that you wish to meet here. Listen carefully to their wisdom and love, for although they have moved on into their next lives, they are able to return here while they sleep, in order to communicate with you and others. In their human life they may remember it as a dream, and it makes the bonds stronger."

Sonia thought her head would overflow with all these strange ideas. It all seemed to imply that souls could pass between the two worlds of Earthly life and the Afterlife. She had heard Jacqueline refer to concepts like the Higher Consciousness, but had dismissed it as nonsense – now she was not quite so sure. If she suspended her disbelief, then it might make sense that just as a soul could return to Earth (as she had done herself, to witness the outcome of her passing), so surely could a soul on Earth visit the Afterlife. Sleep would be the most natural way, so that anything unusual could be explained by human dreams. The more she thought of these things, the more she felt that her daughter's ideas might hold some truth.

※

After the meeting with Geoffrey had proved to be such a positive experience, Sonia did as Mr Fu had suggested, and spent time wandering around the gardens of her Afterlife. As if they had been waiting for the right moment, many people came to greet her – some she had forgotten, some she vaguely remembered: some she would have (in her Earthly life, at least) preferred not to see again. But they all came in the spirit of loving, with not a single comment of recrimination or spite – in fact many of them thanked her for her contribution to their own personal lessons that had led to the development of their souls. It was as if their message was that the harder one's life had been on Earth, the more likely it was that it proved easier to identify one's necessary lessons.

The Ripples and the Tapestries

Now Sonia began to wonder about the element of worldly wealth in her own, and a phrase about a 'rich man finding it as difficult to get into heaven as for a camel to pass through the eye of a needle' came back into her mind. It made her own values questionable – she had started her life in happiness and comfort, but with no great riches. Suffering emotional hardship, she had turned her back on her feelings and determined that financial comfort would provide a cushion for the rest of her days - no matter that it was gained at the expense of other people's emotions. She could now see how it had stunted her own spiritual growth. She had even mistaken religion for spirituality, and had allied herself to a way of achieving status and power that had nothing to do with the teachings she had professed to believe.

Discussing this with Mr Fu at length, Sonia wondered how she could avoid the mistake of confusing things again in her next life. Would she have to pass some sort of test to prove that she had learned the value of emotional riches? What sort of family could she be born into that would provide the background she needed?

"You might want to choose a parent who had also had the same or better start as yourself in terms of Earthly wealth – but who had a more difficult time emotionally. Someone, though, who has managed to see beyond it and who never loses sight of the need for love being at the root of all things. An older soul who was perhaps sent to lead the way."

Sonia suddenly had a flash of insight – *someone like Jacqueline!* She saw Jacqueline's childish puzzlement at yet another episode of her mother's unfair behaviour, rationalised into 'Mummy's poorly again', as she explained to her dolls; Jacqueline, reading the letter, feeling overwhelming sadness not anger; Jacqueline, on the day of the funeral, defending her mother's memory. What she had thought of as Jacqueline's weakness and sentimentality was a persistent attempt to use love to help overcome her mother's unkindness.

Jacqueline's bond with her father could have been even more significant than a blood tie – they had definitely had something very special – could they have both been 'old souls', brought together to offset her own behaviour and give each other much-needed support, remembering at some deep level the quality of love in the Afterlife, and recreating it as far as they were able?

She looked at Mr Fu carefully.

"Will I be able to meet people in my next life that I knew in the last one? Do I get a chance to set matters right?"

"Yes – though it might be in this next life or another; but don't forget that you won't consciously remember why you're there – you have to work continually through your life, gaining insights and piecing it together for yourself. Sometimes souls choose the most difficult settings to work in because the lessons are more obvious. They may choose brief lives just for a single lesson, at other times they choose a longer earth life so that many lessons may be learned. Or, when the lesson is about selfishness and possession they have to learn how to love and let go – that might happen when someone special is snatched away from them just at the peak of happiness."

"Jacqueline said exactly that when her second husband died in the car crash. She said it was the only way to 'move on', as she put it. Strange how I dismissed all her thoughts as nonsense at the time and now they fit into place."

"Anthony had come into her life to bring her greater understanding, and when he achieved this he left, for he had his own development to work on. They will keep meeting in other Earth lives, because they work so well together. Not always as husband and wife, of course, sometimes as mother and child, or teacher and pupil. When they meet, they will know of their past only at soul level, or what some people refer to as 'Higher Consciousness'. That always brings an echo of the peace and love you have felt here, dear lady. Now, shall we continue to weigh up *your* choice of lessons and family? Then we will visit the Patternmakers."

Sonia wanted to choose as many aims as possible, but Mr Fu persuaded her that two main ones at the most would be sufficient for one life at this point in her soul's development.

"There is no hurry!" he smiled. "Don't forget that many of the lessons will be part of your Earthly training and education – from the family values that you are given from the start, and the circumstances and choices you make at every stage of your life – they are the constants of patience and tolerance. But if, for example, you choose the lesson of material possessions, you will be asked to spend part of your life proving that they are not important - whatever the circumstances into

The Ripples and the Tapestries

which you were born. Your achievement will be measured by the way you react – with bitterness or welcoming the chance to learn more about life."

This prompted Sonia to remember a business couple that she and Geoffrey had known. The husband's bankruptcy had been a social disgrace, and they had never been invited to the Hall again. But, supported by his wife, it led him to a new career in caring for others and they had found happiness in their more modest lives.

Could she herself imagine coping with that sort of lesson? The new self that she had become after her visit to the Healing Temple felt that she could indeed. It would be a good contrast to her recent life when possessions and status had mattered to the exclusion of everything else. She remembered that couple again, and the way she had ostracised them, immediately cutting off any contact, lest it should damage Geoffrey's own reputation, and, as she remembered, it brought back the feelings that she had felt when she had been shunned by her school.

That was definitely a lesson she had not learned, or she would have been more sympathetic to the businessman friend. She determined that somehow in her next life she would find a way of spreading understanding and forgiveness. Parents who already had those values would help her along the way, she assumed.

Mr Fu broke into her thoughts.

"The law of adversity applies, don't forget, with all the lessons, especially emotional ones. An infant who is singled out for being neglected in some way is often on Earth for the purpose of learning about the true value of love. No matter how affluent their background, their search for love can be long and hard, but when they do find it, it's more rewarding than anything else. This may be a lesson you choose to learn, dear lady, because you spent most of your last life behind barriers you erected against love in your life. If you start the new life unloved for some reason, your quest will be more compelling, but it will certainly be more difficult for you as an Earthly person."

For no apparent reason, Sonia immediately thought of the scene at the hospital she had witnessed, and Ben's anger at Lucy not being the son he had expected. No doubt he had made recompense many times over, but had the wave of disappointment been noticed by that sensitive new-born soul?

Sonia felt she would never be ready for her decision. The more she thought, the more confused she felt she became. But, eventually settling for the aim of learning that materialism is not important, she had to trust that she would be put into a life where that lesson could be learned, and hope that she would be given a personality that would help her learn wisely and well. As for her chosen emotional task of being in a family where she could demonstrate the healing quality of love above every other thing, she was baffled. She wondered if Mr Fu would allow her to see one or two families who were planning to have a new baby, in the hope that this would help her to choose, using last-minute intuition.

Still maintaining her habit of walking in the gardens, sorting out her thoughts, one day a thought presented itself so suddenly it felt like a lightning bolt. Sonia rushed back to the familiar room and found Mr Fu sitting waiting.

"I know what would be the ideal situation and not only could I learn those lessons, but it would be the most direct and obvious way of making amends for my life!"

Mr Fu did not need her to spell it out, but wanted reassurance that she had seen all the dangers as well as the benefits of such a choice. He carefully listened to her detailed description of how, if she were born into either family, it would provide the direct involvement that meant her lesson could be learned. It would also provide the possibility of a wise soul learning the other lesson from observation at close quarters.

"Well … it's very irregular, dear lady, but I'll intercede on your behalf and see if it's possible."

The memo he sent to God was as persuasive as he had ever dared to be:

> *Dear Lord,*
> *I have a somewhat unusual request to make.*
> *Sonia has decided on a difficult path, and is*

determined to learn lessons that normally I would try to keep for more advanced souls. However, I feel she could do it - provided she has the right people in her life to help.

The problem is, she wants to return to the same family, and I can see that she has a point, but I know it's not usually done.

As it is beyond me to see the whole of the implications, however, I humbly hand the matter to You and will wait for your wisdom to enlighten me.

I remain as ever,
always your devoted
Angel Prince of the East
Master of the Higher Realms
(Mr Fu)

22

The business went well for Ben, but Victoria eventually insisted that there was to be no attempt to recreate the hospitality that his mother had delivered. Her natural apathy to duty came to the fore and she did everything she could to ensure that her life was one of self-indulgence and freedom, with duties parcelled out to staff as much as possible. Ben's love for her began to falter and he was not averse to looking further afield for entertainment and consolation, although he was still insistent that a son and heir would bring fulfilment to them both.

Vicky's phone call to Jacqueline one evening was to impart the news that she was pregnant again – at last.

"I don't know how I'll cope with two – Lucy's going to be four when it's born and she's already such a handful, thanks to all those useless au pairs. Then there's the morning sickness – it's started already, even though I'm barely six weeks. And of course it's due in March – just the worst time of year for affecting our holidays."

Jacqui listened with interest. Poor Vicky – one day she might realise that it was her own attitude that made life hard, and by no stretch of the imagination was it the circumstances. She congratulated her, then added

"Actually, *I* was going to ring *you*" she said happily "To tell you that *we're* going to have an addition to the family here!"

They excitedly exchanged dates and details – realising they could actually produce cousins within a few days of each other. As far as Victoria was concerned, Jacqui was reassuring and helpful, and she soon felt that she would be able to manage things well enough. However, again she adamantly refused to be told whether the baby would be boy or girl, no matter how Ben tried to persuade her when she went for monitoring scans. It gave her some sort of power to be able to keep him wondering – even for a few months – and being more pleasant towards her. Knowing that there was no element of responsibility on her part for the baby's gender did not ease her fears about how Ben would unjustly blame her if it proved to be another girl.

Jacqui had her own personal fears, but kept them secret, and only to be shared with Richard. From the earliest suspicion of pregnancy she had needed his reassurance.

"I simply can't get it out of my head that there will be difficulties with this one. Call it a mother's intuition, but we *will* be able to have all the tests, won't we?"

"Tests, insurance – anything you wish. But one thing I know is that our baby will be the perfect one for us, whatever he or she is like."

Jacqui's pregnancy went well, in spite of her initial nagging doubts, and when the tests and scans showed that she was carrying a single normal baby, her mind was eventually eased and she thoroughly enjoyed the preparations, getting Tim and Ella to help with choosing how to arrange the room that was to be a nursery, as well as clothes and little toys.

By contrast, Lucy proved to be a worry for Victoria, and even her father noticed her stubbornness and wished that the matter had not been raised so soon.

"Don't *want* a baby brother!" she would shriek when they attempted to divert her from inflicting permanent damage to the walls as she rode her tricycle around corridors in the Hall.

"It might be a baby sister for you to play with" her mother cajoled, risking Ben's displeasure, as he once again planned for the boy he felt would be inevitable this time.

Increasingly he put Victoria under pressure to accept prior knowledge of whether the baby was a boy or not, but Ben could not persuade her, even when he went on a prolonged business trip in a fit of sulks, with Lucy's screams of anger ringing in his ears.

"Don't *want* a sister! Want a *puppy*! Want a *pony*! I *hate* babies!"

Vicky tried to console herself with the thought that when the time came, Lucy would change her mind – at present the last thing the Hall needed as well as a stubborn almost four year old, was a puppy.

❦

Yet what did her father arrive with on Christmas Eve? Of course – an adorable golden Labrador pup.

"For my little princess – happy birthday for tomorrow."

The Ripples and the Tapestries

Later, when puppy and Lucy had eventually fallen exhausted in a heap together in the playroom, Victoria rounded on her husband.

"You are the most thoughtless, underhand, arrogant person I have ever met – apart from your mother. Anything to prove that life is to be lived according to your rules and your rules only. How am I going to manage to deal with a puppy I don't even want, and that Lucy will grow tired of in a few weeks if not days? Are *you* going to take it walks and feed it and clean up after it?"

"No and neither are you, you silly bitch – throw enough money at a problem and it usually goes away. I provide you with staff – get them to clean up. Get a girl from the village to be a puppy nanny! For heaven's sake let your daughter have something she can love – there's precious little of that in this house nowadays."

Victoria fled from the room, sobbing uncontrollably. Life was getting unbearable and she phoned Jacqui for consolation. How was she going to manage the last three months before the birth? How would life be if she had another daughter when Ben had set his heart on a boy? How had she ever been such a fool as to marry the self-centred loathsome pig in the first place?

Jacqueline soothed and comforted, promising that they would have time together when she and her family came for their traditional Christmas visit the following day.

"Give it a few days - Lucy will have all sorts of presents to distract her tomorrow. If she loses interest in the puppy after a while then it can be found a new home – I'm sure you could find someone in the village who would be delighted with a pedigree pooch."

"Oh Jacqui – you're always the voice of reason and commonsense. Why can't I be like you, so calm and happy? How is it you've found the solution to life and I'm still looking?

"Hold on there! I don't pretend I've found any answers at all. I just hang onto the thought that nothing lasts for ever, whether it's good or bad, so we need to make the most of the good and look for solutions for the other."

Eventually calming down, Vicky went off to make the final preparations for Lucy's birthday morning that also saw the traditional

Christmas celebrations. The Hall looked splendid, with the tree, as ever, in the far corner of the drawing room, festooned with the decorations that Sonia had purchased over the years.

"Oh Sonia, where are you now? Ben still needs you, you know – I'm not good enough for him in so many ways. If you're somewhere where it will do any good, just have a word on my behalf and let me have a son this time."

Then, shaking her head at her own stupid superstition, she switched off the light and went to retrieve the puppy from her daughter's bedroom.

23

Mr Fu had received his reply, and to his surprise, God agreed. Sonia had deliberated for so long that at last she reached a point of total confusion. The choice of family was all-important, she knew, for her lesson of material importance, coupled with the task of healing with love. An angel messenger arrived with two scrolls, which were shown to Mr Fu. He was very solemn as her studied the contents, knowing the responsibility that lay with Sonia's choice.

"Your unusual request has been granted" he announced as she returned from the gardens "but I am not allowed to show you the details of these files. I can tell you which are the two families concerned – you do have the option of being born to Benjamin and Victoria, or to Jacqueline and Richard."

Sonia looked pleased, yet apprehensive at the same time, as well she might, her guardian thought.

He continued.

"While you have been away, parts of your family have become more divided and there has to be another soul element within the equation. Both Jacqueline and Victoria will be expecting babies at around the same time."

He could not tell her the detail of this next life – that Jacqueline's child would have disabilities, but would be surrounded by love and the restrictions would be physical, not mental or emotional, while Benjamin's child would have a materially comfortable life with many opportunities to develop through emotional adversity.

"I can tell you that one of the lives will be brief, but I cannot tell you which one that will be. Now you may choose which child receives your soul."

Sonia was stunned. Responsibility and opportunity weighed heavily on her shoulders.

"Will you continue to be my guardian angel?" she asked.

"Of course. I will always be watching over you, helping you. You may learn as you get older that there will be a special signal I use when I approve of life choices you make."

"What do you mean?"

"Have you ever heard people talk of a 'gut reaction'? Or sometimes refer to a prickle at the back of their neck?"
Sonia nodded.

"Those are signs that you learn to recognise. Other, external signs can be given – natural sights, such as rainbows; animals or birds unexpectedly looking you straight in the eye - your duty is to be watchful and learn to recognise them. I will make sure they keep coming to your attention – that's part of my job. There is also one other sign that I will tell you just before you leave."

Sonia made her choice, helped by the reassurance that she would always be watched over by Mr Fu. He took her arm for the last time as they made their way to the Patternmakers, and as they paused at the threshold he gave his last and most valuable piece of information.

"You will recognise me by my smile – no matter who is wearing it at the time."

That enigmatic remark was to be trusted, Sonia knew. She turned to give him a smile of her own, and heartfelt thanks – but he was no longer at her side, although she knew that he would never leave her.

Holding her head high, she walked through celestial portals for this last preparation, and into the Hall of the Patternmakers where her own particular tapestry was being designed. It consisted of colours and designs that she had never seen in her last Earth life. Some were bright and glowing, others were sombre and dull. Parts of the design had them mingled in equal parts, and Sonia could almost taste the bitter-sweetness that lay ahead, but the overall impression was that the brightness predominated.

Suddenly she felt herself surrounded, and part of, a swirling mass of brilliantly coloured strands, but whether they were made of light or some material she could not quite tell. Whichever way she looked, Sonia saw intricate patterns being woven – but there was no beginning and no end of the multi-dimensional work. Workers in robes threaded

The Ripples and the Tapestries

their way through the mass; others, with books, entered notes for the Healing Temple Library. Methodical, yet exciting and challenging, was the impression given to the wondering spirit, waiting to be allocated her unique contribution to the rich tapestry of Life.

While Sonia wished she could have said goodbye to Mr Fu, she believed him when he told her that he would be there on her return after the next Earth life, as she had grown fond of the little man who had been the least likely person to guide her through her discoveries. She also hoped that whatever her next life held, she would be able to remember to turn to her own guide, knowing that his wisdom was always there to help her through the difficult times. As she waited for her part of the pattern to be made clear to her, Sonia thought she caught a glimpse of another familiar figure, also waiting. Geoffrey? It could have been, but it may have been a trick of the light.

Helpers darted around, putting the final touches here and there, with Sonia standing waiting with a keen anticipation and barely suppressed excitement. She was shown to a couch, somewhat similar to the one in the Healing Temple.

A shimmering piece of the work detached itself and floated towards Sonia, light as gossamer. The Pattern – *her* pattern, her *life* - floated above her, held by unseen hands. She felt it enter her heart and become part of her knowledge. For a brief moment she felt a surge of energy as the realignment took place and then she was ready. Equipped for her new place on Earth, she was helped to her feet and walked out into the celestial light to begin the journey.

It felt strange to be travelling again, and she had forgotten how the pull of the earth made her feel slightly queasy as she saw it getting nearer.

As she travelled she remembered how she had hesitated for a long time, weighing up the pros and cons of each family – Jacqueline's and Richard's, Ben's and Victoria's – one with all the worldly advantages possible but a coldness in the quality of life, and the other with so much warmth and love.

Which one would be brief? Mr Fu could not divulge that

information, so in the end she made a choice with her heart, and once committed, she was convinced that her decision was the only one she *could* have made - it was to choose the life that would give the most opportunities to make as many amends as possible for her last one, no matter how difficult it might be.

Already her detailed recollection of the Afterlife was fading. Now she was becoming pure spirit, directed by the power of her own choice - a new earthling that would begin to receive impressions of the experiences of life in the womb, followed by the strains of birth and the struggle that surrounds the first breath. Leaving the intensely beautiful celestial light behind, she aligned, and waited for a few more months.

※

Early in the following Spring, after the soothing comfort of the womb, there would be the harsh lights and loud noises that herald any arrival into a modern maternity unit. Protesting with loud cries, the baby would be suddenly quietened by the mother's smile.

A vague memory would stir, an echo of a voice whispering - "… no matter who is wearing it …"

24

It was an early Easter that year, and the usual get-together of the two families was due to take place at the Hall. The Easter egg hunt, either in the gardens, or inside the large house if the weather was poor, was now an annual family tradition eagerly anticipated by the two older children. Lucy, as ever, was boasting to the latest au pair that she knew where absolutely all of the eggs were hidden and no-one else would get even one – she would feed them all to Mindy the puppy who, now five months old, large and boisterous, was proving to be a real handful.

Vicky overheard, shuddered at the thought of the awful effects too much chocolate might have on both child and dog, but decided not to intervene. It was her way of coping with both her daughter and her husband these days, and if it meant that both were given full rein with their selfishness, at least it meant that she had some sort of peace. Vicky had discovered something of the art of her late mother-in-law – of ignoring the things that would cause her too much trouble to solve. Sonia, of course, had gone on to refine this art by only getting involved with things that would bring her rewards – especially the personal satisfaction of being in control of other people's lives. That particular refinement lingered in the air over Victoria, with a faint question mark.
Time would tell.

≈≈

Richard telephoned that evening to let Ben and Victoria know that Jaqui had started labour and he would be in touch the following morning to let her know about the baby. The plan was to be that his parents, who were already at home taking care of Tim and Ella, would take the older children to hospital to visit their new brother or sister, then he would like to bring them over to the Hall as usual, as they were so looking forward to seeing Lucy and telling her about the new baby. Victoria agreed, hoping that it might make Lucy more amenable to the thought of her own imminent brother or sister.

Easter Saturday 2007 dawned, with Jaqcueline still in hospital but with nothing happening.

"It's a false labour" the midwife pronounced. "It happens sometimes. I'll get the doctor to see you and make a decision."

Richard tried to soothe her worries, but not for the first time felt thankful that his own professional training gave him the knowledge that could comfort his wife. He telephoned his parents, then the Hall. Returning to the ward he found she was tired and anxious, but seemed to accept his reassurances and lapsed into an uneasy sleep. He knew she would need this for whatever outcome lay ahead, and continued to sit at her side holding her hand.

Easter Sunday afternoon was bright and sunny. Ben had taken Lucy to Church to show off her new dress, leaving Victoria to stay at home at this late stage of her pregnancy, and greet Richard's parents and the children when they arrived for lunch. Lucy returned too full of excitement to eat lunch, and feeling sick because of the sweets that her father had bribed her with during the service. It was not a good omen. Victoria saw the afternoon stretching ahead relentlessly, without even the comfort of a reassuring chat with Jacqui to look forward to.

Muriel and Ted, Richard's parents, had arrived with Tim and Ella, who were bearing small gifts for Lucy. When she came back from church with her father she tossed them aside without even opening them and unable to contain herself any longer announced that the treasure hunt must start *right now*!

"Anything for a bit of peace" said Victoria as she told the children they should join in before Lucy found all the eggs. Soon, shrieks and calls let the adults know that it was indeed under way. It was pleasant enough sitting on the patio in that warm forerunner of Spring that sometimes comes early in the year. Ben, Victoria, Muriel and Ted, relaxed with drinks, making small talk before lunch. The older couple were naturally anxious about the news from the hospital, but hid their feelings from their hostess.

The three cousins usually played well together, but without Jacqui's calming influence and gift for sensing trouble before it even started, coupled with Victoria's leniency verging on indifference, disaster was inevitable. Lucy overstepped the mark when she pushed Ella off the terrace in full view of all the adults. Ben's patience snapped. He picked up his daughter bodily and carried her to her room kicking and screaming, beating at his back with her small fists.

Flinging her on the bed, he pinned her down by the shoulders and shouted at her to learn to behave like a Woolston, not like her mother, and never, *ever*, to let him down in front of visitors again. His distorted face was only inches away from her terrified gaze – the normally loving, indulgent father had been replaced by someone she couldn't recognise. Her world was shattered; hysterical sobs shook her small body, but Ben ignored them.

He abruptly left the room, slamming the door and turning the key, leaving his daughter to cope with her feelings - alone and unloved.

The embarrassment of Ben's reaction outweighed any effect of Lucy's behaviour. Tim comforted Ella, the adults made the best of things and lunch was eventually over, leaving Muriel and Ted to drive their two grandchildren home as soon as was decently possible, with assurances that they would pass on any news about Jacqui as soon as they heard from Richard at the hospital.

❧

Ben retreated to the Library as soon as they had left, giving instructions that as he had the key to Lucy's room, he would be the one to decide when she would be released. Two hours later, fuelled by misery and brandy, his fury was soon rekindled by another plea from his wife, made as he prepared to go upstairs.

Possibly anything would have had the same effect, but Victoria voiced it, and therefore was on the receiving end of yet another tirade from her husband. She wept, and retreated to the conservatory where, horrified, she realised that she was feeling the early signs that her own labour had started. With barely time to comfort her daughter, now released from her room and delivered into the care of the au pair, she told Ben. He made her wait while he resentfully drank a strong coffee, then wordlessly carried her bag to the car and drove to the hospital.

It was a miserable start that carried a heavy foreboding about the future – their future as a couple, the future of the child as yet unborn, and most definitely the unknown future of their emotionally damaged daughter Lucy who would always carry the entwined memory of the shame of her own actions, betrayal by the person she loved most, abandonment by all those others in her life, linked with the toppling of her priority in the family structure.

25

This time of course, Ben had actually managed to bring himself to attend the birth – resentfully and sulkily. When he realised it was another girl he left the delivery room, feigning faintness. Later, he returned to the bedside with flowers, but no improvement in his reaction.

"You can't even get *this* right" he glowered. "*Another* girl, would you believe." His disappointment could not be concealed, and there was no sign of tenderness – either towards his wife or his new daughter.

Victoria shrank into the pillows of her private bed. Such unfair comments at a time like this – she would make him pay dearly when she recovered, and there would certainly be no more attempts to produce a son and heir. She turned her head away from his perfunctory kiss and, glad of any excuse to get him out of the room, soothed the baby's fractiousness.

In the other hospital, Richard leaned over and carefully stroked their son's cheek. Now several hours old, he looked more normal with the tubes removed, and Jacqui had been able to feed him. It had turned out to be a difficult delivery, with cause for concern at first with the baby, who had problems breathing immediately after his birth. Richard had held his wife close and stroked her hair while the staff bustled about the room.

"You'll be able to hold him soon. They've just put him in the incubator for a few hours as a precaution. It happens with many babies and he'll be fine. He looks absolutely gorgeous – you've given me a son to be proud of."

He kissed her tenderly and waited for her to drift off into sleep before going to see the gynaecologist, dreading what he knew from his medical training would be the likely outcome of the conversation.

"Not enough oxygen… possible risk of brain damage … only time will tell."

There would be the question mark of other long-term effects hanging over them for many years to come, Richard knew, but his trained eye had been able to pick out the early tell-tale signs, and the consultant's words had confirmed the prognosis. Jaqui's eyes held the question as he returned – Richard did not need to give the answer in words, but as they held hands and drank in every detail of the soft little features, Jacqui cradled him to her heart, murmuring "Whatever you're capable of, little one, we'll help you achieve it."

❧❦

They planned that when Richard had collected Tim and Ella and they were all safely back at home as a family, they would explain to the children how special their little brother was and how he would need extra love from all of them.

"Have you phoned Ben?"

"I was saving the news – Vicky went into labour, and you know how short that can be with a second baby – she had another daughter just before midnight last night! Mother and baby are doing just fine."

"Oh Richard! I do hope Ben's pleased. It will be lovely to have two cousins sharing the same birthday and growing up together. I hope we can see much more of them and help little Lucy to feel she's part of a big family."

Jacqui's optimism never seemed to fade, and Richard loved her for that willingness to aim at the best possible outcomes. He knew that no matter what challenges lay ahead, their own son would be cherished and helped to achieve even his smallest successes in an atmosphere of love and support.

❧❦

The two cousins met for the first time at their joint christening ceremony, just a few weeks after their birth. Tiny morsels of life, with so much in front of them and so many hidden depths acquired through many other lifetimes. What had they come to learn, these little ones, Jacqui wondered. What purposes had they chosen? What were the challenges that lay ahead for all of them as these little lives unfolded?

Victoria and Jacqui posed for photographs, with husbands and children, on the terrace, in the late Spring warmth. Looking at the magnificent surroundings, new growth in the trees, early Summer flowers pushing through the soil, even Victoria became tearful for a moment.

"I do wish your mother was here – just so she could know," she murmured wistfully.

"Something makes me think she is" was Jacqui's response, as the babies touched hands.

26

The Celestial realms of the Afterlife contained an air of celebration as an Angel messenger arrived, with a scroll to be treasured.

Memo to Angel Prince of the East (Mr Fu):
Well done, thou good and faithful servant –

GOD

The search continues ...

I turn the last page at some ungodly hour and realise that my glass is empty, as is the bottle which has kept it replenished through the evening and into the night. I'm nonplussed, to say the least.

Quite frankly, it was not the reading material I would have chosen - for this or any other night - and I'm well aware that it's mostly my dedication to Cressy's memory that has helped me through to the end. I've read quotes I half remember from conversations we had. It's unnerving to realise that casual thoughts I'd expressed could be woven into a story this way – and yet where else would authors obtain authentic dialogue, if not from their own experiences?

Not a work of great literary merit (I'm sure she would have been the first to agree), although competent and with some interesting touches of humour in unexpected places; but it haunts me, and I know that over the following days I'll feel compelled to create the time to read part two – not least because of the cliffhanger finish to part one. (Clever Cressy!)

In the meantime I couldn't help wondering exactly where her researches had led. We kept our own meetings on their well trodden tracks, exchanging views on current topics when we met every week or two, or phoned (more often), or emailed (frequently). We would sometimes decide to explore somewhere new, and visit gardens open to the public – a busman's holiday for me of course, but useful too, if she'd managed to unearth one I didn't know, one that I could return to later, if first impressions deemed it worthy of being the subject for an article.

This side of her is something new and unrevealed, and I feel slightly cheated, neither wanting to discover that she had secrets from me, nor wishing to admit that she could not trust me in all things – had she been afraid of ridicule, or even ashamed? I sit wondering who the characters were based on; I can clearly see parts of herself in some of the settings – the flat she allocated to Barbara, for instance, was her own flat – was Barbara in some way a hidden part of Cressy (or a Cressy who might have been capable of Barbara's wayward life in different circumstances) that she brought to the fore?

But I can also see her in Vicky – the businessman's wife, the role of playing second fiddle, expected to do the hard work so the leader may progress smoothly through the difficult passages, giving credit to the virtuoso, although needing equal and complementary skills to provide the background.

Sonia, of course, was undeniably based upon her late and unmourned mother-in-law – a formidable old dowager who would never have allowed herself to recognise her own character presented in that way, even though the cloned attitude towards her darling son, used to portray Sonia's towards Ben, was outrageously identical. (Still the catharsis at work then, Cressy my love ...)

Who was the role model for Jacqui? That ever optimistic, annoyingly perfect third-time wife and mother – was that how she saw herself in some way, how Cressy might have been in an ideal world? What would Cressy's opinion be of a real-life Jacqui? I wonder if I will see the character develop more in the sequel – will there be a great shake-up to rattle her equilibrium, and what would be the catalyst?

Am *I* in there somewhere? The only reference to a gardener was the similarity of the 'guide' (the improbably named Mr Fu) to a gardener at the Hall. Perhaps she had spared me.
There was only one occasion, looking back, when I was aware that she was picking my brains; she'd asked me how I would get children interested in growing things. I asked why and she said it was for something she was writing, but didn't volunteer any further details, and she said it so casually I'd assumed it was a letter to a friend with children. I hadn't come across it so far. On the other hand, I more easily identify myself with Richard – not least because of his capability for devotion, but of course for his down-to-earth scepticism.

However – all this is becoming very deep analysis of a novel that is going to be so easily forgotten, and as it stands at the moment would hardly be likely to see the light of day in any publisher's list.

For a change of pace and subject matter I take a look at her diary. At first glance I can see that this is not her public, flowingly large handwriting – this has been written in an extremely miniature version and will take hours of concentration to decipher some of those closely written pages. It seems to have been turned more into a random journal, with entries on one day spilling over into others, as well as having asterisks and 'see notes' alongside. I turn to the note pages at the back – more of them than usual, as it's a five year diary - but even so, still inadequate. There are many scraps of paper torn from other sources, inserted between the back cover and the end sheet.

Turning back to the diary pages, some headings leap out at me, underlined; 'Sitting' is mentioned frequently, as is 'Healing'. 'Reading with ... ' is always followed by a name, presumably of the person giving the reading. Reading what? Books, hands, tea leaves, cards? I have only a hazy notion of these things – were they research or for her own needs? And if research, then where had the manuscript been taking her? Some of them appear to have been given a rating, none ranked above 5 - although a star and an exclamation mark singled out one of those, which also had a telephone number against it. I inserted a bookmark – just in case.

She had never given me great concern for her mental well-being, apart from the bouts of understandable depression, and had certainly never revealed any tendency to get caught up in cults of any sort. But neither had she revealed any particular interest in any aspect of a more orthodox religion – Cressy didn't 'do God' at all, as far as I knew, yet the clues and the whole tenor of the first manuscript hinted at a 'knowledge' of a subject I never knew she possessed.

Was that knowledge a belief, or had it become one? There are so many questions I want to ask, but the one person with the answers is gone for ever and ... I sighed ... it's my responsibility to read further if I am to carry out the legacy of her wishes and take on the role of literary executor.
If.

Do I want to do it? Who will know if I choose not to spend

further hours reading what might possibly become a second rate novel, if it ever sees the light of day?

No-one, of course, but *I* would, and I would be less than loyal to the love of my life if I neglect this last opportunity to find out more, and I'm *hungry* for more. I can only lay my memories and understanding of her safely to rest when I've found out as much as there is to know.

Wherever it leads me ...

I open the other box.

the tapestries

1

As she saw the infinite expanse which contained her own personal tapestry – woven with strands of colour, some glowing, almost incandescent; others sombre and dark, Sonia felt her sense of wonder growing even more. This was the Temple of the Patternmakers, where every soul came, to be given their individual piece of the immeasurable Tapestry of Life, which had been since before the Beginning and stretched into the as yet Unknown.

It felt as if she were being swallowed into a living creature without shape or texture. Purposeful motion enveloped her; it was like being in a vast ocean of various ribbons and threads, all swirling around her, yet it was far from chaotic. It was warm and richly coloured. The dark tones had no less meaning than the others and she knew that they betokened difficult times; yet they had a hidden profundity – more subtle than the cliched 'silver lining' of comfort that was spoken about on Earth – it was a deep luminosity that beckoned her to peer into their depths.

The language of the symbolic shades revealed there were more, many more, than she had ever seen with human eyes. Fascinated, she became absorbed in the process, until she sensed that it was complete. A piece of gossamer weight was detached – her own piece, to be allocated to herself, no-one else – unique and never to be repeated. It was hers - to make of it what she could. She felt it envelop her like a light mist, then at last there was separateness and she became free to walk from the Temple of the Patternmakers, complete with her own future on earth absorbed into her soul.

Mr Fu had imparted his last precious pieces of advice before she entered the Temple and from now on Sonia's spirit had to make its own way back to the new life that awaited. He had warned her that she would have no conscious memory of the time she had spent with him, yet he knew he had been so essential a part of her new understanding of how her life had been led, what damage she had done, and how she could make amends that he wondered how she would fare. His limitless patience had led to her realise how many opportunities she had been given in her life, how many mistaken choices she had made, and how false her values had been. She knew from her learning that she would not be led into making the same ones, but how different would the different ones be this time?

※

Looking back at her life had been an unexpected development after her death. When he had appeared and informed her that he was going to be her guide and mentor, Sonia had raged with a fury that included all her reactions to what she saw as a betrayal of her beliefs and also her position in society. The detail of the worst of those bizarre experiences was thankfully fading, of those days and weeks (or had it been years?), when she'd had to face the consequences of her actions, and revisit various situations and places in order to see how she had affected others' lives. Time in the Afterlife bore no relation to Earthly time, and there were no ordinary routines to provide a framework for the experiences, so the consequence was that she had no idea how long she had been there; but she could recall trips back – mainly to her beloved home, Woolston Hall – and glimpses of situations she would prefer to forget, yet they had led to productive understanding of the whole process of her soul's development.

Mr Fu thought of the way Sonia had eventually let her pride and arrogance evaporate, then of the rewards - meeting the people she eventually realised would always matter most to her – her husband, her parents: the very ones she had thought in her Earthly life she would never be able to forgive, yet at their meeting all past hurts had evaporated and were replaced by a feeling of love that she had never known before. It comforted her to learn that she would be able to meet them again; they reassured her that she was part of the soul family who helped each other's growth each time they shared a life, and as they talked, and as Mr Fu confirmed, themes of forgiveness and generosity had been decided upon for her next life.

What was perplexing for her, though, was the knowledge they all emphasised – that she would enter the next life with no memory of these experiences.

Oh, she hoped that would not be true. She wanted so much to be able to prove that she had learned from all his wise teachings – yet it puzzled her that she would be expected to start from scratch again – it seemed such a waste. She had once asked him to explain why there was that need.

"To use a particularly harsh example - if your lesson has to be about how to live a life without hope, it's no use giving you foreknowledge when you have to learn from experiencing everything for yourself, and learning what you, as an individual, will make of it.
"I'm sure you can think of children in difficult circumstances who emerge differently as they grow – one child will make a determined effort to succeed in spite of the bad start, another might never succeed with anything – or worse still, perpetuate the difficulties for their own children.
"It's essential that you start your next life having to develop within the family – the particular family you select, that will best help your soul develop. To consciously carry over knowledge from this Afterlife learning would cause such a conflict that many would never survive. In any case, the others in the family will have their own lessons to learn from having you as a baby in their midst, as much as you will have to learn from them. As you respond to their sets of values you will form your own character and opinions. It is the best way of learning - through experience. As you go through your life you will realise that you are always given choices – you can choose to absorb all the family values you see around you and have to comply with, or you can take a stand against them."

She knew it was a difficult concept, yet it made sense when she thought of all the unsatisfactory families she might be born into – why should a soul choose to encounter cruelty, illness, neglect - unless there was a compelling purpose?
This was when she had asked to choose between the two particular families that she knew best. It had taken a great deal of respectful intercession on his part, reminded her mentor, and although the unusual request had been granted, it had been emphasised that she would have to give her choice a great deal of profound deliberation.

Mr Fu remembered the ways he had set out to prepare her – phrases he hoped would enter her deepest subconscious and stay there for times of need - "you will meet people who are able to help you bridge the distance between earthly life and where we are now, and it is up to you to take that opportunity ..."

His parting words, much to be treasured, gave her comfort as she prepared for the unknown life ahead, even though she realised that these words too would be lost to conscious thought.

"... you will recognise me by my smile – no matter who is wearing it at the time."

The journey back to earth was characterised by passing through the belt of mist that obliterated any memories of the Afterlife. She felt her reasoning powers ebb away as she travelled and she became the infant preparing to enter the world.

Harsh lights and loud noises heralded that arrival into the modern maternity unit.

Protesting with loud cries, the baby was suddenly quietened by the mother's smile - or did a wisp of words float across that little mind?

" ... no matter *who* is wearing it ..."

2

Sundays in Guildford had a special atmosphere of their own. This particular family day had started with a precious extra hour of sleep. Ella was now eight years old, and she took responsibility seriously. First thing in the morning she liked to creep into Gabriel's room to see if he was still sleeping peacefully. If so, she would gently stroke his hair or cheek and murmur softly to him or sing a nonsense song, so that her little brother would gradually be woken, and not cry. She loved those precious moments when the two of them were alone in the small room, surrounded by Gabriel's toys and the pictures on the walls that their mother had asked her to paint, even though he would never be able to see them as clearly as she could. His eyes would open but not focus on anything, so that she sometimes thought that he could still see his dreams. It was their special time together, that early morning ritual. Eventually she would listen for sounds of her mother's voice, or Richard padding to the bathroom then downstairs to the kitchen, and know that it was time to go in and snuggle between the covers Jacqui tucked around her.

Four years ago, introducing her children to the man she knew was going to become their stepfather had seemed a daunting task. So many of her friends had chipped in with good advice or tales of catastrophe, that Jacqui was in danger of becoming too inhibited.

They had met at a party, or to be more precise, a gathering where she was helping her friend Barbara. It was not the most auspicious start to a friendship – she had made a start on tidying the flat as people began to leave and was backing through the doorway laden with a tray of plates just as Richard, in the hallway beyond, had been turning to go after thanking Barbara for raising the money for the hospital fund. When he made a short speech earlier she had not only been impressed by his looks, but by his whole manner of quiet confidence, and now, with quick thinking and strong arms saving the tray, she found herself looking up into the eyes of the man she instantly knew she would never wish to be parted from.

Mutual attraction paved the way for an invitation to dinner, subsequent arrangements for other outings and soon Jacqui found she was feeling happier than she had ever thought would be possible again. Richard was everything *she* hoped for, but of course sooner or later she would need to introduce him to the children. Barbara reassured her that it would prove to be the most natural thing in the world, and of course, so it proved, when she had voiced her apprehensions to Richard.

"We'll meet on a day out, then they'll have something to occupy them if they're shy. Having a meal together and being relaxed will be the best way" he persuaded her. They decided to visit a zoo, meeting in the car park and letting the children's excitement override any awkwardness. All that Jacqui had told them was that they were going to be joined by a friend who was looking forward to meeting them, and soon the sight of monkeys and meerkats delighted them all. In fact, after that and several other outings, it eventually proved that the children were more prepared for change than Jacqui herself.

"Are you going to marry Richard?" Timmy suddenly asked one day on the way home from school. Before she could give him an answer, four year old Ella joined in.

"Yes, say yes! We like him so much and I want to be a bridesmaid!"

"Well there's one little thing that's missing" responded Jacqui "he hasn't asked me and I can't ask him, can I?"

"Don't tease!" Ella put on her mother's voice "*We'll* ask him if you like."

"Don't you dare!" said Jacqui, laughing, then sensing someone behind her, turned and saw Richard.

"No, don't you dare, young lady. I'm going to do that – *now* - if you don't mind."

Ignoring the bemused stares of some groups of other homeward-bound mothers, he took Jacqui's hand, kissed it, and getting down on one knee looked into her eyes, and seriously – oh, so seriously – asked the question: and, just as seriously, she looked at him tenderly, looked from one to the other of the children's eager faces, saw them nodding – and replied.

"I think there's only one answer – on behalf of us all, but most of all for myself – yes, Richard – oh *yes!*"

He picked her up and swung her round; then, with hands linked, they walked home as a family. Later that evening he explained that in any case, he'd planned to ask her that very evening after dinner, but decided to meet them coming from school, and well, she'd just have to get used to the fact that he was an opportunist.

સ✧

At first, when Richard became part of their household, even though he knew him quite well, Timmy sometimes felt rather shy of his mother's friend who had so soon become her husband; but Richard's imperturbability had won through – that, plus his tactfulness with established family customs, and a patient willingness to establish new ones.

"Are you going to help me with the man's work?" Richard would ask on Sunday mornings, putting his head round Timmy's bedroom door with a conspiratorial wink, and Tim eventually realised that this kind and gentle man was as fond of him as he was of his mother.

"Ask Madame what she would care for this morning."

Tim would be the waiter and furrow his brow as he made certain he remembered whether it was honey or jam for the toast, then join Richard downstairs to organise the request. As time went by, this part of the ritual became as valued as any other and the ground was laid for some very useful stepfather and son conversations as the kettle boiled and toast was cooked. Then, with great ceremony, they would make the journey up the stairs and discuss plans for the day.

Jacqui made the most of her rest. It was something Richard insisted she should do whenever possible. She lay on the bed, dreamily meandering through the past years since Richard had appeared in her life.

"What a background for anyone to take on" she had said to him in the early days. Divorced and widowed, two children by two different fathers – how can you really want me?"

His unswerving love had proved time and time again that he did, and she had learned the extent and depth of his feelings as they grew closer with time. Third time lucky – against all the odds. She had never dared hope that she would meet someone else who could return her love on the level she gave it. And Richard proved to be the ideal one for all of them; Tim, who was just at the stage when he needed to know there was a man around; Ella, four years younger, who had never known her father Anthony, killed in the car crash months before she was born. Richard had come on the scene when Jacqui's fragile confidence led her to have so many doubts; but he patiently waited while her apprehensions faded, and after they married had again waited for it to be her decision if and when they should have a child of their own.

"Thirty-five or six is no great age to be thinking of another baby" he'd said, stroking her hair as they read the Sunday papers one weekend, after she became used to the idea, then began to long for another child – their own child. They decided to let matters take their own course: she was fit, she kept telling herself and had given birth to two healthy children – the first when she was in a dreadful psychological state, and the second when her emotions were stretched to their limits. This time would be so different. Although, once she had the pregnancy confirmed, she was unable to get rid of a tiny twinge of apprehension – but it was unfounded, she was told – and there was certainly nothing evident in any of the test results. They kept their secret to themselves for some time, as Jacqui felt that many months of waiting would test Ella's patience to the limit. As Christmas approached they were able to talk in terms of the baby arriving at Easter and how the winter would pass quickly with all the things to do.

Both Ella and Tim helped Richard to redecorate the small nursery bedroom and it was a happy time for all of them as they looked forward to their family becoming even more complete.

3

Jacqui had found that she was not the only one to be pregnant. Vicky phoned her one day and broke the news; comparing dates they found that they coincided at around the same time the following Spring, which gave Jacqui a good reason to build up a better relationship with her brother's wife, sensing that Vicky needed more support than she would ever divulge.

Christmas came and went, Easter approached. Although neither of them discussed it in any great depth, they both had an area of apprehension – with Vicky it was totally about Ben and dreading his reaction if she were to have another daughter, while Jacqui could not get rid of the niggling doubt that all might not be well with her baby, although the tests showed nothing untoward at any stage.

When the time came, the joy in the fact that the two cousins shared a birthday was overshadowed by the news of Gabriel's condition. However, Jacqui continued to give support when she could, as did Richard with his honest, matter-of-fact explanations, and Vicky soon settled into the routine she insisted Ben provided - mainly that of juggling a nanny's rota supplemented by other help.

A typical Sunday silence had eventually settled in Woolston Hall, deep in the early summer countryside, but it was not a peaceful silence. Vicky was fuming, sitting in the conservatory with her laptop, furiously battering away at the keys as she composed yet another letter she knew she would never have the courage to leave on Ben's desk. Large lettering reflected her state of mind, as did the colouring she'd chosen to use. Dark red, the colour of congealed blood – thick and bold.

Half an hour ago Lucy had been banished to her own room at the top of the house where her angry screams had subsided into sobs - until she could no longer hear the footsteps receding down the stairs, that is; then she stopped, picked up a book and was soon immersed in the familiar pictures and simple sentences she knew by heart. Nowadays it was all part of her five-year-old's routine – her tantrums and vicious temper resulted in a grip of power she held over her mother and any paid help her parents engaged to look after her. It suited her to gain attention and remind them that she was not to be trusted. She endured her father's reactions – provoking him to the point of violence was an unconscious game she indulged in when she thought he had paid too much attention to her baby sister Rebecca.

This particular occasion had been caused by yet another sly attack on her baby sister, but instead of managing to get out of the way so that she had only to encounter her mother's tight-lipped pleas which usually gave her the benefit of any doubt, she had been caught in the act and incurred her father's wrath. In spite of her flailing limbs, he was still able to pick her up bodily and carry her upstairs, set her down outside her own room, propelling her inside with a push and slamming the door before she could turn to reach for the handle. He turned the key in the lock.

"I'll do some damage to that nasty little madam one day" Ben raged as he came down the stairs, brushing past his wife.

"Don't you think you've done enough already?" she snapped back, bitterly.

"What d'you expect from me? I come home and find screaming children, an incompetent wife, and nannies I pay the earth for, but never here when they're needed. I thought that girl would be around for at least part of the weekend."

"Her wretched mother's ill again and I couldn't get a childminder from the village at such short notice – I told you."

"Wouldn't surprise me if they wouldn't come for any amount of money – there's little pleasure in minding those brats, that's for sure."

He headed for the library and when the door slammed shut Vicky let out a sigh of relief; at least if he spent the remainder of the afternoon falling into a brandy-fuelled haze it would keep him quiet. The worst times were when he prowled around the house or garden, retaining enough energy to keep prodding the situation into another flare-up. She tiptoed into the hallway and listened to make sure that Becca had dozed off again now all the noise had died down, and also listened intently for any sound coming from Lucy's room on the top floor of the house; hearing nothing, she decided to leave well alone. When the au pair or nanny was not there to deal with the situation she had learned there was no point in trying to soothe her little girl – it only prolonged her tantrums. It was easier to leave her to cry herself to sleep, which was what eventually happened if she was left alone for long enough.

But Vicky herself certainly could not relax. Her heart raced and her tense jaw betrayed her emotional state. As she sat down at the table in the conservatory with the laptop, she poured all her vitriol into the letter she would never send, telling herself it was good therapy. What on earth had happened to her ideas of marriage? What had turned it into the nightmare it had become? She thought of the innocent young girl she had been only a few short years ago, when it had seemed that the subtle pursuit of Ben, the most eligible bachelor in her social circle, could result in nothing but the fairytale ending. The only source of discord that she could see at that time was his mother, but she had been so bolstered by the naievety and confidence of youth that even Sonia's reputation had failed to cause her any anxiety.

She had almost completely lost sight of the young man she had set out to marry; "the catch of the county" as one of her envious friends had commented. Why had the tenderness evaporated? It had been there until … until … She kept coming back to that Christmas Day – Sonia's birthday party, then only hours later, Lucy's birth. But he was so unreasonable – it really wasn't her fault that his wretched mother had died, and it certainly wasn't her fault that Lucy was a girl. Her mind continued down the well-trodden route of hurt, humiliation and failure – and continued to encourage the bitterness to grow, even though she knew it was unjustified.

❧

When the telephone rang she was still frustrated by the way the day had disintegrated, and it showed in the flatness of her voice as she feigned a politeness she certainly didn't feel.

"Oh, Barbara, it's you. No, it doesn't matter. Do you want to speak to Ben? Oh, well, yes, I can talk if that's really what you prefer, but I'm not very good company at the moment. Yes, Ben – *again*. He can't handle Lucy when she gets in one of her moods, and she had an appallingly awful one this afternoon."

Then it all came pouring out, as Barbara had intended it should. Alerted to the far from satisfactory situation that Jacqui had noticed more than once on weekend visits, she had agreed to do what she could. Vicky eventually talked herself to a standstill, then listened to Barbara's suggestion.

"Mmm ... yes ... I suppose we could do that. On Tuesday? Well, all right ... Ben will be away on a business trip for a few days. No, nothing planned. I never do plan anything – it's never worth the effort, quite frankly. I can escape for a few hours and be at your place by mid-day. Lucy will be at school, then she's going to a friend's birthday party; Becca will be fine with the nanny and I'll be back home for eight o'clock at the latest. I'm so desperate for some intelligent conversation."

She would tell Ben later tomorrow, when his mind was more on business matters and he would only half hear any news she passed on. What *had* happened to them, she wondered - this was not at all what she had expected when they married. Realising that life wouldn't be easy with her mother-in-law around and notoriously such a difficult figure, nonetheless she naively thought that Ben would be much more supportive of his young new wife – instead of which he had stepped back from any tense situations, simply saying it was her duty to learn all that Sonia had to teach her about running the household that she would eventually take over.

The main problem had been that she was pitched into taking over in the worst of all circumstances. Only someone with superhuman strengths could have been expected to handle Sonia's death, her own child being born, then Ben's resentment due to what he saw as her failure to produce a son.

What a nightmare the whole of that first year had been. Her spirit had felt crushed, and she knew that it was only with the sympathetic help of her doctor she had avoided the worst of the post-natal depression that hovered around the edges of her mind for months. That, coupled with the sheer physical demands of the children and running the Hall, had left her with such negativity that all her fight had gone.

The Ripples and the Tapestries

After what transpired after the funeral, when Barbara had unwisely revealed her closeness to some of the business clients, Vicky had later written to apologise for the unkind things she had said, blaming her health and the stress of the occasion. Barbara was grateful that the gap had been bridged because she could see that she, of all people, could actually help Vicky more than anyone.

Regardless of the fact that Ben had forbidden 'that woman' as he continued to call her, to be any part of their lives after learning at the funeral of Barbara's betrayal of Sonia's friendship, both Jacqui and Vicky had secretly kept in touch with her, which gave Barbara the opportunity to help heal the rift between the two young women. Barbara wanted to retain the contact with the Hall, the scene of so much in her life. Surely Ben would eventually be able to forgive his late mother's best friend.

As indeed he eventually did – Jacqui poured oil on the troubled waters and helped him see that as it was all in the past, it was a useless reaction to have on his mother's behalf, so Barbara had been invited back to the Hall, and had again become the family friend.

Vicky returned to the thoughts she had put down on the machine – skipped through them at random, taking satisfaction from any particularly well-turned phrases - paused - then purposefully highlighted the whole of the text and pressed 'delete' with a sigh of relief. It rid her of the immediate after-effects of anger, but did nothing to unravel the knot of apprehension in her stomach, as she closed the lid of the laptop. Four years on, what had changed? As a couple, they seemed no further forward and she sometimes wondered what kept them together; Ben had his work to escape to, and thinking of that, she wondered bitterly if that was the answer – it was not so much the fact that it would damage his standing if they separated, but the financial consequences of a legal settlement, which would most probably result in the loss of his business.

Where would it all end, she wondered? Her visit to Barbara was desperately needed and she hoped her friend might be able to suggest some solutions.

4

She would never forget Richard's reaction to Gabriel's birth. He was so solicitous, so concerned for both of them yet managed to be completely reassuring at the same time. The eventual confirmation of the misgivings she felt throughout the pregnancy had been a blow for them both, however much they made the best of it, but Jacqui knew he would help her with this, as he had with everything else.

"Let's take as many photos as we can" Richard said "I mean every day, from now on. He's going to be the most photographed baby in the world!"

He'd taken all of the photographs any first time father would – those precious moments after the birth, trying to capture the depths in the eyes that are to be found in the first few moments of a baby's life, then requesting that the nursing staff took one of the three of them. Now the older children were at the bedside and Richard's parents, happy to meet their first grandson, were eager to be part of the family group. The camera was passed around from one to the other. Gabriel slept on, imperturbably.

It was to prove the beginning of a unique record over time, and one that they were so glad they had started. Tim and Ella joined in and with the computer safely storing the results they were able to record every change, every small milestone in Gabriel's life.

When he was ready to come home Richard collected mother and baby from the Maternity Unit, at the hospital where he himself worked in a department at the other end of the building. As he helped her, she knew that no amount of love and devotion would be lacking as their little son grew. Richard's mother, especially, was looking forward to helping with the first few weeks while they were all adjusting to new routines, and was waiting at their house with the older children, who could hardly contain their excitement.

Ella had been trying to think of things that Gabriel might like to have around, and had already been spending pocket money on soft toys. Tim had been more of the protective and practical older brother, making sure that he knew how to install the car seat when it needed to be transferred from one car to another. They had both been pleased that their little brother had safely arrived in the world, and by mutual agreement Richard and Jacqui had told them of only the barest knowledge of Gabriel's condition. They knew that he had needed a great deal of medical attention in the first few days, which was why he did not come home straight away, but Jacqui felt it would be better to explain any details as they arose – for example, he was having great difficulty with feeding normally, so instead of a naso-gastric tube he might have one installed that would take food through the stomach wall.

"I can answer their questions there and then, and see how much more they need to know" she explained to Richard. "It won't be long before they put two and two together and realise that there will be things he won't be able to do."

"There aren't really any guidelines on that sort of thing" commented Richard. "There's support for parents, but mainly for mothers – and not much of that as far as I can tell; after that, it's up to each family to find out for themselves. Specific charities help with advice on practical matters, of course, but the big problem seems to be the variations according to where people live."

※

With Richard's mother helping in the background, Jacqui soon felt capable of managing on her own during the day.

"But I don't know where would I have been without you!" she said, giving Muriel a loving hug as she left at the end of the first ten days.

"Now remember – I'll come here for the day to look after Ella and Tim when you go to the hospital with Richard for that follow-up visit next week. After that we can see how much time to allow and whether you'd like me to come with you or stay here when there are any other visits you feel you can't manage on your own."

Medically, Gabriel was to be monitored regularly for the first few months and a check kept on his progress. There was an appointments system and waiting times were kept to a minimum, as far as possible, for the special needs babies. Nurses were cheery and the clinic was brightly decorated. At this first appointment Jacqui was not quite sure what to expect, and was glad that Richard was with her. Gabriel was weighed and a small blood sample was taken "to assess his immune system" Richard whispered.

"The most noticeable thing about Gabriel is he seems unable to react in the way my other two did" Jacqui found herself telling the middle-aged woman doctor who came into the cubicle. "He doesn't cry, he doesn't smile, and he can't make many sounds – it's very difficult to tell whether there's anything wrong with him."

"I find most mothers saying that sort of thing. No response to good or bad, and it's just the luck of the draw whether you have a baby that smiles or not: but be thankful - at least you don't have one with the non-stop wailing that some mothers have to put up with. He's more underweight than I would like, so it's time we thought of the gastro tube for feeding him. It's a minor operation, of course, and nothing to worry about. Your husband's a great help, I'm sure." She looked vaguely towards Richard and half smiled. "Check at the desk on your way out and make sure they have the correct address then you'll get the letter in due course." She turned back to her notes.

"I shall explode! Didn't you feel she was just the tiniest bit patronising?" Jacqui burst out once they were safely outside and on their way to the car park.

"I thought she was doing her best to be reassuring! She's probably had a long hard day and we're at the end of it – don't be too hard on us poor overworked medics!"

"Sorry, Richard, but sometimes I feel very vulnerable. And as for Gabriel – he's got to have yet another painful treatment. It's too much for one little scrap to cope with." She burst into tears, and Richard understood only too well that this would not be the time to echo the doctor's attempts at reassurance that things were normal for this type of baby. Sometimes the medical profession was difficult to defend.

※

The file of photographs were supplemented by another – Richard had started keeping an account of his son's life. It gave him something to look forward to at the end of each day and was just a factual record of anything Jacqui or the children told him – mostly ordinary things that had happened, like Ella taking Gabriel the first daisies that had appeared in the spring sunshine.

At the same time, Richard had also started to keep a private journal – handwritten in a notebook and, uncharacteristically for him, kept secret from his wife. In it he could record his deepest, and darkest thoughts – things she should never know, or at least, not for a long, long time. He realised that this was a useful form of therapy and as he wrote, passed no judgement on himself – these were his thoughts of the moment, not to be read and re-read, but just to be noted – but for what purpose other than that of the moment, he had no plans.

◈

Jacqui soon felt she was an old hand at anticipating Gabriel's needs. The doctor's comment, though it had rankled at first, made her think about other mothers. As she became used to the clinic visits where Gabriel's progress was checked, she even decided to go on her own one week.

"Kay, it's lovely to have you here, but I'd like to try to manage the clinic on my own next time. If you could just come over in time to collect Ella from school, that would be the best help, then I won't have to feel guilty about disrupting your life."

Her mother-in-law sensed that Jacqui was making an attempt to lead as normal a life as possible. An independent woman herself, she remembered how important it had been to manage on her own at times.

"If you're absolutely sure" she replied, carrying Gabriel up the steps to the front door "I'd really look forward to having time on my own with Ella. She wants to learn about embroidery for a school project and I have some old pattern books she could look through."

There was one mother Jacqui had noticed more than the others, as they always seemed to coincide with their appointment times. She looked too young to be a mother at all – hardly out of school - and she was always alone. This time she was there, as usual, but hardly glanced up as Jacqui spoke to her.

"How's Stacey today?" The baby's mother looked up, startled.

The Ripples and the Tapestries

"I heard you talking to her last time, that's how I know her name. My little boy's Gabriel and he's just three months old."

"Doctor's been called to the wards for an emergency – she'll be back as soon as she can."

The nurse had put her head round the door apologetically.

"Shall we have a cup of tea? I could go back down the corridor to the machine …" Jacqui stopped as she saw the tears falling down the girl's cheeks. "Or I'll stay here if you'd rather have company … I'm Jacqui, by the way."

Gradually the story came out, with occasional sobs. Ria told her that Stacey's father, her boyfriend, had moved out.

"He couldn't stand the crying all the time, he said. Says he agrees with me Mom – it's a punishment for me. But I know loads of girls who've done nothing but drink and smoke – and I don't mean ordinary ciggies – and *their* babies are alright. I wish I'd done away with her, but I was too far gone by the time I asked, and then, when they found out and offered it to me I was too much of a coward. All I could think of by then was that I'd have someone to love me and need me. Not like this, though. I've had more than enough some days."

As she sat listening, Jacqui realised she had come face to face with a member of a world she'd hardly ever been aware of existing. Her own life, however imperfect, had shielded her from many of the social difficulties that Ria had encountered all of her life. She heard about Ria's unknown father, an alcoholic mother with boyfriends who abused both of them, and eventual years of foster care – all this, and Ria was still under twenty years old. Her boyfriend had done his best up to a point, but when he realised the difficult times ahead he couldn't face them.

"I tell you straight – if the Social don't come up with some help soon, and I mean *real* help, I'm going to hand her in. Let them deal with it – and foster homes ain't too bad, if you get the right one."

Jacqui managed to disguise her horrified reaction and changed the subject.

"Have you had any photos taken? Look – I always carry my little camera with me. If you'd let me, I'd love to do that. She's not crying so much today, so I'm sure I could get a good one" Jacqui offered. "I can send it on to you – come on, it won't take a minute."

"It would be rather nice, I suppose. She hasn't had many taken since she was born – just the odd one on my mobile."

Ria relaxed and taking the photos passed away the time until the doctor returned. Ria went in first and waved at Jacqui on her way out.

"See you next time."

Later, as she told Richard about her encounter, Jacqui raised the subject of support for mothers in that situation.

" … and it's isolating enough when you're at the baby stage - she was telling me how she sometimes can't face going out because of the way people look at her baby, then turn away. Her mother doesn't appear to be around much, either."

"You can't save the world" Richard said gently. "No system is ever going to be perfect for everyone – people have to play their part as well."

"But where do you start with a family like Ria's? I felt completely out of my depth and as if I was going to sound so patronising whatever I said. All I could do was to suggest taking stupid photographs."

"But she didn't object to that, by the sound of it - and if that's all you actually do, and she eventually has to hand her baby over for adoption, then at least you can hope that the photos will help her in some way. Come on, my love – you're tired and worried, I can see that, but the bottom line is that we sometimes have to be practical and leave people to find their own solutions and live with the consequences if it's not perfect."

The printed photographs and a covering letter wishing them both well were posted to the address Ria had given her, but there was no reply, nor did they meet again at the hospital. This and other episodes drifted in and out of Jacqui's thoughts, then she continued to doze for a while, feeling very, very fortunate in having the family life she did.

She was unaware, however, that Richard took this and other conversations she reported deep into his own heart, so that later they would form the basis of what was to become their life's mission in a way neither he nor Jacqui could have ever foreseen.

The Ripples and the Tapestries

Returning from their walk with flushed faces, Tim and Ella had raced ahead, while Richard carried their baby brother Gabriel cradled safely in his arms.

Jacqui loved their homecomings. She stepped off the bottom stair and walked into the kitchen just as the two older ones removed their shoes and outer jackets in the back porch and raced to switch on their favourite teatime programme. Richard handed Gabriel to her after their greeting kiss; the baby received her kiss too – wide-eyed and placid, but aware enough to show the slight twisting of his mouth which they had learned to recognise as his only way of smiling. She removed his outer clothes, checked his hands and feet to make sure he was warm enough, then set him down in the comfortable reclining baby chair with a light blanket tucked around him, so that he could drift off to sleep as he usually did, with the comforting sounds of people talking in the background. His routine feed would be later, after they had all eaten.

"Half an hour until tea" she called into the room where the television set was showing the latest children's cartoon "and please turn down the volume so that Gabriel can settle. Richard, there's a message for you – Doctor Hartley, Mummy's old doctor. Would you ring him back some time this weekend?"

"I wonder what's made him get in touch" Richard looked thoughtful. "Perhaps it's some more locum work, although I thought he'd found someone else to do that. I'll phone him while you're getting tea finalised – unless you need me to help?"

"No, I'll be fine – everything's almost ready."

Richard was such a tower of strength, she often mused – how many men would take on the two older children so willingly, then be able to cope with the blow that his own child had been born with brain damage and limited life expectancy?

❧

Whenever Richard's work allowed, they always sat round the kitchen table after their evening meal had been cleared away. It was their family discussion time – a precious part of the day when they all had the chance to talk about events good and bad, whatever affected them. There was always plenty of lightheartedness and laughter.

"... and you never guess what we did when we realised the mud was too deep to go through because our wellingtons are too short? Ella was quite frightened ..."

"No I wasn't" said Ella "I was *worried*, Richard said ..."

"So you should be – you might have lost your socks!" Richard took up his cue from Tim "and we know what might happen to socks that get lost in the mud, don't we?"

"They get used by the mud monsters to make houses!" Ella giggled.

" ... so Richard made up this game of saving the Princess from the mud monsters and gave her a piggy back across the path. He was holding Gabriel at the front of him and Ella on his back, so he looked really funny, like a monster with three heads. I was alright, though, because I've got longer legs and bigger boots – and in any case the mud monsters won't touch my socks; they only like blue ones."

Tim had inherited his father's sense of the ridiculous, Jacqui thought, remembering what had drawn her to Zak, her first husband.

Ella was much more serious. No wonder she had been her grandmother Sonia's favourite in the brief few years before Sonia's death. Jacqui remembered how, when Ella was tiny, no matter how sticky her hands were, however grubby her face, Sonia had always been prepared to show affection in a way that she had never been able to with her own daughter.

The conversation ran its course, then the two older children returned to the playroom to draw pictures – Tim's were always cartoons of strange creatures with feelers that ended in useful tools like hammers and forks: Ella's were elaborately detailed patterns, full of swirls and colour, but very structured.

"What was Doctor Hartley's call about? Does he want you to work for him again?"

"It's *much* more exciting than that" Richard answered, closing the kitchen door so that the children could not hear; "but the implications are huge. Could you bear to wait until we're on our own later? I need to make sure we can give it our undivided attention."

5

"I honestly don't know how you manage it" Vicky said to her sister-in-law "manage all of it, I mean – the children have such different needs, and on top of it all you have Richard to think of."

"I sometimes wonder myself!"

Jacqui tried to laugh it off, but sensed that Vicky was perhaps trying to introduce a difficult topic – maybe get some information that would help with her own situation. "I keep coming back to the importance of talking about everything – whether it's the children's school work or how I can get to Gabriel's next hospital appointment – and we all seem to pull together."

"You and Richard are so alike in that respect. He really is the one for you, isn't he? I never knew Anthony – did it work the same way as well?"

Jacqui paused before answering.

"I don't quite know how to explain it – I always thought Anthony was my soulmate, and I'm still certain he was in many respects, but with Richard it's so different, and so much more ... I can't explain it properly – it feels like one of those things that you can only talk to someone else who's experienced it, and I don't want to hurt you, but ... "

"... but Ben and I obviously don't have that. Yes, it hurts. Oh Jacqui, it *does* hurt. I had such hopes when we married, but I feel as if I've been struggling up the most impossible mountain ever since, and instead of helping me, he's been piling rocks into my backpack as fast as he can go! I can feel myself turning into the person he's always accusing me of being, and I hate it, but I don't know how to do anything about it."

They were sitting at the kitchen table on one of Vicky's 'escape days' Barbara had suggested she planned – days when she left the baby in the care of Nanny, and Lucy with the au pair, so that she could spend time struggling to find out, with Jacqui's help, the person she now was and the one she was trying to be. Jacqui felt hopeful, for the courage of this woman who was married to her brother Ben was, in spite of everything, devoted to him.

Ben, the successful businessman, the man who could be charm

itself to his clients, had developed an increasingly dark side since his mother's death: Jacqui knew, from her own observations, that he was becoming more reliant on alcohol, and suspected that his moodiness and the reactions he provoked in his wife could eventually lead him to seek solace elsewhere – as his father had done. Although Jacqui had been the result of that loving liaison, which was still a secret known only to herself and Ben, she didn't wish to see history repeat itself – it had led to far too much misery for all concerned. But for how long his wife's loyalty could last if he continued to abuse it, was debatable. Vicky had told her of the occasions when her arm had been gripped so fiercely that the bruises showed for days and how her big fear was that one day he'd do that or more to Lucy, who seemed to delight in goading him to a point of fury. Jacqui shuddered slightly at the thought.

"Who does Ben confide in? Does he have a particular friend who could help him see what's happening between the two of you?"

"Not really, as far as I know. I've sometimes wondered if he should go to see Dr Hartley, but he wouldn't want his mother's old GP to know about everything, I don't suppose. Now that he and Barbara are speaking again, sometimes he'll talk with her – the two of them go into the library when she visits and they both reminisce about Sonia – helped by copious amounts of brandy. But I don't suppose either of them gives me a thought."

"At least they find things to talk about – it was a dreadful time when they wouldn't even do that, and Barbara was so miserable at being cut off – I'm sure she'd be willing to help."

"Well, he certainly won't ask her outright, even if he's prepared to admit that there are difficulties. He's so convinced that it's all my fault – my fault for not having the son he wanted, then repeating the same 'mistake' by having Becca: *certainly* my fault for causing his mother's death. That's four years ago, for heavens' sake! Yes, I know it's all nonsense and medically it can be proven wrong, but 'wrong' doesn't come into Ben's self image, so that's the way he thinks. I'm so tired of it all, Jacqui, so very, very tired - and some days I'd give anything to just lie down, go to sleep and wake up in another life."

Jacqui reached out her hand to her sister-in-law, but the energy had almost visibly drained out of Vicky as she spoke, and there was no reaction.

The Ripples and the Tapestries

"We can't have you feeling like this. Have *you* been to Doctor Hartley?"

"No, I went to see someone else. He recommended a long stay in a private residential place then months of therapy, but I really think that it would serve no purpose – Ben would see it as me shirking my duty and it would drive us further apart. If only we *could* talk – but we're both very good at avoiding each other in that huge house."

Jacqui was thoughtful. She remembered those bleak months after Sonia's funeral when Ben had banned Barbara from any contact with Vicky, and had also warned Jacqui not to speak to her, although Jacqui was not one to be told who her friends should be, so had remained discreetly in touch. Vicky had baby Lucy to adjust to, as well as the staffing problems at the Hall, and understandably had no energy to do little else - so Ben was left feeling he had imposed his will without question.

Managing to arrange the occasional visit to Barbara, Jacqui had seen for herself just how much her mother's old friend had been upset – after all, her secret life had been just that – totally secret and conducted with the utmost discretion so that no breath of scandal had damaged the family. In any case, so many years had passed since it all took place. What worried Jacqui most was that Vicky had been deprived of an older friend – as indeed had Ben.

∽∾

It took some time for the right opportunity to present itself, but eventually Jacqui managed to get Ben on his own, and she tactfully insisted they had a heart-to-heart talk about family matters. Lucy's christening was being planned, and it provided the ideal opportunity as Ben had asked for his sister's help with the guest list. Jacqui had been able to persuade him that Barbara should be invited to attend, as a peace offering – and, as she pointed out to him, events after Sonia's death revealed that no-one was blameless as far as secrecy was concerned – especially Sonia herself. However, it was up to them both, as brother and sister, to set a new example for the family by agreeing to let the past remain buried and make a new start.

Somewhat reluctantly Ben agreed to offering the olive branch, but even he'd had to admit that he had missed Barbara's company – not just for her reminiscences about his mother and times gone by, but for her wisdom about business matters, and inside knowledge about some of his oldest clients.

※※

Now, after the intervening years when everything had settled down again, Ben had on more than one occasion spontaneously hugged Barbara and thanked her for becoming part of their family again. The children adored their Auntie Babs and she willingly entertained them when she visited; they in their turn would make sure she had plenty of rest, and delighted in taking her breakfast in bed, where she would recount endless tales of her own childhood in a district of Birmingham – the school she attended with its stuffy classrooms, and the way the children had to line up in the playground each morning, regardless of the weather, to do physical exercises - which they found fascinating. As she talked, the memories came flooding back, and her entertaining way of describing characters and the sometimes embarrassing consequences of her own and classmates' behaviour, brought the characters to life and caused great gales of laughter to echo from her room. Soon the teachers, the class bully, the 'brainiest' boy and girl in the school were as familiar to them as their own school friends.

But she was careful to restrict these stories to her own experiences and not involve her friend Sonia in any of the revelations, respecting what would undoubtedly have been Sonia's wishes to leave *her* childhood reminiscences behind her.

6

As months passed and Barbara was now never far from their thoughts in between her visits, one day Jacqui noticed with great concern when talking on the phone, she was obviously short of breath.

"Take no notice" she wheezed "it's all those years of sophisticated smoking, before we were told it was bad for our health. It will pass."

"I hope you're right, Auntie Babs. I know you gave it up some time ago, but have you been to see the doctor? Just to stop us worrying."

"Oh, my doctor isn't at all like your lovely Richard, you know – I get told off for having middleaged spread, not exercising enough and generally receiving the implication that whatever is wrong it's completely my own fault and they wish I'd go away and stop complicating their lives."

"Look – why don't you come and stay here for a few days? The only proviso I'll make is that you go to your doctor and see if you have anything infectious – if not, then do come and stay here."

"Bless you, Jacqui – I will go, and I'll let you know if I can come. In any case Vicky's coming to see me at the end of next week, and that's only a few days away. It seems to do her good to get away for a day; she tells me I'm her safety valve. Now don't you worry, I'll let you know if I need you in the meantime. If you don't hear from me, I've responded to cough mixture and I'm probably out enjoying myself."

Vicky found out what had actually happened when she went to Barbara's flat as arranged. She had seen her doctor and was immediately admitted to hospital where they diagnosed pneumonia, eventually being released after three day's stay, after reassuring the hospital staff that she would not be on her own. She managed to play the whole episode very low key and shrug it off as if it were of no concern. Arriving the next day, Vicky was shocked by Barbara's appearance.

"Why on earth didn't you let us know?" she asked.

"Judging by the look on your face now, when I'm so much better than I was, you'd have been even more shocked to have seen me then – and there would have been nothing you could have done. So I thought it was better you were kept in the dark as far as possible."

Vicky saw that there was no point in protesting about the events of the past few days, but made a mental note that she and Jacqui should be more vigilant in future. When Barbara dozed off to sleep in her armchair, mid-sentence and worn out with the effort of talking, she abandoned her plan to return home on the evening train and rang Jacqui to explain.

"Jacqui, we have to do *something* – I'll wait to see how she is after tonight; hopefully what she needs is a good night's sleep in her own bed, and I'll stock up her supplies; her freezer's almost empty and I do wonder if she's been bothering to eat properly. Give me a ring in the morning after the children have gone to school and we'll decide how to handle it."

After helping Barbara to bed, Vicky decided to spend the night in the spare bedroom, borrowing nightwear and a robe. Deal with one thing at a time, she told herself – maybe Barbara really would feel better in the morning and then everything would return to normal. Sleeping lightly as she usually did, in order to hear the children's slightest movement, she was wakened by the sound of Barbara's rasping breath. Immediately wide awake, she rushed into the main bedroom and saw her dear friend leaning over the side of the bed, gasping for air. The spasms lasted only for a minute or two, but it seemed an age before steadier breathing was possible, and Vicky's mind was racing through scenarios of calling emergency services and obtaining help. Barbara must have read her mind.

"Don't do it" she commanded in a hoarse whisper "... I saw the notes ... the doctor's notes ... they won't rescuscitate me, you know ...better off ... out of the way ..."

Vicky was horrified, but tried not to show it. She'd have to have a word with Richard and see what he could advise – but in the meantime what could she do? She sat on the bed, with Barbara propped against her, as that seemed to be the most comfortable position for her. How long they had sat there she had no idea, but would have willingly stayed there for hours as long as it helped. Then, when her breathing had quietened down and Vicky thought she might have gone back to sleep, Barbara spoke in a near normal voice – but distant and so full of sorrow that Vicky could barely manage to listen.

"All those years ... Sonia never knew. I sometimes wonder how I managed to keep quiet about it for so long."

"Sssshhhhh Auntie Babs – you talked about that a long time ago."

"No ... not that ... this is ... is something else that no-one knows; no-one at all." Tears started to stream down the thin cheeks. Vicky thought incongrously that the weight loss the doctors had urged Barbara to make had happened of its own accord and she bitterly hoped they would be pleased.

"I *always* loved him; from the first day I walked into that office. I knew then that he was going to be the only one I could ever consider spending the rest of my life with."

Was she hearing correctly? Vicky was acutely alert now and waited to hear more.

"Oh he was so handsome. Ex navy, you see, and all the nice girls ... but was *I* nice enough? Who was I, from a mean little house in the poor end of a Birmingham suburb, to make enough of an impression on such a sophisticated man? He wouldn't even give me the time of day. And of course, I was right. In any case, Sonia decided he was to be the one for her – and set out to get him.

"It broke my heart to see how she schemed and manipulated – how she ingratiated herself with his father, and it was all done with such cynicism. She told me of course – told me her plans each week, each day even. She used to boast how she would get his commitment by the end of the summer, then set out to tantalise him and make promises that she had no intention of keeping – just to keep his interest. It worked. And I had to stand by and watch.

"I used to cry myself to sleep each night, imagining how I would comfort him and show him what gentle adoring love could be like – if only he would notice me. But she had him bewitched, and the more she taunted and teased, the more he thought he loved her. Then, the Monday after his birthday, she came into the office late, with that big diamond on her hand, making sure everyone noticed."

Vicky heard the bitterness in the old voice – bitter pain that had lasted a lifetime, still as acute as that original pain. What must it have cost Barbara to see the man she loved so intensely, snatched by a scheming ambitious woman – to stand by and pretend, and to keep that secret for the whole of her life?

"They were married and we lost touch when I went to work for another firm, thank goodness: it gave me time for the pain to ease. Then some years later, Sonia wrote and offered me the post of assistant for their conferences. Of course I had my doubts, but I was older then, and foolishly imagined that I wouldn't feel so bad. But it *was* torture. I hoped that I would be noticed – hoped for the fairytale ending, but all Geoffrey could see was his old office girl who'd got the ability to keep his clients happy. Just *how* happy, I'm sure he had no idea."

Vicky suppressed a shudder, and tried to forget that she was sitting in a room that must have been the setting for so much of Barbara's hidden past. It was large, elegant and sumptuous, swathes of silk and satin draped themselves over curtain rails and fell to the floor, cascading on to the luxurious dark blue carpet; richly embroidered cushions were piled high on the rose coloured chaise longue; a Venetian glass chandelier complimented the elegantly decorated plasterwork ceiling and the heavily gilded overmantel mirror reflected and expanded the room. The atmosphere was redolent of relaxed and fulfilling times and many of the furnishings had come with their own intimate histories, even before they found their way into her home.

"I loved him so much – I *know* I could have given him happiness. It's all been such a waste."

She sighed and her head rolled forward. For one awful moment Vicky thought she might have taken her last breath. But to her great relief, Barbara rallied herself, sat upright and looked slowly around the room, visibly gaining comfort from the familiar surroundings and breathing more easily.

"Not a word of that to anyone – *anyone* – d'you hear? I just needed to get it off my chest and you're a good friend. " Her voice sounded almost normal. "I'll be alright now, so you can pass me that glass of water then I'll let you catch up on some sleep or *you'll* be worn out."

❧

It certainly was a change, and thankfully one that lasted. Vicky was able to stay another night and make sure that Barbara had everything she needed, then travelled back home to the Hall. She made a lengthy phone call to Jacqui, although, true to her word, she revealed nothing of Barbara's confidences made in the small hours of that anxious night.

Jacqui later discussed Barbara's health with Richard.

"I don't think any of us could have coped with another loss, so we must make sure she doesn't get in that state again. Richard – is there any truth in what she said?"

"About DNR notes, the non-resuscitation? Oh yes, we get guidelines about age and illness and probability of survival all the time. It's ironic – at the beginning of life all efforts are made to prolong it, even though an estimated quality of life could be no quality at all – while at the other it's easy to justify saying enough is enough, and simply take no action, when there could be several years of quite useful life left."

Jacqui looked shocked.

"But older people often have others dependent on them – family members, for instance, and it must affect more lives than just the patient."

"That's part of the huge debate that has been rumbling around for years. I'm a doctor, and, as doctors, we all swear allegiance to the Hippocratic oath. Yet there are many times when I've seen colleagues faced with impossible decisions, and of course the general praticioners have to live with them too – being reminded each time one of the family comes for their own health care afterwards – all the time wondering whether a different decision should have been made, or worse still, realising that it should *definitely* have been attempted. It's the subject of one of the articles I've written – whether or not they'll publish remains to be seen."

❧☙

Refilling their cups of tea one afternoon, Jacqui returned to the ongoing topic of Vicky's concerns about Ben, and offered what comfort she could.

"If you like, I'll have a word with Barbara and just say that you're worried. She's not stupid, and she knows that the drinking is, at the very least, no good for his health. Leave it with me to choose the right time, would you?"

Vicky raised her tear-stained face and managed a relieved nod. It was strange, thinking back to how she had felt unable to relate to Jacqui when they had first met, feeling her sister-in-law irritated her beyond measure by always seeming far too forgiving to stand up to anyone. Now she realised that she just had her own way of getting to the conclusion she wanted without any confrontation, simply by standing back and finding reasons for peoples' actions and words, then finding the right course to take.

She sighed a deep long sigh.

"Penny for them?" Jacqui asked.

"Priceless! No, not my thoughts – *you*! Where would we all be without you? You're like the hub of the family wheel – the still, calm centre, whereas everyone else is running round like headless chickens – which is about the most mixed up farmyard metaphor I could have dreamed up ...!"

They both laughed - Vicky with relief, Jacqui to hide embarrassment.

"If only you knew – but we'll get you there, wherever 'there' is."

∾

Barbara, of course, was only too willing to do what she could. She knew that Ben would be difficult to persuade, but there had to be some way of getting him to talk – and, more importantly, *listen* – to his wife. It would have to be somewhere not too difficult to arrange, preferably a space and a time in their busy lives where they would get no interruptions from the children or staff. Holidays were not easy in the circumstances, and she knew it would be more helpful for a solution to be as spontaneous as possible.

"Leave it with me" she said to Jacqui, then phoned her back the next day.

"Jacqui - how would you feel about setting a precedent?"

"What do you mean?"

"Well, I had an idea that the Gatehouse might be the ideal place for privacy and seclusion, whether for an hour or two or longer, but it's a bit intimidating to expect Ben to fall in with that idea straight away – he'd feel too self-conscious."

"I agree – but where do I come into the scheme?"

"It would be less threatening if it were you and Richard, needing private, uninterrupted time to sort out family plans. Just for this occasion, if Richard's parents could take over for you, perhaps you could make it an overnight stay."

"I'll have a word with Richard this evening. It might be a really good idea anyway – we've seldom had the chance to be completely on our own since Gabriel was born and at home I find I'm always half listening for any sound – even more so than with the other two."

"How is he getting on these days?" Barbara was very fond of both babies in the family, but had a special fondness for Gabriel.

"He's doing really well avoiding any infections. That's been my biggest worry, because of Tim and Ella being at school and in contact with all sorts of viruses – but we can't keep him wrapped in cotton wool, and I've always felt he might be able to build up his own resistance if we treat him as normally as possible. Richard agrees, thank goodness. I know it's going to sound silly, though, but … " her voice wavered.

"Do go on Jacqui …"

"Well … I know it's a small thing, and I know it's physically impossible because his muscles and nerves aren't linked, but oh, I *do* wish that he could smile … it's what every mother wants, isn't it – to know that her child is happy … and I can't … " She could no longer hold back her tears and sobbed down the line, trying to apologise to the friend who had always been prepared to hear and help.

Barbara soothed her, reassuring her that apologies were unnecessary. But it was unusual these days for Jacqui to let the mask slip in this way – she had learned so well how to find the positive outlook she had on life – and Barbara knew it indicated how much tension was bubbling under the surface of the face she presented to the world. The Gatehouse idea had come not a moment too soon, by the sound of it, so that they would be able to have the space they needed together, without any distractions.

※

Jacqui's upbeat outlook hadn't always been in her best interest, Barbara remembered, thinking back in time over four years ago, as

Vicky raged after Sonia's funeral, telling Barbara why she found it so difficult to like her sister-in-law. The "Miss Goody Two-shoes" epithet had summed up exactly what Vicky felt at the time.

Although she could see Vicky's point of view, Barbara knew much more of the background to Jacqui's nature. She had been more like her father, who was also an optimist and always saw something good as a potential outcome of negative situations. But when Jacqui's first marriage ended Barbara had seen that there was a downside to that positive nature, and the struggle that Jacqui had to regain her natural balance hit her so hard because of how she had gladly put everything she could into the marriage. Zak had been the lead singer of a successful band and approaching the peak of his career. Ambition coupled with immaturity meant he was not prepared for parenthood. Jacqui's "mistake" as he'd always called her pregnancy (not taking any responsibility for his own part in the proceedings, of course), had interfered with his music, his promotions and his life – and the inevitable happened;. On his return he went elsewhere for an unfettered welcome at the end of a night's gig, instead of to a young wife racked with morning sickness, wanting him to set up home somewhere more suited to a young baby than their current flat. Zak could foresee trouble – plenty of his friends had learned that babies and show business did not mix. By the time Tim was born, his father was on tour in Germany and sent a congratulations card, enclosing a note saying he wanted a divorce. Zak's betrayal made Jacqui question all the values she held dear, and it had proved to be an almost disastrous learning curve – one that she might not have survived without her good friend Barbara, who filled the gap that should have been occupied by Sonia.

The divorce and unwelcome publicity had been truly awful, and after a period when she felt she could hardly bear to face the world, Jacqui recovered, with Barbara's help. Eventually she met Anthony at a party she'd reluctantly been persuaded to attend and there was an immediate attraction. It was a swift romance, a quiet wedding that was arranged almost before she had time to draw breath, and within months she found she was pregnant again. Such happiness was more than she could have any right to expect, she thought as she laid the table for dinner one evening, preparing to find the right moment to tell her husband the news she had had confirmed by her doctor that day, hoping that he would be as delighted as she was herself. But instead of hearing Anthony's key in the door, the bell rang and she opened it to find a two policemen on the doorstep.

The fatal road accident, the loss of hopes for a normal life, meant that Jacqui spent most of her pregnancy in a prolongued state of shock. Sonia, her mother, again would have nothing to do with Jacqui's problems. Having been so censorious over Zak's behaviour, she was only slightly more accepting of Anthony – but at least he was a professional, after a fashion, although a hypnotherapist was only slightly less off-beat.

Once more it was Barbara who put her own life on hold, and came to her rescue.

✥

All of this was put behind her when she met Richard, and Barbara had breathed a sigh of relief when Jacqui met him at her charity event, when he had been delegated by the hospital to receive the funds they had collected. Jacqui had simply been helping out, never suspecting she was going to meet the man who would change everything for ever. Just a little older, settled in a career which had taken priority in his life - he was a man who could be respected and trusted, Barbara intuitively felt. She had done everything possible to encourage their relationship and the strength of their love that grew day by day. The birth of Gabriel had been a shock to them all. If anyone deserved a period of plain sailing it was Jacqui, but she and Richard willingly shouldered the responsibility of their little son and the knowledge that he would possibly be with them for only a short time.

Now, having heard the strain in Jacqui's voice, Barbara knew that action needed to be taken as soon as was practical. They continued to talk about the Gatehouse and how to introduce the idea to Ben. Barbara undertook to speak with Vicky, and when she did, even the thought of a possible improvement to to her life with her surly husband cheered her greatly.

❧ 7 ❧

Jacqui and Richard sat until well into the night, discussing the implications of Doctor Hartley's phone call and his offer to give Richard first refusal of taking over the practice. They tried to weigh up all the implications for Richard's career, the children's schooling and then started to wonder about where they would live.

"So many things to consider" he said "and not least, could you cope with moving house to a new district? I know it's in an area where you grew up, but many things have changed, so it would be almost like starting afresh."

"But I'd soon make friends with other mothers, I'm sure – schools are great meeting places you know. Besides, I'd be able to see Vicky and Ben much more. *My* concern is for your mother and father and how it would mean moving further away from them – they've been absolutely wonderful with helping us in so many ways, and I wouldn't want them to feel slighted."

"I'm sure they'll be fine – they've always backed me in all my major decisions, and I don't suppose they're going to change now. In fact Mum will be thrilled – she's always seen me more as a country doctor."

They went to bed, talking far into the night, with many thoughts of how life could suddenly take unexpected twists and turns.

When Jacqui phoned with the news of Doctor Hartley's offer, Vicky was thrilled.

"Oh, I'm so glad! He has accepted – hasn't he?"

"Well, we have to think about all the implications, but there are so many good things about it that I can't see us passing this over. Moving house was not at all one of the things on our agenda, and of course, we'll have to find the right house first - but as far as the work's concerned, Richard's the ideal candidate for the practice and it will get him out of the hospital rat-race."

❧❧

Later that day, as she thought of the way Richard had welcomed the locum work when the opportunity occasionally occurred, it had always been obvious that general practice was his first love in his medical profession. He had felt obliged to pursue the hospital career, because that had been an unmissable opportunity which presented itself at the right time. But through Doctor Hartley's generosity he now had a different option, and one which gave his family the chance of living a more suitable lifestyle out of the city, in the countryside.

They were detemined to make full use of the month's grace they had been given, then finally decide. Jacqui was in favour of not mentioning anything to the children until they had made the decision.

"I know we're supposed to be democratic" she said "but I think it will only confuse them. It's too big a decision. What if either of them digs their toes in, and we were forever blamed for dragging them away against their will? Far better to say that this is the way we're going to lead our lives, then make the transition as smooth as possible."

"It sounds as if you've already made up your mind" Richard commented "I thought we were going to stay open minded for the time being?"

"Yes, for the time being - but that's the way we'll have to be if we *do* decide to move, and it's such an important part of any plan that you ought to know how I feel we should handle it, if that's the decision we make."

"Yes, you are right. I totally agree that children shouldn't have to share the uncertainty, just in case it all falls through for any reason – and I also wouldn't want them singling out either of us to blame for taking them away from their friends, for instance."

"We'll be able to make sure they keep in touch – after all, *we* have good friends we wouldn't want to lose touch with. Their friends can visit – and they can phone, text and email these days. They'll also be able to make new friends. It's all about presenting the positive things in the best light, while being realistic about their worries."

"I suggest we get a good night's sleep" said Richard "and tomorrow I'll double check that my qualifications are in order – it's a little unusual to move from hospital to general practice just as I'm about to get a consultancy, but quality of life – for *all* of us – is what matters."

ৎ৶

As it turned out, everything fell into place sooner than any of them could have imagined. Visiting Barbara, while Ben was away on a business trip, happened at just the right time, and no sooner had her visitor been supplied with coffee and biscuits, than Vicky told her what had been mentioned about Richard's opportunity to replace the local doctor. Barbara was delighted.

"When are they likely to move?" she wanted to know.

"It's early days yet – they haven't even reached their decision!"

"Oh, I can't see them needing to take too long over that" Barbara said, confidently. "The only delay will be in finding somewhere suitable to live – after all, Jacqui won't want to be far away from Richard because of the children, and Richard won't want to be too far away from Gabriel, although I'm sure they'll try to make light of any inconvenience involved in the move."

"Perhaps we'll be able to find somewhere they can rent while they look around for a house of their own ... or ... " she looked at Barbara, who smiled and nodded. "You're one step ahead of me, as usual! Do you think they'd accept? It could be for as long as they needed, and there are so many rooms we don't use that we needn't be in each others' pockets - in fact, with the way the rooms are arranged we could divide it without too much fuss."

"Don't overlook Ben's need to have it tactfully presented to him" Barbara warned, "but if you do that at the right moment and give him time to mull it over, then he'll think of it as his own idea, which of course will be the best way. He's very fond of Jacqui, and he gets on well with Richard, too."

Barbara hoped with all her heart that it would happen; she could see nothing but benefits for them all.

And so it was that within days of Jacqui and Richard feeling that the biggest hurdle of their proposed move to Surrey was going to be arranging for somewhere to live, a phone call made it all seem so easy. Ben's plan was that any surplus furniture could be put into storage, and as Vicky pointed out, the timing for Tim and Ella's schooling was just right as the term was drawing to its close, and there was an excellent nearby school where they could transfer in time for the next term. Living at the Hall would be a provisional arrangement for as long as it suited everyone.

Within days, Richard had accepted his new post, plans fell into place, and help was organised from the village to prepare the rooms at the Hall to house the extra family. The excitement of the move for Ella and Tim, and the thought of having her cousins to live with them making Lucy more co-operative than she had ever been, did a great deal to set her parents' minds at rest.

※※

The atmosphere at the Hall lightened daily. In spite of the extra work, Vicky was in her element, making their rooms as welcoming as possible and ensuring that, in particular, the small room for Gabriel, converted from a dressing room next to his parents' bedroom, was as comfortable as it could be. She and Jacqui worked together, and Lucy was encouraged to join in as well – helping to choose pictures, and with mobiles hanging from a central rail that Vicky had suggested installing across the ceiling.

Everyone rallied round with the actual removal from their previous home so that Jacqui could concentrate on Gabriel's need for as little disruption as possible. Richard's parents were towers of strength and Vicky threw an impromptu open afternoon during their first weekend – inviting neighbours and friends to meet their new village doctor and his family. There were hordes of children to be seen, racing round the gardens – some of them Lucy's school friends of course, and some with older brothers and sisters who were Tim and Ella's age.

As a 'breaking the ice' effort it was a resounding success and even Mr Fawkes, the old gardener, who had decided to put in an appearance to safeguard his greenhouses, found nothing to grumble about on the following Monday when he called in at the kitchen to bring vegetables and have his cup of tea with Mrs Ewing.

8

Many times before Jacqui and her family moved in to the Hall, Mr Fawkes had watched from a distance as the Nanny wheeled Rebecca's pram along the paths, occasionally accompanied by Lucy, hellbent on tormenting the infant – poking her with sticks if she could, then running away, screaming with rage if she was reprimanded. He sometimes heard the raised voice of his employer when Ben was outside with his family and Lucy was found getting up to mischief. He noticed that Lucy's behaviour only modified when Miss Jacqui visited with her own baby, Gabriel, and had actually hoped that they could somehow be there permanently. Certainly Lucy couldn't be allowed to carry on the way she did.

But of all the children, Ned Fawkes was drawn to Vicky's baby, Becca, and he looked forward to the days when little Miss Becca could start running round the garden and getting to know the flowers; he'd already seen how she reached out her hands as she was wheeled past the herbaceous border.

"She loves the flowers as much as her grandmother must have done" he commented to Mrs Ewing one day as he took his break for a cup of tea in the kitchen while she was preparing the evening meal.

"I wish her nature could be different, though - by all accounts she's just as miserable and unable to be satisfied as her grandmother was, although Miss Lucy doesn't help, the way she teases her. Thank goodness I wasn't around at the time of Lady Sonia - I wouldn't have stood for it, I tell you; I heard she even changed the name of her maid because it was too much above her station."

"Then things have certainly changed for the better. Now tell me what vegetables you'll want tomorrow and I'll be able to get off home now and watch the football."

His tasks achieved, tomorrow's planned, he lived a contented life - sleeping soundly after his day's work, occasionally having strange dreams of angels, temples and unknown landscapes, yet not remembering details when he woke – only knowing he felt remarkably at peace with his world.

"Those children are going to have a good effect on that little madam

Lucy" he chuckled one day, accepting another of Mrs Ewing's scones. "I can feel it in my bones! They've got their mother's patience, but they're firm with it too – particularly little missy Ella, who's a chip off the *old* block, but in a pleasant way, thanks to her mother, no doubt."

Mrs Ewing knew who he meant, but decided to chide him just the same .

"Don't you go talking ill of the dead, Ned Fawkes. I know we never worked for her, but there's no call for that; and give little Lucy a chance, will you – she's never in the right, no matter what she does, it seems to me, except when Miss Jacqui's around. Have you made any plans for them in the garden?" she asked, giving him a sidelong glance, having seen him consulting the book he had brought from home. 'Children's Gardens' it was called, and had been written years before, when perhaps he had bought it for his own children.

"Well, I thought it might be an idea if I prepared them their own corner so they could start growing veg. or flowers, or whatever they want. Perhaps they'll encourage each other, and it means I can keep an eye on them."

"You'll have to ask – they mightn't like the idea of the children getting dirty."

"I'll find a way of asking" he said, more confidently than he felt.

❧❧

Jacqui never went back on her word to Ben about giving up her right to contest their mother's Will. To all outward appearances they were twins – brother and sister of the same parents. Sonia's cruel disclosure in that awful posthumous letter - that she was the result of her father's affair with his mistress – far from destroying her, had liberated Jacqui, as she now had the explanation for all those years of her mistreatment. Richard's ability to cut through her anguish and find the words to set her mind at rest - "at least you know you were conceived with love" - had given her the magnanimity to deal with Ben's fears and she happily took the formal, legal steps to relinquish her right to claim any part of his inheritance.

Moving to the Hall, at least for the time being, would hopefully mean he'd be completely reassured that she would keep her word. They would make it work well. She was fond of Vicky and appreciated how difficult her life had been during the past months after Becca's birth – she was not an easy baby, and Ben's exasperation that Becca was not the son he craved, to say nothing of Lucy's jealousy and tantrums now that she had a baby sister to oust her from being the centre of attention, were daily reminders that not every family group was happy.

※

Barbara's idea of using the Gatehouse had gradually woven its way into the fabric of their lives. The Gatehouse had already proved its worth as an oasis of calm. Once the scene years before of clandestine meetings, now it was the respectable and respected private place that Barbara suggested could be used in this way. But while Jacqui and Richard had been in favour of trying it, Ben had been reluctant.

"It smacks of hippy commune stuff" he grumbled "all that 'togetherness' and 'peace, man'. Is smoking dope obligatory?"

As planned, Jacqui and Richard had made the first use of it – ostensibly to have a much-needed break and time to themselves to share thoughts about their lives and what their future would hold, now they had Gabriel's needs to consider, and it did indeed pave the way for Ben and Vicky to do the same, with some very beneficial results. Now, once again, after the efforts of moving from their home and setting up their new routines in the Hall, Vicky urged them to take more time out; she'd been worried that Jacqui was not looking her usual self. Although the arrangements were working very well, the move and the subsequent readjustments had been an obvious strain and Richard was concerned that his wife could be getting too exhausted.

"We really need to get to the bottom of this" Richard murmured into his wife's neck as they sat in front of the log fire, more relaxed than they had been for a long time, Jacqui's head on his shoulder, his arm around hers, stroking her hair.

"Think of what you've physically dealt with in the past year – pregnancy and a difficult birth, running a home with the need to take Tim and Ella into account all the time, then all the extra work involved with a small baby who needs regular hospital trips to juggle into that equation – and on top of all this, a husband who decides on a career change that means we all uproot and move home! It's no wonder you feel exhausted ... we *do* need to find a way of helping you."

There was a long pause while he let his words sink in to the silence as they sat gazing into leaping flames of the open fire.

"Are you worried that I'm going to need professional help again?"

Richard knew that his wife was referring to the post-natal depression she had experienced after Ella's birth. She had managed, with Barbara's assistance and the support of a skilled therapist, to avoid a residential stay, but it was not a route she wanted to travel again.

"That's a part of it, yes, but I feel you're not about to do that – particularly now that you've taken up Vicky's offer of sharing all their staff - that will give you more of a break, then whenever you feel up to it you can be more independent again and we can enjoy your home cooking."

"Don't think I haven't been pleased to have that load lifted" Jacqui intervened "it's absolute bliss to join in the evening meals with the others, and not have to worry about organising housework, and having babysitters available – but ...

"Yes, it's that 'but' I'm worried about. We've always promised that we'd tell each other our worries, haven't we? As long as we don't keep things hidden, then I'm sure we can deal with anything. Now can you tell me?"

"Not yet, not until I ..." Jacqui eventually began, then faltered. "Can we leave it for this evening? I do know what I want to say but I know that I need to explain it properly. Please? Will tomorrow do?"

"Well, yes, I suppose so. Look - I know it's difficult for you to put it into words, but it's no use letting it get you down like this – and I can see that it is. You haven't been eating properly for days and everyone can tell you've been crying; Tim and Ella are tiptoeing around in case they've been the cause. For all our sakes we *must* use our time here this weekend."

As they eventually did; and with gentleness and patience Richard discovered that there was much, much more to his wife's strength and beliefs than he had previously seen. So, it was an even more deeply committed couple who returned for their evening meal the next day, radiating a degree of love and understanding that Vicky and Ben could not fail to notice.

☙❧

Eventually, even Ben acknowledged the sense of making the Gatehouse a child-free zone, a breathing space where the adults could escape even for a few hours, while the children were looked after at the Hall, or even to use it as an individual retreat, if pressures became too much.

Ben and Vicky had inevitably felt self-conscious at their first visit, having been reluctant to advertise their need for 'time out', but Barbara had encouraged Vicky to take that first step while she herself was staying for a weekend, and undertook to make sure that Lucy and Becca enjoyed themselves so much that they hardly noticed their parents' absence. It was noticeable that the previously regular arguments began to happen less frequently. As a consequence, Lucy's behaviour, always unpredictable – and particularly so after Becca's birth – eased a little. It was still not safe to leave her unsupervised with her younger sister, but she was a changed child when Gabriel was in the room. She regarded him with curiosity at first, apparently sensing he was different and less robust than her cousins; then one day while Jacqui was changing his clothes and he was whimpering his high-pitched monotone, she began to gently stroke his hand and watch his tiny fingers. Jacqui wisely encouraged her, pointing out his little soft nails and the folds of skin that showed he was a special baby, as she put it to the little girl.

"What do you mean - *special*, Aunty Jac?"

"He'll always be like a baby, Lucy, no matter how big he grows. That makes him special to us, and that's why Timmy and Ella are so gentle with him."

"Timmy told me he might not be here for very long."

"That's also true. That's why every day is important. Look, see how he stretches his fingers when you touch them? It's his way of saying he likes you."

Lucy was very thoughtful.

"I *smile* when I like somebody. Gabriel should smile."

Jacqui turned to get the clean clothes, hiding the tears that were always too ready to come unbidden into her eyes. Thankfully, Lucy's attention was elsewhere, having spotted the old teddy bear in the nursery that once had been her room and was now Gabriel's.

"He can have Teddy Grumps." she said "Look - he's got no smile, either."

Sure enough, the battered bear had lost his stitched mouth. He was a family hand-me-down and had originally belonged to Ben, who took the stitches out when he and Jacqui were playing hospitals one day. Lucy carefully placed him in the corner of Gabriel's cot, where he wouldn't fall over, then skipped happily out of the room.

Jacqui thoughtfully watched her leave then turned back to her little son to massage his legs and feet, as she had been advised would help.

"You're doing so much good" she murmured "she's a different child when she's with you. Keep on with whatever it is you do."

Gabriel's solemn gaze followed her with difficulty.

"I wonder if you see more than with your physical eyes. They sometimes have such beautiful depths that I could feel I was losing myself, looking into them."

She gently moved her hands up and down, round and back, willing his muscles to gain strength, but Gabriel lay as inert as he usually did. Her movements continued up his back instinctively, avoiding the lesion near the base of his spine, gently giving warm sensations to the nerve endings that could receive them, hoping that if she could bring even a second of comfort to him in this contact, she would.

When she had finished the sequence with his arms and shoulders and gently uncurled the tiny fingers, she carefully clothed him with clean, fresh garments and hugged his little body against hers for a long, long moment before laying him down again. His eyes were closed now as he drifted into a peaceful sleep. Jacqui wondered, yet again, at the amount of love she felt for him – no, it was not the amount, it was the *quality* of love that was unlike anything she had felt for either Timmy or Ellie; not simply devoted, but fiercely protective of this precious part of her that would probably not survive infancy.

9

Mr Fu had watched his protegee make her way back to the next life, the mists of forgetfulness swirling about the tiny spirit form as it aligned with the chosen situation. He had so many hopes that this time he would be needed as he waited for opportunities to make contact - unlike the previous lifetime, when Sonia had lived blinkered and secluded in her own unswerving conviction that there was only one way to think and believe – *her* way.

He remembered the efforts he had made after Sonia and Geoffrey moved into the Hall; the role of spiritual guide was so varied. In that instance he had taken the opportunity to attempt to connect with her through the gardener her husband introduced. Surely, he thought, knowing she took pride in the gardens and could develop the conservatory, it would provide him with the contact he hoped for as he waited for the opportunity to fulfill his role as guide to the troubled soul.

The earthly contact had been no problem, it transpired – particularly with the conservatory, which Lady Sonia had decided would be a focal point of the grand features of the Hall – "essential to impress the foreign visitors" she had told him. These visitors had all appreciated living in the grand manner. It was a welcome change from the hotel life that most of them led when they had to travel away from home or their home countries. Wandering around the grounds after dinner on a warm summer's evening provided the tranquillity they craved, and many business deals were conducted as they walked along the secluded paths of the shrubbery, or by the side of the stream that fed the carp pond at the far end of the grounds.

But the hoped-for deeper, more spiritual, contact had never occurred. There was never any conversation - Sonia dictated, ordered things arranged to her taste and no-one else's, and she showed no signs of softening her attitude, and although he returned time and time again, he eventually resigned himself to keeping a watching brief. The gardener retired and the post was taken by another, treated with equal disdain by Lady Sonia, then after her death he in turn was replaced by her son.

Now, having assisted her with awareness of the true purpose of life, the way that souls develop, and with the new life beginning again in the environs of the Hall, Mr Fu had returned to the familiar pathways and expanses of lawn to watch over her in her new life – this time taking over the outward appearance and mannerisms of Mr Fawkes whenever his role as Spirit Guide warranted the switch. At these times he 'overshadowed' the gardener – at others he retreated so that Ned Fawkes, unaware of anything untoward, resumed being himself.

It was a joy to be back again, in the familiar routines, feeling earthly strengths, waiting to see how the more developed soul of Sonia in her new life would enhance the family's soul.

※

The garden which Ned Fawkes set out to construct proved more successful than his employer had thought would be the case. Ben had always been inclined to let Ned have his head – the amount of maintenance that the extensive grounds needed were sufficient, he felt, to keep one gardener busy and Ned always reported on what he had done, with detail and accuracy. So Ben respected Ned's honesty about adjusting his work to allow some spare hours to help the children with their project.

"I'll approve the idea so long as you have it somewhere out of sight of the house" he said, after a moment or two's indecision about whether he should forbid the whole thing, "and I don't want to see any neglected weed-ridden eyesore when I go out for a late night stroll. I like the order and care that my mother insisted upon, wherever I look."

"My idea was for them to have the corner of the walled garden that's behind the existing vegetable patch, sir" Ned nervously fingered his belt buckle "and I know that there's nothing like a bit of growing to remind you that life continues, no matter what age you are."

"Spare me the homespun philosophy, for heaven's sake" sighed Ben, "but I don't expect their enthusiasm to last more than a day or two, so let me know when that point is reached. That'll be all for now."

Ned could hardly disguise his pleasure as he headed for the greenhouse. The children were waiting for him, as he'd suggested they could, and the two girls jumped around in their excitement.

"I'll start preparing the ground tomorrow, Master Tim, and if any of you wants to help with that, then of course you can – but you'll have to come in old clothes that don't matter. I'll find you all some gloves, and the tools, of course."

He was as good as his word, and from somewhere had managed to find child-sized tools for Lucy, and a light weeding fork that was ideal for Ella; Timmy, of course, felt he could manage to wield the proper spade and fork that was waiting in the toolshed.

Ned cleverly managed to sustain their interest. Poorly educated he may have been by the standards of his employers, but he was wise in the ways of keeping their keenness fanned by enlisting the help of first one, then another, to be given the task of harvesting a few vegetables as both a reward for their hard work, and also an encouragement to aim for their own production in time.

He had, of course, chosen a well-nourished section of the walled garden, where few weeds grew after years of cultivation. Also, as the time of year was suited to planting out the onions and shallots to overwinter, he had supplemented those with short-term rows of salad crops that still had time to develop successfully, so that their interest was maintained. Gardening was such a pleasure and he wanted to introduce each of the children to what could turn out to be a lifelong interest. Ella, he noticed, had limitless patience like her mother and would find a lot of satisfaction in growing seedlings in trays and pricking them out for planting on. Little Miss Lucy was different entirely and would need to have quick results in order to sustain her interest – several areas developing all at once would probably suit her best, he mused. As for Tim, well he would have to have a long think about that – it would be so easy to assume he would prefer the woodland tasks, but perhaps he had ideas of his own.

Mrs Ewing rose to the daily challenge of cooking dishes that contained combinations of vegetables she would not have normally chosen, and which sometimes surprised Vicky, but the sight of the normally fussy Lucy eating cabbage with relish because she had picked it herself, was so novel that her mother decided the best reaction was to keep quiet – apart from giving murmurs of appreciation.

10

Life at the Hall had fallen into a routine which brought benefit to them all. They were near enough to a school of excellent reputation to which Ella and Tim transferred with few difficulties, other than missing their old friends, even though they were able to keep in touch by email and phone. Tim made new ones easily, Ella less so, but she was not the only new girl in her class and soon adjusted, with the assistance of a helpful teacher. The 'school run' was now not the sole right of Lucy to treat as a manipulative journey which had reduced many of the au pairs to tears before they handed in their notice. Now that she had the two older children to talk with until she was dropped off at her school gate, she tended to emulate them. The nanny proved to be capable and interested in learning about a baby with the special needs that Gabriel had, so Jacqui, after a few weeks, had felt confident that he could be left with her from time to time.

Jacqui had followed up that Gatehouse conversation, when the conclusion she and Richard reached was that she needed an outside interest of some sort. She hesitated before telling him that the one she had thought of was one that Barbara recommended during her long stay in Chiswick, when Ella was a baby. She had started attending a Yoga class and found it helpful for relaxation; now she had noticed that there was one held weekly in the Village Hall and she had wondered whether to try again. Richard was totally in favour, and it proved to be a way of making friends outside the Hall environment, as several mothers of young children at Lucy's school attended.

Richard, of course, was helped greatly by the fact that he no longer had to commute for an hour at the end of each day, and although his hours at the surgery were lengthy, that was more than offset by the short trip to the village practice. He even had time to resume writing.

Their first Christmas passed with unexpectedly joyful memories for them all. The Hall unreservedly lent itself to the large family gatherings, with three generations under its old eaves; a magnificent Christmas tree was decorated, village carol singers paid their usual visit, church was attended on the suitably frosty morning, and for the first time the memories of Sonia's death played no part. Of course, it was also Lucy's birthday, and although she was the centre of attention - with her cousins around to help and Jacqui organising games - by now she knew she had no need to slip back into her old behaviour in order to be noticed. It was a boisterous, happy time for them all.

After the party was over Vicky, Barbara and Jacqui sat in the conservatory while Ben and Richard, ably assisted by Ted and Muriel, supervised a last game of 'Blind Man's Buff' before tackling the bedtime routines with the younger two children.

"I'm the happiest I've been for years" Vicky said later "and it's all down to you and Jacqui. The Gatehouse idea was a stroke of genius, you can see how it's helped us. Now all we need is to look forward to a year of peace and tranquillity."

"I'll second that" said Ben "here's to all of us, a wonderful end to this year and hopes and dreams for the next – may it be an even better one! Happy New Year!"

They raised their glasses, as did the others, but Jacqui could only pretend to sip – she couldn't bring herself to join in that toast while she had the chill feelings of dread that woke her each morning.

&v&

Richard had never thought of himself as a campaigner. It was not in his nature to be vociferous, and whatever his thoughts about the inadequacies of the health services, of which he was a part, he could not be unprofessional and reveal colleagues' shortcomings in public. He and Jacqui, like many others in their circumstances, made use of the national system for the main part, but had the option to buy into speedy consultations. Nothing was perfect in an imperfect world, but when it came to provision of health care for the family, only the best they could afford was good enough.

Families who had to rely on what was provided, often found that the services fell short of what they had been led to expect. Jacqui's story of Ria had remained in his mind; it pointed out the ongoing need for health and social services to dovetail together properly, in order to provide a joint scheme of support. "In an ideal world ..." he sighed.

Richard was not a great writer. Not in the way that he thought of writers – erudite people who could express themselves clearly and entertainingly. He could produce reports when necessary, wrote letters to senior people and made notes in his Gabriel file. But keeping the journal proved to have unexpected results.

One night, unable to sleep, he found himself writing about his own anger and frustration. It took him by surprise, as he had intended to dwell on the positive aspects of having Gabriel in the family – possibly describing in depth how the older children had learned to adjust their expectations of what their baby brother would be able to do. It was easier for them, in a way, Jacqui had said, as they only had hazy memories of Lucy as a baby, and could make few comparisons.

Yet as he wrote, he was unable to stop his raw feelings of unfairness coming to the surface, as he furiously wrote the words - why did it have to happen to *their* family? Why should Jacqui have to have yet *another* heartbreak in her life? Why should he be granted the son he had longed for more than anything in his life yet at the same time be denied the pleasure of a normal son's achievements? His feelings came spilling out until he neared the bottom of the page.

Putting down his pen, exhausted, Richard looked at the words with horror – that he, with all his knowledge and training, should feel that way deep down, was a revelation. Should he tear up the page in disgust? He decided that in spite of his shame it should be kept, in accordance with the pact he had made with himself to record his innermost feelings. But he clipped those pages of the notebook together so that they should never accidentally fall open. Shaken, he returned to bed and lapsed into a troubled doze.

Just before he woke he dreamed very clearly that he was in a strange desert area outside a tent made of animal skins. The detail was amazing – the landscape was of mountain ranges receding into the distance; no vegetation nearby apart from small scrubland bushes, and when he looked at the tent seeing the way the skins were draped over the poles, he thought he could identify the animals they had come from - bears and foxes, for the most part. An ancient, wrinkled man emerged, carrying a child in his arms. Richard looked more closely and could see that it was Gabriel, but before he could step forward to take him into his own arms, the old man raised him towards the sky; Gabriel changed into a small bird which flew into the air, circling higher and higher, gaining speed as he went, until he eventually disappeared from view.

Richard felt an overwhelming sense of peace as the bird flew above him. Then he woke, still with the calmness that was in such contrast to the previous turmoil in his mind. He lay, unmoving, trying to make sense of it all, not wanting to break that precious spell.

Looking for ...

The chapter conveniently ending at this point, I decided I could take no more of this sentimental family saga. Not my cup of tea, Cressy, I sighed. Oh, Jacqui had been found to have a chink in her armour, thank goodness – well, she couldn't have maintained that martyred angel pose throughout, now could she?

Barbara had been developed and retained flaws that continued to make her interesting. Vicky was coming out of her shell a little - even showing signs of standing up to the pompous Ben, and then discovering the improbable solution of the Gatehouse saving their marriage. And what had happened to the humorous mysticism of the first part? The introduction indicated that the guide was very much part of the story, but apart from the hint that the gardener was not quite as he should be, there had been nothing else.

I went to bed in a bad mood feeling let down, tossing and turning as I tried to work out why. I eventually arrived at the conclusion I was feeling cheated - it would have been so much easier to deal with if I had found that Cressy had managed to write a blockbuster masterpiece. Then I could have had the fairytale ending – published, reaped the rewards, continued to keep her on the pedestal where I had placed her. But as I went on my explorations into the side of her she had kept secret, I was finding that here was a very sincere, yet very human Cressy – and I couldn't let go of the need to find out *why* – why she kept things so hidden from me, her closest friend.

I woke later that night with a start. Rain was lashing the windows, Annie Lennox was singing inside my head –

"... sweet dreams are made of these ... everyone is looking for something ..."

It had pained me to have that reaction to Cressy's hard work and I hadn't slept easily. Who the hell was I, a supposedly empathic reporter on the state of *strangers'* labours of love waxing lyrical over their gardens, to judge the merits of the labours of my dearest friend's fictional outpourings? So much for the hours we had spent discussing unconditional love and all its component parts, one conclusion being that while it should allow for helpful criticism, that criticism ceased to be helpful when the opportunity for change was no longer there.

"... everyone is looking ..."

I turned to the diary again, and having no idea where to begin, opened the thick volume where I had marked the page with a scrap of paper.

> March 18th: Reading - 1st one with D. <u>V</u> impressed by instant knowledge of my past diffs. Brought Ma in - descr. of last illness spot on: also proof of childhood exp. esp in mountains (Wales). Msge: make most of time & don't be put off your search; you're on the right path. G'ma A - D. said she was indistinct as she wasn't used to this, cd only be brief - msge: "<u>I'm so proud of you</u>". I wept a lot. More about past - hurts & helpfulness. Said true friend (felt it was T) was unaware of spiritual side, but through me would come to know. D's comment - <u>we learn from sceptics - they get our thoughts in order</u>!

What - who - had guided me to that particular page: Cressy, *are* you there?

What on earth was I doing, asking foolish questions. *Was* I being the true friend? I would like to think so, but I was far more than a mere sceptic – I was an unswerving disbeliever; I firmly shut the diary, refusing to go down that route - *ever*. The following morning, after more brief hours of fitful sleep, I was glad to get showered and dressed. I concentrated on meeting an impending deadline, mailed it to the marketing company who signed it off within hours, assuring me their photographer had done a splendid job too and their client (a top multi million company) had indicated they would be delighted to use me again. All that positivity cleared my head of the previous night's sourness and I went for a walk in the park, although very carefully not the route which had in previous times gladly led me to Cressy's flat.

I returned feeling much better and thinking much clearer

The Ripples and the Tapestries

thoughts. Couldn't I bring myself to be magnanimous? Just because Cressy had developed a secret side of herself in order to write a book, and had encountered some thought-provoking experiences, why should I be resentful? I returned to the theory that while I thought I knew her inside out, yet here was proof that there was a large part of her I hardly knew at all. I realised I truly did feel cheated by many things that would now never happen – not least the impossibility of my unrequited love being recognised and returned. It had been so much part of my conscious and unconscious thoughts that I wore it like a favourite jacket.

I gave the New Age approach in the first part more consideration - don't criticise what you don't understand, I reminded myself – a lesson I thought I had learned years ago.

Cressy had gone through a phase at school, I remembered, as did most of the girls, influenced by the Glastonbury pop culture of the time, and I thought she had left it behind. In the years since we met again and renewed our friendship it would have been easy for her not to tell me of anything that she suspected I might find fault with – we didn't live in each others' pockets, after all, and there were many hours and days, sometimes weeks, between our meetings, where she went her own way as I did mine. Easy to forget – I would give her the benefit of any doubt that she had deliberately kept it secret. If only I'd known, I thought, I might have been able to weigh up if she'd become unduly influenced – but even so, what would I or could I have done?

If she had indeed been deliberately secretive about it, that didn't mean she'd become immersed or obsessed – could she have been ashamed? But why feel that way (if indeed she did)? The diary entry seemed to indicate that she *was* impressed, at least by "D", whoever that was. I retrieved the diary from its new filing space on the floor and somewhat hesitantly tried the trick again – opening it at random at an earlier date. This time I hit upon a blank double page. The date rang bells – the summer holiday she had taken for the first time on her own - it was not a success, but she knew she had to do it. I tried again, but came to a week of conference events. So much for significance - I gave up and made myself a strong coffee.

Then I tried to be methodical, going back to the first entry in

January 2004, skimming through the pages quite rapidly, basing my search on the format I had stumbled across the previous night – headings, abbreviated notes in that tiny writing – and found nothing like it existed until July 2005. Until then it had been used as a normal diary would be – dental appointments, speaking engagements, noticing that there would quite often be a capital T encircled – plus my own visits recorded, but not in any detail.

I wondered. Turning to the notes section at the back of her diary. There was a general heading of "Dreams" then many entries, some very brief, some much longer; all encoded with a letter of the alphabet - the first 26 in lower case, then as I turned a few pages the upper case took over and the latest one was (P) - so, 42 dreams. Something caught my eye as I turned back to the earlier ones ...

> *Dream (m):*
> *Link: wrote about G. y'day, <u>deeply</u> moving. Was standing on cliff top. Saw N A Indian with baby that changed into bird & flew free: symbolic rebirth/transf. into own element (D says) after being trapped in body. Baby was <u>TROY</u>. Is T not in own element? D suggests not.*

I was taken aback – I could understand why she had used it and sure enough, it was almost identical to the dream I'd read about only hours earlier and the implication about Gabriel was clear. But as part of Richard's theoretical puzzling, and the possibility of the link being that I could be the model for his scepticism ... ?

Well, upon reflection, why not? I don't have to adopt any of this metaphysical nonsense – but what *was* disturbing was this mention of me in conjunction with the mysterious "D" and the evidence that I'd been the subject of discussion. That ended the plan I'd half formulated, of phoning the number – I needed time to think about all of this. What had been discussed and to what extent? What would I find if I did manage to locate her (or him) – what might be revealed? And more importantly, was I sure I would want to hear it?

One implication of the dream, although nothing I'd not

suspected in the plot, of mentioning G. (undoubtedly the baby) in that way, was that he'd died. I sincerely hope that's not the implication for me!

I've decided to do nothing about contacting 'D' - yet.

11

The children were undoubtedly absorbing the benefits of living in more spacious surroundings. Jacqui commented on this to Richard when they were talking of their next home.

"I do think that however difficult my childhood was, the Hall helped a great deal" she said as they sat on the terrace with their coffee one unexpectedly sunny Sunday morning in late February, hearing Lucy and Ella in the distance, laughing as they chased each other through the shrubbery.

"There was always somewhere to be on my own when I wanted to be. Apart from having the huge space in the gardens, we grew up with the lovely high ceilings and balanced proportions. I'd really like the same for Timmy and Ella – the feeling of a space of your own that you can arrange to suit yourself is priceless and I'm sure it can lead to respect of other people's boundaries, to say nothing of the actual privacy it gives. Are there smaller houses around of the same period that we could afford to buy?"

"Not in the countryside perhaps, but in the town there could be more. Are you getting itchy feet already? I thought it suited you here, and now you've started to build up some other interests as well as having Gabriel to look after, I thought you were definitely less tense than you used to be."

"Oh, but I *am*! It's just that I like to have a picture in my mind, and I like to think of a house something like the oldfashioned doll's house that I once used to play with. I named all the people in it, you know, and the family was so good, and no-one ever misbehaved ..." Jacqui paused, looking faraway and wistful. Richard gave her hand a squeeze.

Vicky and Ben walked across the terrace to join them.

"How are the two lovebirds, then?" Ben always teased his sister unmercifully, however much it embarrassed her, although he was relieved that she had such a solid marriage this time. If he ever bothered to pray for anyone else (or even himself on the odd occasion when he went to church these days) it was Jacqui, and to ask that she would be spared more heartbreak.

"We're talking about when we move from here" said Richard "and the sort of place we'd like to live in."

"Well, that's what we'd like to discuss too ..." Ben said; and then, seeing a look of panic in Jacqui's face, hurriedly added "although we weren't exactly going to put it the same way."

"I know you said you would want to move at some stage later on, but we want to put that off" Vicky intervened. "We want to make you a permanent offer to stay – for as long as you wish! Now that you've been here for several months I think we've proved that we can all get on well – any cracks would have shown by now. I know that having your three here, especially Gabriel, has helped Lucy - she's hardly the same child."

"Thank goodness" admitted her father with a heartfelt sigh, then added "You're a good chap to have around, Richard, and Sis helps no end with Vicky's neuroses! Seriously though – wasn't I being serious? – we'd welcome being able to look forward to however many years you can spare us while the children are all growing up. You don't have to give an answer just yet – it's not something you can decide overnight. The weekend will do!"

Vicky gave him a meaningful 'don't overdo it' look so that he swiftly changed the subject.

"How are you getting on with the writing?"

He and Richard had sometimes discussed various topics which interested them both – and although Ben had little actual knowledge of health care, he had experiences of private care that broadened Richard's perspective.

"Oh it's variable" said Richard, somewhat ruefully, but relieved to be able to switch to the different topic until he and Jacqui had talked on their own. "Some days I can write a whole article at one sitting, then sometimes I find I've turned up something else I need to research and everything slows down. What I really want to do is to write a book about our experiences with Gabriel - based on some of the articles, but much more personal - about how we've coped, and also about how we've benefited. It will get done, though, I know I have to do it."

"I just don't know how you fit it all in as well as your practice work."

"Well I must say that since we moved here I've found the pace has slowed down a little. Sometimes I used to feel a whole month of sleep wouldn't go amiss – now it's just a week!"

◈

Later that night in their room, with all the children asleep, Jacqui and Richard thoroughly discussed the matter of where they should live, with all its implications. But try as they might, they really couldn't find any serious flaws with any of the arrangements developed over the past months, so apart from needing to make a formal financial arrangement, there seemed little else to do but accept the status quo. They had never felt they were anything less than welcome and the only point they originally voiced any hesitations about, the children's transfer to new schools, had proved to have been foundless.

The children all benefited from the surroundings, Lucy in particular, with her older cousins to look up to, and they were happy to be with her. Vicky had definitely relaxed with the right sort of company, and Jacqui knew how much she herself appreciated knowing that not only Vicky, but Becca's Nanny could easily be called upon for occasional help with Gabriel. Another bonus was the space for accommodating visits from grandparents – another use for the Gatehouse, and Richard's parents, always willing to lend a hand when necessary, found it so comfortable to stay there, as did Vicky's, when they came over from their Spanish home.

The following evening they told Tim and Ella what their aunt and uncle had offered, and what they had decided. Their reactions were a little surprising.

"We assumed you'd decided ages ago!" said Tim.

"Lucy told me she'd listened outside the library door one day and heard Auntie Vicky telling Uncle Ben that if ever we left, so would she, and she was crying."

"What on earth …" Jacqui was horrified.

"Oh I told her that she shouldn't listen to grownups arguing – they say a lot of things they don't mean. Then I told her we would never go away, ever, and she cheered up. I thought you knew! Have you told Gabriel?"

"We thought you'd like to do that, then we'll all go to confirm it with Uncle Ben."

They had hugs all round and Ella raced upstairs to tell Gabriel, who was being put to bed by Becca's nanny. He looked at her in his usual solemn way as she whispered the news, leaning over the cot to give him his goodnight kiss as his eyes drowsily closed.

※

That Easter they were joined only by Barbara, who stayed for two nights – to the immense delight of the children and some of their schoolfriends who joined them in the Easter Egg hunt that always took place each year. There was a great deal of teasing and calling her the Mother Hen, because she had laid the eggs in their hiding places before breakfast, but she gave them clues about when their search was 'hot' or 'cold', depending on how near to a hiding place they were. The two babies' mothers talked in the kitchen as they prepared sandwiches and cakes, while Ben and Richard supervised the garden activities and made sure that the large pond was well avoided.

"It will soon be time to start planning the party for Becca and Gabriel" Vicky said, allowing herself to pour another glass of wine, after Jacqui declined. "My goodness, we'll have earned this today – d'you think we'll be able to manage it again in a couple of month's time?"

"To say nothing of next Christmas and the one after that" laughed Jacqui. "I still can't quite believe you *really* want us to stay indefinitely. I can't tell you what a difference it's made to my life, being able to concentrate on Gabriel when I need to."

"Of course we want you to – and not to make life easier for *you*! It's for purely selfish motives – just look at how we've changed since you came. Everything seems to be so much easier, and I know Ben feels the same. You're such a positive person, and it spreads! How you and Ben could be so different when you have the same parents and upbringing I'll never know."

"Put it down to my previous life - the one where I was evil as sin, but repented at the last minute and was rewarded by a sunny disposition!"

"Where on earth did you get that idea from? I never knew you were keen on that sort of thing."

"Oh, it was one of Anthony's friends who said that. Some hypnotists get interested in regressing people so that they can explore previous lives,

The Ripples and the Tapestries

and find an explanation for things that can't be explained rationally. Although I never had that done he told me he picked up that detail by intuition. I can't prove he was right, of course – or wrong, for that matter."

"Are you interested in all that sort of spooky stuff?"

"Not really, although – well - promise you won't think I'm silly, but since Gabriel was born I've noticed that sometimes when I go into his room at night there's some sort of very faint light around his head. I never noticed that effect with the other two."

"I'll have to check on Becca, to see if she's a little angel as well – although I know she is, anyway – in spite of her constant wailing!"

※

One of Jacqui's new hobbies was attending the yoga class, held weekly at the Village Hall. Apart from the benefits that the class brought her personally, she welcomed the opportunity to meet others from the village and beyond. An hour and a half of stretching and relaxation, followed by a blissful ten minutes of guided meditation, gave her a calmer outlook each week, no matter what worries she had encountered during the preceding few days. The other women were friendly and she soon had invitations to more coffee mornings and village events than she had time for.

One of the women was older than the rest, but had practised yoga for many years and was great friends with the teacher. They had a wide circle of friends, all of whom seemed to be practising alternative therapies or attending other groups of different interests. Susan made a point of walking to the car park with Jacqui one evening.

"If it's meditation that helps, then you might find a whole day of it useful. My friend Jenny organises them in Guildford. She also sees people privately at home, and she had a message for you - she told me to tell you that although you've already walked a difficult path in this life, you'll soon find your greater purpose ahead. Twins will prove significant."

※

Jacqui couldn't get that remark out of her head for the next few days, and kept looking at the card with Jenny's phone number, although she delayed contacting her immediately. She asked Vicky if she knew what Susan might have meant, and was intrigued to hear that Susan's friend was looked on as a wise woman by the charitable ones in the area, but as the next closest thing to a witch by some others.

"She does card readings and that sort of thing. At one time she used to get asked to the village fete, but then found the Vicar didn't approve, so she stopped coming. I always thought it was harmless enough - although I was a bit spooked when I had one of her short ten minute readings and she told me things about my life that no-one could possibly have known."

"I'll give it some more thought" said Jacqui, and the matter was soon forgotten – by Vicky, at least.

12

The routine of hospital visits with Gabriel continued; none of them bringing very encouraging news; yet, she reasoned, they were not *dis*couraging. He seemed to be stuck on some sort of plateau of development and was still unable to sit unsupported, or communicate in the ways that other babies half his age would. But he was placid and appeared to be in no pain, so at least the spectre of more surgery wasn't raised, which was what Jacqui dreaded more than anything. She and Richard still retained their firm beliefs that they would not subject their small son to any unnecessary or speculative intervention. If he needed surgery or medication then it would have to be for a very good reason.

"I'm not going to have him used as an experiment" she'd once told Vicky when they were discussing Gabriel's teething problems and how she had been told there was a new clinical trial for children's painkillers being undertaken. "It's a double blind trial and they have a 'control group'; what if he's one chosen for the group having placebos, in other words, no medication? Or what if he has side effects? Hasn't he had enough to cope with? No thank you – I'll stay with the proven methods, although as you know, I do try to balance the chemical input with some of the herbal things I've read about, and then there's the massage – just to help him relax and breathe more easily."

At one time Vicky had wondered if having Becca around would be an upsetting daily comparison, but Jacqui's unfailing delight at the milestones Gabriel's little cousin passed reassured her. Becca loved to spend time with Gabriel. The two babies would sit on the soft floor covering in Gabriel's nursery – Becca crawling around to pass toys to him, as he half-sat, propped up by cushions. Jacqui had shown Vicky how to give the massage the hospital recommended, and after bathing their babies they sat side by side with warm towels on their laps using a little light oil and soothing rhythmical strokes.

When Barbara visited them she loved to be part of this scene and was delighted when Jacqui insisted that Gabriel would survive her inexpert attentions. In fact, Barbara proved to be an adept, and also quickly remembered old skills of hand massage for both of her young women friends after they had put their babies down to rest.

"I learned this years ago from a Thai girl" she told them "and I think it's a form of reflexology, but I've never forgotten how beautiful it is to realise we can allow ourselves to receive as well as constantly give."

※※

One weekend when Barbara was staying with them, Jacqui asked her opinion of Susan's friend Jenny, telling her of the message which had been passed on.

"It sounds as if she might be a mystic." Seeing Jacqui's baffled expression she explained. "By that, I mean someone who develops experiences outside the orthodox ones of any religion she may belong to, using intuition and going beyond mere intellect or even telepathy."

"I feel as if I want to go, and years ago in my wild days with Zak I wouldn't have hesitated; but now, although I wonder if it's not just superstitious nonsense, I'd like some explanations for things I've noticed about Gabriel." Jacqui went on to tell Barbara about the light she had seen around him at night, and how she had also started feeling warm and cold spots in his room, although the heating was kept at a constant temperature; and lately she had begun to notice an occasional faint but distinctive smell of the perfume his grandmother had aways worn.

"I just want to make sure that no harm can come to him."

"Would you like *me* to have an appointment with her? Then I could report back and you could decide."

So it was that two days later Barbara found herself standing on the doorstep of a neat house in the suburbs of Guildford. A pleasant, middle-aged woman, dressed in classic twinset and skirt that would not have looked out of place at any sedate committee meeting, greeted her warmly.

"I'm Jenny" she said, ushering her guest into a hallway where the main feature was a huge shallow bowl on a low table, containing many large polished stones of all colours, shapes and sizes. She led the way through to a comfortably light and airy conservatory at the back of the house.

"This is where I work – we're not overlooked here and I find the garden is quite helpful for people who need a soothing outlook; I often get the birds outside joining in with the meditations."

She sat opposite Barbara at a small table, leaned over to a tape recorder on a nearby chair and switched it on, then from a silk handkerchief unwrapped a deck of cards with beautiful illustrations of angels.

"As you can see, I don't use the Tarot; I used to, and from my point of view it doesn't matter, but I find pictures like these are easier for most people to look at."

She shuffled the cards as she spoke, then fanned them out on the table, asking Barbara to choose five from anywhere in the pack, and place them face downwards. Barbara did as she was directed and the reading began.

✷✷

Later, telling Jacqui, she said what convinced her from the start that Jenny was genuine was that although she turned the cards one by one, she hardly glanced at them, telling her significant things about her life. Not just platitudes about difficult times, but specific details about unrequited love and substitute love, successes and failures in business, and her present situation where banishment and heartache four years ago had been replaced by acceptance.

"But listen to this part of the tape" she said, and Jacqui heard for the first time the voice that would subsequently impart so much wisdom in her own future.

"There were many misunderstandings and many secrets undisclosed, among the people you looked on as family, although they were not your blood ties. I have a tall distinguished gentleman, a businessman but once a naval man, standing here who is closely related to the dear young friend who told you about me; he passed over ten years ago. He tells me that you still secretly carry a photograph of the two of you together, taken many years ago. He was never able to be yours in this life, but will wait for the next."

Jacqui was sitting open-mouthed.

"I never knew you ... oh, Auntie Babs!"

"Shhh – this is the part I want you to hear."

"This young friend's peace of mind is more important to you than any of your own worries. You have often been able to help her in the past, when she was unable to receive help from the very person she should have done. Will you pass on a message from that lady to her? The pen was poisoned by revenge. She will understand."

Barbara stopped the tape and looked intently at Jacqui, who had gone pale.

"That's something *I* don't know, isn't it?"

"The letter ... the letter you saw Ben give me in the library that night before Mummy's funeral. I can never disclose ... but it *was* about revenge. Barbara, how can she know so much?"

"All I know is that you now have proof that she has some extraordinary powers. It's up to you whether or not you go to see her yourself, but I really think she could help you in some way. She explains people's purposes in life so clearly."

※

This time Jacqui didn't hesitate and immediately arranged the appointment. She found Jenny's voice over the phone even more gentle than it sounded on the tape. She drove to Guildford the following day and was shown into the conservatory, just as Barbara had been.

She was half-prepared for setting her own doubts and incredulity on one side, but remembering that Barbara had told her that Gabriel had never been mentioned in any context, she could not believe the first words Jenny uttered once they had settled down into their chairs.

"There's a child who is special in every way – not just to you, but for mankind. His life will influence people's ways of thinking long after he has left earth plane. He has been entrusted to you and your husband because of your own special qualities. He's named after an angel and already has a special light around him."

Jacqui sat, tears streaming down her face, but with a rapturous smile. This woman *knows*, she thought: she knew Barbara, she knows me, she knows Gabriel – and I need to hear *what* she knows about him.

Jenny did not produce the deck of cards. As she explained to Jacqui, there was really no need when she could tune in so specifically right from the start.

"I shall tell you what I hear and see, and I'll try to get the spirits to wait if you want to comment or ask them any more questions - but remember we're dealing with people who have passed over and some of them may not be used to the process."

She switched on the tape recorder, relaxed in her chair with her eyes shut, and after a slight pause began to speak.

"There are several people who have passed, queueing up to speak to you. I have one here who meant everything to you, but you were together for only a short time and I feel ... *here*" she suddenly leaned forward, pressing her hands against her chest, "I feel a sudden death, an accident. So sudden he felt no fear, no pain. He wants to make sure you know that, because he knows you've always worried. He's also saying that he had already guessed your news, and he's so proud of the result."

"Oh Jenny, that's Anthony – he must be talking about me being pregnant with Ella; I was going to tell him that evening, but he was killed in the motorway accident on the way home. Does he *really* see what Ella's like? Sometimes she's so like him."

"... he will be there to protect your daughter in life, so that she will have the wisdom, as you do, to see past the immediate, and look beyond to the true purpose ..."

Jenny continued to tell Jacqui many things that she only half heard after that, so overwhelming had the first statements been.

"... it's time for him to move away and let someone else come through, but not before he tells you that you were his true soulmate, and to remember the daisy chain."

Jacqui sat transfixed. The daisy chain was the symbol of their love - the first time he told her that she was the soulmate he had been searching for, she was sitting on the grass in a London park, making a daisy chain which she laughingly put around his neck. Sorting through his papers two years later she had found it, dried and preserved, between the pages of his diary.

Later, as she told Barbara, she wondered if it was all just some sort of telepathy, where Jenny was tuning in to her own mind in some way.

"But if she is, it must be a remarkable skill. You can make up your own mind when you're ready, but for now, just accept that the messages are accurate, wherever they come from."

"Then just listen to this part, Auntie Babs, where she describes ... oh ... I'll just play it back for you ..."

"I have a gentleman I've met before, but not with you ... he seems to be on a father level ... he's turning to someone else behind. She's very indistinct, yet I feel she's known to you in the closest possible way." Jenny paused. "I don't quite understand, but he won't explain. She's very beautiful, but she's fading away ... she doesn't speak, but I can see she's sending a huge aura of pink light to enfold you in her love."

"I think I know who that is" Jacqui could be heard whispering, choked with emotion, feeling a maternal love matched only by her own for her children.

"... he's still there; your father. He knows how much you have always loved him and tells you that he has often been near since he passed, but he finds it easier to come to your son in his dreams. They were close, weren't they ..."

"Timmy adored him. There was a special bond between them from the beginning, and Tim often used to say he saw his grandfather in his dreams. I don't know if he still does – it's the sort of thing you don't expect a twelve year old to talk about so much."

"...your father will help him, through coming in this way, whether or not Tim remembers; if he goes to sleep with a problem on his mind, he'll just think he's woken up with a solution in his head, but it's actually a gift from his grandfather."

"Isn't that wonderful? You know, I've always talked to Timmy about his grandfather – I didn't want him to lose those few memories that meant so much. He was only three when he died, but he still has that photograph in his bedroom where he can see it; the one where he's holding my father's hand so tightly, and they're smiling and looking at each other as if there's no-one else in the world."

"... he's asking you to think kindly of him if you hear things a daughter shouldn't really know; there are so many things he regrets but he's setting them to rights as best he can. He's been joined by the other lady – the one with the letter, although she doesn't have it now as she knows you received the message; she's carrying a spray of orchids instead which she'd like you to accept."

"Can you ... can I ...?

"You can say something if you'd like to – she can understand through me."

"I want to tell her the pain has gone. It went the morning after I read the letter, when Richard helped me to let go of it."

"She's nodding. She knows Richard helps you most of all, and she's saying that the two of you have far more than she and your father ever did. She means blessings, not riches. They are both moving away now, but say they will return when you need them."

The tape clicked off as it reached its limit.

༄༅

Barbara sat silently, deep in thought. They had adjourned to the upstairs sitting room after their evening meal; she was staying for an extra couple of days, as Vicky had gone to visit friends for a long weekend, and Jacqui welcomed her offer of company and help with the children.

"Barbara - Jenny made a very telling comment afterwards – she said 'a great house with so many secrets and so much undisclosed love'. Was she talking about the Hall, do you think?"

"Hmmm. I think she might also have been referring to the family; a great house in the Shakespearian, Romeo and Juliet, sense. Sonia's death seemed to open a Pandora's box, and many family secrets came to light." She gave a slight shiver. "How many of us *really* know the people who share our lives? Although sometimes I think it's just as well we don't."

"Well, whatever she meant I'm sure she was right. It says a lot, though, doesn't it, that we can trust her with knowing these things and using them to bring comfort. Thank you Auntie Babs, for giving me the courage to go. She's a lovely woman and I'm so glad I did. I have a feeling I'll see her again, although perhaps not straight away – she's given me so much to think about. I'm not going to tell anyone else about this for the time being; it's too precious. I hate having any secrets from Richard, but I feel he's not ready to understand it just yet and I wouldn't be able to explain, as *I* don't understand it properly."

"I know what you mean. There are so many things we don't know enough about. I've played my tape several times, and at one point I know I heard Jenny's voice change. I could have sworn that it was someone else talking; a man I used to know – one of your father's business friends who had a distinctive manner of speech. That, and all the other things, convince me that she's genuine although I don't know how it happens."

"But have *you* found that any of it helped you?"

"Absolutely. Would you believe - after all this time, I've been able to come to terms with my mother's attitude; she came along to tell me that her own mother had ill-treated her as a child, and *she* knew no better. It makes sense when you think of the way things were fifty, sixty years ago."

Agreeing that, for the time being at least, they would only discuss this with each other, they spent a quietly thoughtful evening – eventually talking about the joint birthday party that was planned for Becca and Gabriel in a few weeks' time.

More clues ...

Well, at least this shows how Cressy takes her own experiences and weaves them into the storyline, doesn't it ... I have my own views of course, on how these 'fortune tellers' can prey on the vulnerable, and I'm surprised that the level-headed Barbara was the one Cressy chose to lead the way; but perhaps that makes it all the more convincing.

References to unsatisfactory relationships with mothers – was Cressy in cathartic mode? I'm trying to remember if she made great reference to her own, but can't recall much more than the usual childhood memories of holidays and school – very little about home life at all. Did she keep that hidden under wraps too? There are always so many questions that we think of after someone has died – it's too painful to dwell on missed opportunities, but I can't seem to let it all rest.

I suppose I sound like a very amateur psychologist trying to get to the heart of what made her tick. *That* was an unconscious (Freudian?) slip – 'get to the heart': these years of hoping I could reach it by patiently waiting, but getting no confirmation one way or the other that she noticed or even cared. Oh for sure, she cared enough to enjoy our time together, but not enough for anything other than a companionship I knew was too precious to risk losing by a clumsy declaration of my feelings. Would it have made any difference? Hard to tell – I'll have to rely on intuition and hazard a guess that I was probably right to be cautious; yet here I am, even now trying to reach that heart and understand, although she's gone and I'll never know ...

What drives me? Is it searching for 'closure', to use the current term? But I can't let it rest. *What* can't I let rest? Am I forever doomed to wander around, searching for explanations I will never find, the burden of it feeling like the albatross around the Ancient Mariner's neck? That 'evidence' she seems so eager to attribute to this Jenny (or her own experiences with "D"?) would be beguiling to anyone with current or longstanding problems. When it comes to it, human behaviour usually fits into various patterns with fairly obvious sources, so the way Barbara describes 'coming to terms' with *her* mother's behaviour is classic and pretty standard. She could have achieved that closure with any half decent therapist, I'm sure. Cressy's attitude towards her own mother-in-law (almost certainly portrayed as Sonia) was to maintain survival mode, by which I mean that she let as much as possible pass by without comment or effect, and only allowed herself to become directly involved with practicalities.

But I do remember her telling me of her total delight on one occasion when, in her 'dutiful daughter-in-law' support role at the private hospital Maud frequented in latter years, she caught a look of sympathy from a nurse who had just encountered Maud's acidly critical tongue.

"It was the one time I spoke up, albeit indirectly. I told the nurse, with great relish, that Maud was in deep shock and was therefore responsible for neither her actions nor her words. Maud either didn't hear, or chose not to, but I felt so good about it, for *ages* afterwards!" I chuckled at the memory.

I wonder how she's going to develop the storyline? I feel there's going to be much more of Jenny. I turned to her diary again, looking for a later entry where she referred to 'D' – ah – here's one included in the notes she made soon after a day when I'd been to see her:-

> *D rec'mends look through life for 'threads': start with simple ones: they = life lessons. N.B. repetition stops when lesson's learned - <u>except for 1 more, for checking purposes.</u> E.g. not being heard - can see pattern from earliest days. Praps this writing helps - no-one can stop me! Can't risk telling anyone & not being listened to/heard (not even T tho I desperately wish I cd) until have produced i.e. <u>published</u> s'thing for world to see. Proof that I <u>can</u>.*

So there I had my explanation for being kept in the dark. I remember her telling me at various times how she had tried in vain to explain some of her feelings to her husband, but found his scornful reactions so hurtful that she learned to hide them away – even from herself, she felt, in the end. As for her fears about his loyalty, he was either not prepared to listen, or by that time was already immersed in finding fresh interests. She'd told me about his business trips, but then rationalised it to herself by dismissing any thoughts about unfaithfulness by telling herself that if she wasn't tempted to stray, then why should he? They had made their marriage vows and she decided to trust him.

"I only wanted to get him to realise that it wasn't easy having to take responsibility for everything while he was away" she volunteered one evening as we took cushions outside, to sit under the old apple tree in her garden. I'd pruned it the previous year and it was promising to show the benefits of a little proper care.

"It didn't become any easier when Greg went away to school, oddly enough – that's when Paul decided that as I had all this time on my hands, as he put it, I should become involved with the charity work – but it was as much to help his business as anything. I made it the commitment it has become and it stood me in good stead when everything else fell apart. I don't know how I'd have coped without something to focus on, and then, thank goodness you came along."

She smiled across at me and my heart lurched; how soon would I be able to tell her? Subsequently, I lived in an emotional chaos of visits, spending time together, alternating between hope and despair for months until my next assignment, to some of Scotland's finest gardens, where I made use of the distance, gave myself a 'good talking to' as my father would have said, and resigned myself to platonic friendship.

The opportune warmth of early summer evenings had to be seized, we'd decided, and during that year, the first one after we met again, we'd spent our time piecing together the gaps as much as creating our own level of companionship. It was when I'd hoped that by listening and helping her gain a different perspective she'd realise that I had more to offer than the marriage which hadn't, by any stretch of imagination, come anywhere near the expectations of either of them. Paul sounded as if he might have been the type of man who would respond more to a wife less anxious to please – if he'd perhaps had to work more at gaining her affections, he may well have shown her a little more respect; a little like the character of Geoffrey, who Sonia had trapped by treating him so poorly.

I had, I realised, fallen into a trap myself – I was starting to identify Cressy's characters with people in her own life. I vaguely remembered a topic of our school days; the history of the novel

– when there was apparently a debate in the latter half of the nineteenth century about whether or not it was permissible to use direct quotes made in real life, or should the novel be pure fiction and therefore not include passages which could be traced to their source by contacts of the author. My own feelings now, I must admit, were less ambiguous than they had been when it was theoretical; encountering passages in her text gave me a sense of secret valuing, and I was pleased that she'd found our talks worthy of recording in this way.

We met more frequently in those early days of our renewed friendship, and I remember many evenings when we would be talking long after the bats had emerged to feast on midges, straining to hear their high-pitched squeaks; eventually, reluctantly, acknowledging that the evening chill had set in and I needed to make my way home and get some sleep. I felt useful during that time, believing that my willing shoulder would hasten her return to normality - buoyed up by my hopes that one day she would be able to see me in a different light – when time had healed, when scales fell from her eyes, when she had overcome the residue of Paul's betrayal and was ready to start again.

I've never thought of myself as a person to experience great regret – I usually pick myself up after an upset, roll up my sleeves and throw myself into my work. This search for the real Cressy is different, however – work is proving to be no solace. All the 'what might have beens' come crowding into my thoughts far too often for comfort and I seriously begin to wonder if I'm becoming unhealthily obsessed.

Thankfully, there's the probability of a lengthy trip in the offing. If I concentrate, perhaps I could finish reading the papers in the second file, then methodically read the diary so that I could question the mysterious D, and hand it all over to my agent for a verdict? That night I managed to sleep a deeper, apparently more dreamless sleep than I had for a long time.

13

It was a birthday party to remember, they all made sure of that; Becca and Gabriel sat side by side – Becca in one high chair, Gabriel propped in his special one, which comfortably supported his body and head. Their digital cameras recorded all the highlights, and everyone made sure that the ceremonial blowing out of candles was captured perfectly.

They had, in the end, decided to make it a family affair. Vicky's parents were so pleased to see how their second granddaughter and her cousin had grown in the months while they were away, and arrived with arms full of lavish gifts both for Becca and Gabriel. Richard's parents would not have missed it for the world and had trawled the local shops to find beautifully handmade clothes for both of them.

Barbara had also been included in the invitation – by now, they knew no family occasion would be the same without her, and she brought gifts of small silver animal treasures; a rabbit for Becca and a mouse for Gabriel.

The following day, a Sunday, dawned bright and sunny so they were all able to go for a family walk when they had waved farewell to Vicky's parents as they set off to visit to their sons – 'doing the family rounds' as Colin and Marie always referred to it. Barbara, however, had elected to stay behind as she was uncertain if she could keep up with the younger ones, and offered to entertain Becca for as long as their walk took them. Vicky made no comment about this, but felt it showed how her illness had taken its toll; however, as Barbara often pointed out, there was no halting the ageing process & one's 'bounce' could quite easily disappear after a setback.

***

The grounds of the Hall were extensive and beautifully landscaped and it was an opportunity for Richard's parents to see them at their best in the early Spring sunshine. Gabriel was in the carrying pack on his father's back, Jacqui walked alongside with Vicki and Muriel, Richard's mother, while Ted and Ben were deep in conversation, having recently discovered a mutual interest in motor sports; Tim hovered within earshot, as it was also a pursuit that interested him, and he was hoping that his next birthday might include a visit to one of the local events. Ella skipped ahead with Lucy, once her little cousin had established which route they were taking.

"My favourite, please" she begged "the witchy one – can we?"

The 'witchy one' was so called because of the ancient landmark in the woodland. It was now in its last stages of natural decay and because it posed no threat to other trees had been left to its own slow return to the surrounding earth that had been its home for over two hundred years. The lower boughs had gradually sunk to the woodland floor and started to rot in among the brambles that had invaded over the last few years, resembling an invading shroud. Mosses cushioned the exposed gnarls – beautiful bright green mounds, with their own delicate maroon stems and flowers. Ella had promised herself that this year she would like to spend a whole day by the tree; there were rabbit burrows nearby and she could think of nothing better than taking a picnic and spending time there by herself. The tree sometimes came into her dreams and she wanted to draw it – perhaps if she asked Richard to photograph the tree she could practise at home.

They all wound their way up the incline to the top of the hill that was reputed to be an ancient fort with vestiges of a surrounding defensive ditch. As they went higher the trees became more dense – beeches, for the most part, but there were some ancient yews towards the top and their special tree was one of those. The girls grew quieter as they walked into this thicker part of the woodland, their feet sinking into the leaf mould of the previous autumn. A hush always seemed to descend at this point and even the birdsong was less noticeable. The path became steeper and emerged from the main body of the beech trees and the yews took over on the west side of the hill – a few more twists and turns and there she was – their own witchy tree, arms outstretched to greet them.

"Look, Gran" Ella said to Richard's mother "can you see her face? It's made from the twisty trunk and where branches have dropped off."

"Screw up your eyes a little" said Richard "then you get the hang of it better."

Muriel did this and sure enough, the face could be seen – a little lopsided, but definitely there. Ella stood on tiptoe against the trunk, carefully placing a daisy that she'd brought all the way from the Hall into a crevice made by one of the low branches separating from the trunk; a habit she had developed ever since her first visit.

Jacqui took Gabriel out of the back pack so that Richard could take photographs of all of them in turn. Finally he arranged them in a group and set the camera to take a delayed shot, racing to take his place at the back of the others.

Tim, Ella and Lucy suddenly started a vigorous game of hide and seek between the trees, then started to gallop down the gentler path which would eventually take them round the lake to the back of the Hall. Vicky and Ben ambled contentedly with the others; having others there meant that they no longer took these walks for granted and had visited their grounds more often in the past few months than in the past few years.

"I'd forgotten how beautiful an English Spring can be" Vicky mused, as they slowed to look at drifts of anemones and celandines, trying to spot primroses hiding in long grass, and lagged behind the others. "We always seemed to miss it when we had our early holiday abroad, and there's really nothing like it, is there?"

Ben reached for her hand to give it a squeeze, then continued to hold it. At one time Vicky would have kept this contact as brief as possible, pulling away, but now her reaction was a warm smile. She shook her hair as the wind ruffled it, tossing it out of her eyes.

"We don't need to escape so much now, do we?"

"Silly old thing!" he said affectionately, without embarassment, and they let the moment lapse into a companiable silence as they followed the others.

∽

"You all look so windblown and healthy!" commented Barbara as they divested themselves of jackets, coats and shoes, making their way to the conservatory, where drinks and biscuits were waiting. Ben took the camera into the lounge, where the large television set was installed.

"With all the wonders of modern science ..." he said, striking a dramatic pose as he connected the camera to the set. "... here we have the intrepid travellers of Woolston Hall exploring the hinterland of Surrey."

The girls had fits of giggling at the various poses, particularly of the group.

"Show Mummy!" Lucy kept saying.

"I'll print the good ones later." Ben volunteered, knowing that Richard liked to keep his family albums up to date, and also appreciating the reason for doing that.

Their day lazed on – one of the memorable gatherings that the Hall was designed for, Ben felt, as he sat with the others later in the evening after the two sets of grandparents had left, gazing into the roaring fire, remembering childhood events when there would be such a busy atmosphere in the public part of their home as the business meetings took place. But this was so much better – family gatherings had somehow become more meaningful since his sister's family had joined them.

In the old days the Hall lent itself to being divided into two almost equal parts, and Sonia had made certain that family life was kept separate. Although Ben had allowed Vicky to make whatever alterations she felt would improve the large house, it had been difficult to see beyond the old tradition and it was only when Jacqui and Richard moved into their rooms that the other part somehow became incorporated into the whole.

The two couples sat until well into the night, all of them feeling the closeness, not wanting to be the first to break the warmth that linked them. They shared stories of the children, then of each other. Ben began to realise how much of Richard's solid childhood had given him the qualities that Jacqui needed – the dependability that seemed to be able to help them cope more easily with the many problems they had been dealt. They were able to pull together in ways that he and Vicky were only just beginning to discover, and although it felt strange, he welcomed this new part of their own marriage – it had not been easy to see past the continuous arguments and blame, but somehow it had happened and he was glad.

14

It was only a few weeks after Gabriel's first birthday, that Jacqui became aware of a tight knot of apprehension one morning when she woke and crept into the room which adjoined their own bedroom. Yet there was nothing visibly wrong. She checked that he was not too warm or uncomfortable. If anything, he was less fractious than he had been of late. She shrugged her shoulders once she was satisfied there was nothing to be concerned about, and yet the feeling would not go away. Should she mention it to Richard? Returning to their room she looked at her husband, still asleep, and decided not to bother him, as she knew he had a very busy schedule that day.

"I couldn't worry him that Gabriel is unusually well and placid" she told Vicky later that morning "but I can't quite get rid of this feeling."

"Why don't you go for half an hour's walk?" suggested her sister-in-law "Blow the cobwebs away while Nanny and I hold the fort."

"I'll just check him again before I go."

There was still no change in her son's condition. He'd had his morning bath and gentle massage as usual, and was sleeping peacefully, his head turned slightly to one side. His breathing was regular, his colour normal, so Jacqui decided she would have a short, brisk walk. The weather was warm for the time of year and there were a few old autumnal brown leaves underfoot as she walked along the gravel path towards the shrubbery reliving her own childhood memories of days when she escaped outside if she could, leaving her brother to his own devices. Sitting on the curved marble seat set against the neatly trimmed hedge Jacqui wondered why she believed in guardian angels and their ways of helping, yet couldn't contemplate a specific God – perhaps it was just that angels felt more approachable. She asked for help – for Gabriel to have the best quality of life that was possible; for all of the family – she ran through their individual names, as she always did; and finally she asked for the strength to continue to care for them all, whatever their future was to be.

The remainder of the day passed as usual – a small lunch with Vicky, more time with their babies, then before long the return of the children from school announced the end of any more opportunity to brood about what Jacqui had decided was imagination. Richard's surgery had finished late and he looked drained. There would be no point in mentioning anything now and worrying him about nothing. He needed a restful evening, but still found the energy to talk with Tim, read a story to Ella and spend several minutes with Gabriel, as he always tried to find time to do.

Their first floor sitting room was within earshot of all the bedrooms, a thoughtful arrangement by Vicky that had reassured them considerably, and in any case gave them the privacy they appreciated.

"Everything all right?" asked Jacqui.

"Absolutely fine – they're all tucked up now and will soon be snoring their heads off, I'm sure!"

If Richard had noticed anything he would have alerted her, Jacqui knew, so she made a determined attempt to relax for the remainder of the evening until it was their own turn to retire to bed, Jacqui returning to Gabriel's room for a last check, as usual..

◈◈

The atmosphere in his bedroom was different. Sometimes, Jacqui had noticed recently, the air felt much lighter and she could have sworn - as she entered the room at night to make sure he was peaceful - she could feel a tingling sensation, but it was nothing sinister. Only after checking could she slide into bed herself and fall asleep; a very light sleep, so that she could hear the faintest sound. There was almost an air of expectancy, and yet there was no visible change in that small body she loved so protectively.

This particular evening she sat for a long time by his bed, oblivious to everything, but willing her son to – to what? Stay with them for just a little while longer? Was that fair? Or selfish? She was so wrapped up in her thoughts she didn't hear Richard join her, and was startled to feel his hand on her shoulder. She looked up and met his gaze, then they held each other closely for a long, long moment as they looked at their son. Throughout Gabriel's brief lifetime they had each unconsciously rehearsed this moment so often that now they somehow sensed it was about to happen it felt unreal – like an old film that was about to be re-run again.

"He needs me to hold him" Jacqui whispered, and Richard reached into the cot, gently lifting Gabriel into his mother's arms.

They had been warned it could happen this way; a sudden infection would meet no resistance, and even before medical help could be summoned, he would have given up his already tenuous hold on life. Checking their son's pulse, Richard found only the faintest of intermittent flutters.

※

They had spent countless hours discussing all the implications, when they first knew the extent and prognosis of Gabriel's condition. Well-meaning friends, and not a few of Richard's medical colleagues talked brightly of the children who survived years of life well beyond expectancy. It would have been easy for both of them to get swept along that route – believing that any quality of life was better than none.

Yet Jacqui had always questioned the validity of that atttude and eventually raised the whole thorny issue with Richard.

"I've not reached this conclusion out of fear – goodness knows, it would take more courage to resist the accepted ways of thinking and the intervention of all the preservation techniques – but, to me, it matters more than I can ever begin to say. Although I know Gabriel should have his chance of life with all the love we can give him, no matter what we have to sacrifice, I equally strongly feel we have to accept that he should live his *natural* span, then we should let him go."

Richard had been startled by this. From the moment of discovering that Gabriel had a serious condition, he had seen Jacqui's fierce protection and had witnessed her boundless patience and her non-complaining devotion, even when she was almost overwhelmed with the exhaustion of caring for Gabriel's needs. The implications of what she said threw all his assumptions out of balance. He had indeed assumed that Gabriel's life would be preserved for as long as possible, and that if it meant prolonged episodes of hospital treatment, then that was the route they would take – as a doctor, he could do nothing but agree with that.

Now, suddenly, here was his wife objectively and rationally suggesting that if an opportunity arose where they had a choice in the matter, they should definitely *not* take that expected course of action.

Jacqui saw his expression and felt his struggle so keenly as he attempted to grasp all the implications. She reached for his hand.

"Don't say anything right now" she murmured. "I just needed to tell you how I was thinking. I don't want you to agree or disagree with anything I've said, until you've had as much time as you need to think it over."

Richard buried his face in her hair, speechless. They sat quietly together for some time, until Gabriel needed his next feed and Jacqui went to prepare it.

It was a few days later, during which time Richard had discreetly approached medical friends with experience of human rights cases, that he broached the subject again.

"Jacqui, I've given it so much thought over the last few days. The only conclusion I've reached is that you're absolutely right in one respect – that is, we make any decision based on what's best for Gabriel. The problem I have is that we're continually being told that medical developments are happening all the time and there may be a breakthrough one day which will help Gabriel have a better quality of life – although to what standard we could only guess. All I can suggest is that we make no hard or fast decisions – there never will be any way for us to know definitely what his true quality of life is like – we have to guess, and we must just hope that he's content to be who he is. Which means I have no definite answer for you."

"Thank you for being so honest, Richard. I'm convinced we'll know at the time. The main thing for me has been that I *could* say all that to you and tell you how I felt, without having to fear you'd criticise or dismiss it out of hand. But one thing I know - I hope we never lose this closeness and freedom to talk in whatever way we choose: talking to you is – oh how can I describe it without sounding sentimental – it's somehow like speaking to another part of myself who's only just been discovered."

✌

That conversation had recently been at the back of Jaqui's mind, but although she wondered if it was a forewarning, there were no signs of any alteration in Gabriel's condition. He'd been sleeping no more than usual, the routine of feeding through his gastro tube had been no problem, and although she made notes every day with one hand as she held him with the other and soothingly hummed to him while he went off to sleep, there was no noticeable difference in his habitual responses. It was purely maternal instinct that made her feel that time was short.

But that night they both knew the time had come. Jacqui held Gabriel against her, Richard put his arms around them both and they willed unlimited love into their son as he took a few sparse and shallow breaths.

It could have been for a minute, or a handful, that they stood in that way, then Gabriel opened his eyes, looking from one to the other with a light of comprehension. But before they could comment, his face softened and his expression changed.

He *smiled.*

It was the one response they had never seen, yet longed for, all his short life – that smile which, of all things, Jacqui had longed for him to be able to show as she tried to do everything she could to bring him comfort in his restricted world.

Now, here at last, in what they knew *was* the last moment of his life, his smile was there for them, as a gift like no other.

His eyelids closed with the sigh of his last breath leaving his weak little body, then he was no longer with them. They could not bring themselves to move, still gazing at that now peaceful face until eventually even the faintest traces of that smile could no longer be seen, although Jacqui and Richard both knew it would stay in their hearts forever.

Eventually Richard prised himself away and gently woke Tim, then Ella, so that they could join them. They had always known that it could happen to their little brother – Jacqui had never made any secret of Gabriel's expectedly short life, although the solemnity of knowing that the end had been reached deeply affected them. But gentle tears and shared hugs helped the healing begin, for all of them, as they took it in turns to stroke his hair and hold his hand for the last time, as he lay peacefully in his mother's arms.

※

Later that morning Jacqui and Richard took Ella and Tim to tell Mr Fawkes about their little brother. They found him in one of the herbaceous borders where he had recently been dividing some of the plants.

"I'm right sorry to hear that" he said in his deliberate way. "I liked to see him being wheeled about the garden with Miss Lucy running round, and her such a happy child to be with him. But he'll be peaceful now, I dare say."

"Thank you, Mr Fawkes, I'm sure …" Richard's voice faltered momentarily. "We thought we'd like to get a tree to plant, but we'll need your advice".

"And we'll need you to dig the hole" added Lucy. Timmy and Ella stood close together, waiting to put their own request.

"I'll bring you a book I've got and you can choose. I don't know if you'll want a tree that flowers or one that grows strong and tall, but the pictures should help. It's just the time of year to be thinking about it, too."

He had wisely chosen the right tone for the children, knowing that any grief, regardless of age, is helped in the early stages by having something practical to plan.

Jacqui nodded - not trusting herself to speak - to Ella to put her own request.

"Mr Fawkes, could we have flowers from the garden for Gabriel's funeral?" asked Ella.

"Of course you can; anything you want and I'll help you pick them fresh. Just let me know when you want them ready. And if you want to plant some later on his grave you only have to say. "

They all thanked him and as he turned to continue plying his hoe, from the corner of his eye he watched them go back up the path, wishing with all his heart he could do more; but knowing that grieving was a natural process and had to take its own course. He had so much respect for Miss Jacqui, having heard from Mrs Ewing about the many losses and troubles in their lives and it did seem unfair that some people had to have more than their share.

~*~

The funeral took place a few days later, with the close family, Richard's parents and Barbara, and although they sent out no official invitations, many local people came to offer their condolences to their doctor's family. At their familiar church and singing a hymn all the children knew, the service felt so natural; the vicar beckoned, Tim led Ella and Lucy out of their seats to stand by the small coffin and describe the favourite things they had liked doing with Gabriel. Jacqui had left them to decide together what they wished to say and smiled encouragement, although she leaned against Richard, nervously twisting her fingers together.

Tim was selfconscious but composed. Resting his hand on the coffin he surprised his mother by revealing how he had now made up his mind about his future career, thanks to seeing the effect his little brother had on all of them.

"Gabriel brought out the best in everyone who met him. It was a great gift, and now that I can see how rewarding it is, I'll want to work with children like him, in some way."

Ella was tense, although determined not to show it. She, more than anyone apart from Jacqui, daily felt the loss of her little brother. Her message was simple and brief.

"Gabriel, you know I'll always love you. Thank you for sending me the dream last night – it was great to see you running around at last and you looked so happy."

Lucy had rather more to say. She described how she had chosen the pictures for his room and how she had decided Teddy Grumps was to be his, then she added

"I've made up a rhyme that I can say to you every night.
You've gone to be an angel; help me to be one too.
I'd like to show you I can be good all day like you.
Thank you Gabriel!"

... and she ran back to her mother's side, scrambling into the pew next to Vicky, who sat with baby Becca on her lap – Becca, born on the same day as Gabriel, but who still had her whole life before her. Ben sat on the far side of his wife, with tears streaming down his face, having seen a quality in his elder daughter he never knew existed.

Vicky and Ben had already found that Gabriel's death affected them even more than they had expected. Vicky had, in time, eventually grown used to the contrast between her own baby and Jacqui's, though she felt awkward about enthusing too much, as Becca achieved the usual milestones of infancy. This had eased in the time that Jacqui's family had moved to the Hall and she had seen Gabriel every day. Somehow, seeing at first hand the tasks that had to be performed daily and hourly, and the devotion and patience that Jacqui and Richard had with their son, gave her more patience with her own child. Becca had not always been an easy baby in many ways, but Vicky had learned, then began to wonder if it had more connection with her own attitude, and something about a relaxed mother leading to a more relaxed child. She dared to look across the top of Becca's head to her husband, saw his tears, and realised she loved him all the more for not hiding his sorrow.

✦

The service drew to a close and they proceeded to the area for the family graves in the churchyard – Geoffrey and Sonia's now well established and well tended. Richard carried his son's small coffin, with Jacqui at his side. The small family group walked behind the coffin, all now very solemn; even the birds seemed to quieten their songs for a few moments.

Traditional words were said at the graveside, the coffin was lowered into the ground and they each took their turn to throw flowers onto its lid – white camellias from Jacqui and Richard, a small bunch of golden pansies with bronze faces from Lucy and Becca, a daisy chain from Ella and marigolds from Tim: Ben and Vicky had brought a spray of orchids from the conservatory – Sonia's favourites - a gift from them and, by proxy, from the grandmother Gabriel had never known.

The grandparents stood at a short distance, with Barbara, all deep in their own thoughts. Richard and Jacqui stood closely together, their arms around Tim and Ella. Vicky held Becca against her shoulder, Lucy leaned slightly into her mother's side and tightly pressed her father's hand against her cheek. Time stood still.

"Let's go home" said Richard eventually, and as he turned for a last look at where his first-born son now lay in peace, a ray of sun illuminated that part of the churchyard – then, out of the corner of his eye he thought he saw a small child sitting on the grass beside the grave. It lasted a millisecond – so brief and unbelievable that he told himself it was a trick of the light ...

... and yet ... it *was* there ... indelibly, in his memory ...

15

It was difficult for all of them to adjust to the changes since Gabriel's death. There was so much missing in all of their lives – for Ella the high spot of every day had been racing to his room when she came home from school, telling him what had happened and chatting about her friends and teachers: although he could not comprehend, he responded to the sound of her voice and, lying in his cot, moved his head towards hers if he could. Timmy, too, had gaps in his life which his little brother had filled – particularly at the weekends when the family usually went for walks and Tim was able to have Gabriel on his shoulders in the special backpack they had managed to find for him. Since they moved to the Hall Lucy had also taken more part in their family outings and would skip ahead, finding interesting flowers to show her baby cousin.

The garden became a natural haven for the older children, and Ned Fawkes gladly kept them occupied with sowing seeds in trays in the greenhouse – there was nothing like starting new living things to counteract death. He remembered only too well how it had been when his wife died years ago and how, for a time, bereavement seemed to take the purpose out of his life. It was only the rhythms of seasonal routines that gave him the incentive to keep on, and many a tear had surreptitiously fallen onto the soil as he worked in those dark months. He sighed. She had been too young, so full of life, and no-one could have foreseen the tragedy of the blunder that turned routine minor surgery into a nightmare of irreversible reaction to anaesthesia, a heart attack followed by several days' coma, and the heartbreak of having to take the decision to turn off her life support equipment.

Their son and daughter had gone to live with Sal's mother in Northumbria, and although he regularly kept in touch and went to visit whenever he could, and always would, it would never be the same as the life he had originally intended for them. They had done well, nonetheless. Jimmy had followed in his father's footsteps, had been able to train at horticultural college and was now managing the practical side of a large garden centre. Vivienne was married, with a husband, house and career in teaching to take care of - and she was very happy, he could tell.

Sal would have been so proud of both of them.

～⚘～

He remembered that morning of Gabriel's funeral when he went to the garden early, to check that the flowers the children wanted were at their best. Lucy was insisting on making a daisy chain and nothing else would please her, he knew, so he had found some Spring daisies by one of the sheds in longer grass and had dug up the clump of soil to bring into the greenhouse for protection. She came along after breakfast with Ella, and the two of them made certain it was the best daisy chain they had ever made, carefully slitting the stalks with a pin, then threading them together. The bluebells had flowered in profusion this year so Tim's choice caused no problem; their deep blue colour and woody scent brought back memories of Mr Fawkes' own childhood, when people from the neighbouring town could be seen gathering them in armfuls to take a little piece of the countryside back home with them.

"They'll be alright" he'd commented over his usual morning coffee in the kitchen. "With Miss Jacqui as their mother they've got a head start on life, and that's for sure."

"I hope you're right. I know she's got her husband to lean on but she looks so frail sometimes – as if a puff of wind could blow her away. I worry that she's not eating properly, too, even though I try to make all the meals she used to enjoy when they first came to stay."

That evening he sat in the comfort of his village home, dozing in front of the fire. The evenings were still inclined to be cold at this time of year and the flickering flames were a comfort at troubled times. He *was* troubled. The family's grief had affected him more than he could say, reminding him of his own past grief and the long road he'd had to take, putting his own feelings to one side so that his son and daughter could lean on him; taking his tears to work and letting them fall on the ground he loved to tend. He wished, oh how he wished he could spare each one of the family the heartache he had known.

He dozed and dreamed – or at least, he thought it was a dream

– the now familiar one where he was in an old building like a very ancient church, walking in a sort of corridor with massive pillars that seemed to stretch for ever upwards into clouds. It made no sense and he always seemed to be walking there without end. But this time he felt himself moving towards a great circular room in the far distance, and as he entered through the doorway was momentarily blinded by the strongest light he had ever seen, coming from a being in the centre of the room. As his eyes adjusted he could see that there were other figures, standing around, but they were somehow not stationary – they seemed to be linked by a quivering radiance of energy like nothing he had ever seen before.

He felt compelled to bow low before the central figure, who reached out a hand – projecting a shaft of light into his innermost being. A phenomenal strength entered him and he knew that he need never again fear he was alone – the memory of that meeting would remain engraved on his heart until his last breath.

The fire crackled as he roused with a start, but it was just the last spluttering of a twig resting on a heap of ashes. Ned looked at the clock on the mantelpiece and realised he'd been there for only a few minutes, although it felt much longer. Rubbing his eyes, he took a few moments to remember the dream, and he could still feel the strength he'd received. He went to bed, puzzled but with a peaceful mind.

It was not long after Gabriel died, during a conversation with Barbara, her longstanding confidante, that Jacqui suddenly and uncharacteristically revealed her deepest feelings.

"*Why oh why* did we all have to be punished like this?" she wept with bitter, angry tears. "I don't know if I can go on trying to keep everyone else's spirits up. Some days I feel as if it's useless pretending that life's worth living when my baby's not ..." she started to sob – wrenching sobs that seemed to come from somewhere deep inside her. Barbara put a comforting arm around her shoulders.

"I know I have the others to think of, but all I can see when I close my eyes is his little face and that smile and I'm worried that I'll wear out the memory, but I can't not have it and I feel so false trying to keep a brave face …"

As she became incoherent and her body shook violently it was all Barbara could do to hold her close. Wisely she let Jacqui's grief take its course and waited until it ebbed away, leaving Jacqui pale and exhausted. They sat, both shaken by their emotions, for some time afterwards, until at last Barbara broke the silence, poured her a glass of water and spoke gently.

"Have you told Richard about this?"

"Yes – yes, of course – but I've been quite matter-of-fact and couldn't let him see me falling apart, or he'd just have one more worry on his mind."

"But he, of all people, needs to know how upset you are."

"I can't risk it."

"Look, I've had an idea – one of the things that helped me get through the time after my mother died was to join a meditation group. Does it still run – the one that was held in the Village Hall when I used to be here? It's not just sitting in silence – we used to chant or sing or move around the room – anything as long as it took us out of ourselves, then we'd have a relaxation and wind down."

"It might help me to have a little space outside the home, I suppose" Jacqui said later to Richard, although a little dubiously, having told him what Barbara suggested. "I sometimes feel as if the walls are closing in."

"It's *certainly* worth a try" Richard immediately responded. "Anything would be welcome that could stop your mind racing over and over things and help you slow down."

He understood only too well the reasons for the way she had been throwing herself into too many practical tasks, trying to fill the great void that had been left in her life. As he also had, he thought ruefully; but somehow men seemed to do their grieving differently, and the distraction provided by needing to return to work was part of the acceptance of a sad fact. He had found a great deal of support from the local patients at the practice and was able to keep on an even keel.

By contrast, after a burst of energy, Jacqui would have a corresponding downward swing of mood that left her feeling tired, listless and only able to manage the most basic routines for a day or two.

They grieved as a couple and grieved as a family, sharing memories of the days they had all been together. They all were deeply affected and as time passed Lucy, in particular, seemed to be more so. She could often be found sitting with Teddy Grumps in what had been Gabriel's room, and she had become noticeably quieter and more thoughtful than before – her tantrums and rages seemed to be things of the past, which was such a relief to her mother and father that they looked no further than that. Jacqui spent a great deal of time listening to both Lucy and Ella's memories of Gabriel, and helping them come to terms with the reality of Gabriel no longer being there; but Richard knew, and was as concerned as they all were, that underneath her brave exterior his wife was feeling lost, and welcomed any interest she showed in doing something for herself. He certainly did not want her to return to any kind of breakdown.

She had attended the meditation with a friend from the village and returned in a thoughtful frame of mind, but calmer than he had seen her for many weeks. He knew better than to prompt her with questions, just contenting himself with his usual hug and gentle kiss – she would tell him when she was ready, he knew. He did notice the welcome change spreading throughout the intervening days as she looked forward to the next meeting – she was calm, more at peace with herself and life in general.

༺༻

As the weeks passed, Jacqui began to return more to her old self. Richard could feel his burden of care for her easing noticeably as she was better able to retain her emotional balance. She had still not gone into any details, and he had wisely waited. One evening she said she was ready to tell him what had happened, now that she was sure she was not mistaken.

"The first evening I was there we sat in a circle on chairs, and the lady who was leading the group, asked us to make ourselves comfortable while she led us into a state of relaxation. It was very much like the relaxation tapes that Anthony used to make for his patients, so I felt happy with that. I was able to concentrate on my breath and go with the prompts - walking down a path to a sandy beach where I could sit on a rock at the water's edge.

"Then - oh, Richard, it was unmistakeable - I felt a small hand in mine. I knew without looking that it was Gabriel. Just for a moment it happened, but it was a warm little hand; stronger than it had ever been when he was here with us, and I *knew* it was him. It brought me such peace that I didn't want to leave that spot. I didn't want to hear her begin to talk us back into the room. Of course I wondered if I was hallucinating, but when she asked if anyone had anything to share with the others, one of the group said she'd seen a small child happily playing. Then someone else said they had too, a little boy who kept looking at his arms and legs and moving them, smiling all the time."

Jacqui looked at Richard apprehensively. He said nothing, but his mind was racing – how could he destroy this illusion that brought such obvious comfort to his wife? Hallucination? Yes, it must be, and a common one too – as his own experience had been at Gabriel's funeral; it was the reason why he'd never mentioned what had happened. Mental processes were such complexities that at times of stress the brain's wiring mechanisms could become disordered. His pragmatic medical mind struggled to find the words that his heart wanted to say to his wife, to help and not disillusion her. He failed to find any, so put his arm around her shoulder.

"I couldn't say anything to anyone" Jacqui continued "it was too precious. I've never seen him so clearly again, but at two other meetings he's been there waiting for me. Once I definitely felt him hold my hand again and another time he was just a smile – the one he smiled when ... when ... oh Richard ... please *please* believe me ..." her tears choked any more words.

What could he do? Richard held her to him as she sobbed. She knew his attitudes to such matters. All of this was something they had long ago discussed in the early days of their relationship, exploring their common ground in beliefs and values. She herself, at that time, had no firm convictions of faith; they had settled for an orthodox attendance at church every now and again, appreciating the music and atmosphere rather than joining in with the stated beliefs. As far as death was concerned, when Geoffrey, Jaqui's father, died and Tim was only three years old, Jacqui had encouraged him to think of his grandfather coming to visit him in dreams, but that was the way children could be comforted. Both Tim, and subsequently Ellie, had been happy to accept that was what would happen - as they did later, when Sonia died.

Should this new interest of hers be regarded as a simply an instinctive attempt at comforting? Even the other group members' experiences might be explained as due to their own heightened receptivity, and a reflection of Jacqui's unspoken distress.

"I believe *you*" he said at long last "and I promise I won't comment until invited."

"An air of amused tolerance would suffice" Jacqui said wryly, with a glimmer of her old self-mockery that had been missing for so long.

He still hadn't told her about the impression he'd received just after Gabriel's funeral, nor did he tell her that he'd explained it to himself as a trick of the light, combined with overtiredness – even now he didn't really find that logical explanation convincing.

16

They waited for Jacqui's tears to subside. The two women, one half the other's age, were sitting in Jenny's conservatory, full of Jenny's passionate hobby - orchids, which reminded Jacqui of her home at Woolston Hall and Sonia's orchids in their own conservatory.

After Jacqui's initial reading, it hadn't felt necessary to pursue matters - for a while, at least. Then Gabriel's death and the consequences took up all of her energies and it was not until some months later, after attending the yoga classes and having the experience of feeling Gabriel's hand in hers, that Jacqui felt ready to contact Jenny again. Their subsequent meetings had started with the type of counselling Jenny referred to as holistic – incorporating spiritual aspects, as well as more orthodox techniques, then over the ensuing months, when they occasionally met at Jenny's home, it was part of Jacqui's search for answers to some of the events which puzzled her, as Barbara's reading had implied would happen.

From the first, Jacqui had found the meetings helpful. This was a therapy she could understand, and one that somehow made more sense than the orthodox counselling she had undergone after Anthony died, unaware that she was carrying his child. In another way, it also linked with the period of her life when she was with Zak, her first husband – when everyone was interested in what was called 'New Age' topics, so some of the terminology was familiar. When Jenny referred to 'soul journeys', for instance, she knew the theory of souls coming into a life that would provide the best opportunities to learn lessons; likewise, karmic opportunities to redress the imbalance and debts of previous lives. But theory was one thing, actual experience quite another, and Jenny handled Jacqui's bruised soul with sensitivity and great care.

The first counselling session had consisted of Jacqui gaining confidence and trust in her new helper, and as she gave her a brief account of the way her life had turned out, yet with no sign of self pity, Jenny marvelled at her courage, as many did. However, she also knew the capacity for strong-willed people to close down on their uncomfortable emotions and rationalise them into intellectuality. Seeing past Jacqui's forbearance, she could sense a well-hidden area of immense anger.

She raised the subject at their next session and immediately Jacqui denied any capacity for anger, as Jenny had known she would.

"Tell me what anger means to you" she invited.

"It's selfish frustration - bitterness and attempting to control and manipulate" Jacqui responded, unconsciously also describing the late Sonia's emotions.

"Tell me what *your* anger is like" provoked Jenny.

"I don't have …" Jacqui stopped, paused, then said in a small voice as if confessing a great crime "well, that's not quite true – but I have ways of dealing with it before it comes out."

"Why do you do that?"

"So that it won't hurt anyone – that would be wrong. I step back, calm down, then work out what's needed so no-one gets upset."

"Hmmm. Do you feel hot or cold when that happens?"

"What a strange question; colder rather than heated, I suppose."

"Have you ever really lost your temper at *any* time in your life?"

"I think I did when I was small, but I can't remember properly. That might have been the incident Anthony's hypnotherapist friend found, but I was too afraid to go back to him. Can *you* explain it?"

"I'll explain what I can see. You know I often get pictures as I listen to someone – well the reason I asked you about the temperature is that I saw you carrying a huge box across an expanse of snow. It felt like the Arctic. It's your own Pandora's box – do you know the old story? The box contained all sorts of nasty things – demons and hideous beasts that had to be let out one by one. But when they had all been dealt with, there was still one thing left in the box – do you remember what that was?" Jacqui shook her head.

"It was Hope. There *is* always hope – and we use that to attempt to improve things in our lives. We hope for something better to happen. When we give up hope we may as well die, and some people indeed have a living death from that point on."

"Do I *have* to dig out the anger?" Jacqui asked, apprehensively. "I'm so scared that I'll turn out to be a really awful person."

"Don't look so terrified. We can do it safely, together, and in a way that you can handle. It won't take too long, even though there's a lifetime of it. It just happens while you relax."

"But what if I *can't* take it? I don't want to have to experience anything upsetting – I've had too much upset in all these years" her voice became tense and Jenny reassured her again, with a soothing tone of voice.

"You won't experience it directly. But not now, not today ... today we'll just do the relaxation on its own. Everything will happen in its own good time"

Jacqui looked at Jenny's kind face, reached out for her hand and found the reassurance she needed. It was strange how someone who was a complete stranger only a comparatively short time ago had become so much part of her life.

She nodded.

Jenny found some music to play almost gently in the background, lit a scented candle, and made sure Jacqui was comfortable in the large adjustable chair with a soft blanket over her body.

The relaxation technique was familiar, and Jacqui found her tensions melting away as Jenni spoke quietly from her chair nearby. Then her words led Jacqui into deeper relaxation, visualising a place which she could recognise as being safe and comfortable, and asking her to remember the feelings of warmth and security.

"This is *your* place of safety where no-one can reach you; available for you to return whenever you wish ...." Jacqui found herself in a small valley by a stream and floated through impressions of flowers and fields, mountains and oceans. Eventually she reluctantly heard Jenny's gentle voice calling her back, back to the room where they were sitting, with a deeper sense of peace than she had felt for a long, long time.

❧

Over time, these counselling sessions developed into friendship and, due to Jacqui's interest, informal tuition. Jenny's knowledge was the result of a lifetime of study and she had been well-known in psychic circles for many years. Jacqui was content with having her private sessions, and did not feel the need to get drawn in to all of the activities of workshops, residentials and more groups, and the time that would have involved. Her priorities were always her family – Richard and the children – and she would never let anything come between their needs and her availability.

Richard was tolerant. Anything that helped his beloved wife was good, but at the same time he was also alert to any dependency that might arise. As the months passed he relaxed, and whilst he could not agree with everything Jacqui told him, he listened and did not challenge. Time enough for that later, if ever – it was enough that she was obviously coping better each day and could continue to talk freely about Gabriel's short life. The daily strain she had been under ever since his birth had naturally taken its toll, but Richard knew, as any doctor would, that it would help enormously when her mind and body had built up their natural equilibrium again.

※※

Jacqui found comfort in being able to phone Jenny when she'd had a particularly difficult emotional day, then began to gather enough strength to stand back from the actual events and with Jenny's help see the positive influence of Gabriel's life – not least with Vicky's children. Lucy had always been different when she was with him – gentle and kind, although Jacqui had always thought it was more connected with the example Ella set, but then realised the situation had developed a side of her that had lain hidden under the defences she'd had to build up in order to survive her parents' behaviour.

A favourite game for Lucy was to pretend that Becca was Gabriel, and the strange thing was that Jacqui thought at times that Becca might indeed have taken on Gabriel's personality – gone was the fractious toddler who made incessant demands, and instead, an amenable little girl took over, who liked nothing better than to be wrapped in shawls and cuddled by her big sister.

Vicky wondered if it was healthy to let their interests centre so much on Gabriel, but Jacqui asked her to tolerate their play as it seemed to do no harm. They discussed it one morning in the drawing room, standing by the french windows as they waited for their coffee to cool, looking out over the expanse of parkland.

"They'll grow out of it when they're ready, I'm sure, but for now it seems to bring them comfort. After all, cuddles and hugs are good at any time, no matter who they're from."

"True. Even Ben would probably agree with you there, and at one time I never would have believed that!" Vicky paused, wondered whether to continue, then decided to tell her sister-in-law. "Please don't say I've told you, but we've been thinking about having another baby, only Ben feels a bit awkward about it so soon after ..."

"Oh *Vicky*! Are you? *Really*?" Jacqui was obviously and genuinely delighted.

"Not yet – well, I mean I'm not pregnant yet, but ... it ... it won't upset either of you, then? This time I feel it would be so different for us, and it will be a very welcome baby. You've taught me about real mothering and I feel much more confident now. You don't realise what you – all of you – have done for us as a family and ... and I want to say thank you for being ..."

Suddenly lost for words she turned and hugged Jacqui, who immediately responded. Tears welling up for both of them, they stood together, thinking their own thoughts and marvelling at the strange twists of fate that had brought them to this point, where they had become the best of friends.

17

Barbara cherished the family where she was now welcomed and appreciated as an unofficial aunt. Once retired from her role as personal assistant to lady Sonia, and as her powers of attraction had dwindled, so too did her opportunities for companionship of the type which she could sustain. Her secret role, as what she preferred to think of as 'private friend' to the select business clients whom she could trust to be discreet, had naturally ebbed away as they retired, or died of the type of disease that designated their position in the society of that time – heart or liver conditions being the commonest.

For too many of those past New Years she had sat alone amongst her treasures, drinking a toast of her own to her own special memories of 'absent friends' - the list increasing in proportion to the fresh memories she had acquired throughout the year. Those 'friends' she made were only too aware of the need for discretion and, as ever, attended to their own family priorities. Locally, she was a well-recognised figure, but one who was noted for her reluctance to be little more than a recluse - even now she had effectively acknowledged her retirement age and allowed her social life to curtail itself. Occasionally she might be seen taking a taxi to the West End theatres, although it was a bitter-sweet reminder of times past when she would have a companion for such outings. She had long grown accustomed to her solitary status and the emptiness of the basic, yet most significant components of a fully satisfactory life, what Jacqui's friend Jenny would have called "the natural order of things", had been missing.

For years she had shrugged her shoulders and firmly shut the lid on what she thought of as sentimentality; it had been her own choice to live her life in this way, after all, and she had benefited materially, if nothing else. Yet now they seemed worthless - objects, that was all they were, and replaceable in case of accident.

What *was* irreplaceable was the welcome she received when she had arrived at Woolston Hall after that time of Ben's banishment. There had been so many visits there in the past, provoking so many different memories every time she travelled again up that familiar driveway between the tall trees. She had fought her way out of those years by taking advantage of one situation, then subsequently and so very discreetly building on that until she had forged her own lifestyle, defiantly denying even to herself - *especially* to herself, she thought - that she was missing out in any way.

That period of mistrust and suspicion, particularly on Ben's part, after revealing more of himself to her than to anyone when his mother died and his wife gave birth; then how she had subsequently seen him at his lowest point as he floundered through the following days, embarrassed him beyond measure, and the only way he could deal with those reactions was to freeze her out of their family scene.

Maintaining contact with Jacqui, and subsequently Vicky, she had heard about and recognised how Ben's attempts to firmly clamp a lid on natural human emotions and prevent his grief from surfacing affected his wife and children – especially Lucy. As he took refuge in applying himself to his business, he formed a hard shell of behaviour that could at best be brusque, at other times downright rude. His childhood of indulgence had insidiously woven its way to a dependency on his mother, and, as Sonia had thought of herself as invincible, so had Ben expected her to be indestructible, so that his anger was selfish and more to do with the betrayal he felt at the suddenness of her death, and Barbara could sense him developing the hardness that denial of emotions brings.

But that was all in the past, and nowadays her arrival was so different. Sitting in the car she gave a slight shake of her head, to clear it of the unsettling thoughts, and reminded herself that now she always entered the house as a truly welcome friend. Time had eased all the negative feelings, and that other period of absence due to her prolonged illness and recovery had merely confirmed her valued and welcome place in the fabric of their family life.

Today, Barbara's car had been seen by the children, who came running towards her as she parked on the gravel driveway opposite the main door. The memories continued to return – of her first visit, when Sonia could hardly wait to show her how proud she was of the achievement of owning this house – the circular drive, the shallow stone steps and pillars of the portico, the balanced proportions of the 'age of elegance', as she always referred to it. She almost expected to see Sonia standing at the doorway, waiting to greet her, but it was the younger generations now – Vicky and Jacqui and their children who were there.

She looked at them fondly, as they came down the steps and hopped around the car – Tim, now in his early teens, showing unmistakeable signs of his father's dark good looks and sense of mischief; Ella, his half-sister, happy and chatty on the surface, yet with an air of solemnity that was never far away; Lucy, Ben's elder daughter, who had at last left behind her tormented years of infancy and early childhood and suddenly, just after Gabriel's death, had become a gentle, caring child who was so much more like her Aunt Jacqui than anyone else.

And there she was – Jacqui – Barbara's favourite friend and reminder of her oldest friend Sonia, holding Becca's hand. When Becca found a sudden moment of shyness, plugged her mouth with her spare thumb, twisting out of sight behind Jacqui in self-consciousness Lucy noticed her little sister's unease and went to her side, to allow Barbara to envelop Jacqui in a huge hug. Then they each in turn had their own hugs – even, eventually, little Becca.

∽ယ∾

When all the excitement had died down and the children organised into an early tea and quieter pastimes, the adults settled themselves on the terrace in the gentle dusk of early summer, with sherry before their later evening meal.

Barbara, Jacqui and Vicky were joined by Ben, on his return from the office.

"Richard's phoned to say he might be a little late" Jacqui said "surgery never closes on time, as you well know."

"But he doesn't regret the move, from what you tell me? It can be very demanding."

"Oh no – it was the best thing that could have happened. Much more his style of working and it has given him the time he needs to write." A shadow of pain momentarily passed across her face and her eyes grew moist.

"I'm sorry, Auntie Babs, I still get caught out at times."

Vicky reached across and patted her sister-in-law's hand comfortingly.

"It's less than six months, you know – it's bound to happen."

Ben looked slightly uncomfortable and busied himself refilling glasses.

"Can we leave all that until later? It will be time to eat when Richard comes along, and I call a truce. What do we have on the menu tonight, Vicky?"

As his wife announced home-grown asparagus soup, spiced chicken salad with new early potatoes, and declared ignorance of the dessert, having left it to the inspiration of the now well-established Mrs Ewing, Ben thought back to the days and months of despair after his mother's death when he thought that Vicky would never be capable of running the house. What had changed her so dramatically into the woman she now was? Not given to introspection, he failed to make a direct connection with Jacqui's ever-increasing friendship and influence; being a fairly uncomplicated thinker, he only rarely put two and two together to make any more than four – but since Jaqui's family had moved into the Hall things were definitely better.

Using the Gatehouse had been a stroke of genius on Jacqui's part, although he would never have admitted it. No longer used for residential staff (Mrs Ewing was from the village and the au pair boarded with her) the two couples had made full use of this private space. It had saved his marriage, Ben knew – Vicky had more than once said how much she had needed time to remember who they both were before parenthood, grief and responsibility had overwhelmed them. In the Gatehouse they could adjust to the people they had become and gradually Ben's resentment faded, as Vicky softened towards him and they rediscovered the qualities in each other that first attracted them.

18

"There's something I've been wanting to ask you" Jacqui settled herself onto the now familiar cane chair, having arrived for another session with Jenny. "Is there a greater purpose in reincarnation than just the individual's development?"

"Do you mean a group of people, or perhaps a family?"

Jacqui nodded.

"Well, let me start by asking what *you* see as the the purpose of belonging to a family, or indeed a group of any sort?" responded Jenny.

"Well ... we grow up with our family and learn about support, then with a group it's the same sense of belonging, which leads to mutual understanding among all the individuals in it."

"Good answer, but that's the ideal, isn't it? What about all the occasions when people's behaviour is less than ideal?"

"Belonging to a family gives you the chance to put things right *because* they're your family and you're in touch. Confrontation, apologies, forgiveness, that sort of thing – you have to learn to do that or the whole structure falls apart. That's why there are so many fractured families, I suppose – they've never learned how to handle their differences. It can apply to groups, too – you have to have an overall purpose that keeps you heading in the same direction."

Jenny nodded, then waited quietly for Jacqui's next question. She loved the way this young woman wrestled with concepts that differed vastly from her orthodox upbringing and was sufficiently openminded to examine ideas that had puzzled so many people for so many generations.

"But what happens if, for any reason, that can't take place? People can go to their graves with unresolved issues - 'unfinished business' - to use a common phrase."

"That's where the idea of Karma makes sense to me; they can return to deal with it in a later life, when the conditions are right."

"Is that what people call karmic debt?"

"Absolutely, and although we usually think of reincarnation as a philosophy which had its roots in the East, there are traces of it in ancient scripts from all parts of civilisation. Nowadays - with more openmindedness among people and the opportunity to study many points of view, it has once again become more tolerated.

"I've always explained reincarnation to my beginners' groups as the oldest form of recycling" Jenny continued "and it certainly can provide a way of returning to the same group in order to put matters right. After all, if you've killed someone in a previous life, you've lost your chance to make amends; in a subsequent lifetime you could have the opportunity to *save* their life in some way, or even return it to them, by being their parent. But don't forget, Jacqui, I'm only telling you what makes sense to me – I'm not going to try to convert you to my ways of thinking."

"But if it were actually true it would also show you the other side of the coin" Jacqui commented thoughtfully "you see, I had a dream the other night, which was so vivid it worried me. I was a really awful man who illtreated everyone he knew and died a miserable death and I was shocked that even though it was my subconscious mind, that there was even a *tiny* part of me that could feel that way. So could it be a previous life and is it a reason for me being able to forgive people like that in this one – am I offsetting the Karma? You said that if you learn from experiencing the whole process from more than one aspect, your soul would be better developed."

"Exactly so - and if you accept that the whole process is about soul development, the more evolved the soul becomes, then the more subtle the lessons become. The individual's soul is one thing, though – but there is also the family soul and the community or companion soul; think about those groups of people and how much we can influence each other."

"Mmmm, I've heard of this idea of knowing many people from a previous life, and certainly there are people I've physically met for the first time, yet who seem very familiar, as if I *have* known them somewhere else, although logically I know I can't possibly have done. How do I know what we might have to settle?"

"Sometimes you don't until you look back at events - why someone came into your life for a time, then left quite suddenly. Take Anthony, for example – did you have that feeling of having known him before?"

"Oh yes – we were always commenting on it, and we called each other our soulmates."

"And so you were – soulmates are very close – whether it's in a romantic way or not. Sometimes the purpose is to deliver lessons that can only be put across with harshness. From what you've told me about him, Anthony *had* come into your life for a purpose – you told me he had restored your self-esteem after your first marriage."

"So are you saying he could have done something against me in a previous life, then turned up to put it right in this one?"

"Yes - in the same way we get opportunities to put things right in *this* lifetime, I believe that opportunities come along within different lives – particularly when they were significant events that caused harm."

"But if that were so, why did he have to die? Why couldn't we have continued with our lives and been happy?"

"Because at that moment he had fulfilled his life's mission in restoring you to a point where you could move on independently of him. So he had to leave you in some way, cruel as it seemed at the time. Betrayal wouldn't have been at all appropriate, as his mission was to restore you, so it had to be his death."

"I can understand what you're saying, but death is so final, and we'd had so little time together. Could that one achievement have been the sole purpose of his life?"

"As far as you were concerned – yes. Before he met you he would have been learning the skills he needed and developing his natural gift of being a 'restorer' in people's lives – that was why he entered the profession he did. His other purpose, of course, was that he had fathered Ella to carry on his memory for you. She has her role to play in the family, as you all do."

"So the difficult times have all had a purpose in a process of rebalancing or developing my karma?"

"What you have to remember is that neither of you had any *rational* memory in this life of what went on in that previous lifetime, or any others – although we can sometimes access those memories by using techniques linked with what people call our 'sixth sense' – that is, a state of altered consciousness. That's why hypnosis can be used. Similarly, some people learn to enter their own state of trance."

"Anthony used to say that there were some patients' phobias that he couldn't deal with in the ordinary way – there was no cause to be found in their current lives, yet when he asked them to go back to the root cause, they would start describing another life entirely, and it was often something that happened as they died, although not necessarily the direct cause of it, that had led to their phobia in this life."

"It's a well-known theory, and certainly there are some well-documented cases which make it sound very convincing; but the critics say we're now so bombarded with information all our lives that our memories store pictures and stories that hide away in the deepest recesses of our memories and we can't be sure of that information, even under hypnosis, being unaffected by them. Some attempts at detective work have been made, linking historical dates, even names, with records, but the results are far too patchy to be convincing for the sceptics."

Jacqui sat reflectively digesting all this information.

"Jenni – I can see how this gives our lives purpose and I can see the need for there to be people who provide the lessons; I suppose it could even explain why some people go through their lives being thoroughly unpleasant – to make us sit up and take notice, but why do some people have really uneventful lives?"

"As you say, not *all* lifetimes have difficult episodes – some are relatively plain sailing, and I'm sure set out to provide us with reassurances that this can be so. If you can accept that our souls have to learn all sorts of lessons, then it would make sense that some lives just show us how to sit back, take it easy and enjoy the benefits.

"Now, I know we could go on talking about this for hours yet, and I'm sure you'll be able to think of examples of all these different soul purposes when you have some quiet time – but that's enough thinking to give you for one day.

"I suggest it's a good time to give you some relaxation before you go home, so that you'll feel calm for the days ahead. We can ask for things to be revealed only when you're ready for them."

❧❧

Jacqui eagerly agreed, as she always looked forward to this part of their time together. Jenny had once told her that the first of life's lessons was always patience, and she was certainly in need of that in so many ways. The relaxation was soothing, and although she had so far never felt any of the major sensations that people sometimes described, she was content to let the usual peacefulness wash over her.

Jenny stood behind her, quite still, with her hands near to the younger woman's shoulders but not touching, as Jacqui closed her eyes and tried to relax. Some days it happened quite easily. This time it seemed slow to happen, then ... suddenly she was aware of a picture in her mind's eye; she was in a house, in an attic, to be precise. The room was quite dark and indistinct, as if it had been unused for many years, and there was an old woman in a dark floor length cape, her face obscured by a hood, indicating to her that there were many shelves of books. Jacqui knew that she was being invited to look through any or all of them, and although their quantity was, on the face of it, quite daunting, she felt that she would be able to in the future. She moved towards the window which looked out on to the street below and observed other people going about their business. Turning back into the room she noticed that the lady in the cloak had gone, the room had become lighter and then the picture faded. Time had no meaning, she felt nothing but peace, then Jenny was murmuring in her ear "come back when you're ready."

Sipping some water, Jacqui told her what she had seen.
"Oh, I'm *so* glad - you've met one of your guides! Shall I explain?" Taking a nod for an answer, she continued. "Those books represent the knowledge that's waiting for you. The fact that it happened in the attic shows you were experiencing this at your highest level of understanding at this time, and the guide is showing you that you're ready to take your learning further.
"It would be really helpful if you could start to keep a record of any dreams you have, and try to work out their deeper meaning, so that we can discuss them. If you can learn how to recognise these guidance dreams and find out your personal language of symbols, it will help you enormously."

And more ...

As I read through that last chapter, and particularly that account of the meditation, I could feel myself actually entering into the state of mind Cressy was describing. Now, while the state itself was comfortable and indeed comforting, I was glad that I could pull myself out of it before I became seduced completely. Elementary hypnosis techniques, of course, but very powerful for someone like me who had never experienced them first hand. And to feel the effects as I read a book? Did Cressy know what she was doing?

I've decided that this is an appropriate time for me to let things settle. I can't pretend to understand all of the contents of the plot that Cressy has started to weave, and that dream 'coincidence' really unnerved me. Yet somewhere, recently, I had read an article on telepathy – as Jacqui had asked Barbara, could this be a form of telepathy linking in with Cressy's mind at some level that enabled a feedback, or where a forecast could take place?

But surely that level would be quite remarkable in itself, and I didn't think I was taking note of all of the plot; if truth were to be told, I was skimming much of it, or had done with the first section, as it was easy reading matter anyway. The second part continued in the same manner as the story of the family developed, but when Jenny was introduced the whole tenor of the book changed and it had become almost a teaching manual in places. Nothing I would have sought out for my personal learning; even so, I felt compelled to read on.

I've just found another entry in her journal which might shed light on things ...

Tea with T. Long eve xploring ambitions. Mine v much based on what haven't ach'vd. T's on lack of depth in life of worldly success – aware s'thing's there but deferring it until old age - ha!!!. My Sp. side opens so many options – I want T to share, but know have to hold back until time's right. Hope T catches up or will b waste of <u>another</u> lifetime!!

I remember that evening – not too many months ago, in fact. We sat well into the night – Cressy wanting to tell me about all the past opportunities she felt she'd missed because of duty to husband and son. When I commented with something along the lines of 'there's always something positive in the most negative experiences' I was castigated for being an unbearable optimist; cushions were thrown, as I recall, and we decided to let the matter rest in a fit of giggles.

It started me thinking, though. Have I missed out, through not exploring this section of life, this spirituality of hers? Had she been looking for signs that I could perhaps embark on the same route, and if so, why? Why did it matter to her that I should catch up and not 'waste another lifetime'?

The implication is that, of course, by now she has really taken on board the notion of reincarnation and yes, it has a certain intellectual beguilement – promising, as it does, that things may be set to rights and that we could indeed have another chance to solve all sorts of mysteries. Yet if that were indeed so, why aren't we allowed to remember; why do we have to start from scratch each time?

I wonder if that's something she's raised with 'D' ... two pages on I find she has:

Y can't we remember? D recmends caution. See Dream (w)

I turn to the back of the book and look for the entry.

> *Dream (w): in school building – junior sch. V crowded & rowdy. Escaped to seniors but almost the same. Rescued by H'master & taken to library. On table is necklace of pearls, am told to put it on. Immediately step through some sort of veil into grand room and see groups of people in earnest discussion, with notes being taken. No emotions apparent – just a sense of purpose and calm. I wake with that same calmness.*
>
> *D confirms H'master is guide, taking me from low levels of learning to appropriate place. Pearls are precious (don't cast pearls before swine). Veil of remembering opened for my benefit. Yes, souls*

are planning next lives, lessons being written down.

D says we don't remember until we're tuned in to this higher level & after studying carefully can see the overall plan. It's wrong to cast pearls until the recipient can see their quality for themselves - and only a guide may judge that moment.

I wonder, if she had still been alive, when I would have been allowed to graduate from being one of the swine?

19

Jacqui had tried Jenny's suggestion, starting to keep a note of any dreams she could remember. That was easier said than done, she found; her sleep pattern was sometimes quite erratic, and quite often she slipped out of bed, went downstairs and made herself a mug of cocoa before creeping back into bed – usually managing to do that without disturbing Richard.

Sometimes she noticed a pattern to her dreaming. The ones she woke with in the middle of the night were often the ones she could link with daytime events and reflected her concerns about the children and Richard. These dreams were often difficult to recall in any detail. But occasionally, and particularly when she returned to bed after sitting downstairs for an hour or so, waiting to feel drowsy again, she would have a startlingly meaningful dream of such clarity and detail that she began to call them her 'significant' dreams. These were the ones she discussed with Jenny, and as she learned from them she began to piece their symbolism together, trying to understand the code, and finding that her dream world was populated with messages and messengers – all connected with her spiritual development. Jenny would sometimes lapse into quite old-fashioned language as she explained what was happening.

"It's because we're dealing with archetypes and ancient happenings from the early part of time" she would explain. "There's no use trying to say things in a modern way because it doesn't fall into place so well."

Jacqui learned that these 'significant' dreams were from her Higher Self – the part of her soul that was accessed through a particular level of dreaming, or in deep meditation; this was her own personal instructor who knew what she needed to learn, and when. The dreams often took on the quality of what Jenny called 'visions' and the intense detail of the settings made them unforgettable. One morning, she had a vivid example of this.

"I was walking in a lane and looked through an opening in a hedge, so I went through. I made my way through weeds and undergrowth and came across a strange pre-fabricated building at the edge of a forest" she told Jenny. "There was a door at one end, and I was surprised to find the whole length and width of the building was filled by a swimming pool. The only way to reach the far end was to swim. I entered the water, moving effortlessly and powerfully, submerging myself three times, then coming out of the water and through the doorway at the other end, into warm sunshine and green meadows."

Outwardly Jenny remained calm and matter-of-fact, but inwardly she rejoiced.

"It's a baptism, representing you moving from one level of spiritual development to another. The weeds represent the lesser quality of your spiritual life that you can now leave behind, and you have no option but to enter the pool for a cleansing and baptism. It's significant that you submerged three times – that's not only to draw your attention to the importance of the dream, but it has the qualities of an initiation. Tell me what happened afterwards."

"I found myself in a nearby house, preparing for a party. Everyone was very welcoming and I realised that the party was for me. I looked around for Richard, but someone told me he'd been delayed and would come along later. I felt quite alright about that, even though it would have been nice to have him there from the start."

"The house represents your Higher Self, as you have learned. The gathering is of old souls who have been waiting to congratulate you and celebrate your baptism into the family of souls who are aware of their purpose in life on Earth. You will meet them at different stages in this life, as they are the ones who will help you to learn. Some will bring you easy lessons, with others it will prove more difficult."

"But what about Richard?"

"You try – tell me what *you* made of that."

"I thought about that for a long time and the only explanation I can find is that it's because he's not with me at that level. But the good news seems to suggest that he *will* be with me at some stage."

"You're quite right, although whether or not he joins you is his own choice – he may not be ready for some time, depending on the develpment of his spiritual journey."

"I have to try so hard to be patient about that!" Jacqui exclaimed. "He shows signs of understanding, then backs away if I try to talk too much about it all."

"Don't overlook the difference between conscious knowledge at the ordinary human level, and the subconscious wisdom of the Higher Self – it's all being stored away so that when he does get to the stage when he starts to believe, it will come to the fore and everything will begin to fall in place. Do you remember how you started to recall puzzling events from years ago, and found that the spiritual explanations were the only ones that made any sense?"

※

Jacqui certainly did. She had never thought of herself as a deeply spiritual person, or one with special gifts, but Jenny had recommended a book which included a description of 'out of body experiences' and Jacqui realised that one of her escapes from her troubled childhood had been to do just that – lying in bed at night she would find a separate self floating up to the ceiling and sometimes out through the window. It was very real, but she had always thought of it as a 'wide-awake dreaming' and something that she supposed everyone did. In time, she began to ignore them, then forgot they had ever existed. Reading through other parts of the book, she realised that it was often simply a matter of terminology, and because she'd had no-one to discuss these matters with, she hadn't learned they had other names.

Jenny taught her how to use her meditations to tune in to some of the very subtle energies, and how to recognise different levels of consciousness, as well as recognising the physical signs that were her personal vocabulary of being in touch with people who wanted to contact her from the spirit world. As well as feeling Gabriel's little hand, she learned to recognise the different energy of her father when he had messages for Jenny to pass on to her.

※

"Why are they the only ones who keep returning to me in this way?" she asked one day.

"Because they are the ones who have chosen to give you guidance at this stage, and as they were the strongest love link in earthly life, it's easier for them to make contact."

"But I would have expected Anthony to be around as well, and there has only been that one occasion – the first time I came, when he gave me the message about the daisy."

"That was the one and only message that was needed, my dear. Once he had given that he was free to go and do the work he's supposed to be doing with others, because he's such a developed soul."

"Oh, Jenny – that does make me feel sad" Jacqui couldn't prevent a sigh escaping, then pulled herself together. "But at least I had *that* message. There's so much to learn about all of this; every question I ask leads to so many others!"

"And that's as it should be – *I'm* still learning new things every day, and the work gets more subtle as I go on and more is revealed. However, let's return to where we started today - remember, the full impact of dreams occurs if you remember to apply the dream to your own personal spiritual circumstances. The confusion that some people find is when the prompts come from something that happened quite recently, so they dismiss the underlying significance."

"Like the one I had this morning perhaps ...?"

Jenny nodded encouragingly.

"... well, I was waiting for a place in a car park at the supermarket and drove round and round, then I saw you, waving to me, pointing out an empty space. On an ordinary level I might have ignored it, as I knew I'd be seeing you today, and yesterday I went to the supermarket, so it was something very up-to-date ..." she paused for a moment, then continued with the other explanation "... but it did have significance, because if the car represents the spiritual part of me, and you are a guide, it all makes sense on *that* level."

"You'll soon be making me redundant" laughed Jenny "but make sure you continue to tell me about all the dreams you can recall – it's such a useful way of seeing how you're progressing."

20

Becca was telling Vicky about one of her dreams.

"Mummy! I woke up this morning and Gangan was sitting on my bed"

Vicky had become accustomed to her small daughter's accounts of Sonia, the grandmother she had never known, appearing in her bedroom; she had sometimes heard Becca chatting away as she played with her toys.

"What did she tell you this time?" she asked, remembering that Jacqui had advised her to treat this as normally as possible.

"She didn't talk. She was playing with Gabriel. He had a new teddy bear."

"We'll have to tell Auntie Jacqui – she'll be so pleased!"

Privately, Vicky told Ben later, she wished that all this would stop; but although he understood what his wife was saying, he also knew that his sister needed to have every scrap of comfort she could – and it certainly did seem to bring Jacqui comfort in some strange way.

"Who knows what we'd be like in the same situation" he said, putting his arm around her shoulder and drawing her close enough to kiss her cheek. Vicki smiled up at him; she had taken time to learn to trust and adjust to the new, demonstrative Ben, but after all the strain of recent months great progress had been made and they now held conversations that they would never have held before.

"It was worth all the embarrassment and tears" she'd told Barbara after their first weekend in the Gatehouse "I thought we'd forgotten how to talk at one stage - but there's a long way to go."

"You've made a good start – just keep practising as often as you can. Don't overlook the simple things – turn and look at Ben when he comes through the door at the end of a long day, instead of saying hello over your shoulder. I know it's supposed to be old-fashioned, but deep down we all like to know that we aren't taken for granted."

Vicky was so relieved at the changes, as of course was Ben, but it was not all plain sailing. Lucy's behaviour had been the subject of one of their most painful discussions in the Gatehouse one weekend. They had raged at each other, neither wanting to accept any blame, although in her heart Vicky knew she was a weak mother. Ben had been accusing, feeling he could never do the right thing, and their arguments always returned to the subject of the puppy that he had bought Lucy for Christmas, not long before Becca was born. Vicky saw it as a selfish act on his part, wanting to put himself in a good light with his older daughter, and had felt powerless to say or do anything, as it would only make Lucy resent her. On this occasion the only conclusion they reached was that they should seek professional help, which they did with visits to a counsellor Richard recommended.

She approved wholeheartedly of the 'time out' element of the Gatehouse and agreed to see them, both individually and together. So, as time passed, it was a much wiser Vicky who could look at her own mistakes as well as Ben's, and forgive herself as much as she learned to forgive him. She and Jacqui had long talks from time to time and was helped as much by Jacqui's sisterly memories of Ben's original personality as she was by the psychologist. She began to see how having a domineering mother whom he adored had been emotionally restricting in its own way – all he had learned was how to please one person. But, while she doted on him, at the same time he had also witnessed her behaviour towards Jacqui, which, as he grew older, puzzled him more than he admitted. It did, however, result occasionally in him being protective of her.

Although undoubtedly Vicky was mistress of the Hall, Jacqui was inevitably the hub of the family, a role she was comfortable with and handled wisely. The individual members of the family began to blend together in a remarkable way that they could never have foreseen at the start, and in spite of the sad events connected with Gabriel's life and death, there was much happiness and contentment so that the Hall, which had housed so many differing occupants and purposes over the years came into its own as the solid, secure family home it had been designed to be.

The Ripples and the Tapestries

Richard continued to write and when his articles started to get published in professional periodicals he was soon in demand for speaking engagements. He allowed these extra demands into his life very cautiously, until he was reassured that his wife was able to handle his extra hours of work, and that the children understood why he wasn't always available. He sometimes incorporated their 'Gabriel tales' into his work, as these illustrated more succinctly how a family could be affected in the minutest ways by having a child with special needs in their midst. He became more and more convinced by colleagues' reactions to his material that there needed to be a bridge between the professional attitudes and the all too human needs of the family. Jacqui's story about Ria haunted him and eventually, as he researched information he needed for his work, he'd discussed a case with a colleague and realised it had to be her.

He did not risk telling Jacqui what he discovered – Ria's baby had been considered to be 'at risk' and had been removed from her care to a foster home in a different town a day's travel away; she was not encouraged to keep in touch, in case it became too unsettling for the child. Having lost the purpose of her life, it was not long before she lost the will to motivate herself to do anything with each day and sank into a deep depression that overwhelmed her. Her mother could barely cope with her own problems, so Ria had no support to help her through the worst time of her life.

Due to her age and circumstances Ria fell through the net of the services who could deal only with the most vulnerable members of society and her plight went unnoticed until she was found wandering at the side of a motorway late one night in pouring rain. Paramedics wrapped her, unresisting, in a blanket and gently helped her into the ambulance, one of them bending to retrieve a photograph she'd dropped – of herself holding a small smiling baby; she grabbed it fiercely and clutched it to her as the rescuer tried to talk and find out who she was.

Richard's colleague had seen the photograph. On that wet night he had admitted her to the mental health unit of the hospital where her baby had been born and had noticed that the background of the photo looked vaguely familiar, then realised that it was the waiting area for the special needs baby clinic. Looking again at the child, he could see how the photographer had carefully angled the shot so that her deformed skull was hidden by the folds of a shawl. Some mothers, he knew, wanted no such disguise, but for a mother in her circumstances it could have been important to have that memory of a baby who looked healthy and happy. The only other information he was able to give was that she was eventually discharged, but had failed to attend any outpatient clinics.

✌✎

Richard realised as he wrote, that there was an increasing and urgent need to start work on the book. This case study could be woven in (without identifying Jacqui's role, as he knew she would prefer to be anonymous) but *he* knew and recognised it as yet another example of the gift his wife had for intuitively knowing how to bless people's lives. She had the special quality which he'd immediately responded to when they first met, and at some level he couldn't define, he knew that they were destined to be together for ever, no matter what happened in their lives.

21

Jenny looked forward to receiving guidance from her new contact, who had eventually revealed a name she could use. She was accustomed to the ways of her constant guides – the ones who had helped with her own development throughout the years, but he was different. This Mr Fu, she realised, was entrusted with the most difficult cases of souls' analysis and recovery – and Sonia had certainly been that. She felt honoured that he should make himself known to her at this time, and knew that it would be guidance for the highest development of everyone concerned.

He appeared in her dreams in the middle of the night, always at the same time and in the same circumstances, in his robes, at the end of a corridor in an upper floor of a high academic building, waiting for her to approach. Jenny, by now half awake, would reach for the pen and notepad she kept on the bedside table. Years of practice had taught her how to take notes automatically.

Always the topic would be additional knowledge and insights with regard to soul themes, showing how Sonia's progress had eventually had a beneficial effect on the family soul because of Jacqui's great capacity for understanding what had happened and also realising that she could, by her own behaviour and reactions, counteract the damage that had been done.

"That is the true progression of humanity" he said one night, broadening his discourse into a more general philosophy, "and why you often feel that no progress is being made within the context of civilisations – indeed, it sometimes appears to be going backwards and making no new discoveries, only rediscovering what the Ancients knew - but that is an illusion.

"Civilisation is unimportant in this context – whatever physical settings humans occupy during their earthly lives, they are the ones which provide the opportunities for their souls to experience the life they have chosen, and for the situations to occur that provide the best opportunities for the subjects that they have already chosen to learn –

not only for their own higher good, but also for the family soul and their group or community soul.

"Bear in mind that these are all being encountered simultaneously, just to make things more complicated, so there is often a discrepancy between all aspects – spiritual, emotional, physical and mental – and it takes a very special teacher to be entrusted with the concurrent development at all these levels. Your usual guides will be available for any assistance in the general way, but I will be overseeing the process, as the timing is crucial.

"Soon your pupil will be thoroughly prepared for the next level of information. By then I will have shown you what it entails, so that you can lead her through the intricate details in ways she will be able to comprehend. You are as adept at teaching on simultaneous levels as she is at learning, so neither of you will be deceived by the simplicity of the conscious explanation, knowing that there is so much greater detail being passed to her Higher Self."

※

Jenny ensured her notes were as detailed and comprehensive as she could make them. Her task, she knew, was to simplify the information before she passed it on. As he explained the finer details of Jacqui's soul progression, he impressed an urgency on her – it was as if he wanted to make sure that her protegee understood as much as she could in as short a time as possible.

Jenny was troubled by this urgency and worried about its possible implications. She asked him why it was so necessary, but he would only give her the enigmatic reply he always used -

"All will be revealed."

And with that she had to be content.

※

Jacqui continued to find information – or to be more precise, it found her. Sometimes she would be in the local library waiting for the children to choose their books, when she would feel draw to one for herself. They were not always in the religion or philosophy section -

she could read a novel and find it gave an interpretation of a spiritual experience that she had not thought to ask Jenny about.

"Jenny, I've come across a term we haven't used before, in a book someone lent me - Twin Souls. It all sounds a bit confusing and I don't really understand the difference between those and Soulmates."

"I wondered when that would be brought to your notice" Jenny said thoughtfully, "but I didn't think it would be quite so soon." She looked somewhat troubled. "I'll have to be very careful how I explain this, as I don't want you to get any wrong impressions. First of all, let's go through the other categories to make sure you're absolutely clear about them - Companion Souls first."

"They're the ones we meet with in this life, in order to learn specific things. We've met them in previous lives and then, in between lives, agree to meet again when we're planning our life tasks. But of course we don't remember any of that by the time we're actually here."

"Yes, that's so. Now then – what about Soulmates? I once asked you if you could identify those people who you felt had had a significant influence on your spiritual development: at the time you could only think of your father and Anthony – and, of course, Richard – but we'll leave him out of the equation for a moment. Have you remembered any more?"

"Well, there was a strange, but disappointingly brief encounter with a girl that I'd known at school. It was not long after I'd realised that Zak and I were drifting apart. We accidentally bumped into each other while shopping one day, had a coffee together and I was in such a state I couldn't help but tell her about it. She advised me to get out as soon as I could, and *she* mentioned Karma – saying that the system would sort out revenge far more effectively than I ever could. At the time, I supposed it was something to do with the old saying 'as ye sow, so shall ye reap'.

"I had a terrible time, but I found that I *could* cope, with the help of Aunty Babs, and of course, the bonus was that I had Timmy. I knew it was all making me a stronger person, and far from seeking revenge, I was glad when he found someone else."

"Did you ever feel that Zak was a person you'd known before you met?"

"Oh yes! That was what we both felt. At the beginning he used to call me his Soulmate. Do you think we were, Jenny? I get puzzled by this because I also felt this way with Anthony – can you have more than one Soulmate?"

"You can encounter several during a lifetime – some are harsh and some are helpful, but they are the souls who have been entrusted with aspects of your emotional purpose and development, whereas Companion Souls help you learn about the day-to-day matters that come along, such as forgiving and having patience. They may be everyday lessons, but they can take *years* to learn, and some people never do, or only get part way, then have to do more in later lives."

"Did I ever tell you that a long time ago I met a woman at a Psychic Fair who told me Anthony and I had been together four times before?"

"I sometimes get messages about that sort of thing, but it's not my usual way of working. You could try going back to the hypnotherapist to get more specific details about that, and even the lessons you came to learn – it depends how curious you are. Another option is to ask for more information in dreams, although not everyone can do that so easily."

"Like Companion Souls we meet and work with our Soulmates when there is an important emotional lesson to learn, and I'd like you to go away and think about what these might be.

"But to return to your original question – Twin Souls are very different. Put very simply, Twin Souls were originally one soul, who became divided and separated, in order to develop independently. Whilst they are living all their various lifetimes apart, every Twinsoul has a deep longing to meet their other twin, as they aren't complete without that happening; it's like the pull of the strongest imagineable magnet. Once encountered in an earthly life, the unmistakeable potential of their joint power is revealed. There is always a Divine purpose to that meeting - a particular task for them to accomplish together for the greater good, and they know at their deepest levels that they have this significant purpose to achieve in the future – both on Earth or afterwards."

"What happens if they meet and one is more developed than the other?"

"What made you ask that?" Jenny looked intently at Jacqui.

"It was only a thought that popped into my head as you explained."

Jenny was suddenly aware of the presence of Mr Fu in the room and was startled, because he had never appeared while she was with anyone. But he smiled benevolently from one to the other, so Jenny knew that the time was right and that the guide would help her find the right words. She took a deep breath, knowing where the information would lead.

"As I understand, it does happen that one is more developed than the other, and the developed one will realise the significance of their meeting, but the other will not – not in *our* terminology, anyway. I've also heard it's possible that neither of them recognise this for what it is at first, and indeed, they may even be together for years thinking they are Soulmates, before they are allowed to understand that they have a higher purpose.

"The most likely situation is that they develop a relationship at a level that both can understand, such as getting married or working closely together in their careers, which can last for many years. Sooner or later though, if the undeveloped soul can't 'catch up' with the other one's developed spirituality, circumstances part them. Even though this is temporary, until they meet again once their earthly lives are finished, it is an extremely difficult experience for them to tolerate, as you can imagine, because at their souls' level they know they should be together for evermore."

"*Is* it possible for one to catch up spiritually with the other?"

"It is, but you must remember that we're talking about unusual events when we consider them even meeting in the first place. However, *nothing* is impossible when dealing with these highest matters. I've been told they're recognisable by the power they have when they work together – a special kind of energy that eclipses anything else."

She looked across anxiously at Jacqui as she finished talking, wondering if her young friend was actually going to ask the question that hovered in the air between them.

"People comment on Richard and myself – how close we are and how much love we have. How can I tell whether it's earthly love, soulmate love, or indeed this other type of belonging?"

Jenny glanced at Mr Fu, who had put on his most inscrutable face, even as he planted the reply in her mind.

"It will be revealed to you in unmistakeable ways, but only when you need to know."

※

Jenny made certain Jacqui was 'grounded', as she called it, before she would let her leave for the short drive back home. After she put a cup of tea in front of her younger friend and they chatted about the children, she did a final mental scan to see if there was any need to warn her about traffic conditions, but this time all the roads felt clear.

They shared a long warm hug, then Jacqui drove away, feeling her usual elation mixed with curiosity, and wonderment that she had found such a wise friend.

Musing over the afternoon as she made her usual notes, Jenny realised how taken aback she had been by a surge of emotion as she finished her explanation; it was as much as she could do to keep her voice normal while she talked of more mundane events. That evening as she meditated, slipping into a deep level of consciousness, a guide of immense energy and surrounded by an intense light appeared. He came with a clear message.

"It is ordained that these souls <u>will</u> know, and in that moment of knowing will come Home. Fear not, all will be well."

Answers ...

It feels like the right moment to phone this person 'D'. I hear a welcoming female voice on the line.

"I'm sorry, I only know you by your initial, but we had a friend in common ..." I get no further.

"*Troy!* Oh, I'm so glad you rang. I didn't know how to contact you. Cressy never gave me ... when are you coming to see me? We have so much ground to cover and in any case, you've reached that part of her story where you need to hear from a third party."

"So you know about the book? I've almost finished reading it."

"Yes, of course, and it was such a labour of love for her. *She* knew its purpose, thank goodness, but she also had to trust that you'd be interested enough to do the detective work."

The torrent of her words does nothing to disguise the tone of relief in her voice; I wasn't suprised to hear she'd been hoping to hear from me at some stage. We arrange for our meeting to take place on a day when she has absolutely no other commitments, and it fits in nicely before a trip for which I had just been booked – a combination of talks and filming visits to hidden gardens in Virginia USA, tracing the legacy of British influence on descendants of the colonial settlers.

A few days later, walking down the path which Cressy had trodden many times, I experience a feeling of familiarity, but dismiss it as anything other than a recollection of something I'd read – in all probability Cressy had utilised it in the book, as Jenny's house. Diane had sounded friendly on the phone, but I'm not quite sure what to expect. Opening the door then ushering me in through the corridor which led to the conservatory Cressy had described, she turns and holds out both hands to me, looking me up and down as if to reassure herself that I was actually there.

"You can't imagine how many times I've thought of this moment, and longed for it too – you will have the explanations for anything you care to ask for. Cressy will join us, too, I'm sure."

I must looked startled at this, so she hastens to reassure me that I needn't be fearful.

"It's just part of the way I work, Troy, and what better way of healing people than by putting them in touch with their loved ones? But we don't have to if you'd rather not. Sit yourself down and talk to me - about yourself, about Cressy - and anything else you can think of. The coffee's made and the whole day's available."

I begin to relax within minutes, feeling Diane's gift for putting people at ease, her manner reassuring me that her normality is unexceptional, even though her singularities are so unusual. She listens intently, nodding her head as I talk about events that she must have heard Cressy describe. As I pause to pour my third cup of coffee, she dabbs her eyes with a tissue.

"Tell me about your pain – I can feel it so keenly."

"You know?" I ask, wondering what Cressy had divulged. But I was still not absolutely certain that Cressy had known, so how *could* she have told Diane?

"I know, yes - more than Cressy ever told me. *Her* pain was that she felt she was a great disappointment to you."

I'm astounded. My poor darling Cressy – if only you had said as much, I could have swept you into my arms, kissed away all those fears and set both our minds at rest. Disappointment? *I* am the one who feels inadequate – particularly after I've found that she had been keeping this side of her life hidden, while it was so obviously something she believed in. I can't hold back the tears for a moment longer.

Diane sits with me, waiting. I weep for lost opportunities, for my unrequited love, for what I see as the sheer waste of it all. Picking up my thoughts, Diane comments softly and tenderly.

"It *wasn't* a waste, you know. There is a message to the world in that second book – a message of great hope.

"Let me explain a little more. You've probably begun to realise – when she started writing she used her own research and some of her experiences and it started as a portrayal of the Afterlife, put in a way that would be understandable for the averagely unaware reader. That was fine – it mirrored her own stage of development, then something new started to take place - some of the passages she wrote were happening at the time of writing. That was slightly scary, she felt, but she adjusted to it. Then, as she was planning the second book, the sequel, her own development began to speed up - and I must say she could absorb and understand the most difficult concepts really quickly. She started including them and so it became a parallel to her own understanding."

"I don't know that *I* understand - is it the idea of the Twin Souls? If that's what you refer to, it all seems a bit far-fetched to me and bears no relation to anything I've experienced or heard of before. Just a twist of fantasy, I thought – but I don't mean to offend you" I add hastily as I see her face cloud over.

"Oh no, *that's* real enough, and as we worked together Cressy knew it - from the inside, as it were, and knew it had to be part of The Tapestries."

I can't see what she means.

"How did you both work at the book? How did it start?"

"Oh, the writing was all hers, but the start of it, well, it was very like the passages in the book describe it – a friend of Cressy's had been for a reading and told her to come to me because she was so upset after her mother's death. Like Jacqui was after Gabriel died - that was how she had most of her material for the story – she lived it, then wrote about it. That was why your friendship meant so much to her – she needed to experience that quality of companionship and support in order to describe it convincingly – you and Cressy 'were', to all intent, Richard and Jacqui. Your scepticism came in handy, too."

"But Jacqui and Richard were the greatest of all lovers, and …"

"She didn't dare risk that – don't you see? If you'd actually had the romance in your lives it would have influenced the necessary part of the story, and it would either have never been written or it could have turned out so differently that it might have destroyed it."

Lost in thoughts of 'what might have been' for several minutes, I eventually rally and asked the unthinkable.

"But the Twin Soul idea; are you saying that she thought …?"

"More than that – she *knew*. But, as she gets Jenny to explain, few of the Twin Souls get to be together in earthly lives. What really concerned her was the way that she'd begun to write about things that were yet to happen – you see, the trouble with general predictions is that very often we can't tell when, where, or to whom in any great detail."

"Then what about those predictions that she weaves into the

storyline? Does that mean that if *I* start to believe, I will die?"

"Don't forget, it doesn't have to actually happen - there is always choice. You can choose to remain a cynic, and even if you start to understand that part of the story, see it as allegorical - it was not until Richard actually *fully* realised and felt it in his heart, that the prediction could happen. If that happens to you, you can see it as the old part of you dying and the new you living on with the knowledge."

It was too much to take in all at once and Diane realised this. As she rose to switch on some music before heading to the kitchen to assemble a salad for our lunch, she reached across and briefly touched my arm in a comforting gesture – so similar to the touch I had felt in Cressy's flat on that final visit I could have sworn...

A hauntingly sweet melody now plays in the background and I settle back in the chair, eyes closed, feeling that this is the closest to the real Cressy that I will ever get. I feel a disconnection, as if I'm floating out of the room, then somehow 'see' in my mind's eye, a gateway into a meadow. I try to open the gate, but it is firmly padlocked and, frustrated, I have to turn away, although just as I do so I have a fleeting impression of a figure in the distance. Could it be? I shiver and rouse myself from that half-dreaming state just in time to prevent myself from getting lost in the yearning.

Diane returns, we adjourn to the dining room for the meal she had been preparing and the conversation takes on a much lighter tone while we eat. She has a fund of stories from the days when she was on the psychic merry-go-round, as she put it – appearing at shows in various venues, meeting all sorts of characters among the professionals as well as the public who attended. As she talks I realise what a very positive character she is, seeing potential good within the most negative situations, and always advising the 'take a step back' approach, in order to see the bigger picture.

"This is where people like me get their peace of mind" she explained. "If I couldn't take that step back, I would soon get caught up in the traumas that people bring to me, and wouldn't be able to help. It's the same with any form of counselling - you can become close, but still need to retain an element of detachment in order to be most effective.

"In the end I had to give it up - I was in danger of too much toxicity rubbing off and damaging me. Some people can do it for years and have no ill effects, but I was told I had to stop ..." Seeing my puzzled look, she elaborates " ... by God, the Creator, the Universe, the Big Guy - whatever you want to call he/she or it."

"So - forgive my ignorance - how does this message come to you?"

"Sometimes it's a voice in my head, sometimes it's something I wake up hearing. Do you know much about that?"

I must have looked startled. I was remembering Annie Lennox and *'everyone needs something ...'*

"No. No - " I say hastily "- it's nothing important; just one of the odd things that happened when I first started reading the diary."

"I never knew about the diary until you mentioned it. That was how you found my number, was it?" I nod. "Did she say much about me?"

"She listed dates you'd met, and she added comments you'd made in answer to questions she put to you, but I've not come across more than that - it seemed to be very much a working notebook or journal. The only thing that's strange about it is the way she writes - it's full of abbreviations, tiny and cramped, not at all like her usual style."

"Hmmm - I've heard of people doing that when they're writing about the higher things, but I don't know why it happens. Perhaps to deter prying eyes."

We sit, with the remnants of our meal uncleared, coffee pot at the ready. She knows I'm hungry for information - *any* information I could glean about my beloved Cressy, and tells me about many of their sessions together, filling in the background to what sounded like a full-blown spiritual awakening and development; rich in its content, wide-ranging and effective in its delivery.

"But *why* couldn't she tell me?" I hear myself bleating like a cheated, lovesick youth.

"Because she knew it wouldn't be *your* path and would cause too much pain for either of you to attempt to keep in step with the other. At best, you would have been humouring her, in the name of love - at worst, she would have held back her own development, also in the name of love. It can be an uneasy relationship between souls, when earthly desires want to take precedence. Think of it as not so much a holding back *from* you, but her gift *to* you – a sacrifice she made on your behalf, of withholding her feelings from you.

"It demanded great courage – she sometimes wondered how she could go on, having the torture of physically spending time with you, talking on the phone, emailing, texting – all the modern methods of communication which, although so helpful in one way, mean that contact can be almost too frequent - yet at the same time, having these wonderful experiences she couldn't risk sharing with her dearest person in the world."

I feel an overwhelming sadness as I listen. All the 'what-might-have-beens', the 'if onlys', crowd in and threatened to engulf me in waves of grief. Diane has spared me nothing, but it is exactly the honesty I need in order to understand the nature of Cressy's feelings for me.

"This will be the only time we meet" Diane said, "and I'd like us to make the most of it. You may feel you've got what you came for, but I need to know what you're planning to do with the book she left for you. She asked me to find out."

"I've been in touch with my publisher" I replied, "and although it's out of her usual sphere of operation, she has contacts. One of them has suggested that I could include the two sections of Cressy's story with my own quest. Disguise it in a way - if I prefer to do that, of course - and it could be marketed as a modern mystery, with a fictitious author's name. Even today's events may need to be included in the story, so it's very much a 'work in progress', as they say. May I ask you a favour?"

"You want me to respond to any enquiries in the event of your premature death, don't you? Don't look so surprised – it's no use me having the extra powers if I don't use them!" She chuckles infectiously.

Her teasing response lightens our serious mood, and I willingly agree to her suggestion that she should give me a period of healing before I leave. Making our way back to the conservatory, I settle again into the chair as she switches on another CD – this time of beautiful plainsong chanting that resonates deep within a part of me I feel I have forgotten for centuries.

The low volume is the perfect background for the visualisation

The Ripples and the Tapestries

she uses – new to me as an actual experience, but familiar because of reading the book. I *recognised* the pathway down the incline, the tree branches meeting overhead then thinning out as the hedge grows sparser and the pathway sandier - the sight of the shoreline, the feel of the soft sand as I walk onto the beach, then the firmness at high water line. The smell, the warm sun and the sounds of the gulls as they wheel in the sky takes me back to childhood memories, although the setting is new. There are the rocky outcrops I remember from the book, and Diane's voice gently making me aware that as I step around them I will meet a friend.

I know ... I had *always* known she would be waiting ... we move towards each other in agonisingly slow motion, yet savouring each moment as we draw closer at last and share the embrace we have never had. No need for words. It feels as if it will last for ever and we never need be parted ...

But from far away and all too soon come Diane's words, helping me return from that special place; reminding me that I will be able to retrace my steps at any time, to feel *that* love and closeness the two of us had denied ourselves in our earthly lives.

Somehow, I return to my work. The deflation I inevitably feel during the following days is soon overtaken by the need to prepare for my trip. Even so, I make sure I allow time to read through the last pages of the book and add my final notes.

It is a compulsive deadline I somehow *have* to meet, and I feel Cressy urging me on.

22

One Friday, towards lunchtime, Ben tried again to telephone his wife, but her mobile was switched off. She was probably having her hair done or talking with Jacqui, he assumed. A few years ago that would have irritated him intensely, but he shrugged and turned back to his paperwork, then put down his pen and enjoyed the feeling of being less 'driven' these days than ever before. The business was in good shape, his clients were of the highest standing and his mother would, no doubt, be proud of him and the way he had developed the family concerns. Ah, his mother ... his mind wandered back to the years they had all put behind them, and although she was seldom mentioned now, when she was, it was with a different attitude. Although no-one else would ever know the contents of Sonia's letter apart from Jacqui and Ben (and of course Richard), the passage of time and Jacqui's generosity had served to erase the vindictiveness of Sonia's action.

Barbara's presence had also helped, he thought; nowadays, she could often be prevailed upon to tell humorous (or sometimes scandalous) anecdotes about the weekend business parties that were held, and Sonia's unawareness of the 'extra-curricular activities' that went on, telling it all in a way that skilfully avoided giving any embarrassment to Ben. She made it sound like the traditional theatrical farce, although sometimes with far more at stake than family honour – international consequences could have ensued were it not for the discretion of Barbara and other staff.

"But bless her for her innocent arrogance!" she had once said. "Sonia was like Queen Victoria – if she hadn't experienced something she refused to believe it could happen in her world – so, as long as everyone kept things secret, she knew her world was perfect."

Vicky, once she had overcome her resentments and depression, had returned to the girl he had first known, Ben mused. Jacqui had a lot to do with that, he was certain, and maybe Barbara too ... he was pleased to turn into the driveway each evening as he returned from the office, knowing that he would be welcomed by one or more children and told tales of the latest events in the village or school or taken to the vegetable patch to admire the latest crop they had grown; Lucy's enthusiasm in particular hadn't waned, which surprised him, but perhaps she had something of her grandmother in her.

◈

He'd decided to leave the office slightly early, telling his secretary to handle any enquiries, although at that time on a Friday afternoon it was unlikely there would be any futher calls – and called at a florist to buy some of Vicky's favourite flowers – the heavily scented lilies she loved. Turning into the driveway he saw the gardener in the distance with Lucy and Ella in their gardening clothes. They heard the car's tyres on the gravel and enthusiastically waved as he came to a halt.

Vicky emerged from the shrubbery where she and Becca had been chasing one of the three kittens that had been born a few weeks previously in the greenhouse, unknown to Ned Fawkes, who hadn't the heart to take them away. Once Lucy had discovered they were there she immediatey adopted one for herself and the other two on behalf of Becca and Ella - so it was fait acompli, and the Hall now had resident cats. The little tabby was enticed out from the bushes with a paper 'butterfly' on a piece of string.

"What shall we do this weekend, Tuppence?" Ben swung little Becca high into the air. "Would you like to see the horses?"

They often went to the nearby stables and Becca showed a keen interest in riding. It would soon be time to get her started thought Ben – he could just imagine her riding in the local Pony Club, then progressing to three-day eventing and maybe the Olympics – as ever, his ambition knew no bounds.

Vicky carried the flowers and linked her arm with his as they strolled back to the terrace. She went to the kitchen to find a vase for the lilies while he sat and waited for her return, half-listening to Becca chatting to the kitten, now worn out with its exertions and lying on the warm stones, lazily washing a paw.

Reappearing with a tray of tea and fresh baked scones that Mrs Ewing had left ready in case anyone called.

"Life doesn't get much better than this ..." he said contentedly as he piled cream and jam onto a half-scone, and sensing the mood he was in, she felt that this would be the best moment to pass on the news that would define their future together.

"Well, it depends on you, but it might ..."

"How could it? I've got you and the girls and all of this!" he indicated the view across the rolling fields to Box Hill in the distance.

"Ben, how would you like a son to add to your troubles?"

For once in his life he was speechless.

"I didn't want to say anything until I was sure, but I went for a scan this morning and decided I'd like to know this time." She looked anxiously at him. "You don't mind, do you? I know we'd vaguely said it might be a good idea, but we hadn't actually agreed anything and it's a huge surprise to me. *Please* say you don't ... oh please say *something* ... anything ..."

He went over to her chair and cupped her face in his hands; she saw the tears of joy welling in his eyes and knew she needed no words after all.

23

It had been a successful Conference, with many world medical figures of renown in attendance or taking part. Richard's paper on "An Unmissable Opportunity for Choice" had been delivered in his inimitable style – with insight and even humour at times. But he made no attempt to disguise his emotions; why should he, when they were what prompted him to write about this most difficult of subjects?

He portrayed his wife's devotion and his own professional dilemma with great dignity – explaining how only too often, even fellow medics, those in charge of a 'case' hid behind their 'rules' and swept people along with little or no room for discussion or individual decision. The profession was more accustomed to people wanting to prolong life at all costs, and had in fact compounded those views with their hovering fears of litigation if it did not take place. Squeezed out, only too often, was any respect for the parent who said "this will be too much for our child – let them go without more intervention, any more fight – because the quality you foresee is not quality at all."

Richard and Jacqui both knew that Gabriel had been fortunate to have his final crisis at home. He had gone with peace and love in the gentlest of ways, in the arms of those who mattered most to him. His brother and sister had also been able to understand this natural process, and their inevitable sadness nonetheless contained a marked quality of acceptance, having had the likelihood explained to them from the time of his birth.

Richard's final quote, as he said, was from the book he had recently published, and was the example he wanted to share to illustrate how it was possible to experience the dignity and peace of death.

"I'd like you all to hear how it was for us - then reach your own conclusions ..."

"It had been so gentle. There was no sign of stress on that innocent little face. I held him closely while Jacqui lit candles, then I handed him back

to her while there was still some warmth in his little body. I went to his brother and sister's rooms to gently wake them and explain. They joined us in his bedroom. We encouraged them both to stroke his cheek and talk to him. Tim whispered to him about being able to meet the grandfather he'd never known, who Tim could barely remember; Ella kissed him, and told him he'd be able to learn how to run and play in the place he was going to. Jacqui continued to hold him closely for a long, long time.

It was only when we were all ready for the family phone calls to be made that she laid him down in his bed, and we found we were all able to weep tears of parting and take the first steps along our long road of grieving."

Richard's description of the event, dignified, but with a few inevitable brief pauses in order to retain his composure, was undoubtedly moving; and like no other argument, was strong persuasion for understanding and allowing the individual needs of a family to be accepted. The end of his speech was greeted by a long silence. He stood, head bowed for a few moments then gathered up his notes. As he turned away from the lectern, the applause began and swelled. Some of his audience stood, visibly moved by his words.

He found his way through the crowd of delegates with great difficulty, so many of them wanting to congratulate him with a quiet respect and empathy.

Eventually, as the numbers thinned, he was able to make his way to the refreshment table, then, with cup in hand, looked around for a quiet place to gather his thoughts. An elderly man stood not far away and Richard thought he vaguely recognised him, so nodded in acknowledgement as he made his way to stand nearby, with his back to the remainder of the room.

He had second thoughts. No, it must have been a trick of the light – in any case, it could not have been *that* man. However, there was certainly an uncanny resemblance to the gardener at the Hall – he could have passed for an older, close relative. The man moved nearer and started to speak in a compelling low tone.

"You have delivered your message well, Richard. The immediate effects will be evident and will take you by surprise; the far-reaching effects of this child's purpose in being born to you has atoned for the previous life. Now it will continue to change attitudes for many more years to come, but you are soon to be involved in other things as yet undreamed of."

Richard smiled pleasantly, not feeling a need to reply or question, although he did not totally understand. The old man continued to look earnestly at him as he spoke again.

"The unique forces that are at work with, and within your family will give each and every one an opportunity to show themselves at their ultimate best. It will not be easy for them, but your wife has paved the way and you yourself will soon come to realise that her words are true. The message has been delivered and that part of your work is done.

"Now you will be able to join forces to work with the cosmic message. We will meet again soon and then you will understand. All will be well."

With that, he smiled. Richard's heart almost stopped; the smile was so much like ... it was almost as if Gabriel's face had been superimposed on the old man's. He realised that he was probably staring quite rudely at him, so turned away on pretext of finding a place to set down his drink.

"Forgive me, I don't know your name ..." he began as he turned back, ready to shake his hand – but there was no-one there. No nearby door could have provided his exit, and although he looked around there was certainly no-one of his description making his way through the other delegates.

His reactions were mixed – prosaically he could tell himself that there was a rational explanation and the old man must have been capable of moving more swiftly than he thought. He might also attribute the whole thing to overtiredness, yet he could remember the gist of what he said quite distinctly.

He would tell Jacqui later. The final words echoed in his head – "all will be well" - and brought him comfort for the remainder of the day before he returned to the hotel.

※

While Richard fulfilled his Conference duties, Jacqui had been buying gifts for all the children. Then they had planned to stay for a further two days in New York, sightseeing, but they found that the newspapers had covered the Conference in detail, and the TV stations, ever quick to pick up a human story, were ringing the hotel, beseiging them when they went out, and asking for interviews.

It seemed easier to agree to shelve the sightseeing and agree to the interviews the following day, so that it could be networked, then carry out any further plans for last-minute shopping and fly home as arranged, the following morning. There was to be one interview with Richard alone, for the serious medical fraternity, then another appearance on the leading TV chat show, with both of them telling the human side of what had happened.

※

The producer looked down from the control room at the two figures as they sat down in the studio holding each other's hand, rubbed her eyes and spoke to the famous show host through the headset.

"Can you see that light around them – like a *halo*? These two are phenominal – I've never before seen or felt so much love!"

She had no time to reply, but as ever, the consummate professional host introduced them both and the reason for them being that day's studio guests. Then, as Jacqui's clear voice described details of how she had been told the news of her baby's condition, and how she had made her pledge to their new-born son - "*whatever* you're capable of, little one, we'll help you achieve it" - the tears in her eyes showed how this still touched her, as it did every member of the studio audience.

When the programme was shown the switchboard was jammed – even after the first few minutes. Emails were pouring in. Something had happened that afternoon, in that studio. The phrase that kept being repeated over and over again was "so much *love*!"

The Ripples and the Tapestries

They eventually escaped into the waiting taxi, to emerge later, laden with parcels, then disappeared to their room to phone the children, who were very excited to receive another call from them. Vicky was eager to hear about the TV show – "I'll tell you all about it when we have a moment to ourselves" Jacqui promised; and Richard confirmed their arrival time with Ben, reassuring him he would let them know if there was any delay.

"Time for dinner, I think – room service this time, as we don't want to see any more people, do we?" he said, after their call had finished. "Then we can tell reception not to put any more calls through and I *must* tell you about the strangest thing that happened."

❧❧

Later that evening Richard told her about the elderly man who had spoken so compellingly about messages and work to be done. Jacqui looked at him strangely, then began to show Richard the notes she'd made after her conversation with Jenny about Twin Souls; she explained that she'd waited as he'd had so many things to think about – not least the Conference, but she felt an urgency to tell him about it now - it wouldn't keep until they returned to England.

She needed to make certain he understood correctly, briefly reminding him of the structure of each family soul - Companion Souls meeting time and time again for general life lessons such as patience, selfishness, financial attitudes and many more which were needed to benefit the social group; how Soulmates occupied a different level and were for more specific lessons for the individual soul's progress, often within personal relationships. Twin Souls rarely came together, but when they did it was always for a higher good – often to influence global attitudes by setting an example in some way.

Well rested the following morning, and with everything prepared, Jacqui and Richard reached the airport in plenty of time for their flight. They were met by one of the airport staff.

"I saw the show, and noticed you were on our passenger list" he said. "Our Chairman has seen it too and insists that we upgrade you, with his personal compliments and a request that if you have time to spare in London, he would like to meet you in person."

They looked at each other, bemused.

"Go with the flow!" said Richard, squeezing Jacqui's hand gently.

※

Once they had settled into their comfortable seats they could continue the conversation they had begun the night before, which soon became so important to them both that sleep had been immaterial. It was only the thought of being able to continue that led to them eventually turning off the light. Jacqui had slept peacefully, knowing that at long last her beloved husband was ready to hear the full explanation.

"But what made you think there was a possibility that we might be not just Soulmates, but a pair of Twin Souls? After all, I had no greater reaction of togetherness than I'd have expected from what you call a Soul Companion ... that sense of having known you before."

"It was a case of piecing all the clues together" Jacqui said. "One day, not long after we'd met, I wrote down our common characteristics, our shared viewpoints and moral standards. We covered a lot of ground in a few conversations – I don't suppose you even remember.

"Everything that was important to me was apparently equally important to you. You attributed that to life experiences – what I valued was precious because I *hadn't* known it as I grew up; you had been raised in a home where they *were* the fabric of life. But the important thing was, they matched, although at the time I thought it was just because we must be Soulmates.

"Then some time later I wrote another list – this time it was episodes in my life that had puzzled me about the intense responses they provoked. Are you interested enough to hear all this? It *is* important that I explain."

Richard nodded. He could sense her earnestness, and now was an ideal time, wrapped in this cocoon of unreality as they flew, thousands of feet above the sea.

The Ripples and the Tapestries

"I knew I'd always been searching for someone, from the time when I first began to think. Sometimes I'd think I caught sight of him – I knew his height, I knew what it would be like to be at his side, I even knew his name. I was misled on occasions, of course, but the search went on – until it ended the day *we* met! But, looking back, we *couldn't* have been allowed to meet before – not until the timing was right, or our purpose wouldn't have been achieved.

"At the time, I was so happy to have found the true love that I could match, after all that had happened in my life. Now, after all that has happened in *our* lives – yours and mine together – I know we not only share the deepest love possible, there will never be any more separation."

Richard leaned across the armrest and kissed her cheek.

"I have something to say to you, too. I haven't ignored the things you've shared with me when you've come back from Jenny's. I knew that you were gaining strength from what you learned from her wisdom, and ways of looking at life.

"You asked for 'nothing more than an air of amused tolerance' as you put it, but although I started with that, something has happened to me as well, and it started when I saw Gabriel siting at the graveside. Then, I could feel my heart expanding as I wrote the book and described your reactions to the times we've gone through. Your courage has been immeasurable as you've helped everyone to accept what was happening; the ways you responded to Gabriel's life and death – unselfishly and unquestioningly, gave me the strength *I* needed. Jacqui – I do feel this 'as one' aspect of us being together.

"Twin Souls? Oh yes *indeed* - I've caught up with you at last!"

"It is ordained that these souls will know, and in that moment of knowing will come home. Fear not, all will be well."

The voice was clear, and they each heard it, feeling an indescribably deep peace sweeping over both of them as they looked into each other's eyes, sealing their wonder and love with a tender kiss.

The pilot had had no warning of the freak storm and the thunderbolt which was drawn to the nearest object in the sky. In a split second their world suddenly disintegrated into twisted metal, fire and gases that eventually scattered into the depths of the ocean below.

24

The headlines screamed around the world. No other publicity would have achieved so much, thought Ben, as he read more details of the crash and long columns of speculative journalism. He was quoted from his brief statement made later in the day outside the front portico of the Hall, TV cameras adding to the unreality of the situation. He had seen it happening to other people often enough, but nothing had prepared him for what felt like a gross assault on his emotions.

He refused to let Vicky think of appearing – the children needed her, above anything else and he needed to keep the press out of their lives if at all possible. The senior officer asked for the reporters to respect the family's need for privacy as they tried to come to terms with their loss. The well-worn phrase sounded crass and intrusive

"Just how *do* we come to terms with this?" was his reaction as he hurried indoors.

On that dreadful morning he and Vicky had held each other closely for a long, long time after they answered the door to two police officers. They were lost for words. It was not something that anyone could be prepared for and they heard Ella coming down the stairs, followed closely by Tim.
"They must have heard the door bell; how on earth do we tell them?"
"We must, straight away, before they find out from anyone else" Vicky said, looking meaningfully at the officers and shaking her head. They understood and tactfully withdrew into the hallway.

Somehow they managed to do it. Ella and Tim sat stunned, not wanting to speak or knowing what to do - just holding each other's hands, later joined by Lucy and Becca who hugged and kissed them and wiped away tears. Ben took them to the kitchen so that Mrs Ewing could fuss around with offers of hot chocolate and biscuits in front of the fire.

Barbara arrived within the hour, in response to Ben's earlier, urgent phone call. All she could think of as she drove was to send up an agonised plea to whoever she thought might be listening –

"Why can't you leave them alone? Don't you think they've suffered enough?"

Of all the people in the world – why did it have to happen to *them* – to her adopted family who had already been through so much? How would they cope with this most devastating blow to the very heart of the family group? Had they suffered?

The reports postulated various theories, including a bomb – how could *that* be, with all the security that was in force at airports? She arrived at the Hall at the same time as the first of the press photographers, and swept into the drive without pausing, scattering them with a continuous blast on the car horn.

Tim and Ella looked relieved as she hurried into the kitchen to gather them into her arms, oblivious to everything other than a mutual need for tears and contact with their Auntie Babs, who always understood. Barbara let them take her to the sitting room and then carry her overnight bag to her usual bedroom.

"It will give them something to do" she murmured to Vicky as they embraced and Ben hovered in the background, unashamedly waiting his turn. "Remember how Jacqui encouraged them to take part in everything when Gabriel died? We must do the same now."

Richard's parents made their way to join the others at the Hall, and Vicky's mother and father were also on their way from their home abroad. Vicky knew that they would all be helped by coming together to share their grief. She and Jacqui had once had a long discussion about grief in its many forms, but what she remembered most was hearing her sister-in-law say that the best way was to share it.

Almost as if she'd had a premonition? No, that was silly, she thought, then remembered that Jacqui had hugged the children for so long before they left for New York. Almost as if she never wanted to let them go ... but her mind must be playing tricks. She must *stop* - it was her turn to be strong for all the others, as Jacqui had been in the past.

The remainder of the day passed slowly, oh so slowly. Sympathetic officialdom took over, when they could manage to talk to them. There seemed to be so much red tape. At long last the strangers left and they managed to sit down together around the table in a brave attempt to eat a meal and make some attempt to resume normal life, even though normality had forever disappeared, it seemed.

❦

The ensuing days blurred together, a memorial service for the couple who had made such an impact on the world, held in the church where Sonia had held sway, and the family group had honoured Gabriel. On this occasion there were many more than the church could hold. The village was thronged with people who had personally known Jacqui and Richard and many more who wanted to demonstrate how these two lives had affected them in some way. Many more had sent letters of sympathy and for weeks the post brought sacks full from all round the world, from audiences who had been touched by the message of Richard's book and wanted to let his family know how the couple's lives had given them the courage to deal with their own children's health problems.

Unnoticed, Jenny attended the memorial service, sat in the corner of a pew near the back of the church, lost in her own thoughts. She witnessed the grief all around her, she understood people's sorrow, and of course she felt her own sadness at the thought of never seeing either Jacqui or Richard again, but she also felt joy. This was where her beliefs in the continuation of life led her and indeed, where her gifts had allowed her to be aware of what had happened on that day.

On the morning of the crash she was sitting in her conservatory, and had just closed her eyes in preparation for the meditation she used when linking up psychically with those in her care. Her priority was always those who were away from their usual surroundings – checking that all was in order - so it was to Jacqui and Richard that she first tuned in.

In her mind's eye she became aware of an intense white light approaching from a distance. A speck at first, it eventually grew close enough for her to see that it was not just a steady ray of light - it whirled and twisted upon itself; then as it became larger still she could see that it was formed of two separate lights which were spiralling around each other. She could feel the force that it generated as it slowed in front of her for a moment – then, picking up speed again, it gathered momentum and went upwards and outwards into untold galaxies, spiralling round and round until it joined other lights in a larger and larger mass until all of them were indistinguishable one from another.

It was a sign, she knew. She held her breath and waited to be told. Sure enough, Mr Fu's unmistakeable voice came from behind her shoulder –

"... they are home .. all is well ...."

Catching her breath, she waited - feeling peace and love at the level of her Higher Self, yet knowing the message was connected with her beloved Jacqui and Richard, and had implications that her earthly self wanted to reject. Gradually she came back to her familiar surroundings and became aware that the telephone was ringing in the distance. It was Barbara, phoning to tell her the news about the plane crash over the Atlantic, anxious, even in her own state of shock, that Jenny should know as soon as possible.

From that moment the telephone was in use for the rest of the day, and she lost count of the times she relayed to friends and colleagues how they could help by holding the couple in their thoughts, sending love and healing to Barbara, the children and the family. It happened day after day, and they sensed it joining with the worldwide surge of compassion.

This was the first sign of the impact that the couple had made. Their TV interviews were shown time after time and money poured in from people who wanted to help in practical ways – the start of what was eventually to become the Gabriel Trust, helping parents of babies like Gabriel by providing specialist support and counselling.

Jenny wished above all else that it had not had to happen in this way, having to admit that the knowledge her human self was given was sometimes almost unbearable. It was only by being helped to step back to see the wider picture, that she had been able to survive this. She had her own circle of group support and those who brought her comfort, but even so it was difficult not to have ordinary human reactions and she was glad to meet Barbara again within a few days, to tell her at first hand the impressions she had received.

"I've never known that to happen at anyone's passing" she confided "but it does make sense, thinking of the Twin Soul aspect. My guide has told me they were reunited with Gabriel's spirit and are spending time with all the family spirits before moving to their next tasks."

She and Barbara sat for a long time, sharing silent thoughts.

~

Gradually they all picked up the pieces in their own way and life settled into new routines as gaps were filled. Vicky and Ben willingly and lovingly absorbed the children into their home and their lives, even though it had never been a formal arrangement in Richard and Jacqui's joint Will. Ben responded to Tim's needs in particular, and showed how he had absorbed much of the example Richard had provided. He spent hours with his teenage nephew, almost as if he were guided by an unseen hand. Vicky became so proud of his skills, often remarking to Barbara that she had the husband she'd always known he could be. For her own part, she became more confident in the way she organised life for the girls – Ella was admirable in the older sister role and Vicky's two daughters, Lucy and Becca, responded to her example, and showed it in the way they loved the new baby when he was born.

They were of course deeply affected by the events, but not emotionally damaged – Barbara's commonsense support and ever ready willingness to help saw to that. They all kept as many memories alive as they could, and although they travelled their individual paths of grief at their own pace, somehow they managed to keep pace in the ways that mattered. Gabriel's tree was no longer a sapling on its own on a gently sloping part of the lawn, visible from the Hall; it was joined by two more strong ones, with a wooden seat placed nearby so that it became a natural place for quiet meditation, looking out over the countryside they had all loved.

Barbara continued to keep in touch with Jenny. That kindly woman made sure she was available whenever Barbara needed comfort, and passed on whatever information she received from her guide.

25

Jacqui and Richard's spirits were held together by that look of love, as they left the fragmented scene. Other spirits from the plane surrounded them, then encouraged by the welcoming hand that Jacqui held out to the closest one, soon linked one with another until a chain of spirit energy was wafting through the ethereal realms – supporting each other and feeling no fear.

As they were propelled across oceans and into a landscape of amazing beauty, Jacqui and Richard felt themselves gently detached from the others, then realised that they themselves had started to merge. The Twin Souls were indeed again becoming one.

Approaching a distant temple across fields of flowers, their Twinsoul felt an immense peace and belonging. From the steps of the celestial building a small figure came running towards them, waving excitedly.

"*Gabriel!*" they exclaimed, each extending an arm towards him. He joyously leapt into their embrace, perfect in every way, radiating a happiness that showed itself in a very special smile – the one he had smiled only once in his earthly life.

26

Mr Fu was the one to give all the explanations, of course. As he sat, looking at the spirit throng that surrounded him on the steps of the Healing Temple, with contacts being made that had not happened for lifetimes, he thought of the varied missions that so many of them had set out to accomplish.

He held up his hands for attention and began ...

"We are all, at this moment, part of a very significant family reunion, and it is a great privilege to be a part of the very unusual developments that have taken place. Some of us have spent longer here than others and are more aware of the world of Spirit, so you will have to forgive me if I cover topics that you know.

"Let me start with our meeting place here, at the place we all return to – our Home. We - that is, our spirits - return here after our earthly bodies have finished their souls' tasks. When on earth, the various parts – the physical body, the emotions and the mind - develop that individual's personality and characteristics in order to experience the opportunities for that soul's growth. That process never stops, and when you return here you are helped to see how the new learning fits in to the soul that you are and will always be. As you all look back at your latest lives you will see situations that repeated themselves again and again – which, as you now realise, was because you didn't learn the lesson the first time."

He looked towards Sonia and smiled gently.

"You are all now experiencing the chance to sort out the details of why you kept trying - and sometimes failing - to discover something that you knew was the purpose of your life: this is one of the reasons why there *is* return after return, and meeting other souls you know. You are part of their ongoing learning process just as much as they are of yours.

"Let me now take you through the sequence of how you have each played a significant part in each others' learning ... "

The group settled expectantly. They had all encountered him at some stage in their earthly lives, whether they recognised him or not, for he was the Guardian and Guide of the Family Soul as an entity, and of each individual within it.

"Your recycling process has been taking place from the time when your souls were very new and undeveloped. You haven't all progressed at the same pace, naturally, due to circumstances and personalities. As you will have observed, there are periods when you get really stuck – you may have responsibilities or restrictions that weigh too heavily for you to have any energy left to do anything other than carry out your duties, and just exist. That in itself is part of your learning and development. There has been no pressure of time, and you have all done what you can at the pace you set yourself, and how the family soul group agreed it would happen.

"The only exception to this has been my dear friend Sonia, as she was called in her last life. When she arrived here she had to have a period of, of … quarantine, I suppose you would call it, so that her spirit didn't contaminate the family spirit. It really was that bad, wasn't it, dear lady?"

Sonia nodded in agreement from where she sat with her earthly family spirits around her. As with all of them in Spirit, she had no emotional attachments, but she now had a keen awareness of the details of her life and the amount of work she had undertaken in order to benefit the Family Soul's future work on earth. She now felt no emotional pain as she thought of the damage she had done to so many other people – that was an earthly sentiment - but the responsibility for ensuring that there would be improvements was something that they all felt very keenly.

"She, as you all have had to do, looked at her actions, the effects they had on others, and from them evolved the purpose of her next life. A healing life."

The Ripples and the Tapestries

Gabriel, who was sat on Sonia's lap, looked intently all around. The two of them became enveloped in a strangely beautiful light that wound its way around them both before it faded.

"Gabriel was Sonia's chosen life when she returned, as you all know. Sonia's learning here had given her the opportunity to demonstrate that she could become the opposite of her previous existence – and Gabriel personified love. His physical condition gave people the chance to love him purely and naturally, in a way that Sonia in her previous life would never have permitted – even if she had believed that such a love could exist. Now, having lived it, her soul's development has enhanced the family spirit."

His audience nodded in understanding and agreement.

"But now I need to say more about Twinsouls – in some instances there is a Twinsoul, divided at source, separately developing in different families, until the time is right for them to meet again within one family. It means the culmination of many, *many* lifetimes of hard work in order to reach the stage of development where they can work together – even if they are not aware of the spiritual significance at the time – or, as has been the case with Jacqui and Richard, where only one of them has been aware to some extent, and the other not at all until the last moment.

"As you may know, the Twinsoul purpose is to find and take the opportunity to work for the World Spirit in some way – to raise awareness of something that should be part of *every* Family Soul on earth. This was the purpose for Jacqui and Richard finding each other, and their personal Twinsoul discovery liberated them into a level of development that will benefit mankind - spreading understanding of the needs of children like Gabriel.

"Once that had started and their purpose was fulfilled, they could be set free to work on an even higher level – and now they have spent time with us to make sure *we* understand what has been achieved so that *we* can continue their work, as they will no longer continue to be part of this family in the way that we know.

"The work is already continuing, and the remainder of the family who have all benefited from knowing Gabriel will be joined by others who move from here back to earth plane to meet and grow together. All the Family Souls in existence will become involved as a new era of awareness takes its hold on humanity. Changes in communication, which have already begun, will rapidly ease the way towards understanding among all peoples on earth.

"There is still a long way to go, but you, my dear family, have been instrumental in making use of the opportunities you have had. Bless you all for your courage, and be assured that every one of you will have the opportunity to contact me when you need. Don't forget what I always tell you – you will recognise me by my smile ..." he paused ...

"... no matter who is wearing it!" they all chorused.

Jacqui and Richard, their earthly mission accomplished and now together for ever, went round the group one by one answering questions, reassuring those who would have them stay for a while longer that ways would be found to stay in touch. Having spent time with old friends and long departed relatives, then Sonia, Geoffrey and *their* parents, they sat beside Jacqui's mother Maria, and Gabriel. This was no occasion for speech.

The family willed each other to gain the utmost from these precious moments – moments that would form the basis for those eternal human instincts for belonging to something larger than comprehension; moments that might possibly remind their future earthly selves of a vague memory, as they connected with higher beings or had experiences that transcended all rational explanations.

∞

The current of energy was subtle but immensely powerful; it enveloped the group, taking substance and swirling around them - a misty shroud of shimmering opalescence, gathering momentum as it spun, rising as it grew in pace, separating from their dimension even as they watched, then becoming an intensity of light so strong that even spirits could no longer bear to look.

Eventually, only the group remained, the Twinsoul now no longer visible – already starting the new journey into the highest realms where its new purpose would be revealed.

※

Gabriel beamed his angelic smile, and handed his grandmother a daisy ...

The knowing ...

I turn over that last page reluctantly, yet relieved to have reached the end.

There is a shift, a change in my ... my what? My heart .... my soul? I have been undoubtedly out of my depths with the metaphysical, yet it has somehow worked its way into my thoughts ...

What cruel twist of fate had led Cressy to write about the plane crash? Surely she couldn't have realised that she was foretelling her own fate, and yet there had been hints I'd encountered along the way, which implied she knew very well what she was doing and the way they must be incorporated into the story.

Was this what she had been trying to show me? Was this why, on this occasion and no other she had written her *"To be opened ..."* note, preparing me for what she had in some way foreseen?

I look back over our time together and it is not only *my* reluctance to declare my feelings, I can see now – but hers as well. A physical passion would have muddied the waters for us both, and the remainder of our lives would have undoubtedly been placed 'on hold'.
How many friends had we seen go down that route, only to find that eventually the second time around didn't greatly differ from the first, and it would only be a question of time before the same problems reasserted themselves. Those who decided to stay with their decision could perhaps be said to have learned a little about repeated lessons, in order to achieve a level of forbearance that allowed them a reasonably successful period of emotional maturity to look back upon, and a companionship which would just about withstand the age and infirmity process; those who couldn't do that, for the most part moved on ... and on ... becoming more embittered or depressed. There seemed to be little to recommend either as a long term goal.

I would not have wished for that descent, and nor would she, I am certain. But what has been the point of what we had? Am I missing something? Surely she could not have seen me completely in the role Richard had occupied – I can comfortably wear the sceptic's mantle - but to be the other half of this Twinsoul concept ... in spite of myself ... ?

I think of the emotional undercurrents we'd both been delighted to discover when we met at school. The devastation we had both felt when parental ambitions parted us – Cressy to tread the conventional path and succeed – partially, at least. Me to go through the same motions, then escape into a life where anything was preferable to the betrayal of who I wanted to be. There was no option then but to lie low and lick one's wounds, throw myself into work and wait for the rawness to heal. The school reunion had reopened those wounds and hidden currents - for both of us, but even in these enlightened times it seemed preferable to wait for dust to settle rather than go straight for the unspoken solution we both wanted – contenting ourselves with glimpses of what might have been and possibly still could be, once we made up our minds to risk everything.

Cressy had written of the power of the Twin Souls. At times our own power was almost tangible as we talked and laughed in those all too few summers. Heads would turn to share in the pleasure of seeing two people so much in tune with each other. Could that power last? Was that earthly power the basis for her writing, and was the supernatural only a construct of her imagination? Yet I'd noticed a subtle and gradual change in her writing as she went deeper into the fantasy, until the final chapters seemed to contain a quality of something outside herself.

Then there was that cruel coincidence of what she called predictive writing – the air crash – surely it was no more than that. I turn to her last few diary entries to see if she had left any further comments for me. There were the usual lists of what she needed to do and last minute appointments before her flight on the Monday afternoon.

Three days before she left she had put my familiar T in a large circle, underlined twice and with an asterisk each side for good measure.

Told T about Twin Soul theory - said I'd

> *come across it in a book; Adam & Eve were 1st ones. Greeted with hoots of derision as fanciful nonsense. We were pretty drunk at the time - T may not remember it - p'raps as well: knowledge might be a dangerous thing - look what happened to R when he realised!!*
>
> *I know what waits 4 me - always get same signal with predictions - D will know too, but won't say anything. All affairs in order - left letter for T. Ready to go ...*

So she *did* know ...

That had been our last evening together, that Friday. Yes, we did get pretty drunk - heady with our mood as much as the wine we drank, partaking of our 'last supper' as she insisted on calling it. If she already *knew* - or at least thought she did – no wonder it seemed so important to her that the evening was perfect. Did I remember the revelation about Twinsouls? I vaguely remember Adam and Eve coming into a disjointed conversation, but the detail escapes me. Just as well, if I had *that* reaction - I can be very scathing, especially when fuelled by Chilean red topped up, I now recall, by a particularly well received nightcap of vintage something or other - or was it Benedictine? It all became a little hazy and the taxi was a welcome final note to signal that evening's end. The following morning she phoned to tell me she'd hidden a letter for me in the dressing table jewellery drawer.

Seeing the news on that Monday evening made me determined to go to the flat and retrieve her letter. When I phoned the odious Greg, uttering condolences and concern, and his only reaction was to say he'd be getting rid of all her things as soon as possible (even before the funeral arrangements had been made) I arranged to meet him there the following day - privately arranging with myself to get there very early.

Now I am also off on my travels. I have to pack the final few things, and on the way to the airport tomorrow I'll call in at my agent to leave the manuscript and all these notes in her safe hands - perhaps she'll give it a glance while I'm away. She's a very prosaic person and should be able to give me an honest appraisal when she's ready.

I'm so glad I have the outpourings, the George Eliot, your diary - and so glad I now know more about you, my darling love, than I ever dreamed I would – and relieved that I can believe Diane when she says you would have been taken out of your body and would feel no pain.

... and yes ... *now* I understand and believe in my heart – so, wherever you are, I will be part of you as you are of me. Scoop me up in your beliefs, my angel, so we may no longer be apart, staying entwined forever as the Twinsouls that we are.

Footnote:

This remarkable story is published in its entirety, as it was presented, by the late Helen Wells, better known as Troy Treadwell - the gifted gardening correspondent and author, who was killed in a motorway accident on her way to the airport. She was on her way to research assignments in the U.S.A.

I welcome readers' comments –

please contact me on

lyz.harvey@btinternet.com